SUMMERLIGHT

By
ERIC LITTLE

Preface

Ten cycles ago we found the most beautiful place in the galaxy, an inside-out world of fable where the sun always shines. It all began when we found ourselves in desperate straits, pursued by a pack of hunterShips set on our trail by the mad Raider Queen. We ended up running hard for a monstrous event horizon deep in the Chaos Sea, and accidently stumbled on the amazing world of Summer. Unfortunately, the mad dogs of the Raider queen stayed hard on our trail, and several hunterShips followed us through the Door into Summer. We went to ground on a massive abandoned island. Meanwhile, they wreaked havoc and death on the sleepy communities they found. It wasn't long before they found us too, and we fought off over four hundred Raider shock troops in a fierce showdown. But we wiped them out and carved ourselves a home the Raider queen still hasn't found.

The Ranch was born in blood and fury, but a decade of peace gave us time to discover what it's like to have a real home after wandering the galaxy for so long. Hard work and sweat, problem-solving with abandoned alien tech, and building were the most satisfying things we'd ever done. We have a home now, a fledgling nation, and not nearly enough people to go around. But we can never forget that there are still hunterShips out there somewhere hovering around Summer, hagridden by a daughter of the Raider queen carrying as many as a thousand Raiders; all marooned, unable to return home without our heads.

We always knew they'd be coming around one day.

1—Koen of Summer

"Incoming, seven life signs, in addition to smart-bad-tech," Dread growled in my implant. While wandering wildlife crossing over onto Ranch-land was not unusual, smart-bad-tech accompanying them was.

I activated my implant. "Raiders," I broadcast Ranch-wide as I strapped up. *Raiders are the worst.* Baling-wire-muscled psychopaths distilled into pure mean by the refining that their Queen-mother subjected them to. They were driven mad by this of course. *But if enough people share it, is it really madness?* I shook my head, shedding these distracting thoughts like raindrops in a downpour.

The important new-data was that Raider shock troops multiply exponentially, with more of their terrible forces arriving by the minute once they establish a beachhead—you absolutely must stop them before that or all is lost, and all that remains is a rough journey into the Dark.

Navire joined me in the passageway, tossing me a sad smile as we trotted rapidly through the halls of Fort Lilith to where Katy the Sledge was waiting. Behind us, the defenses of the Fort began locking down and shifting to siege-mode. It might have been an excess of caution, but these days I always err on the side of security. I have more to lose now than I ever had before.

When we got to the landing, Katy the Sledge was already waiting, wearing her favorite battle-train. It was purple and shiny and layered in dull, carbon-fiber bumpers that could bust through just about anything—Katy liked to keep her options open. As usual, she greeted us with smoking-hot music as we climbed in; today she was playing a classic Strut with White-haired Jack on keyboards, East Gravtown style. Lotsa dancehall energy. It was very-fine. I slung Navire a smile with just a little heat tucked in here and there. A crooked grin flew back my way. Then we subsided into the introspective quiet that seasoned fighters exhibit before battle.

Katy took off at high speed, as always. We crouched and held tightly onto the vibrating handles set in the scattered stanchions across the deck as we hurled through the tunnels beneath the crystal ranges of the Ranch.

Or, as Katy the sledge put it; "today we ride a hell-bound train into battle, with sizzling Gravtown horn laying the beat. We ride to protect our home from the bad-guys, to create immersive battle-art. Today we ride to fight the good fight!"

My daughter can be a little dramatic at times, but her heart is as pure as platinum and she _is_ a teenager. Such things are not exactly unknown.

When Katy screeched to a halt dramatically, (as usual), we stepped out into the smaller cross passageway. It was too narrow for Katy's battle-train to take us any further. I had to make her promise not to rip her way through; she was pretty disappointed. All dressed up and then she couldn't even get into the dance! Sometimes life sucks when you're a teenager.

I touched my implant, shifting my stealthsuit into full-recording-mode, sucking in all spectrum Signal. I now appeared only as a man-shaped black hole in the bright crystalline world of Summer. Light itself bent to me as I full-body recorded everything I experienced.

"The Raiders have fully breached the Fort Medusa corridor, and are apparently looking for Control," Navire breathed in my implant. "I didn't expect this kinda strategic thinking from a bunch of monsters. I think that maybe these Raiders have evolved a bit, this far from the Raider queen. While my eye-gnats show them to be as physically scarred and wiry as we remember, these guys are no ordinary Raider shock troops; they're too organized," she added.

"Why do you think that?" I asked.

"They've bypassed several easy targets already; seems as if they have a mission and goal. Not standard Raider behavior the last time I looked. Might be evolved predators shooting for apex," she continued through my implant.

I felt a sub-dermal thrill flood me; such rich material to work with was rarer than you might think.

While today Navire was wearing a familiar hard-body crafted for battle, she also rode my implant at the same time, painting new-data on the fringes of my perception. The Children of Electron can do that.

We heard them before we could see them. As we drew close, the Raiders came to an uneven stop in front of us, leering and waving at us mockingly. This band of bad looked like they'd been put together outa barbed-wire and stone-bones, all pressed together with spit and scars and old leather. They never stopped moving or occasionally roaring in challenge. Their implants had them too wired for anything else.

Kinda noisy for pros, I decided, but this behavior was still different somehow. They didn't find us particularly scary but at the same time nobody was closing to fighting distance, either. That was when Navire painted pink tutus and clown noses on them through our implants. I busted up. They didn't like that.

It never occurred to the bad-guys that there may be a reason why only two of us showed up; truth was, one of us was only backup.

I sighed. Not the sharpest knives in the box.

"Don't be disappointed, Koen; there are always unexpected surprises and there's sure to be lotsa Boom," consoled Navire, although she knew it was material for art and the actual challenge of a complex fight I desired. I slung her a micro-wink. It was good to have friends.

The leader was the loud one in the middle of the pack, predictably surrounded by other hulking bad-guys in all kinda battle dress. Much of their armor looked as if something had been chewing on it. Of course, they were heavily strapped, with lotsa Boom and no shortage of pointy-things. They were also clustered too close together; they either had too much faith in their armor, or simply weren't used to people fighting back. Otherwise their discipline was unexpected though. Definitely not pros of our caliber but still something new.

In front of the soft-bodies were two massive Weiss hard-bodies somebody salvaged from a defunct deadShip. Defunct because the Weiss weren't around anymore; to the best of my knowledge, their civilization was completely extinct. They had blown through the galactic stage and left no mark but for a single exception; a handful of strange artifacts known only for the savagery of their weapon systems and an inability to turn to the side with any speed worthy of modern combat. I was guessing these clowns were the frontal attack kinda guys.

I step into the Now.

Immediately I am almost non-verbal, and it is hard to process even linear new-data. Peripheral concerns like language and intellectual thought slough away, leaving me in a timeless state known as base reality. I am profoundly aware of everything around me, without visually focusing on any one item.

I accelerate to my left. When I reach the corridor wall, I rebound off it, to close in on the nearest hulking hard-body's right side. I snap my nine-sectional corrosive whip under its main guns as they trail just behind me in silver and orange Boom. It stops firing and begins to list to the side as I accelerate on past it. I am very hard to track in full-recording-mode.

Navire spins up the other side of the corridor, dual auto-shotguns pouring heavy metallic crystal shards across the bottom half of the second archaic monstrosity. As it falls, it begins to twist slowly (at least to me) to follow Navire in a hailstorm of ceramic/metal projectiles from a massive hand cannon clutched in one hand.

How quaint.

It also manages to take out two of its own slower comrades in thunder and fire before Navire finally removes its belly with a slap-grenade. (That's where the logics are). It crushes a bad-guy's foot when it drops.

Despite Navire's encouragement, I am beginning to experience a bit of disappointment at the quality of my opponents. I fan a crescent of implosive grenades across the tunnel above the remaining Raiders. Two more fall, with what remains of their imploded forms cascading to the ground like a shower of overbaked cookies. I check Navire; she's in high tide mode, sweeping her opponents before her like the seventh wave. She leaves nothing standing in her wake.

The remaining bad-guys, including the leader, separate automatically into a triangle with me at the center. They moved very well, and I can tell they have trained to fight as a unit.

I smile. This was more like it.

I settle into the fighting stance of Lui Xing-yi, sinking deeper into the eternal Now. It feels kinda like when a stone drops down through the water, and comes to rest in the quiet places. There's no doubt when you arrive.

Time crawls around me, and the peripheral noise and the concerns of my life fall from me in a sort of bright white light. I completely lose the ability to speak as my whole being sinks into the instinctual hindbrain's world of angles and counters.

I simply… am.

I feel no moral conscience, no second thoughts, or hesitations. There is only movement and counter, and I can perceive their embryonic moves in the posture of their bodies with absurd clarity. That's the way it always begins: le Danse Macabre.

My right hand automatically tucks my steel whip back into its pocket under my left armpit. When the moment reaches fullness I move to my right, in the direction of the primary target, the boss-guy, as if I were about to go after him. The bad-guys cautiously draw closer, spaced equidistantly apart.

I am merely a black fissure in the world, not actually invisible; the closer they come to me, the easier I am to see. I shift my body and wait for them to take the bait. With painful slowness the other two move to intercept. When they're finally close enough, I rotate ninety degrees and become Rooster; unleashing a continuous Xing-yi Charge on my secondary target, 'big-guy' on my left. I engage him with a collarbone split and knee break that flow into a whirling continuous fist.

I pass over him and he never gets back up.

Skinny-tall-guy moves to the center of my simple universe.

I rotate back to the bully on my other side and become Dragon, redirecting both of skinny-tall-guy's powerful strikes as well as a kick, without losing inertia. Then I crush his throat. He falls down.

That leaves boss-guy, now the center of my uncomplicated universe.

I move towards center. Again, a collarbone split and knee break, and I finish with a graceful Crane hammer fist through his solar plexus and central vertebrae. In that moment I become Crane extended, in perfect stillness; motionless in a timeless instance of touching the Dark.

When I came back to myself, the world, as always, seemed different. Somehow newer, shinier; more filled with potential. Sometimes I wish I could see the world this way all the time, but as all things good and bad, it eventually passes.

Nothing lasts forever.

***

After the clean-up, Navire and I caught a ride to the recording studio at Control from Katy. Control is buried hundreds of kilometers deep beneath the continent of massive crystal forests that make up the Ranch.

We had hundreds of sensory-tracks to edit, in addition to my first-person view the Stealthsuit had recorded. Navire's miniature eye-gnats had also covered the fight from every angle—she didn't much care for surprises. She continuously monitored my feed real-time, for tactical new-data during a fight. Her threaded consciousness can handle the massive Signal load without breaking a sweat.

My battle-art footage is then reduced to a concentrated poetry of motion. This is Navire's real forte—to sculpt the new-data into something better than real.

My job is to create the raw new-data. During the editing, I also brought a certain recognition of pivotal moments, not to mention a cadence that defined the flow of the full-immersive fight recording. This was a first-person recording that was completely indistinguishable from 'reality' when played. My fans could relive the experience over and over. And did. For a moment they became someone else: me, better than real with all the boring parts cut away.

We were in studio for four days.

What emerged in time was very-fine, if a bit limited by its length of forty-eight blinks. This small piece quickly became very popular; then Parkar gave it ninety-five points, and we sold out in minutes. We never make more than a few thousand numbered copies, so they were always in high demand.

2—Koen of Summer

The Ranch is a very big place and has four border forts at the points of the rough diamond shape that our island nation resembles.

It is covered with enormous crystal forests and rugged amethyst ranges that begin a few kilometers above the gaseous rivers between the Ranch and the other city-states. The light rivers were pretty much impassable, although we still got wandering critters once in a while. The river's semi-solid wastelands made for a good security barrier, and the two-kilometer high cliff overlooking the toxic waters didn't hurt either.

There is a rhythm to my days on tour.

I am a hands-on kinda guy or a control freak, depending on who you talk to. I just think that good stewardship of the land requires personal involvement. So, when I wasn't away on a mission, I regularly went on long tours that covered every Fort, terra-formed Crystal, and project in progress. It took about four weeks for the whole tour. I inspected, troubleshot, and got a fresh feel for each of the stations along the way.

Katy the Sledge loved to travel, and usually pulled a mobile command center, dining car, and four or five luxurious pullman cars for us to live in. After a long workday, dinner time was usually a party, where anyone might drop by—and usually did. This maintained the family ties with our scattered Ranch hands, mostly the lost children of Eden grown strong and healthy in their adopted home. We always enjoyed celebrating the synergistic alchemy of good food, great conversation, and fine wine, beer or smoke together.

These were ties that bound us, as well as tending to make sure the big problems didn't sneak up on us and catch us by surprise. It may not have seemed like much at the time, but it would be these small pleasures and simple evenings that later nourished us through the Dark times.

The four fortifications of the diamond were Fort Lilith, Fort Cerberus, Fort Charon, and Fort Medusa. That's where we were headed first, Fort Medusa.

We approached our second stop after Medusa Control, with Katy the Sledge sliding dramatically to a halt, as usual. I was glad that we were holding on to the large handles attached to the stanchions dotting the deck of the transit car, the first of Katy's passenger carriages. She had timed the music so that the last notes lingered in the air as she slammed open her doors and liltingly announced that we had arrived at Crystal Four—The Bamboo forests.

I rose to my feet eagerly, Navire at my side. The Gardener, joining us enthusiastically, laid a long hairy arm across our shoulders. We'd all been looking forward to this stop.

Stepping out into the Crystal Four garden is like stepping out into the clear air and sunlight of a tropical planet at dawn, although this description doesn't begin to do it justice. It is so much more. I looked up through the sky and transparent crystal into the inside-out world of Summer.

Overhead a large lightstorm was working its way across Far Summer. Violet and bronzed straw surged across the sky in slow motion combat. The wastelands separating the island-nations of Far Summer were visible as giant blue/white fractures in the sky. From here, they looked like enormous glowing cracks in the world.

That is, of course, how the light gets in.

The interior of this seventeen-kilometer long crystal had been completely hollowed out, leaving a quarter of a kilometer of thick crystal on all sides. All surfaces of the huge crystal had been polished to extreme clarity. We were bathed by vintage light in delicate hues, cascading down upon us in undulating waves. The overall impression was almost overwhelming in its beauty. It is one of the most beautiful places we've ever been.

Then you look down and see the bamboo forest.

The tall lean bamboo trunks were clustered in areas that at first seemed to be separated by color. The old warriors leaned protectively over shorter, more diverse groups of work-horse bamboo. Patches of brilliant white reflective grasses interrupted the ground between clusters. It was beautiful and timeless and somehow haunting.

Directly in front of us lay a rough tiled path, accented in bright green. The path is built of salvaged ship hull fragments embedded in scrubber-moss. It snake-walked into the gently swaying forest of down crystal leading away from us. It had an organic/metallic mélange going on: very Hive, very Auntie Tao. We had lotsa hull fragments anyway.

This morning Navire was wearing a new hard-body I'd never seen before. She was rocking a slow moving tree-like nymph of immense grace and power. Impossible, blue-green iridescent body with branches for arms and myriad thick roots that slipped through the earth without resistance. Even her head was treelike, with enormous vermilion eyes and a mouth built for laughing. Her trademark crooked grin was showing. That's how I always knew it was her, in anything she put on to wear. Navire sank her roots deep into the soil as we roamed downwards through the giant bamboo forest, tasting its metallic salts and organic compounds in broad spectrum swatches.

As we got deeper in, the quality of the light in the forest grew noticeably richer with the organic reflections and gained a golden hue with light turquoise highlights. The canopy was blushing purple behind the green.

Navire and I and the Gardener strolled comfortably through the forest. As we walked, Navire painted an analytical new-data flow of Crystal Four's stats through my implant. It appeared as a carmine waterfall of new-data in my right eye's peripheral vision. The coral contrasted nicely with the rich bamboo background; Navire's artistic side was showing.

The Gardener passionately shaped verbal new-data about the forest into concise word-pictures that spoke richly of the land and its underlying ecosystem. He wanted to import a species of tree-frogs but was having difficulty finding a proper niche for them. He wouldn't introduce them unless they fit just right. I told him we had plenty of crystals and he chuckled. Said it seemed indulgent, but didn't say no. We'd find a place for his singing tree frogs before long.

The trail slowly worked its way downhill.

A breeze wafted through the forest, carrying rich, organic scents of minty chlorophyll and pungent loam. It was easier to see looking up; the tops getting busy. The breeze traveled down from Up-Crystal to play the wood winds in a weaving pattern as old as time. Navire slow danced to its tune, sliding frictionless through the deep, organic-rich soil. She wasn't alone.

It was a good morning.

After walking long enough all data became old-data and your mind wanders down unused passages. I was thinking about our days. Man wasn't designed or meant to sit down at desks all day and be carried everywhere by comfy-tech. I had attempted to achieve a balance at the Ranch. We walked a lot of places by design. It gives you time to think, and your body needs it to stay in fighting trim. Besides, after cycles living aboard a liveShip, walking someplace not particularly close stretched more than your leg muscles. Oh, some Ranchers stay buried like a tick in their Control for years, but eventually all old-data gets purged, including Ranchers. You stop moving, you start dying. I learned that when I was very young. Long story.

I always know the walk was just right when sweat breaks out across your forehead but hasn't got in your eyes yet. About this time, we came around a corner and saw our destination. It had been constructed entirely of the bamboo and the plant fibers had grown around it, the simple-to-the-point-of-elegant open air structure was a masterwork of renewable engineering. Again, almost Hive--which was my home for half my life, so I guess you bring some things along with you no matter where you go.

The open air building was a brewery fully staffed by the E.

I stumbled upon the E, when I was fighting in an obscure war halfway across the galaxy in a place called Amber. What had begun with a long-missing regent had degenerated into a Machiavellian nightmare of siblings consumed with 'climbing to the big chair'. The battle had lost all semblance of honor. When my prince was captured and blinded, we scattered, running for our lives. We all got broken up and I found myself with a badly injured Smitty, and my army's MP force, a Ronin warrior tribe of small, hairy mammals called the E. We were conned into taking a ride out, and barely escaped as the redoubt was being brought down around us by heavy weapons fire and the Amber Imperial guard. That was one bad day. Still wake up in the night sometimes. But that's another story.

The E were a lost cast-away crew who had finally given up looking for old-Home after a century or thereabouts. We were crew, and when we decided that it was time to stop wandering around and build a new-Home, everyone got to work. They were with us in those heady, early days of building the Ranch. Not that its finished, we're just getting started. The Ranch has lotsa elbow room. Enough people is the problem.

The E work together extremely well. They have a fluid communal consciousness that raised efficiency to an art form. There are tradeoffs—it gets a bit loud around them, what with everyone talking at the same time. Very chaotic but worked well for them.

Also, they worked for beer.

Admittedly prodigious amounts of it, and it had to be *good* beer.

The E stand half a meter tall and are covered everywhere in short velvety fur the color of cinnamon. The standard two arms, two legs, and one head. They were adrenaline junkies and entirely fearless. The more dangerous the job, the more they liked it. This has made them the favored shock troops among the knowledgeable generals, and now there aren't a lot of them left these days. (Although it seemed like I'd been seeing lotsa kids the last few cycles.)

Normally, they wore extensive battle harnesses that covered most of their body, with the odd tuft of cinnamon fur sticking out here and there. They favored large (for them) knives or short swords of high carbon meteor-iron. Assorted Blade, but the emphasis was on things-that-slash. Lotsa straight razors. Not to mention Scimitars, and something that reminded me of primitive Kukri. Long and intermediate range Boom. Salvage tools. Anti-personnel mines. Blowguns and toxic darts. The usual. The long and short of it is; the E made very good friends, and bad enemies.

Luckily, we were in the family category.

Oh, and they were essentially indistinguishable from each other. That wasn't as bad as it sounded. They traveled everywhere in constantly changing groups; you never saw just one E. You got used to it after a while, and it helped that they were voracious gossips. Eventually you ended up addressing them as the same person, as if they remembered your last conversation. And they did, kinda. Gossip mutated a bit as it was passed from E to E; so extended conversations with them entered surreal territory rapidly. Still, it worked, after a fashion. Got the job done, and beers all round. Lotsa beer.

In fact, during the early days, our trade balance with Gravtown quickly grew out of balance due to the prodigious capacity for fine ale the E embodied. I had to find a better solution for our trade imbalance before our $cred rating went completely to hell. It was the import costs that was the monster in the hen house.

That was how we got into the brewing business.

Turns out that the E not only have very high standards for the barley nectar, but they also make very-fine beer. Back in those days, they were reliant on vendors for acceptable brew, and I got tired of seeing my best men screwed around with, so I kinda arranged for them to learn how to brew their own. The E enthusiastically applied their high standard to production and aging of fine ale in all its glorious manifestations.

Over the years as we wandered the ever-changing Chaos Sea, the E adapted and incorporated local practices and new innovations they came across; substituting local ingredients that were widely available. In the quiet times they even supported the tribe by brewing great beer.

Despite their brew skills, they remained a warrior culture. I was proud to fight by the E's side… or drink, for that matter.

The Gardener had studied the process, consulting with the E brew-masters, and quietly trading seeds with his fellow Gardeners in the colonies. Eventually he planted part of Crystal Eight with five and seven row John Barleycorn. Then he planted over sixty rare and downright arcane hop varieties. The Gardener originally expected the E to choose a handful of strains for use and move the rest to cold storage until they could be sold off planet.

Turns out the E are *very* good brewers. Used over thirty different hops in their Imperial IPA, and the flavors never muddied; they layered. One on top of the other. It was glorious.

Which brings us to now.

Here we were, all thirsty and hot, walking up to an E brewery in the middle of a towering bamboo forest hanging in the sky, bathed in cascading waves of vintage light. Sometimes the pieces of the day all fit together perfectly.

We stepped inside and eased up to the polished bamboo bar. We were surrounded on three sides by deep forest. It was a riot in celebration of life; turquoise Verde, and bone parchment splashes slashed by Summerlight flowing down like honey on the pungent air. The shade was cool on my skin. On our fourth side, a small group of E were pouring draft Gold Ale and a hop-monster they called Sister Scythe (The E usually giggled when they said it—seemed to be some obscure off-color joke only the E understand).

On stage, a small Stomp band was deep into its afternoon practice; they kept stopping and restarting. At first it was irritating. The lead horn wouldn't let them progress further until they had the first part down. Repetition after repetition until it began to have a kinda rhythm to it, with the pause always on the beat. The gradual progression of the piece crept down the back stairs and grew bolder, louder with each new step. You just knew it was up to something naughty.

The torch singer was beautiful; she had the elongated body of a being that had never known planetary gravity growing up. I didn't know her, which rarely happened. I glanced at Navire and she dropped the singer's stats in my implant.

Now I remembered—one of Josephine's rescue projects outa east Gravtown. She was a former bad-girl, equally skilled with a microphone and exotic blades. Had an affection for tools of mayhem in general, but I couldn't fault that, so do I. Her new name was Barbo.

She belted out song with low-pitched attitude, promising trouble of the feminine type, the kinda trouble that men should know better than to get too near. Her eyes found mine in an invitation as old as time; which was both blatant and rude as hell to Navire. I inhaled deeply and Navire suddenly focused on me with the gift of discernment. She put an iridescent hand on mine—Navire can easily tell the difference between anger and attraction in my heartbeat. The Children of Electron do that.

The Gardener smiled sympathetically at me, as old friends will do in these situations. Navire seemed amused by the whole thing.

I ordered the Sister Scythe all round. Everyone smiled or snickered as expected even if we didn't exactly know why it was funny. It was like that.

The first round was lugged over by small groups of chattering E. It was served in tall frosted goblets that were sure to keep you busy for a while. Everybody grinned. I took a long, slow pull off the sweating amber nectar.

It was very-fine. A toffee, whiskey barrel's caramelized vanilla. IBU near threshold. So rich and dense that you wanted to slice off a piece and chew on it a while. Very refreshing, with just the right amount of complex flavor profiles. You didn't feel obligated to fall down and worship it. Just… enjoy. It was true-yummy.

I slowly set the tall crystal glass back on the bar and looked around in satisfaction. After an amused glance at the torch singer Navire smiled back, a mouse of froth left on her upper lip. It quickly vanished, and we both pretended we hadn't seen anything.

The Summerlight filtered down through the purple bamboo's swaying heights. It streamed in gold/emerald ribbons, slicing through the softer, azure shade. A gentle breeze bathed us in jasmine and citrus hops. Cold Beer. Good tunes. Fine company. Beautiful surroundings. I smiled and ordered another round.

The Stomp band made it all the way through the new piece, and it was tight. Bad-siren-girl had figured it out, but still snuck me a smile. I looked the other way. Some guys can't help stopping to smell the roses on the way home. But I had a flower of startling beauty beside me and wasn't even a little tempted by lesser blooms.

***

The days shuffled past as we toured the Fort's Crystal gardens; a water garden of tiny islands filled with lilies and blue lotus and trout. A budding temperate rainforest still under construction. An orchard of key lime and mango trees. And the newest, Crystal Fifteen: Bayou, soon to be complete with delicious Umami river eels and cypress knees poking up everywhere.

Each massive Crystal had been hollowed out, polished to optical quality, and planted with a different eco-system. Because the Crystals thrust out of the surface of Summer at different angles, each terrain had a grade of anywhere from seven to forty-two percent.

This made for good hiking, and the water always chuckled musically downstream. There were a wealth of waterfalls, high-arching bamboo bridges leading to switchbacks, and plenty of private niches with fabulous views. A couple of remote E breweries for when you need to walk off those calories; and maybe need a buzz. Ripe fruit you could eat right off the branch, juicy and dripping with sweet flavors. Minerals tainted the crystals in delicate hues, adding delicate nuances to the Summerlight as it passed through.

Every day we covered a different Crystal, unless something needed my attention for a while. I don't mind getting dirty and breaking a sweat. It was good, honest work. Good kinda tired at the end of the day. I slept like a baby those nights. These were the fine days; the kinda days you remember in feelings more than visuals. Times when the survival of our civilization wasn't in doubt. Innocent pleasures to be remembered well, later, out there in the Dark.

We usually spent about four or five days at each of the Forts when we were on tour. Three days working, then one off; four-part beat made for good life rhythm. It seldom got boring, and we tried to always leave the gardens for the better. You know; worked hard and had fun.

After a while the Ranch gets in your blood, and leaves us all better for it. It feels good to finally have a Home after all those years of wandering. I discovered that having something worth fighting for tends to bring out the best in us.

When we headed to Fort Cerberus, Katy the Sledge was obsessing on classic Stomp, playing live-jam from the masters; (so few left; they that burn brightest burn fastest). By the time we had worked our way through the Fort Cerberus Crystals, a week had passed, and we had covered the roots from New Harlem colony, to the Neo-tune and early Strut cycles. Katy has impeccable taste in music. Still a little room to grow in some other areas, but I had nothing but faith in her. Teenagers change daily, and you had to pay attention, or you'd miss something vital. Most days I got it right.

I like the kitchen and dining rooms at Fort Cerberus best.

This night, Katy the Sledge and the Gardener were cooking dinner, and everyone was getting together for one of those long, wonderful nights of great wine, good food, and long conversations of the kind you seldom found anywhere else. Not that we got out much.

Navire was wearing a new hard-body to dinner. She was styling a punk street-fighter girl with lotsa tattoos and asymmetrical anime-girl hair in a shining lavender that burned your eyes if you stared at it too long. Smudge across one cheek, accenting citrine topaz eyes. Worn, high quality body armor and boots that were born to kick ass. Kinda dark mahogany/gold motif going on, I noticed.

She was strapped up with dual Wing-chun butterfly swords tucked into her shoulder blades. A surprising number of Blades within easy reach, including quite a few throwing daggers braided into her lavender hair. Slap grenades and her customary ivory handled needlers. Boot daggers and tox darts. Basic Formal ware in Gravtown.

Tonight Navire was a former bad-girl with a big heart, a tarnished angel gone human. She was wearing a familiar lopsided grin, and it seemed like too long since I saw her.

I shined her an idiot grin with a bit of wicked tucked in around the corners. Her eyes widened for a micro-blink before she smiled back, shining like the sky on a hot Summer's day.

Katy the Sledge, who lately had decided she absolutely loved trying on new bodies like some kinda deranged fashionista, was wearing a leopard-girl hard-body—a jaguar, if I was correct.

She was dressed in an intricate rig that covered her body in weapons and tools and all kinda Boom. Her spotted fur webbed her body under everything, and she was sporting six centimeter black retractable claws that clicked the floor in a strident beat. She looked very grown up tonight.

Dread was wearing a humanoid hard-body for once, dressed as a very urban young man of means and good taste. Of course, he was still strapped from here 'to the Dark', I mean, Dread was still Dread, no matter which body he wore to dinner.

But this night, he was dressed in fine golden linen and bronzed leather with shining ebony skin (never mind the bits of pointy-things and Boom tucked here and there). Navire said it was a good look for him. Maybe he'd even smile.

Pasteur was slowly making the rounds, with lotsa shoulder slaps and a quiet smile. His ursine body was thick and immensely strong. Short thick fur rioted in red earth colors all over the place. His tooled leather, (some scaled reptilian type), harness was strapped with lotsa blades and a wealth of Boom.

Somehow, conversations with the warrior monk always had a layered complexity that rang true and made you ponder things beyond your ken. He had a paternal flavor that made you feel safe if you needed that, and a sense of humor that was both salt and pepper.

The Gardener was moving quickly, but fluidly as he and Katy balanced the timing of the various dishes. They were cooking so that the dishes would arrive at the table together in a synergistic harmony of flavors and textures. The aromas pouring forth were amazing.

Dread opened up a Champagne from Nouveau Reims, a pinot-dominated, finely tuned magus work of rainier cherries and brioche dripping with butter and drizzled in a delicate acidity that made your taste buds tingle. Everything was wrapped up in a small bubble deluge of nose tickling mousse that was delightful. It was very-fine.

First course was a florescent pink, chilled borscht drizzled with sour cream and dried Moro chilies sprinkled generously across everything. The Gardener's innocent beets had been living happily in the rich soil of Crystal Garden Three just a few hours ago. Now they were a delicious pleasure to consume. Sigh. At least they ended well! (I know. But guy humor seasons my days with these absurdist thoughts. Small smiles are under-rated).

The rich borscht was accompanied by rounds of hot, fresh-baked pizza rustica flatbread finished with course-ground black-sea salt and olive oil liberally splashed around. Hot and cold paired with a Semillon white wine that comfortably shared the stage without trying to take over. Balance was good.

We sat at a large, comfortable curved table set in a half-circle around Fort Cerberus's central kitchen/alchemical station, chatting and watching the action. We could all comfortably see everything (and each other) as the Gardener skillfully juggled culinary tasks in teamwork with Katy the Sledge. They danced through the work to the beat of a Strut number straight outa Gravtown. Oldtown dancehall tune. Neo-classic horns ushered in the moment. Bawdy piano hammered out the melody to drums bonged by a madman guzzling bootleg absinthe. I couldn't sit still in the presence of that. Just couldn't.
We didn't.

When we sat back down, all sweaty and smiling, the next course was just being served. Crystal Thirteen Ocean prawns had been blanched in a lime juice/serrano chile bath, then vacuum chilled at the perfect doneness. Mounds of split limes, and pulped horseradish punctuated with ramekins of hot sauce and alabaster sea salt covered the rustic platters filling the table. Piles of warm damp cotton napkins of generous proportions. And right in the center of the table was a small mountain range, consisting of steaming fresh corn, baby red potatoes, Turin artichokes (Chrystal Three), and the aforementioned spotted prawns.

How do you eat a mountain? Answer: messily, with lotsa napkins and Vino Albarino in the big bottles.

One bite at a time.

***

I first met the Gardener on the back-side side of nowhere, out there in the dark places. Navire and I and Smitty were running a freshly salvaged Residential space station we were planning on flipping, to generate $creds for a Ranch project. The Gardener somehow built an oxygen-generating Garden outa scrap and latrine biologicals. He began with nothing but passion and hard work; soon he was feeding us all. We got to know each other pretty well. Navire liked him and I knew him to be a man of honor. He stood about a meter and a half tall, with long arms tipped by claws built for digging. He had limpid black eyes large enough for me to suspect his original world was low-light. He had longish chocolate fur which was usually well groomed, and he smelled really good. I know that sounds kinda funny, but constantly growing aromatic plants had saturated his scent in juniper and blood oranges. Sometimes Tarkuna, too. He was peaceful, and easy to hang with in comfortable silence. This is a sign of good people everywhere.

Eventually we sold out for a tidy sum and dropped the waste disposal contract and moved on.

I offered the Gardner a home at my new Ranch on my way out. We told him that we had gardens to tend, in a fabled place where the sun always shined, and everything thrived with hybrid vigor. Entire eco-systems to design and build. A Home in paradise. Family.

He smiled that rare but true one and came with us. We worked hard, started a Home with the E, Smitty, the Gardener, Navire, and me. Everybody was happy. Life had a simple purpose to it. I slept well in those days.

We never discussed my art, or missions, because that wasn't the kind of thing the Gardener found interesting or important. But he could talk all day about the glories of a copper-based plant system vs. a chlorophyll eco-system. My eyes would eventually glaze over and I'd move on, just to stay awake. Didn't mean we weren't friends.

However, I'm afraid that I am also responsible for creating a world class wine snob that strapped up with ethereal memory in full Δqm^x quality. Sight, nose, mouth, back-nose, throat, finish. The works.

I had started it all one evening after work when I introduced the Gardener to the wonders of fermented grapes. Garnacha, I think. Several bottles with tapas scattered through the evening lent a certain cadence to that night. He just couldn't get over the fact that a human developed such a sublime thing. See, his people had never even thought of fermentation. Deliberately drinking something spoiled was a bad idea. Crazy. Now the Gardener had abruptly become aware of a huge blind spot in his weltenshang.

He didn't like it at all. Being ignorant in such an art was simply unacceptable for a Gardener. Fortunately, such things were curable, and the Gardener was nothing if not a consummate professional. He dove into the study of the Vine a like a broke pearl diver.

He lived, drank, and loved the Vine.

Sometimes these days you got the impression that he thought wine was wasted on most humans, present company excluded. I learned a lot about wine during that time, and we were gradually amassing a collection of nice wine from odd corners of the galaxy. Eventually he began to bug me for rare genetic samples of the Vine and began collecting Δqm^x tastings of all the fine wines. This eventually became a high usage of resources, aka expensive. But the scales balanced overall, so I didn't say anything.

Besides, I enjoyed the Δqm^x tastings quite a bit as well.

After all, he had close to thirty crystals about seventeen kilometers long and eight kilometers wide to fill with vegetative life and bio-environments. And now he knew exactly where to start. I just made sure to provide diverse enough genetic samples of the Vine AE in all its glories and manifestations. This made him happy and kept him in the Crystal gardens.

We both got more done that way.

3—The Prince

Prince Anodos patiently waited for exactly the right moment to leave the confines of the royal palace; timing was never a problem when the possibilities spread out before you like a map you could read in your sleep. The prince was very handsome and no longer a child, as of yesterday. While he was still young, his painful gauntlet was over; he was even capable of breeding now. The court still regarded him as a teenager in the long-lived life cycle of his kind, but he knew he was more. He was a seer of the first water, a future leader who would walk the fabled golden path through the myriad possible futures into the light. The golden path was much more difficult than the other possible futures, but in the end, it would bring millions through the darkness. Prince Anodos knew he was destined to save uncounted lives and even entire civilizations. The downside was that it was clear that walking the golden path meant grave personal danger, and bad odds all around.

Even with all his advantages, he wasn't assured of success. This didn't bother the prince. He could see everything clearly, even if he and his race were optically blind. That was of little meaning though, because the royal line could still perceive some forms of radiation, electric and magnetic fields, entropy and gravitational waves; and, well, all the possible paths that lay down that road.

To be a seer was both a burden and a gift, and a great responsibility. He had heard that so many times growing up that it had become a null sound, without meaning or value; a boring drone of white noise from the mouths of his trainers. His teachers and the royal tattoo artist-priests, who had painfully inked his long elegant body since the age of four, had drilled this into him. Literally.

Princes and princesses of the royal line are not happy children. They are neither giggly nor prone to boisterous play and pranks. Oh, they laugh or smile sometimes, but never as wholeheartedly as the other children. The trade-off for foreknowledge is a dampening of happiness. All the adults say so. Repeatedly. The elders believe this is necessary to produce a seer of the first water and have adapted the tools of the artist-priests to produce a precise level of pain. Regular, painful experiences every day, every month, every cycle, throw a damper over life. With great power comes great pain. They said that a lot, too.

Sometimes Anodos wondered what it would be like if he were a commoner, to be happy just because it was a sunny day or something. He couldn't really visualize it, and none of the paths came from there. It was mystifying.

There is something in this ritual tattooing of genetic lineage, mystical protection glyphs, and piercing of a predilections' nature, that is physiologically arduous. Assassination isn't the only reason few of the royal line survive to adulthood.

Adult females are capable of producing a handful of eggs every six cycles. Each stage of the development of the young shaves off a few of the clutch; some entire hatchings never make it to adulthood at all. Anodos was the last of three surviving royal heirs to the big chair. This was not a good place to be. The intrigues of court awaited; another even more deadly gauntlet to survive.

Anodos knew that he was an awesome sight—females had been known to faint upon seeing the full majesty of the giant salamander's crimson spotted body. He had grown to young adult size: over six meters from nose to tail and would continue to slowly grow throughout his hopefully long life. Every centimeter of his skin was heavily inked with rare compounds known to enhance clairvoyance and luck. Every symbol had meaning millennia old. Even his lineage was laid out in meter after meter of tiny script. There were no pretenders to the throne among his people. The process of inking took decades of painstaking work and resources few could afford. A prince of the line in all his glory was unmistakable.

That was the problem.

Once upon a time it was traditional for the young newly-adult princes and princesses to embark upon an adventure, out there in the uncivilized wastelands of the frontier. They learned to walk the futures in a harsh classroom; very few ever returned to take their place in the monarchy. However, those who did return were a force to be reckoned with and usually ended up ruling the empire.

This practice had fallen out of favor centuries ago, and the monarchy was weaker for it. These days' intrigue and duels accounted for the majority of deaths among the nobility. The royal court's older scions were well-known for arranging the unpleasant endings of potential rivals that might one day compete for the throne.

It was all about the big chair in the end. A royal scion that survived life in court was extremely dangerous; they had been well-blooded in duels fought with potential futures and strategic paths blazing. Only the most dangerous seers thrived.

Anodos knew he was inexperienced, and the futures before him dwindled and darkened should he tarry in the only home he had ever known. The Golden path led elsewhere anyway, and he was destined to follow it. To linger was to invite death, and this is how he came to be sneaking out of the palace, accompanied by only two bodyguards: the Stones that Speak.

The Stones that Speak had been his personal guard since he could remember. They had saved Anodos' life many times over the years. Their loyalty was unquestioned. The Stones were massive; over twenty meters long and powerfully built for battle. Their warrior tattoos had infused and toughened their skin into a flexible armor that deflected most anything. They were quick too, unexpectedly so. And their bite was worse than their bark. Much worse.

The little-used hallway they found themselves in was quite dusty. The young prince had never been in a place like this. It was dirty, something he had only heard of but never seen before. It was unexpectedly exhilarating.

Eventually the Stones that Speak halted in front of an inlaid stone mosaic. It took up an entire section of the wall and depicted an ancient battle between some long dead king and a horde of pale daemons on their spindly two legs and bony arms swinging unfamiliar weapons. They were quite ugly, and the royal warrior was cutting large swathes through the tiny figures with tail and claw. Anodos thought it was boring, and impatiently twitched his tail. This must be a very old section of the palace. Nobody did mosaics anymore. What were they waiting for?

One of the Stones that Speak delicately pressed a series of inlaid stones with a dark finger; suddenly the entire mosaic shuddered and moved up into the ceiling, exposing a dark tunnel that slanted down. A cool breeze rose from the opening carrying the scent of wet stone and mesquite and something long dead. One of the Stones that Speak rotated his enormous head back to calmly consider the prince.

Anodes hesitated for a moment; the Golden Path beckoned, but he had never actually been outside the palace before. He felt balanced on the knife edge of fate; behind him was inevitable death by intrigue. Ahead, the Golden Path threaded through a great abyss, eventually emerging into the light only he could see. After a few blinks Anodos smiled to himself and plunged forward into the future.

An hour later they emerged into a red stone gully shaded by twisted burgundy mesquite and divided by a creek that sang softly as it danced its way among the sand and boulders. Harsh sunlight sliced through the squat trees in spears of bright heat.

The prince wasn't used to being hot and didn't like it much. There wasn't enough room to bath his pampered skin, but he was able to splash his sizable head and belly. The Stones that Speak didn't seem to need a break, dividing to scout the immediate area for threats.

"It's time to move on, the smuggler's ship waits for no one," one of the Stones said.

"I'm ready," the young prince stated bravely, "Let's go." The future paths narrowed quite a bit here; in some he died by ambush, in others from exposure, his skin peeling badly from the harsh sun and wind.

Anodos walked the most comfortable of the paths, accompanied by his ever-present bodyguards. It took a long time to reach the landing spot where the off-worlders waited. His skin was still too dry for comfort, but he didn't complain; princes of the royal line had dignity. All his teachers said so. The Stones that Speak seemed invulnerable to discomfort and drew near to closely flank him as they approached the strange creatures.

The aliens stood tall, on two thick legs and had two long, loosely jointed arms tipped with long, sharp claws. They had unattractive noses that poked bluntly out of their flat faces, and small mouths that didn't look like they could do much damage in a fight. They had strange artifacts and gleaming knives strapped all over their battle harnesses. Tufts of dull blond fibers stuck out here and there; he thought it was called hair or fur. Anodos found it to be quite ugly, and his visions hadn't included the dank smell wafting off the whispering smugglers, either. The smelly aliens stared at him, occasionally rumbling to each other without taking their eyes off him. He understood their awe; a prince of the royal line was magnificent in appearance. Most commoners go their whole life without even a glimpse of royalty.

One of the Stones that Speak made his way up to the small group of aliens and reached into one of his concealed flesh-pockets, pulling out a small pouch. The aliens seemed nervous, and several fondled well-worn artifacts of dull metal or the sharp things on their harnesses. The Stone that Speaks raised his massive head four meters high; towering over them, motionless as only Anodos' people could be. A hint of pungent salt crept into the scent pouring off the odd-looking creatures. Behind them stood a disreputable lander with a few non-essential pieces missing and burn marks in all the wrong places.

Anodos could see a few paths that led to conflict and the aliens' deaths, but in those futures he died shortly thereafter. Most led to the lander and a fourteen-kilometer long liveShip in orbit around his world. He took three steps forward, and two to the left, settling into the best of the futures available. The off-worlders seemed to relax a bit now that he was in full view.

The largest of the aliens spilled the pouch's contents into his paw, rumbling with approval at the sparkling nodules. Several of the other creatures crowded around, focused on the treasure, but two of the aliens remained on alert in their guard positions. Anodos approved. This boded well; as they followed the Golden Path in search of lost Summer, there were going to be a few close-calls. Maybe more than a few. Well-trained servants could make all the difference in the days to come. The Pirates of Thunder didn't know they were now in the service of the royal heir. This was just a quick side job for them to raise $cred; they had their own desperate mission.

***

One of the Stones that Speak was in front of the young prince, methodically jogging along—the salamander equivalent of jogging, more like waddling sideways, not pretty but it covered ground amazingly fast for such a massive body. Anodos had to hurry to keep from getting run over by the Stone that Speaks behind him. The ship was vast, maybe larger than the palace complex itself, although he hadn't thought that was possible. The broad corridor they were in stretched almost the entire fourteen-kilometer length of the ship.

Anodos was tired and wanted a bath but the Stones insisted that he train for the dangerous trip ahead. He tried to explain that he could see trouble coming and didn't need all this exercise. They just looked at him with serene confidence and upped the pace again. He stumbled and kept up, but he was breathing in a very undignified manner. Neither of the bodyguards seemed to be uncomfortable, radiating a solidity normally only found in boulders and mountains. Thus, the name.

They were called the 'Stones who Speak' for a number of reasons.

When they wished, the Stones could become so motionless that they faded into the background visually. Specially inked warrior tattoos helped with that. They physically loomed over the smaller, younger

25

people of their race in the same way a wall or monolith did. The Stones that *Speak* rarely did—this lent a weight to their sparse words on the rare occasions they did speak.

The young prince made it to the top without getting run over by one of the Stones that Speak. That was a first.

Of course, he had known this would happen today.

They were in a large cargo hold of the massive colony ship known as Thunder, one that was used to hanger the ship's landing craft. They were climbing the walls to build his muscles and speed. It was working. At first, he had only been able to climb five or six meters high. When he stopped, unable or maybe unwilling to go further, the Stone that Speaks below him had nose-butted his rear upwards, pushing him further up than the young prince had felt comfortable going. Prince Anodos was shocked the first time this happened; back home in the palace you could be put to death for touching royalty. Not to mention offending their dignity. Of course, back home he'd probably be dead by now, a victim of ruthless court battles. The young prince simply hadn't been paying much attention to the futures spread out before him, secure in the care of the Stones. They were in a flying fortress far from anything, tearing through deep space. What could happen?

Apparently more than he realized.

He vowed to be more aware of his surroundings in the future, of the paths laid out before him. He needed to keep his eyes on the Golden Path. As he rested at the very top to catch his breath some eighty meters above the deck, Anodos felt the simple satisfaction of athletic accomplishment. This was not something he was familiar with; princes seldom expend much energy on mere physical tasks. Dignity and all that. He found that he liked this feeling.

The hard exercise also had another effect. He was beginning to automatically select the best short-term outcome of the futures thrown at him with fire hose intensity. Always before, the sheer complexity of the paths ahead took all his concentration. Now, with his subconscious taking over the minor first steps of his path, he was able to see ahead much further. Instead of minutes into the future, he could sometimes make out the nearby future paths hours ahead.

Of course, this was much different than the moment of his Awakening, when he had seen the Golden Path laid out across the cycles in all its complexity, all at once. That shining experience was burned forever into his heart and mind. The details had faded a little over the past three cycles, but the emotions he felt, and the drive to walk it remained as strong as ever. He was going to help lead millions of people through the coming darkness, into the light. He did remember that the Golden Path truly began in an inside-out world.

A legendary place known as Summer.

4—Koen of Summer

We used the proceeds from the new release of my battle-art vignette to increase Ranch security. We began by purchasing a "lost" carrier class freighter complete with cargo. (You can buy anything in Gravtown). The ship was stuffed full of mobile sentry-guard units that were only three meters across. There were hundreds of them. They bristled with arcane Boom and antiquated particle beam weaponry, plus full spectrum sensory units that broadcast in Γqm^x. The units had terribly inadequate Signal transmission speed, but Smitty said that this was fixable. At least it was almost full spectrum Signal.

Dread, who'd methodically appropriated the role of "head of security," was very pleased, although you really had to know him to tell. He immediately began to design a complete survey of our Ranch land with Navire by implant as we worked. It would be the first survey of its magnitude. Long story. At the same time Smitty and I dug into the guts of one of the sentry units to learn exactly what kinda tech we had on our hands.

Navire and her team of E focused on strip-searching the logics and pre-programed decision-trees. They found lotsa old-data from ten cycles ago, the last time they'd been used.

She was operating at full speed now, crunching numbers and running diagnostics at a full gallop. I knew she found it lonely operating at battle speed and blew her a pale kiss by implant.

There was a very primitive, heavy frame that held everything together and it would be an excellent chassis for the new Ranch sentries we were going to 'Phoenix' from the antiquated tech. Navire was relentless in her inspection, delving into every byte and cranny. Eventually her hard work paid off, uncovering a handful of remote-access back doors and tar pits, and a sleeper waiting for the right moment to broadcast our position to someone.

Γqm^x— *Gamqum: quantum messaging encrypted to Gamma standards.* Δqm^x *or Delqum was far superior.*

We weren't sure who.

Navire tried to follow the trail, but the multiple recipients were re-broadcasters layered on top of each other like pastry sheets in a really good baklava.

Smitty and I decided that our work should start with the shields and weaponry.

I took the shields and headed down to my forge to run some ideas through my forge's Smith. He was dwarven fabricator-tech and went by the name of Biljaok; a true master of the art. He and I went way back; he didn't have much of a sense of humor, but he was a genius at weapons and bad-tech.

I was interested in the chitin armor we had picked up recently during a salvage operation. It was incredibly tough given its weight and had very efficient reflective properties. Biljaok studied the material for a bit and said we could make it, suggesting a layer of bamboo fiber woven with carbon filaments in a flexible amber resin, followed by a very thin chitin layer, then another weave layer until it resembled old-school jawbreaker candy. I liked that, but also wanted to be able to reflect back Signal to its source and fry it. That took shaping the surface of the three-meter sphere in such a way as to focus light, to form coherent pulses salted with microwaves from the weaponry the enemy turned on us. There's a certain elegance in using the enemy's own fire to hit back.

Smitty headed to his forge to start analyzing the Boom and designing a new heavy H_2O cannon for the sentries. This was one of Smitty's favorite activities; creating tools of mayhem. Any excuse in a storm—building new guns was always a good time.

Me too; I liked being on a mission. No gray, I was a black and white kinda guy back then; a clearly defined goal. Everyone working together, focusing on a common purpose. It was when I felt most alive, and so far, it was turning out to be a really great mission.

The E were running around excitedly as usual; not satisfied just making beer, the little guys loved building weapons too. They were the foundation of the forge, the backs upon which great weapons were crafted. Plus, they never minded cleaning up and doing the hundred little tasks that created the whole. As long as they were getting well paid. In good beer. Lotsa good beer. Which they made for me…

Navire completely re-engineered the logics and ended up almost rebuilding them from the ground up. Nevertheless, it was going well; she was almost ready to install Ranch protocols and our proprietary decision-trees. After that, we would install full Ranch security and battle protocols and then we'd be golden as a Summer afternoon.

Navire ran best at accelerated speed, as was her custom when working alone or being short on time. It was more efficient, but when we were together, she always matched my biological processing speed. Navire is always kind in the small ways.

Smitty and his forge crew of E came up with a unique way to fire heavy H_2O shells at a truly frightening rate. Kinda noisy, but sometimes that was fun too. The adjustable caliber cannon could fire a wide range of Boom. I liked that part—precision firing that could either disable or destroy in a blink. The surgical use of overwhelming power was best done by a pro.

Like us.

Pasteur came up with sleepy-time flechettes that could lights-out anyone in less than a blink. They were biological in nature and came pre-loaded with toxins of great purity and strength.

I think that flechettes are bad-tech at its best.

Very small, completely silent and precise, so fast you can't even see them hit. Virtually instant effect. Very effective on soft-bodies, but not so much on the hard-bodies like the one Navire was currently wearing. That's when you strapped up with mantis leg flechettes and shredded your target into small pieces.

I once met a man that wore his on the back of his hands.

He ran a bar while secretly waging a one-man war against an empire. Put thousands of enemy soldiers to bed for nine-month naps. No one ever suspected him as he hunted enemy soldiers in their own stomping grounds. He later became known as" the Man Who Never Missed", but that's another story.

Eventually it was time to go to the Boom Grotto.

Katy the Sledge took us over; she hung out there a lot. Teenage angst and Boom went together like chocolate and hazelnuts.

The Ranch was huge; and our primary facilities were buried deep within the densely layered crystalline structure known as Summer bedrock. We drilled whatever spaces we needed—there was lotsa room beneath the giant crystal forests, so we over-engineered as a habit. It didn't hurt that we'd inherited this place from a race of Rime giants. Everything important was already built on a grand scale.

One afternoon we were drilling out a chamber to conduct weaponry experiments in, when we unexpectedly we broke though into one of Summer's occasional caverns. The dense crystal layers made standard mining survey scans useless. While that was good security for us, it also made for the occasional surprise.

The exposed chamber was massive in nature and hadn't seen light for uncounted millennia. The grotto was sterile in nature. Not even a lick of moisture, only brilliant crystalline mineral deposits laid down by an ancient ocean as it slowly evaporated eons ago. Our lights reflected in a million facets, magnifying it so that it covered kilometers instead of just meters.

Smitty and I looked at each other while our teams of E watched us closely. I cracked grin.

"This place is just ideal for blowing up stuff, no?" I asked, although I already knew the answer. The E broke into spontaneous knife dances and blade juggling while gossiping at the top of their lungs.

That was answer enough.

So we did.

I challenged each of my leaders to succeed in winning the impromptu competition, each beginning with the same resources. I had brought three of the sentry-guard units with us, so each team could modify and simply demonstrate their unit's new abilities.

Each of us was separated by about fifteen meters. The shining Spheres were so bright that it was hard for my soft-body abilities to distinguish details; seems that they were very efficient at concentrating and reflecting ambient light. When everyone said they were ready, I nodded to Pasteaur. His bad-tech flechettes weaponry went first. Best to start with the quieter tech, if not as easy to see.

The bio-mech targets down range had no actual intelligence; that would be too creepy. They <u>were</u> quick, though. The armor they were wearing simulated the degree with which they would take damage in battle. A good test recorded a widely varied level of damage infliction new-data. This research could be valueless unless it was calibrated for a wide selection of resistance, as was our habit.

Pasteur's sentry guard opened fire with sleepy-time ammo.

About forty percent of the targets hit went down instantly. If I hadn't known where the fire came from I wouldn't have even realized a weapon was in use. Then Pasteur rapidly switched to toxin ammo and another twenty percent went down. Although, not as quickly this time. Again, undetectable.

The huge ursine monk snapped his wrists downwards as he changed ammo on the run. Then his massive paws snapped back up to blow everything in its wake up with mantis-leg flechettes. The few remaining targets silently exploded into wet shreds.

"This guard unit is capable of extended non-stop fire for a period in excess of twenty-five minutes. You can disintegrate a small building in a fraction of that," Pasteur explained.

"The flechettes weapon system allows measured levels of aggressiveness that include non-lethal crowd control. Anyone can blow something up, but I can reward bad behavior with an instant time-out nap."

Pasteur stretched his long arms overhead and grinned. Then he turned to face Smitty and his team with an expression of patience and gentle expectation. He was very aware of exactly how irritating Smitty found this.

I exchanged a micro-grin with Navire and turned to give Smitty my full attention.

Smitty stood tall, over two meters and powerfully built; he was after all, a smith, first and foremost. Hadn't always been that way, but where else does an aging fighter go when the young ones come up?
The forge.

It has always been a natural progression for certain fighters. No one can forge a weapon like a warrior that has fought and bled for his art. A warrior who intimately knows le Danse Macabre, if of old. Such a smith could wrap elemental chi into the very metal of the battle-art quality weapon he produced and quenched in sweat and blood.

The weapons produced by such a smith were considered master-class, and the very best of them seemed to thirst for the death of the enemy with avarice and a dark lust.

This kinda weapon was not for everyone; it takes a strong personality to fully master such a blade. Or Boom.
One of those.

Smitty wore a battle harness that was literally layered in bad-tech. Heavy on the pointy-things. He firmly believed you could never have too many blades in a fight. Didn't skimp on the Boom, though. His primary weapon, however, was his war hammer. Smart-tech. It was an archaic Child of Electron, with densely textured memory banks and potent processing speed. It was encased in a huge metal hammer covered in runes that glowed sullenly, except in battle. Then they shone with a brilliant electric-blue intensity.

The hammer was more than a weapon; it was both powerful and creative, with two main modes. It had one form and personality for creative forging, and a very different one for battle. Smitty was holding the one for building right now and regretted once saying that he had forged it as a replacement for his long lost hammer Goibhniu. His new hammer had kinda developed an attitude about this, and tended towards sulky. It was prone to lashing out out when Smitty talked about his first-forged.

Hammer envy, I guess.

"The sentry units have the armament to control most situations they encounter, with a diffused intelligence that can be upgraded, in order to increase processing power," the red-headed smith began.

"Once the targets have been selected, the six auto-cannons are calibrated, and open up with variable heavy H_2O ammo. By spinning and rotating at high speed while firing, multiple targets can be destroyed very efficiently," Smitty understated, with a micro-glare at Pasteur.

He then announced "Firehole!" and stood back.

Quite a few missiles and Boom, moving too fast for us soft-bodies to count, tore through the quiet air of the Boom Grotto, aimed at us. Smitty's sentry unit whirled too fast for me to perceive, (Navire replayed it for me later at a speed I could follow), strobing Boom. It was over in a few blinks; nothing even came close. My implant had muted my hearing, of course, but my head still hurt from the barrage. It was extremely noisy. We were all very impressed, even Pasteur. We all clapped heartily, but I'm not sure Smitty could hear it.

My turn.

I smiled politely at everyone and began.

"The layered armor we've come up with can resist extensive Boom, but there's lotsa Signal based weaponry out there, from coherent light to pulse based. We've come up with a passive ricochet surface that in essence, returns fire to the enemy using their own firepower. There is, of course Signal loss, and the return fire is currently only about thirty-five percent of the original attack. Still, this will degrade the enemy's weapon potency as the battle progresses, and requires virtually no additional resources," I explained, before also declaring "Firehole!" and gesturing at my sentry unit.

Target mechs bearing assorted Signal weaponry opened up in silent, bright fury. Within several blinks, a few of the attackers began melting and going dark. Shortly thereafter all the enemy forces stuttered to a malformed, liquid halt.

Not bad, I thought before immediately shushing myself. It just didn't pay to tempt Lady Luck's attention these days. I knew this from experience. Long story. I might have been a little worried too, despite our extensive testing within our allotted time period. New concepts seldom work the way they're supposed to so early in the process, but then Biljaok was <u>very</u> good.

I moved on to the second project that Navire and I had cooked up.

"I used to think in terms of 'large weapons equals big Boom. Larger equals more Boom.'" I smiled wryly.

"Today we are taking a different approach. By the time we're finished, we will have one sentry per three-hundred square kilometers of Ranch land. While the individual unit's armament is fully capable of resolving any problem within their quadrant, it is unable to take out large, ship-sized targets.

"However, the multiplexed fire of hundreds of units, coordinated with precision and accuracy surpasses any individual weapon we are currently capable of producing. We can vaporize a target on Far-Summer with almost one-hundred percent accuracy." I paused for effect.

I knew it was kinda dramatic, but I've always wanted to use the word "vaporize" in a threat. What? It was guy-humor. Too many corny space operas in my teenage years, maybe. It didn't matter that Navire rolled her eyes. I still thought it was funny. So did Smitty. Dread didn't get it. The E did though.

"Navire's hard work has paid off in a Signal transmission system that can link every guard unit together into a single gestalt," I said, nodding slightly to Navire; she never, ever, missed a nuance of body language. The Children of Electron are like that.

Navire smiled widely, making eye contact with everyone before beginning. "I tore everything out and built these guys up from scratch, using Hive-tech to fill in the gaps," she began. (We like Hive-tech).

"The decision-trees are our standard Ranch systems. The units can run on independently, carrying out orders using sophisticated guard and problem-solving systems for the everyday kinda situations. They can also link with any number of other individual units to multiply their intellect and their processing efficiency, as well as speed. Firepower too." she said softly; everyone was so focused on her description that they instinctively leaned closer to hear better.

"There is a third mode; puppet. We could wield them as extensions of our arms and legs. The combined firepower could burn a moderate-sized ship to cinders in blinks." Navire paused for a measured moment, then continued in a soft tone. "This is powerful. We don't like using innocent smart-tech like throw-away meat puppets. You use this kinda bad-tech only when you run out of all other choices. Desperate times of survival. Like that," she said.

Everyone knew what she meant. I slung a true smile her direction, and she micro-grinned back so quickly that no one else saw it. Just me. I like that. Intimacy unseen in a full room. Shared secrets only you two know. It has its attractions.

Everyone's attention focused on the sentry unit hovering about fifteen meters in front of us. About two hundred meters away a busted up corsair deadShip had been positioned so that any attending Boom would be channeled away from us.

Navire chanted the ancient war cry: "Firehole!" and all the spheres cut loose. Then there wasn't any wrecked ship, just a glowing hole in the Boom Grotto floor.
And a very big bang.

Everyone clapped and hooted.

Navire was modest but pleased. She even blushed a bit. The Children of Electron are like that. At least in the beginning.

Afterwards we met at the E brewpub inside Fort Lilith and hashed out the details over ice-cold golden ale with seaweed chips and that hot sauce that burns so good. Thirsty work really, and the seaweed chips from Crystal Thirteen pulled their salty share to keep the barley nectar flowing. Smitty and Pasteur can really put it away, for soft-bodies like us. I'm really glade Navire's memory isn't damaged by our excesses. Good times.

5—The Tyrant

The Tyrant Jenny-Rose and her team were coming in fresh off a difficult mission, exhausted to the point that it would require days, not hours, of rest to completely restore the Horde to their full operating potential.

The Tyrant's Horde was employed by Dacca Corporation, deployed out of the Corp-nation colony of Tepito, on the planet Deffey. They were hostile takeover specialists in the Acquisitions department of the company's Division Forty-Seven and were quite good at their job.

Jenny-Rose had taken over the Horde nine cycles ago and had gradually distilled and shaped her team into its current size of just over five hundred highly-trained soldiers, down from a force of over twelve hundred. The previous Tyrant had been quantity oriented, with a habit of throwing more and more bodies at a problem until it was resolved. That hadn't worked out too well for him in the long run. They never did find his body, but no one was really looking that hard.

She, on the other hand, was quality oriented, and had forged her Acquisitions team into a loyal, potent force that was highly respected. The Horde had enriched her boss significantly over the past seven cycles, and his stock in the company had risen along with his \$cred balance. Nothing made the company happier than high \$cred earnings, and when the upper management was happy, everybody was happy, because their \$cred balances were growing like wildfire too. That's the way it works in the Corp-nations.

Life was could be very good when your star was rising.

Unfortunately, not everyone was equally pleased with her manager's rise in fortune and prestige. While he had always held his own with the other regional managers, his success in the company had drawn too much attention. In the Corp-nations, it rarely pays to come to the attention of upper-middle management.

Upper-middle management consisted of detail oriented, highly-evolved sociopathic predators who had painstakingly worked their way up the corporate chain, generating massive loot and an equally large trail of bodies in their wake.

The Tyrant's boss had come to the attention of such a woman, sub-Director Jane, who found it in her interest to weaken a competing region by eliminating him. This was not a simple task; Jenny-Rose's boss was well protected by the Horde, so careful planning was necessary. Unfortunately, highly-organized sociopaths also enjoy that part, especially in the laissez-faire office arena of the Corp-nations.

The sub-director's plans came to fruition in the ninth cycle of Jenny-Rose's leadership of the Horde.

It began with new orders that came through as the Tyrant Jenny-Rose was checking in on four wounded team members currently dozing in the commercial ship's doc-box. She didn't like traveling on public transports, but the exit strategy of the mission she was wrapping up required it.

The Tyrant was, as always, surrounded by her command troika. Mick, the communications and sabotage expert, tapped into her implant and relayed new orders to her with a concerned expression. At her nod, he forwarded them to her other two troika commanders, Erika and Antonio. From the looks on their faces, they didn't care much for them either.

"I don't like changing ships, especially at a dump like Nigel's Star," Erika stated quietly. She rarely got outwardly excited about things, but still managed to convey her feelings with great effectiveness.

"I'm more concerned about the part where we transfer to a ship I've never heard of—why all the mystery?" Antonio asked grumpily. "Why can't this wait until we have a chance to catch our breath and a few hours of sleep—the men need downtime," he continued.

"That's the way upper management does things—never an explanation or reason for the hired help," Mick clarified, "What concerns me is the Δqm^x itself; it didn't carry any of the sub-texts from our chain of command. These orders originated somewhere else, someplace high enough in the company to give us all nosebleeds. It smells bad," he concluded.

The Tyrant nodded in agreement, still looking at her resting, injured men.

"Our orders don't mention who we're meeting, or why the Horde has to accompany me, but not to jump when upper management says to, has very well-defined repercussions. The strategic choice dictates that we report in person as ordered… and that's what we'll do," she added softly.

Her troika nodded and immediately began organizing the Horde for the change in plans.

To Jenny-Rose, it felt like another asset grab by unknown parties.

Her people were considered both highly-effective and valuable, and it wouldn't be the first time someone in the company attempted to appropriate the Horde, to co-opt her team. Odd that they hadn't waited until the entire Horde was involved; seventy of her fighters were still home, back at the enclave, watching over everyone's families and children, and of course, her boss as well.

The Tyrant took what should have been adequate precautions.

Unfortunately, she was dead-tired and hadn't anticipated that everyone on the new ship would be determined to murder her team and dispose of their remains in the depths of the Chaos Sea.

The Tyrant wasn't one to let it show, but she would carry the weight of that failure for a very long time.

Nigel's Star _was_ a dump, but they'd all seen worse. The worn-out orbital facility was perched on the edge of the Chaos Sea, seemingly on the verge of falling in as it rounded the dull red sun each orbit. The Chaos Sea took up the whole sky at this point, but there weren't many windows in the station, and she suspected that was deliberate.

The less-than-delightful smells of unwashed humanity permeated the very fabric of the corridors and the vendor stands were serving tacos made from some kind of off-brown mystery meat. With over four hundred soldiers, there was always someone hungry enough to venture a bite; and his comrades watched him with varying expressions of curiosity and distaste. Most of the Horde took advantage of the moment to snatch a bit of sleep; good soldiers rarely waste such an opportunity. The soldiers of the Horde were very good.

6—Koen of Summer

In this corner of the galaxy, you were always aware of the Chaos Sea. It was simply too big to ignore, taking up the entire sky in a slow boil of debris and dust. You could find all colors in there if you looked long enough. And you simply couldn't help but look.

It was simultaneously scary and fascinating: beautiful death in a boiling gas maelstrom of almost infinitely complex movements, with the occasional bent-time whirlpools the closer you got to the Horse latitudes. Navire said it was sorta like a new kind of music; she spoke of barely-glimpsed oddling rhythms and shifting alien tonal-notes. Beautiful and deadly, she had heard its siren call for as long as she could remember.

The Chaos Sea was made up of trillions of space chunks that had once been parts of planets someone called home. It held gas cloud neighborhoods with thousands of planetary systems. All the assorted cosmic debris that was left over from building solar systems. Dwarf systems and massive dark planets. Comets and moons and burned out suns. Wandering derelict residential stations. Frozen worlds covered in strange ruins and atmospheres locked in ice and snow.

Everything was mixed up in a dense, sparkling dust cloud the size of a moderate galaxy, a cloud that concealed everything within. Chaos indeed.

Everyone said you could find anything in there; anti-matter nodules, rare metals, valuables of all sorts… and even, if you were lucky, alien deadShips.

These silent, dark ships were populated only by ghosts and memory banks that sometimes held entire worlds, not to mention loot of all denominations. That was our favorite part.

It'd be unfair not to mention the lost castaways either, or the rare species and bizarre life-forms clinging to life in the strangest of places. Of course there was also lotsa crashing debris and crushings of worlds.

Archaic Boom and deadly static discharges churning in soundless fury, as far as the eye could see.

The Chaos Sea had been gently drawn together over time into a slow swirling maelstrom, perched on the edge of a colossal event horizon. A massive black hole nibbling on a Sargasso Sea of celestial junk and smashed planets, belching iridescent gas clouds and cosmic flotsam of galactic proportions.

They said that lost Summer was buried deep within the Chaos Sea. Most people considered it a myth, like old-earth or honest carnies; mention of it primarily showed up in late night action-romances. But all myths begin with a kernel of truth.

Deep in the Chaos Sea, on the very border of the Horse latitudes was a dark wasteland of burned out stars and dead planets. That's where Summer hid. It was a dark jewel turned inwards, you couldn't even see her until you were too close to stop. It was a sudden monstrosity outa nowhere, with a gorgeous soul that was hidden from the outside.

Summer had begun as an enormous planetary-sized ocean, buried deep within the magma of an immense planet in an unstable binary system. With time, the magma cooled and the giant sea slowly lost moisture to the surface where life began. Layers of mineral-tainted crystals were deposited on the shore of the subterranean sea without interruption for countless millennia, until an enormous geode was birthed. It was a geode noticeably larger than a standard planet, still deep within a mammoth world.

It remained buried for untold millennia. Life arose on the immense planet's skin, looking like nothing more than algae blooms on stagnate pools from space. Eventually vast cities arose that were nothing like what we think of as cities. Life became crowded, and the madness known as war spread like wildfire. These unremembered people destroyed everything left in a mad scramble for the few remaining resources. They sundered their world in fire with weapons that a sane people would have never built. When the giant planet finally disintegrated, the geode that would become known as Summer tumbled free of the rubble to spin silently through dark space, for a very long time.

That was the first part of the story, anyway.

Then one day, two things changed.

First, an impact. We don't know with what, but it was big.

Second, the geode began breaking apart very slowly.

When the cracked and apparently fatally damaged geode was drawn into the Chaos Sea, the roaring maelstrom swallowed the broken geode planet effortlessly, leaving no trace of its passage.

Sometime after that, an old-data tribe we called the Builders had strung long brass hued spun-carbon tubes between the enormous fragments of the planet sized geode, holding the pieces precisely in place. Then the huge gaps and cracks between the pieces had been stuffed with frozen gases of various types. Whatever was handy at the time, I guess. No shortage of raw materials in the Chaos Sea. The off-white packing material in the cracks absorbed broad spectrum wavelengths eagerly, almost hungrily. A potent, luminescent fungi was inoculated into the ice. It eventually spread webbed mycelium throughout every meter of the frozen packing ices. The fungi thrived over time, absorbing starlight through its outer surfaces, and generating bright light that flowed down from its interior surfaces.

From the outside, Summer spins invisibly, folded in the velvet night of space.

From the inside there are jagged white cracks across a glimmering sky that was never dark. It's astonishingly beautiful, especially when a lightstorm is working its way across Far-Summer.

The inner-side of each massive fragment was in essence an island. An island covered in myriad crystals that hummed and color-shifted with the reflected mycelium-light of billions of faceted mirrors. The Ranch was one such island.

The larger crystals that covered Summer were clustered in groups of seven to twenty-four, sunk into beds of smaller and sharper crystals. Those were surrounded by smaller beds. And so on.
There were literally countless reflections.

Inside Summer, the light is strangely bent, focused, and scattered. Mycelium-light gains strange textures as it bounces from crystal to crystal a few trillion times. It's very bright, though. There is no night in Summer, only the occasional strange light-tones of a lightstorm passing through. They even say that there are light waves still circulating under the crystal forests that were new when the Builders first lived here.

The forges had been busy. They had turned out over six-hundred rebuilt sentries that were shiny-new and already deployed across the Ranch, surveying every meter up close and personal. Dread hadn't wasted any time.

"I can't produce effective security without knowing what I'm guarding, intimately," Dread explained for the I-don't-know-what time. He had a point.

"You've never had a real survey of the Ranch lands—there could be anything out there!" he continued.

"We've been kinda busy," I replied with a touch of defensiveness. The early years had been very exciting, defined by not-enough sleep, and even, some argued, too much hard work. That had left little time for the niceties. The problem for Dread was that security always came first. Couldn't say I disagreed, but he hadn't been here back then. Didn't know what things had been like at the time. My eyes met Navire's.

"Found something you'll want to see; it's like nothing you've ever come across. Beneath the Shimmering!" he growled several hours later. You had to really know Dread to tell that he was pumped. Luckily, I did.

I nodded politely at Dread and we all began to strap up. I was already wearing my Stealthsuit, and Navire was ready for anything, her hard-body all Valkyrie and blond with dangerous curves and lotsa blade. Katy the Sledge was auditing everything through our implants, and she got noisily happy, like she always does when we decide to go somewhere new.

We had come off tour a month ago, and I was already feeling the itch to travel way down in the spring wells of my feet. I think we all did.

Katy dropped a Stomp on us by implant from the east side of Gravtown with Wild Man Taw on sax, and chorus tube-metal throbbing heavy dancehall beat. Then Jelly Girl started keyboard, way off and quiet, creeping closer and louder with every ivory note. We all grinned at each other as we slipped bad-tech into convenient nooks and armpits, sheath and holster.

Time to move.

Today Katy the Sledge was wearing a new train, smaller and more compact than usual. It was dull metallic gray with lotsa shielding and was strapped up with an extensive array of weaponry. Pulse and Coherent light guns, heavy H_2O cannon, even an antique rail gun. She was strolling Steampunk style, laced tightly with arcane laser and chemical based Boom. So grown up and ready for anything. I just smiled at her for a moment, trying to capture the moment before she grew up completely.

They do that. Children.

We left Fort Charon and traveled for six hours before arriving at the Shimmering.

Dread was right.

Orange-red needles of crocoite crystal jutted ten kilometers high around the perimeter, a crimson beach circling an ocean of light.

The Shimmering.

You could see it all the way from Far-Summer, but I'd never actually spent any time in this particular corner of my own backyard. The concave, citron limonite floor of the ocean of bright retained the radiance that the crimson needles reflected down from the sky. The light bathed in its own reflections and spread out in brilliant molten pools that shimmered so intently that you couldn't look directly at it.

But that wasn't what Dread had brought us to see.

Katy the Sledge slammed to a stop dramatically, as always. She had timed the music so that the last note ended as her doors shot open. Had to admit; my little girl had great timing. The sudden quiet, combined with the hot glare, created a surreal impact.

I stepped out into an egg-shaped clearing in the needle forest of cerise crocoite crystals that guarded the light sea's borders. Katy hitched a ride on my implant. I could feel her looking over my shoulder.

Dread took point, while Navire and Pasteur flanked me, and the Gardener covered our rear with Smitty. We soon found ourselves at the entrance of what turned out to be an extensive labyrinth cave system honeycombing the light-ocean's floor. We trotted down into the maze, thoroughly enjoying the warmth and golden sunlight. I'd spent more than enough time out there in the cold dark places—we all had—and had learned you had to savor the small pleasures and warmth, then tuck them away to see you through the long night.

Sections of the maze's ceiling opened directly to the liquidesque light-weave of the Shimmering. It appeared that the heat had gradually melted wide holes in the light-ocean floor. These somewhat organic skylights opened down into the grottos and passageways of the labyrinth beneath the Shimmering. Some overhead sections were translucent, slow-pouring Summer's concentrated golden light down in sensuous waves of warmth and honey across our heads and arms. Other skylights pierced the dim caverns in brilliant spotlights ten or fifteen meters across.

The Gardener was beside himself, chuckling and making comments about plant-friendly environments and chlorophyll heaven as we moved through the maze.

We came to a stop in an oval cavern pierced by sizable light falls and golden crystal-altered sunlight seeping down in easy waves. It was magnificent. I turned to the Gardener and grinned.

"Looks like we finally found the right place for your tree frogs!" I said.

He nodded happily and began explaining what kind of bio-environment he thought we should create in detail-rich word-pictures. He was talking kinda fast and his eyes glowed with bio-luminescence or fanaticism or maybe just happiness.

One of those.

We all subtly stepped back a few paces before our eyes began to glaze over and get all sleepy. Been there before.

Time to move.

***

I had been playing with an idea for a few months. Sometimes all the things fall into place so naturally that the idea just becomes reality. Or maybe it just seems that way. Hubris has its attractions.

We now knew that there were legendary creatures hiding out there in the Dark places; Apex predators, virtually invisible before they struck. They were simply called the Keer. Each one a six-meter long ant-shark-like jack-in-the-box of sudden death. The ate people now, ever since they had tasted 'long pig' for the first time. Keer racial-rapture had ensued, and a deadly religion was born. Dining on Rock-lice just didn't cut it anymore.

The reason you never saw a Keer coming was because of the fine silk down covering its entire body. It had amazing properties, among them invisibility, and this was priceless. Well, not priceless, but two cycles ago a Corp-nation middle manager had traded three entire prime planets for a quarter kilo of the down. This turned out to be a bargain.

A small number of miners had always prospected in odd life forms and rarities. Suddenly a dead Keer was the holy grail of instant fortune and fame. The amateurs flocked in and a vast majority of them were never seen again.

Currently the Keer got a lot more miners for dinner than the miners got Keer. A lot. Nobody really kept track, so we didn't have exact numbers, but it appeared that the Keer were ahead about nine hundred to one. Of course, a large percentage of these newbies wouldn't have lasted in space more than a few months anyway. Lotsa ways to die out there in the Dark. Sometimes its better all at once than some of the alternatives.

The inherent problem I saw in the current situation is that first you had to find one (no small task), and then kill it to harvest its down; these rare creatures decreased in population as you harvested them. More work for less, always going the wrong way down the slope.

On the other hand, the Ranch had lotsa room.

If we could herd the Keer, then we could harvest them every cycle, without having to roam the dark asteroid belts of the fringe systems searching for something you couldn't see coming—something hungry, with a taste for people meat. And it was freezing out there. Not my favorite. Spend enough time in the Dark, and it's hard to get warm again.

However, everything thrived under Summer's light, maybe the Keer would too!

These warrens running under the Shimmering would make an excellent pasture, if we could seal off all but a couple of the entrances. I felt a smile blooming; maybe we could move the damn chickens here too.

That was how Pasteur came to be part of our family; it all started with the damned chickens. I had wanted a new protein source for our table and for export to the Gravtown restaurant market. (You got tired of fish after a few cycles).

When you've spent the first seven years of your life desperately hungry, there's something very satisfying about being in the food business. It sorta made me feel safe and powerful at the same time. I guess we never outrun our early imprinting. And it didn't hurt that the $cred balance with Gravtown was healthy—most people there ate every day.

Some didn't. The poor have always been with us.

After some research, I decided on a modified dino-chicken with significant muscle tissue and long legs; they dressed out about twenty kilos of pure meat. They bred true and produced large eggs for consumption as well. Sounded great! I bought four hundred embryos in stasis to start, thinking that would be enough to establish a stable flock. I assumed the Gardener would be raise them, because he was so gifted at growing things. Problem solved, time to move on.

Wrong.

I really should have asked the Gardener before I bought the chickens.

In a rare moment, he flatly refused, saying that he, "doesn't have time, or desire to have anything to do with those filthy creatures."

He said to "get someone else to do it, someone who cared about such things." I was speechless for a moment, which suited the Gardner just fine.

Turned out everyone else, including me, was too busy to take on a new project. After talking it over with Navire, I decided to go back and ask the Gardener's advice. He listened patiently, then said he had someone in mind, a shepherd he could send for. Someone trustworthy. Someone good with animals and people (I would eventually realize that he didn't actually see much difference between the two).
Someone that would fit in around here and take care of the disgusting chickens for us.

Ten days later, Pasteur showed up.

He was an ursine, a highly intelligent bear species with unusually good rapport-building skills and a gift for healing. He was also physically quite powerful, with a short fuse balanced by a nurturing instinct.

In combat he was a serious opponent, never to be taken lightly. Hairy and long limbed, he usually charged in with a slow, limber uppercut that evolved into an unstoppable full body charge. His razor tipped talons would swing up hard enough to slash through flesh and bone, torquing all the way from his feet up through his massive arms, and culminating in a loose slap that rang bell.

A very friendly guy, but not someone to mess with, and he was good with the chickens. I thought that would keep him busy.
I guess I really need to work on my assumptions.

Before I knew it, Pasteur was involved in seeding Crystal Thirteen Ocean with Dungeness crab, magenta lobster and oyster beds.

Now, I sure do like fresh shucked oysters on a hot afternoon at the beach in Crystal Four. I mean, cold beer and gorgeous lightstorms over the water? What could be better? I could easily visualize a sultry Caribe tune beating across the gleaming alabaster sands stuck at three o'clock in the afternoon. Cool ocean breeze in the shade. Maybe a shot of grappa. Maybe two. Summer's eternal afternoon light pouring down on the salt air like honey.
What's not to love?

I assumed all this would keep him busy, so I didn't say anything.

Like I said, I really needed to work on my assumptions.

7—The Prince

The Chow sisters of Thunder's crew filled the young prince's afternoon with lessons in breaking and entering locked habitats, bypassing security protocols, and what they called ghost walking. It was new, and interesting fun, he found, and exercised a different part of him than the climbing challenges that the Stones came up with every morning. It was new-data of a sort that Anodos had never realized existed, much less imagined that he would find useful someday. Until he began to walk the Golden path he simply expressed his desire for something and it was quickly brought to him. He had never been hungry, or thirsty or exhausted before.

He had no need for such skills back then, but then he'd also been pretty bored, anxious to reach adulthood and leave the palace like the heroes of old. Since leaving, the young prince certainly hadn't been bored for any significant length of time, that was for sure.

He had, however, discovered many new experiences: being hot, cold, uncomfortable, thirsty, muscle aches, and rude servants that turned out not to be servants after all; it was quite a list.

The most difficult of the new alien concepts to wrap his thoughts around was the concept of theft.

All his life he had experienced servants putting away his things. Just because something wasn't where you left it didn't mean it was gone. It was put away for later. You just had to say something and there it was again, shiny and clean. That was the way things were in the palace.

Here in the vast liveShip named Thunder things were very different.

He met the twins quite by accident. He had just cooled off from climbing by swimming in one of the liveShip's H_2O reservoirs, and was hurrying to his quarters to relax, when he abruptly realized that his future paths diverged about ten meters from the door. He was at an important branch he hadn't foreseen; if he hurried along as planned, the

Golden path faded almost into obscurity. It didn't completely disappear; it was just harder to see. If he cautioned the Stones, and walked very quietly, the Golden path was shorter, and strengthened in brightness.

There were intruders in his quarters, and they couldn't be servants, because he now had none. Perhaps they were crewmen in awe of his presence, and were cleaning his quarters out of respect? Except he had experienced little respect in this hollow, soulless place of metal and synthetics and not-servants.

Anodos nodded subtly to the Stones, and they stilled, fading into the surrounding bulkheads on either side of the mammoth passageway. The young prince moved as quietly as he knew how, creeping up to and through the hatch entering his suite. Apparently, he wasn't all that quiet, because the intruders had somehow concealed themselves and then darted out into the corridor behind him unseen, at least by Anodos. However, the two scarred human siblings hadn't counted on part of the wall detaching itself and pinning them to the deck with a meter-wide paw. The pair of thieves were struggling uselessly to escape when the young prince retraced his steps to regard them with curiosity.

After a moment, he nodded towards his chambers and the intruders were rolled inside. The Stones that Speak blocked the exits of course, and the prisoners couldn't take their eyes off the fifteen-meter-long salamander bodyguards towering over the room. The scent of pungent fear flooded Anodos' nostrils as he curiously examined the Chow sisters.

They were quite unlike anyone the young prince had ever met, but then pretty much everyone out here on the periphery of the empire were unfamiliar. They had removed several things from his den and concealed the items among the false skins everyone seemed to wear out here. He thought they were called clothing or cabinets or something. Anodos didn't understand why the Chow sisters had taken his things and decided to ask.

"Are you in need of these small-tech items for some reason?"

The sisters were having a hard time taking their eyes off the Stones and didn't respond to his inquiry. He stepped much closer and raised his triangular head to peer down at them. They didn't smell any better up close, but at least he had garnered their attention.

"Why?" he asked again.

"We were needing to exercise our skills; it makes us feel good," replied the sister with the left side of her face heavily scarred. The other sister had the reverse side of her head damaged. She nodded in agreement. Maybe they had been in an accident?

"What particular skills require you to be in my quarters?" asked the young prince, cocking his head to his right side. This conversation was growing increasingly bizarre.

"We are thieves," replied the quieter one, looking down. Her sister thrust her chin forward belligerently, daring him to do something. He didn't have a clue as to what she was anticipating.

"What is this 'thieve'?" asked Anodos.

The sisters exchanged a knowing look, conveying *something* without any need for of body language or gestures.

Anodos was getting even more confused. Were they referring to mating? He had heard that it could be a sensitive subject, especially if your lineage wasn't purebred nobility. They <u>were</u> female, and a prince of the royal line was basically irresistible, but Anodos didn't think they were compatible; much less did he find them desirable. He might've been mistaken. He asked again.

"What is thieve?"

"We sneak in places, solve the puzzle of the lock, and remove things of value. We take them with us and secretly leave before anyone realizes we've been there," explained the quiet one. Her sister nodded this time.

"Value is relative," stated Anodos. "Who are these things of value to?" he continued. "Is sneak how you exited the room without me seeing you?"

Now it was the Chow sisters who were confused.

The quiet one tried again, looking up at his massive head with a mixture of defiance and curiosity. "It's like a game where the mark tries to hide important things where we can't get them, and we win by getting them. We are very good," she finished.

The prince considered this. "What happens when you lose the game?" he asked curiously. They were silent for a moment before the belligerent one replied.

"We were caught one time. Before that, our faces matched."

He glanced away, experiencing the relatively new emotion of embarrassment, or maybe awkwardness—but he didn't have the experience to say which. He looked at the nearest Stone.

The Stone that Speaks shook his massive head in silent dismay. No help there. Looked as if he'd have to figure things out on his own. Unfortunately, just because he could see the possible near-time futures didn't mean he understood what he saw. He thought about it, trying to understand.

How did ordinary people acquire what was necessary to survive? Did they all play this game? Since leaving the palace Anodos had noticed that not everyone was able to eat when they wanted, or sleep in a safe den. It had been a shocking realization for the young prince; he had never thought about such things before.

The galaxy was much different than he expected.

Anodos was no stranger to pain, the cycles of ritual tattooing had been deliberately painful; this was thought to ensure both wisdom and compassion in future rulers. His heart went out to the unfortunates once he realized that they had no servants to feed them or palace to rest in. His personal experience with chronic physical pain had unexpectedly developed empathy for other's suffering.

This came as quite a surprise to the young prince. After all, he had been taught from birth to rule his civilization, to perceive power in groups and alliances. To use that power effectively, and to wage war without mercy, to completely destroy the enemy when the time came. Not to feel sorrow for the suffering the Chow sisters must have endured. Anodos had mistakenly assumed that their scars were ritually applied to willing volunteers.

But that wasn't the way of things out here on the frontier.

He didn't much care for this game, suddenly realizing that it felt wrong to take someone else's things, when apparently there weren't always servants to replace it automatically like back home. For the first time he fully understood the concept of "mine" versus "theirs."

This made things much more complex. Life just wasn't as simple as he'd believed. He focused on the Chow sisters again. These skills would be valuable in this new world he'd opened his eyes to. Not to take from those with little, but to reacquire what others had taken from him, because now he also had no servants to automatically replenish his, what were they called? "Possessions", that was it. His stuff.

"Teach me," he commanded.

So, they did.

8—Koen of Summer

In the fifth cycle of the Gardener's stay at the Ranch, we produced a modest harvest of a drinkable fruit-forward red wine, and a forgettable white. I shared and understood the attraction of the Red, but true balance demanded the appreciation of White wine's delicate forays into the light as well. Making good wine was always about the balance. I learned that studying, of all things, Lui Tai Chi. The internal martial arts embody balance in all aspects of my life. Apparently even wine!

When the Gardener began to ramble on about sparkling wine I was forced to politely stop and reorient him. The red had promise but the white needed lotsa work. I explained that we were not going to produce a wine that didn't adhere to our now elevated and expensively educated tastes. I knew we could do better, and we needed to make a wine that we actually wanted to drink. Anything less, and we were just wasting everybody's time.

The Gardener reluctantly agreed and saturated his waking hours with new-data on the Vine, particularly on the white wines of the Loire Deau colony.

With more research, I found that some of my favorite white wines were being beautifully expressed by the new-school Loire winemakers (intent on one-upping dad and creating a new legacy), letting the Vine express itself it all it voluptuous glory. *Hedonists all*, I thought at the time, *My kinda people*!

That was the kinda wine I believed we were capable of producing here at the Ranch.

Loire Deau colony had developed a clone of Savenniere that had adopted well to low pressure eco-systems—and it thrived in intense sunlight. That was important, because it never got dark in Summer. It was always three o'clock in the afternoon. Night never fell here, and I was good with that. I'd spent enough time out there in the cold.

Summer was an eternal afternoon in that timeless moment between noon and twilight, frozen halfway between mid-day and a sunset that never fell. I absolutely loved living here. Nothing else I had ever experienced compared. Nothing.

It appeared to me as if the extended sunlight might produce high sugars and a generous number of extractable flavor profiles. The good kind, I mean. I mentally crossed my fingers for that hard lady, Luck.

With her help, we might be able to make a classic Savenniere white wine of dense, layered complexity, redolent of lychee nut tarts with graham cracker crusts and a salty apricot butter bombe filling. That was the plan, anyway.

We decided to go forward with that, and focus on learning one varietal at a time.

Navire left for Gravtown at high speed, wearing a corsair liveShip hard-body we'd scrounged together. She loved flying at full speed through the stars, much like a thoroughbred stallion does the quarter-mile. She said sometimes the stellar wind just lifts your mane, and you find yourself running full-on into the light. It's not really about reaching the destination. "Balancing on the cusp of forever" she called it.

She picked up the Vinifera clones waiting at the Zona Rosa docks as scheduled without a problem. Then Navire flew back to the Ranch in the usual eight days. The Gardiner was thrilled with the new genetics and immediately disappeared into the vineyards and transitory vegetation of the pubescent vineyards of Crystal Fourteen.

***

Fort Cerberus is a well fortified bastion of safety, sunk deep into the crystal layers of the northeast quadrant of the Ranch.

The main crystal clusters overhead (Eighteen through Twenty-six) thrust up out of the surface like the frozen image of a liquid explosion, a motionless splash seventeen kilometers high. It had sharp faceted edges, tinted in delicate hues of rose and bright cherry. The monoclinic peridot crystals were surrounded on all sides by razor-sharp, kilometer-high Kunzite shards pointing outward like a battle collar on a really bad dog. This was powerful protection, but we really weren't passive-resistance sorta people. We were the "you can't have too many blades in a fight" kinda family. Unfortunately, while there was no shortage of personal bad-tech around here, our biggest guns were insufficient to handle the kinda large scale battle the true professionals brought to town. I had a feeling that there would be a need, sooner or later.

Fort Cerberus <u>was</u> defended by some over-engineered Boom, and there were also several coherent beam weapons that usually worked. We now had a small wealth of untested armored sentry-guards, and even a few archaic heavy-metal and neutron canon salvaged from derelict deadShip's we found in the Old Garage. The implosion mortar fields and stealth missiles came much later.

Fort Cerberus was going to be our flagship battle center and future big-gun fire control. It did have full Δqm^x pods that you could run a war from, or implant-experience five-star meals and catch the latest action-romances from any character's point of view. If you couldn't sleep, there were the extensive crypto-analysis logics to solve puzzles with and endless salvaged memory banks from alien deadShips. Whole worlds tucked away in there.

But that way lies the danger of a static death. Some people liked it so much they stopped coming back to the real world, and just sorta faded from the big stage without even a whimper. Most never actually took the effort to reproduce, so at least such weaknesses didn't get passed down the line.

***

And then there was Dread.

In the sixth cycle of the Ranch, Navire and I had unexpectedly found ourselves scavenging an alien derelict deadShip. We needed additional sources of revenue to continue building the Ranch, and this was what we knew best.

An eddy of clear space had serendipitously opened up during a milk-run back from Gravtown, about thirty hours into the Chaos Sea. Exposed in the clear pocket were the remnants of an ancient battle. What really drew the eye, though, was an oddly shaped dreadnaught-class deadShip. It had sustained massive battle damage, with entire sections of the ship missing and carbon-charred from the ordinance it had been subjected to. Somehow, the broken vessel still had a tattered sense of dignity, despite its condition.

Floating in disarray around the derelict were a number of destroyed fighters, maybe nine or ten; it was hard to tell with all the scattered debris surrounding the dreadnaught. Someone had beat the hell out of them, and it was pretty obvious who. The liveShip had put up quite a fight before it died.

It looked to us as if the liveShip had been pulled down by a pack of hyenas, but she had gone down to hell dragging a sizable honor guard along with her.

It must have been one hell of a fight.

We couldn't help but be curious who these people had been. Besides, it looked like no one had salvaged the wreck yet; it could have been hidden in the backwaters of the Chaos Sea for weeks or centuries. No way to tell. We approached cautiously, as always. Navire wore her standard three hard-bodies for breeching deadShips, and I rode shotgun.

The armory was empty. They fought until they there was no more Boom, then died defending their stations with bad-tech of the edged variety.

Good warriors. Auntie Tao would have liked these people.

I liked these people.

When we searched the bodies, some things didn't make much sense. There were at least six different species of aliens that I had never seen or heard of working together. Plus, a scattering of those I'd come across here and there out in the Dark. The significant thing they all had in common was what appeared to be some kind of bio-magnetic implant attached to the neck on the left side of their skull. It was an odd fusion of tech implants in some kinda of biologically based communication unit.

Shiny.

I took lotsa samples. New-data implant tech was always valuable.

I felt some disappointment that I never had a chance to know them, these kindred spirits who had gone violently into the Night, fighting the really-good fight.

When we got to the bridge, we found most of the officers still in their command pods. Not much left of them, until I got to one of the primary pods with lotsa armor. Commander's chair, I think. Anyway, I found a beat-to-hell disabled hard-body among the vacuum-cleansed corpses left on the bridge.

Both legs and one arm were badly damaged or missing. His torso was bent sideways, and his neck had a big hole in it, but he was still alive. A Child of Electron, buried in this broken body, yet still fighting to live, to carry the battle on. Helpless, but not scared. I don't think anything could have frightened him at this point.

Sometimes anger carries you further than you could imagine.

Again, he had a certain dignity that is independent of circumstances. It was rare, but potent, and usually found in the most unexpected of places. Like this forsaken place. I carefully picked him up.

He said his name was Dread.

I took him home and gave him canon for arms and missiles for feet, not to mention massive memory storage and a mission, with good people counting on him. I gave him a Home to defend. A family. Friends.

And lotsa of Boom to play with.

In the time since, Dread has become very devoted to me.

It was kinda hard to tell what he was thinking in the beginning, but after a while I learned to read him like a favorite book. He was actually sorta sentimental, but I don't think very many people saw that side of him. He wasn't ever afraid to let his deadly side show through when it served a purpose or two.

Back then he didn't understand the concept of "bluff." He was still capable of great subtlety, but outright falsehoods, and lies? He'd rather just shoot you and be done with it. He wasn't built that way. But he could play a part, if he had to. Just didn't like it. Tasted bad on the palate. Wasn't the way the good guys rolled back home. But he learned. I felt a bit guilty for teaching him, but deceit was something I learned early, and it was an invaluable art in war.

I think we are all shaped by our beginnings, and he was no exception. I didn't remember being innocent, but I saw Dread lose his. Wasn't one of my favorite memories; paths not taken and all that.

Dread had eventually become our Ranch security chief, and now guarded the Ranch, (and me), with unsurpassed loyalty. Man had serious skills. Dread was a good man, but deadly at the art of War.

"War" is such a small word to hold so much. There are many types of warfare, and Dread excelled at most of them.

We just added a few more.

He was skilled in symbolic battle, economic and trade war, as well as cultural and political infighting. We added dirty tricks and illicit business deals with bad endings. Literal dead ends to metaphoric battles of many flavors. He was already a hard-leverage specialist, a byzantine plotter, and a real layer-upon-layer planning kinda guy.

Did I mention, lotsa Boom?

That said, Dread usually preferred the precise application of force if possible; too much was crass, and too little didn't get the job done. But a little pressure here and there, nicely orchestrated and well-timed, often accomplished the goal with a minimalistic milieu that he found innately satisfying.

Anybody could just blow someone up.

But Dread found that tasteless and crude. I guess we all did. It wasn't amateur hour, and Dread was anything but unsophisticated at le Danse Macabre. Truth was, he was not someone you'd want unhappy with you for any reason. In fact, I was pretty sure that Dread's reputation protected the Ranch from the bigger fish on Summer as much as the Boom part.

Probably more.

In the end, Dread had become the public face of the Ranch, while I was the true power behind the big chair. I liked it that way. Good security.

***

Fort Charon was kinda like a giant spider web carved in gemstone. Spanning hundreds of kilometers, its crystalline antenna wove back and forth across a hollow of the mountainous landscape known as "The Well."

The actual Fort was buried deep within the jawbreaker layered bedrock, but also had hidden aerial probes spanning the entire quadrant on the surface.

Fort Charon was the Ranch's new-data collection center. From here we could listen in on a whispered conversation half a geode away, if we wished. It could also access the Gravtown nets, Δqm^x postings, and on a good day even reach the colonies outside the Chaos Sea. Dread spent a great deal of time here.

This was also where I published my works from.

I especially liked the ocean Crystal Thirteen at Fort Charon; the tinted beryl giants were particularly suited to water habitats.

But the ideal environment produced by the tinted Crystal-filtered Summerlight was the vineyard. Something in the subtly focused mycelium light was special, producing grapes of singular quality and delightful skin-thickness and flavor.

The sixth-cycle red was quite nice, downright yummy in an unpolished but friendly style while remaining relatively complex. Different than the last vintage; viscous and delightfully rich on the palate, this higher-alcohol red wine was definitely better than our previous vintages. Despite the limited yield, I decided to bottle this one for distribution in some of the nearby colonies.

We also used the virtually unlimited crystal around us to cut one liter octagonal spheres for our first declared vintage. The white was better than previously, but the acids were still out of balance and the sugars were not very high. Still had a way to go, which was unusual, because most of us thought a serious red was harder to produce.

Our white wine was definitely lagging behind.

The Gardener brought up the sparkling wine issue again but didn't really put any heart into it because he knew the white had to be up to par first. Besides, we needed higher acids to produce a sparkling wine anyway, and the Gardener felt that playing with the PH in the lab was the hallmark of a dilettante.

I decided to distill the white, because I didn't want to drink it.

Navire suggested that we order some toasted oak barrels from Nouveau Armagnac colony and I thought it was a great idea; we had a positive trade balance and needed to balance the books anyway.

When Salvatore the tug got back with the barrels we transferred the raw ethanol into about thirty of them and tucked them away into a cool dark nook of the Ranch's cellars, deep within the layered bedrock. And then I forgot all about them for a long time.

This cycle's harvests had been good, thanks to a new adjustment in our growing medium. See, I had always thought that by feeding and watering a plant well, the Vine would produce the best fruit.

But no, the Vine is different.

It doesn't produce great art until it has suffered. Fought for survival, thirsted though the long day. Bled on the sand.

Kinda like people. Seems like the best ones I've known have gone through hell and survived, emerging transformed into better people who grace the earth with kindness and empathy.

Or ravage the earth with sound and fury, slaughtering everyone in their path.

One of those two. I forget.

So, we stopped feeding the Vine so much nitrogen and compost.

We encouraged the Vine to grow deep in search of water. The lower gravity in the Crystal garden allowed her to dig deep with her roots, over seventy meters down. Why not? After all, the ranch had plenty of pulverized crystal.

This cycle the harvest had been reduced by thirty percent.

Clusters of grapes had been sacrificed to concentrate all the Vine's flavors into their remaining berries. Skin-to-juice ratio had increased because of the smaller berries the Vine's struggles had produced.

At crush, the difference was immediately apparent; more raw tannins in the air, and a darker, more compact must.

That cycle I found that I enjoyed the every-four-hour work of pushing down the must with large mushroom-shaped paddles to submerge and increase skin contact with the juice (the kinda work most wineries automated). The Gardener and I and Navire worked side by side in the Crystal Eleven Vineyard all through that eternal day. Katy the Sledge spun sub-harmonic boosted Island Music through our implants that kept us working and swaying through the warm eternal afternoon of Summer. The Summerlight poured down, the mineral impurities of the giant crystal adding a faint violet tinge to the richness of the hot rays. Sometimes sweat is good, unless it runs into your eyes. Some days, even if it does.

I eventually came to the self-realization that the simple rhythms of Harvest brought out a sorta peacefulness in me, allowing me to live more in the Now than usual. That it was a timeless gestalt lingering on in the eternal afternoon of Summer's mycelium light. I found that there was something special in working hard together with people you like.

In building something better, as a team, there is a careless sort of trust that begins to blossom. (Something I usually avoided in my early cycles). You develop a sense of shared accomplishment, a sorta quiet triumph, with someone who understands how hard you all worked to achieve your goal.

I hadn't known the like since I left the Hive.

I hadn't realized how much I missed it.

* * *

I remember when I'd first come to the Hive; I was being chased by angry gangsters. I was about seven; a skinny, tough little boy whose only friend was his smart-knife, an intellectually damaged Child of Electron named Bella. We lived in the unincorporated wastelands outside a Corp-nation city, fighting for survival for as far back as I could remember. I remember being constantly hungry.

Not an "I missed breakfast" kinda hunger; it was a gnawing hole in my middle, a searing need that would have made me do anything if it wasn't for my mother Bella. She said I was a good boy, although I didn't always feel like one. I wanted to be one, though, for her.

Looking back, I see how hard our life was, but we didn't know any different and so it was okay. We would make silly jokes to distract us from our needs—mine for food, and her for her falling power-levels. I thought everyone was as hungry as we were, and that's why people sometimes did terrible things. But we never did. Then the gangsters caught us. They took Bella, and I barely got away.

After that I was so angry I wanted to kill someone, and for a while I thought I was turning into a bad-guy. But something else happened instead.

I think that when a child sees too many terrible things, one of two things happen. He either turns into a bad-guy himself, or he develops a core hatred of injustice and evil. He tries to help the weak ones who can't fight for themselves. That was how I felt when Auntie Tao took me in and trained me to be strong, to fight the good fight. It was hard for her, because I wasn't like the other Hive kids, but she found a way to help me fit in and still be me. Long story.

Anyway, Raiders are scum just like the D Street boys in District Thirteen, and I'm not that little boy any longer. But sometimes in the night I still wake and reach for Bella before I remember.

9—The Keer

The Keer tracked the lone asteroid prospector with innate precision.

It appeared to be a Bob, the holy sacrament of flesh it had heard so much about in the Dream. As far as it could tell, all Keer who tasted of the sacred meat became instant converts to the Church of Good Taste. This Keer was fascinated by the tales of the converts as they spread the word of Bob. The tales were almost unbelievable, but the disciples were fervent in their testimonies, and their belief in the sacrament was unmistakable.

Before the discovery of Bob, Rock-lice were the height of cuisine for the gourmand, ant-shark-like predators.

Rock-lice had been the single, boring flavor of culinary experience for millennia uncounted. There was nothing else out here, so the Keer had been satisfied with their lot in life. A Keer's life was simple; it waited, hanging motionlessly onto a tumbling rock for up to a decade if necessary. When it finally spotted dinner, it instinctively calculated the trajectory to the juicy Rock-lice, leaping into space from its lonely vigil with great precision. Keer pounced on their dinner with a speed that was downright shocking. It gobbled up its prey completely in a few blinks, and then settled into a nine-month digestive stupor.

That was when it entered the Dream.

While its body was utilizing all its resources to digest the tough but tasty Rock-lice, the Keer's mind was propelled into a group consciousness shared by other digesting Keer. Not unlike a big cocktail party where everyone was pretty buzzed, and constantly talked about food. Except without actual words—the Keer were not really sentient. Yet.

But now… well, Rock-lice simply didn't cut it anymore. All everyone was talking about was the succulent Bob. After millennia, there was something new, something better; something so remarkable that it had become simply all anyone could talk about!.

This Keer had dropped out of the Dream several cycles ago when it finished digesting its last meal of, you guessed it, Rock-lice. This time the Dream had felt different. For the first time in memory nobody in the Dream had wanted to hear about its dinner. It had still had a pleasant time in the Dream, but Rock-lice had become so boring lately and no one cared about yesterday's cuisine anymore.

The Keer was in no hurry, studying the Bob as it scurried around the small asteroid hitting the rock to break off small pieces and then regarding them with a shiny eye attached to one of its spindly appendages.

The Keer only physically move when attacking; but the Bob wasted energy in motion that served no distinguishable purpose. It was recklessly burning calories as if it had an unlimited supply of dinner. Did it eat stone? Maybe minerals and ice like the Rock-lice? Such thoughts drifted past without attaching themselves to the Keer's mind for contemplation; the Keer was only interested in dinner. That took up all its mental resources anyway.

The tiny organic ballistic brain at the base of its head supplied the trajectories necessary to pounce on the Bob. This also triggered the Keer's transformation into its hunting form.

Dinner was imminent.

The six-meter, ant-shark-like body elongated to almost nine meters; its middle pair of legs shortened and folded into previously undetectable niches. The rear set of legs grew thicker, more powerful, in anticipation of launching itself from its tumbling boulder into open space. The Keer's stomach began brewing potent digestive acids while the connective tissue between its torso and head segment expanded until it resembled a long tube, covered in a fine down and ornamented with one-meter-long razor-edged hairs springing out all over like mutant barbed wire.

The predator's front legs were curved forward, to scoop dinner into the expanded mandibles of its huge jaws. The Keer's mouth had expanded to dominate the entire front of its head—if you could have seen its head. Keer-down covered it completely, concealing everything from perception except the inside of its mouth and its mandibles. If you could see those, it was far too late to even scream.

Dinner time.

The Keer launched itself through the stone rain, dropping out of the night in a stoop that would only end with fresh Bob in it's tummy.

At the last moment, the Bob seemed to sense something, turning to look over its right shoulder.

The Keer fell right over him, gobbling up the Bob and landing on its closing jaws in two blinks. It stuck right where it had landed, its interior grinding-teeth making short work of the unlucky prospector, transformed to shredded bits in its industrial strength stomach. The Keer groaned in pleasure at the tenderness of the rich, fat-veined meat. It was quite unlike anything it had ever tasted. Even the inorganic shreds of the spacesuit gave a crunchy counter note to the succulent flesh. The meat itself seared the palate, melting quickly in the mouth, on taste buds that had never truly known warmth before.

The Keer's rear section softened and slowly collapsed over its body as it shifted into digestion mode. Its body shortened by almost half, and eventually was completely covered by the draping tough skin. The irregular covering settled and hardened bit by bit until the edges were sealed to the rock where it landed. Only a few antennae projected from its snug hideaway, concealed by its priceless down. Within a few hours the antenna connected to its sisters among the stars and it was propelled outwards.

That was when the Keer fell up into the Dream.

Ruddy orange light bathed everything equally in the endless cavern that was the Dream. Many thousands of Keer wandered back and forth, happy to be there and gossiping about food, all without sound. Everyone was pretty buzzed, and eagerly clustered around the members of the Church of Good Taste as they described the glories of Bob with rapt attention.

The Keer would have smiled had it a mouth capable of it.

It began to share its experience, and this time, _everyone_ was interested in what it had to say.

10—Koen of Summer

I looked around Control's conference room at my team. My family.

Navire, slinking a familiar body of café-skinned beauty and lopsided smile, Dread in the usual battle rig and quiet competence, Katy the Sledge wearing an elegant chromed Meza body of long limbs and sophisticated accoutrements. The Gardener was as he always was, and Pasteur with his rust colored fur rioting out of his massive battle harness in the usual uncontrolled chaos. Smitty was leaning back in his chair, wiping carbon dust from his hands with an old rag. The E were unusually quiet, which still wasn't saying a lot—they just couldn't help themselves from at least loud whispering and gossiping.

I had everyone's attention as I leaned forward.

"I've been thinking about a new project for some time. I think we need to do it," I began, looking around.

"After ten cycles on the Ranch we have eighteen fully developed Crystal gardens. Two more under construction. Less than eighty Ranch hands, most of them E, the rest outa Eden, some Rime-tech mechs, and us, to get everything done" I said.

"We have a Ranch larger than any of the colonies, and just a small army of sentry-tech to oversee it. We still have yet for the main Raider force to hit us and Dread suspects that some of the bigger Ranch islands are probing our defenses with the goal of annexing us should we be viewed as vulnerable. These recent raids may not be as random as they appear," I explained, looking over at Dread.

He put both of his massive arms on the table as he leaned forward.

"We are not as powerful as we appear to the other island nations. Deception in the art of war is time-honored and inexpensive compared to actual battles," Dread added. "So far, we have been able to maintain the illusion of power, but the truth is that while we are highly skilled in the small-scale conflicts, we are not ready to fight large forces of the kind some of the other island-nations of Summer can field, much less a thousand Raiders with a plan. We need more resources," he finished in a quiet voice.

Most people wouldn't hear the pain he felt at admitting his difficulty in defending the Ranch, but we were family and had known each other for a long time. The E got louder, and notes of belligerence crept in here and there. I tossed a micro-smile Navire's way; she caught it and threw it back.

The little guys were absolutely fearless warriors and would defend their home with sound and fury. And lives, if it came to that.

I was going to make sure it didn't.

Everyone else was silent as they digested this. It never occurred to anyone to question Dread's analysis of the situation. No one was smiling now.

"I'm sure Koen didn't bring us all together just to depress the hell out of us," stated Pasteur in a low grumble. He rolled his shoulders and neck, then laid his gaze on me with a palpable weight.

"So, what is this new project and how does it relate to our problems?" asked Katy the Sledge in a bright cheery tone, belying the general sense of unease.

That was the question I was waiting for—the children of Electron never miss a cue, regardless of how subtle. And this one wasn't.

"Our Ranch is underdeveloped; we use less than one percent of the surface crystal ranges. Lotsa room out there. I've come up with a kinda crazy idea to use some of that land."

I paused for a blink, then continued.

"I want to herd Keer," I calmly stated.

The Gardener choked on his limeade, sputtering yellow-green liquid onto Katy the Sledge and Pasteur (who patted the Gardener's back enthusiastically with a paw as big as the Gardener's head). Katy let loose a battle-train whistle that drowned out all sound in the room for a moment, glaring at me the whole time.

Some of the E were bouncing into the air whooping, while the others were busy explaining to their brothers and sisters what a Keer was. More whooping. Dread slowly leaned back in his chair with a reluctant smile creeping onto his face. Smitty was on his feet shouting at me; the words "idiot" and "rock head" were the sweetest of the endearments he showered me with. I had bounced the idea off of Navire earlier, so she was the only one in the room that wasn't shocked. She still had some glower left over to bath me in, though.

It still went better than I expected.

After we cleaned up the spilled drinks and everyone had calmed down, the real conversation began.

"Keer-down is the rarest and most valuable substance in the galaxy," I was re-iterating, "the down from one harvest would be enough to secure the future of the Ranch! By the second harvest we could expand our operations at a tremendous rate. We need these resources to bump us up to the next level of Ranch development. With the $creds we could hire and train a force large enough to protect the Ranch for good," I paused and waited for the questions.

"Exactly how do you hunt down and capture an invisible beast that wants to eat you?" Pasteur asked with not a little sarcasm.

I played it straight, despite the guy-humor response 'very carefully' that wanted to pop out of my mouth. See! I'm learning!

"Keer-trap," I suggested. Everyone shared unconvinced looks around the conference table. Maybe I wasn't entirely insane after all.

"How would you know if you even caught anything?" Katy asked with a bit of snarky tucked in here and there. Well, maybe more than a bit. They're like that. Teenagers. I smiled sadly, wondering just how long she'd remain one.

"I thought that if we filled the area outside the entrance to the trap with clouds of long micro-filaments of something very light and strong, maybe the threads would naturally attach themselves to the Keer as they passed through. We may not be able to actually *see* the Keer, but we could perceive the filaments wrapped around the Keer's body. The Keer should be completely unaware of their new visible coat!" I suggested. Lotsa maybes and might's but the concept was valid. It was all I had been able to come up with so far. Maybe with all of us working together, we'd be able to come up with something better.

11—Auntie Tao

On any given day, Auntie Tao was simultaneously holding over thirteen thousand private conversations, and orchestrating the myriad research departments of the Hive, as well as overseeing the productivity of the reclamation departments and a handful of widely varied covert operations. (Auntie Tao still always had time to talk to you). She was also in full control of everyone's implants and was currently applying pharmacological pressure to correct bad behavior in any of her local drones.

Auntie Tao was a Child of Electron, and had lived thousands of cycles, slowly distilling into a woman of great depth and insight. She was one of our oldest leaders, and unique among the Children. Many considered her enlightened or more. Even if she wasn't flesh and bone people.

Of course, everyone in the Hive loved her—and if they didn't, that too could be adjusted.

But she rarely encountered that situation these days. Her people relied on (and sometimes worshiped) the unique blend of friend, fierce protector, and imperial authority that she had evolved into over the past millennia.

Auntie Tao nurtured the weak, building their confidence and leading them to their strengths. The queen of the Hive protected them from the evils found in all other cultures—and themselves.

In the Hive, there were no bullies, or murderers or monsters. No child abuse, or hunger, and everybody had a purpose in the Hive. With Auntie Tao you always had a friend to whisper your secrets to, that would guide you every step of your life. You were never alone. Ever. The Hive was safe. You were safe.

Home meant all the good things and none of the bad.

It was quite a change for a starving seven-year-old who grew up fighting to survive. Long story.

Ages ago Auntie Tao had developed a business plan that was downright elegant in its simplicity. First, she moved into a decaying urban neighborhood, or mining outpost, or the unchartered wastelands outside a major Corp-nation city. (That was where I first met her).

Her financial teams would buy up abandoned and undesirable properties through third party blinds, until she amassed a large contiguous estate measured in kilometers, not city blocks.

Then her external security forces would descend in force on the property, running off all squatters and animals of every type, including the human variety.

On their heels the construction force hit dirt, and began throwing up thick, thirty-meter-high walls. These new perimeter walls were riddled with lethal defense nests filled with enormous sentry wasps. (The Hive never had graffiti problems).

The next teams to hit dirt were the reclamation squads, accompanied by mech and bio-tech equipment that reduced all the buildings and debris to a coarse powder. Other teams would then strip the existing residue and dirt of contaminants, often yielding surprising amounts of valuable metals, and useful compounds (as well as myriad toxins that came in handy for all sorts of endeavors).

While the soil was being cleansed, her financial teams would bid on the city waste refuse contract with the civil authorities (utilizing the traditional bribery, low bids, and occasional hard-leverage to accomplish their goal). It was always easier when the contract was secured before anyone realized who was bidding.

The Hive broke down the city's trash with amazing efficiency born of a thousand cycle's experience. The organic waste is simplest; it's composted with specially bred bacteria and enzymes. The metals are separated out and purified (then usually sold right back to the people that paid her to get rid of it). The plastics and nonorganic garbage are industrially cleaned and shredded. Then it is woven with an air-hardening resin to produce anything from custom furniture to small buildings.

This allows the Hive to sell building materials very cheaply, and also tends to promote growth in the previously devastated neighborhood.

Growth in nearby populations is good for the Hive.

The composted black gold you've developed from the city's sewers is plowed into the once-ravaged soil the Hive is rebuilding. At the right time, the Hive plants intensively (the produce and fruit of the Hive is pure, prolific and very affordable) and cultures gardens, orchards, and even grains from wall to wall.

A new Hive is built like an iceberg; plants on top in the sun where they can be seen, massive underground caverns and residences below—as well as vertical gardens, recycling facilities, and forges that can produce just about anything. It is really a small concealed city beneath the orchards and gardens everyone knows about. By the time the Hive is fully established, the neighborhood has low-cost produce and grains and fruit for sale, directly out of an add-on market module attached to the outside of the un-breach-able walls.

A stable food supply draws people.

So does a free health clinic.

Like century rain in the desert, life springs from the cracks and sands of the wastelands when the Hive blooms. It was amazing to witness. Even better to help build.

This is all part of the plan, because the Hive recycles more than general waste.

It recycles people too.

The local community saw them as human garbage, but Auntie Tao gathers up the discarded and forsaken, the last-chancers and the rock-bottom-hit. Desperate people who had lost hope and couldn't really remember why they're still holding on so tightly.

The sad and former bad, the hard-hurting souls that came to the free health clinic; all were a fertile field for the Hive to harvest.

Nobody else cared, Auntie Tao had realized all those cycles ago. Everyone needed Purpose in life to feel worthwhile. The Hive had what everyone needed.

Every*thing* they needed. A purpose. Home. Guidance.

Auntie Tao brought them into the Hive, implanted them with the latest Hive-tech, and healed their torn souls and broken bodies. After that, she was always there, listening and gently whispering in your implant through the lonely night. Auntie Tao saw everything you saw, shared it with you, and subtly guided you into the right decision-tree. Your hormonal balances were a jazz piece she played with skill and wit.

Sooner or later you would begin to Hive-think automatically. And life was good after that. It really was. Of course you were very grateful to Auntie Tao, and would do anything for her. Anything, without thought or hesitation.

You owed her everything. Your life itself.

When you were part of the Hive, you were, maybe for the first time, part of something greater than yourself. Perfect teamwork. Dedication. The knowledge that part of you would live forever in the Hive. Stability. Fun (but never the cruel kind).

You were an intrinsic part of a tribal culture that group-identified instead of being all about you. In the Hive you had a clear purpose in your life. Your life had meaning.

You were valued.

That was the part I craved when I was seven years old and first adopted into the Hive.

Well, that and food. Lotsa food.

The only purpose I knew before was survival. I had never known the feeling of home, of family. Auntie Tao gave me both. I owed her everything in those early days, like so many others before me.

However—every ten thousand or so new adoptions into the Hive, something didn't quite go as planned. Someone who could not, or would not, submit completely. Someone who simply refused to be fully absorbed into the Hive. I guess some of us have a steel core forged in fire that simply will not be sent quietly into the Night.

The choice for Auntie Tao was simple. You could inject them with memory wipes and leave them in the wasteland from which they'd come where they would come to with no memory of the past cycle, a pocketful of $cred, and a good knife—some skills completely bypass that kinda memory.

Or, you could train them to be an elite Hive operative.

Someone capable of being dropped into enemy territory, and creating an insurgence from rubbing two sticks together. Someone used to a certain autonomy and freedom of movement. Someone who could understand Corp-nation politics, and still be Hive. Someone who understood the nomads and asteroid miners and spun tango through the dancehalls of east Gravtown, but still sang Hive battle language with skill and nuance.

Someone you could trust.

Someone like me.

Old-data.

12—The Tyrant

When the tramp freighter docked, a ferret-faced spacer came to get them. The spacer had thin, elongated limbs that said he had never known planetary gravity in his youth. His eyes were the dead pools of a killer, but that didn't bother the Tyrant, it was the hint of a secret unshared that his thin lips insinuated.

She met her troika's eyes and they immediately straightened in unspoken response; Antonio sent a quiet warning through his implant to the men and women of the Horde. She could see the subtle ripple of movement as the "heads up" order spread. Erika stepped in front of her in unconscious protectiveness. There wasn't a man or woman here that wouldn't gladly give their life to protect her.

The Tyrant and, of course, her troika, were insulated by her personal guard as they entered the battered freighter in good discipline. They followed the long-limbed killer without worry, after all, they were fully-blooded warriors, and outnumbered the ferret-faced man four-hundred-to-one.

Being professionals, they maintained security regardless. This whole situation stunk worse than Nigel's Star, and her people had a pretty good sense of smell.

The spacer was soon joined by an all-purpose hard-body someone on the liveShip was wearing. The hard-body had a barely noticeable Signal lag in reaction time and appeared to be an unspecialized human hard-body of a type that would attract little notice in any crowd. When three more hard-bodies fell in behind them as they walked down the wide main corridor of the ship, alarm fireworks started going off all over in Jenny-Rose's mind. She gave the hand signal for "boogie-time imminent" as she stroked her implant and boosted. Her troika boosted too, and the rest of the Horde followed suit a blink later.

The skinny spacer apparently noticed the hand sign as well. A blink later, his crew knew too, and le Danse Macabre manifested, not unexpectedly, to spin wildly across the dance floor.

The ferret-faced bad-guy was strapped with plenty of Boom, but it was with twin broadswords that he began his attack. His hard-body had quickly turned to fully face them with a broad-sword sliding out of each sleeve. The assassin quickly moved straight-line at the Tyrant's team with the two whirling blades spinning in his arms. He was cackling madly and apparently having a hell of a good time. The Horde had seen most everything, but Jenny-Rose could tell it was still starting to irritate some of her team.

She snaked out her three sectional staff and began wrapping the razor sticks around her body in an increasingly rapid tempo, as she slid forward in a series of strikes and extended strides right through the long-limbed spacer.

Then, the mad, thin-boned spacer no longer mattered.

That was when the corridor walls on both sides of the Horde dilated open and heavy fire ripped through their ranks. Eighty-two men fell within the first few blinks.

The Horde War Cry burst from her lungs, followed by a terse gobbet of battle language streamed through their implants. Everybody reversed direction and began to retreat the way they'd come aboard while laying down Boom and smoke in their wake. They dragged what was left of their fallen brothers and sisters with them. The Horde didn't leave anyone behind. Ever.

When they got to the airlock they'd entered by, the hatch was empty; there was only dark space out there in the port screen.

The Tyrant didn't let any of her horror show.

A Tyrant never does.

She met her troika's eyes briefly. They unconsciously adjusted their body posture, focused on her with every bit of their being. Her troika's subordinates stood taller as well, and the subtle posture-change spread like a wave across the rank and file.

Yes, it was true that they were too late. Their ride home had left them behind, and they were dropping like a stone through the uncharted depths into the myrid dangers of the Chaos Sea.

Plan B time.

The Tyrant barked another snippet of Corp battle-language; explaining the situation, their new objectives, and the precise attack formation in a few short sentences. They were headed to Control: from there maybe they could turn the Ship around and get the hell out of here.

The Tyrant Jenny-Rose trilled battle language again, sending out scouting triads (three warriors working closely in a team) in front of them, and to each side passage as they went by. One triad hunted down the engine room to secure them while another searched for environmental control.

None of them were ever seen alive again.

The Tyrant's forward teams rapidly advanced down the main corridor in battle formation, moving like well meshed gears in an intricate clockwork. They had drilled in it so many times that they could do it in their sleep. Leapfrogging forward, always covered by each other, they were as irresistible a force as the incoming tide.

High tide was coming in.

It still didn't help as much as Jenny-Rose expected.

The enemy was extremely aggressive, highly experienced fighters. They were relentless in their attack, never pausing to stake ground or re-assess their probabilities.

They just kept coming. A dozen of the Horde's warriors in the forward-teams were gone in a blink. The Horde was drilling through the enemy, but the bad-guys didn't seem to care about losses, most likely because most of them were wearing replaceable hard-bodies. When one of the Horde put down an enemy hard-body, the assassins just put on a new one and went for the throat again.

By now the dead were covering the ground in an uneven flood plain painted in crimson and copper. Forward progress slowed to a crawl.

The cost was terrible, but they finally made it to the Control.

It was, of course, a trap.

Sixteen of her men entered the liveShip's bridge before the room exploded in fire and shrapnel. The explosion took twenty-seven soldiers outside Control as well, injuring the ones the Boom didn't send directly into that Darkest Night.

There would be no new course for the falling deathtrap they rode down into the depths of the Chaos Sea.

For a timeless micro-moment everything paused, and then started again all in a jumble.

The Tyrant felt her lips curl back as she screamed the War cry (implant and out) and accelerated in a curving course that brought her to her surviving men in seconds. She hovered protectively over the fallen bodies while firing a flechettes scattergun with a bore the size of a human fist. The other fire-teams flowed past her, carrying the fight to the now-fleeing enemy. Medic triad fifteen saved five more, but they kept spilling into the Dark.

Jenny-Rose's heart was breaking. She let nothing show.

Tyrants never do.

The enemy was making a hasty retreat to the hanger bay, leaving their hard-body fighters to cover their exit. At Mick's direction, his subordinates chased them in thunder and Boom, determined to secure the bad-guys' exit vehicle for the Horde. Mick's place was with the Tyrant, managing the battle with Erika and Antonio, the other two members of the Tyrant's troika. Antonio suddenly barked battle-language; his guys had found a solid defensive position nearby, but it needed fortifying. Erika snarled a battle-language strategic statement, warning that the bad-guys would blow the hanger lock on their way out, sucking everyone out to a cold and Dark end. Antonio's cargo-hold suddenly looked a lot more desirable. The Tyrant couldn't continue to lose men at this rate; there would soon be nobody left.

Jenny-Rose growled a slice of battle language, and sixty-five percent of her remaining team veered off for the defensive position, with the other thirty-five percent pressing an assault on the entrance to the hanger bay. The hard-body assassins outnumbered Mick's guys, but the Horde fighters were the distilled essence of professional warriors. Today they fought for the lives of their family, their battle siblings—and sometimes that makes a difference.

It did that day.

The Tyrant's build-teams sealed the cargo hatch as best they could and searched for ways to reinforce it; there wasn't a lot to work with. They were reduced to welding scrap to the deck in tactically significant positions around the kill-zone located just inside the air-lock.

There wasn't enough scrap.

"Position our fallen strategically. They can't be hurt any more now," she said softly, hating the idea, but protecting her surviving people was more important. Tyrants make the hard decisions. That's their job.

The entire hold shuddered violently, knocking a few of the walking wounded to the deck. They pulled themselves back up, every one of them, and went about their duties as if nothing had happened.

Not their first time in the big city.

The aftershocks were almost as rough. The doomed ship didn't have much longer.

The Tyrant made a hand gesture and her troika drew close, surrounding her in a semi-circle facing mostly outward.

"All immobilized wounded fall back to the locker. Antonio—position the forward fire-teams as best you can. Make sure they have a secure position to fight from. Mick—lay down implosion mines in the kill-zone at the airlock entrance. Flash bangs at eye level and sticky grenades overhead. Make sure the bad-guys have a warm welcome. Erika—see to getting the wounded settled, and then reallocate the snipers into new three man teams. We've lost so many that it's impossible to rebuild on the fly. Assign new partners," she finished. A drop of sweat beaded on her forehead, not quite ready to trickle down into her eye.

Assigning snipers to new teams was not a small thing in the horde.

Her troika immediately got to work, a well-oiled machine built for battle. A wave of calmness seemed to spread out across the horde in tandem with the operational orders, radiating from a center around the Tyrant.

The horde excelled at organized mayhem, they'd known it of old.

Everyone worked calmly as fast as they could, acutely aware that this was only a brief chance to catch their breath before the enemy came a knocking once again.

They didn't knock.

The bad-guys skeleton-keyed the airlock and cut open the hatch to find a large, dark cargo hold with indistinct piles of junk scattered around. A few hostile hard-bodies peered into the darkness, searching for the Tyrant's horde, but nothing stirred in the lightless space. Rose's people held their breath, waiting for the fight to begin.

When the enemy's implant scans shifted visually into thermal-heat mapping, they got all excited; some of them were snickering gleefully as they unleashed the unholy hell of an auto-targeting plasma cannon. The dark was split by the blue-white brilliance of the plasma strobes and Rose's team members began going out like candles in a storm.

She lost over a third of her remaining force in the first two minutes alone.

They were the longest two minutes of her life.

The Tyrant felt her concerns fall away from her in a shower of blood and pain, leaving nothing but Intent, burned clean of impurities. She had never been as deadly as at this moment.

She was fully in the Now and absorbed all the new-data flooding her un-buffered consciousness with an efficiency unknown to humans of the past.

The Tyrant began to move forward into the strobing plasma fire, firing her own scattergun relentlessly. Her troika moved forward with her as naturally as an ankle walks in concert with its knee.

They were a mud-slide of death pouring downhill, irresistibly carrying the fight to the enemy. When they demonstrated the enemy was not invulnerable by taking down their plasma cannon in a wealth of boom, Rose's people screamed in triumph and tripled their efforts to destroy the enemy.

It's not always the guys with the biggest Boom or sharpest blades that carry the day, although that helps. Sometimes a strong jian and well-honed teamwork can turn the tide. Heart makes a difference at those times.

But often it's more basic; the strongest will to survive when everything is going to hell all around you. And the determination to send a big honor guard ahead of you.

Sometimes it's just being the last line of protection between your brothers and that Darkest Night.

This time it was all of the above.

The enemy attack began to falter and slowly drew to a static, poorly situated stop.

In the center of the killing zone.

The Tyrant Jenny-Rose strode forward, fully immersed in the eternal Now.

She coordinated the counter-attack in terse gobbets of battle-language that rang through her team's implants with an elegant simplicity. Her team reacted almost at the speed of thought. They leapfrogged forward, shining with a terrible beauty like the angels of old, as they swept forth into battle.

They were unstoppable; Will itself made solid and deadly.

They blew the attackers into a thousand pieces.

The surviving enemy began falling back.

Rose's team continued to push them off-balance and followed through until the enemy had exited the cargo bunker and were attempting to close the landing hanger airlock.

Rose barked a "stand your ground" battle-command and her remaining warriors shivered into motionless statues, teetering on the edge of exploding into motion.

Rose found she was inhaling in rapid, deep breaths that seemed uncomfortably loud in the sudden quiet. She quickly regulated her breathing.

In battle language she ordered her people to fall back to the defensive position in the rear locker and fortify. Only ninety-seven soldiers remained of the over four-hundred souls.

Her team methodically prepared themselves to go violently into that Dark night. Jenny-Rose heard the enemy blow the main hatch as they left. All that remained was a cold silence that sucked body heat like a glacier wind.

Then someone knocked on the door, and fate proved to have a sense of humor.

13—The Keer

The first encounter between a Keer and a human was in a remote system way out in the dark places. The human was an overweight prospector used to living on cheap calories, corn whisky and solitude. His name was Bob.

He was a simple man with little patience for crowds, or even people in general. They talked too much. He liked the quiet of space, the way sound didn't carry. When he hit town, though, he always ended up in the Strikerich Bar and Grill.

Sometimes you just needed to be around people, just to keep your head on straight. The whiskey helped him relax amidst the raucous crowd, even hold extended conversations. Sometimes noisy was okay, but it got old fast and he eventually found himself longing for the quiet of the night, out there in the Dark.

That was his home. He was very well adapted to his solitary environment, even thrived alone, so long as he came to town every so often. He preferred his human interactions in bite-sized pieces.

The Keer was a highly experienced rock-lice hunter who hadn't eaten in a very long time. The Keer could feel that Darkness looming, and when it spotted the oddly behaving giant rock-lice it focused upon it with its whole being.

It had heard of occasional parasites (in the Dream) that made the rock-lice twitchy, but this one was quite different. It moved around a lot, poking at rocks and consulting some shiny thing in its paw. The rock-lice was badly deformed, probably the result of some kinda accident; it only had four legs and was balancing on just two of them. The Keer didn't care. It was still meat. The organic ballistic calculator in its head plotted a direct trajectory; it wasn't very far at all. The starved Keer threw itself across the empty spaces between the asteroids as it stretched into its elongated hunting form.

Dinner was imminent.

When it fell out of the sky to gobble up the faux-rock-lice named Bob, everything was was over very quickly. The presumed rock-lice only had time for a quick multi-band Squeal before being shredded in the famished Keer's gullet. Then it settled down to digest dinner and entered the Dream effortlessly.

Bob turned out to be the most delicious meal any Keer had ever experienced.

Now, the Keer are intimately acquainted with every aspect of dining on rock-lice, all they talk about in the Dream is dinner (except without words). But this was something new, something amazing, something life-altering. Eating Bob was a religious experience, transforming in its depth and intensity on the palate.

The Keer-who-ate-Bob began to preach about the experience, and droves of Keer epicureans clamored for space near enough to hear the prophet. After all, millennia of the same thing for dinner got kinda boring for a race of gourmands.

The Dream was a fertile plain to sow, and the Keer-who-ate-Bob cast out seed with abandon. The seed took root quickly, and before long, the prophet and Bob were all anyone could talk about.

Many Keer were skeptical of the prophet's tale, and wanted to find the truth out for themselves, others just wanted something new for dinner, and it sounded like Bob was just the ticket.

A few Keer were jealous of the notoriety the prophet now enjoyed and wanted some of that for themselves. Whatever their reasons, everyone wanted some Bob.

At this point in history the Keer were not truly intelligent and wouldn't be considered sentient by the scholars who studied such things. They didn't have a real language; however, they _were_ apex predators, with all the cunning and hunting instincts such predators demonstrate. This included a small organic ballistic calculator in their heads that allowed them to plot complex journeys through the remote asteroid belts that made up their hunting grounds.

The prophet visualized the asteroid belt where it encountered the Bob, and the coordinates were distinct enough that the other Keer thought they could find it. There were always Keer entering the Dream and Keer reaching the end of their digestive stage that produced the racial co-consciousness of the Dream. As they fell out of the Dream back into an unforgiving galaxy, most plotted the trajectory and threw themselves through the black stone rain, headed for the place of new legend. The galaxy is a very big place and as spread out as they are, contains a great many Keer. Almost to a one, they began traveling. Only a few would get there quickly, most would take ten or more cycles to get there.

To the land of Bob.

14—Koen of Summer

The Keer had many followers now in the Dream. They wanted to partake of the sacrament of Bob and evolve too. This required that they find more Bob. The new pilgrims weren't really very smart at this point, so it took quite a while to come to a conclusion.

The place to find more Bob was the place they were found before.

Oddly enough, that was the same conclusion that we had come to, as well. Regarding the Keer, I mean.

We were kicked back in the bar-car Katy the Sledge was towing for us while we were on tour. Dinner had been wonderful, and we were lingering over Porto and stilton cheesecake. The topic had been the same all night, although it had already made it past the argumentative stage and had moved on to the "what if?" part. The wine helped.

"But we need a <u>big</u> Keer-trap—only way to do it is start with a big enough herd to expand rapidly," I was expounding enthusiastically in a confident tone. Why muck around?

Navire and Katy felt I should proceed slowly, try it out with one Keer first. If that went well, then a second Keer could be added. The E, who had been drinking at twice the rate they were pouring for the rest of us, were spontaneously bursting into bouts of whooping and slinging blade around.

Smitty was eying my cheesecake and leaning closer so slowly that it took me a moment to catch the movement. I casually moved my shoulder and arm between the smith and my desert. He'd already polished off a rather large piece, and I was still taking my time. Talking was thirsty work, and I'd been concentrating on my yummy desert nectar, a Porto from a really good cycle. Vintage Fonseca Dynasty. Very-fine.

"What did we do with the ship that carried all the sentry-guard units?" the Gardener suddenly asked (during one of those rare quiet moments we seldom see after eight at night when we're touring).

I sat up quickly. "Yeah!" I unnecessarily added. "What did we do with that freighter, after all?" I wondered out loud, more than a little buzzed. But it'd been a long dinner with lotsa wine that tasted too wonderful to just ignore. What are you going to do? Spit it?

"Smitty stashed it in the old Garage," Pasteur volunteered. We all turned to look at Smitty.

"It was taking up space we needed; tucked it away for later. Knew it would come in handy sooner or later," he said after a moment, almost savoring his unexpectedly becoming the center of attention.

Smitty has definite pack-rat tendencies.

It came in handy just often enough to remain a positive trait. I didn't find the same comfort in piles of broken tech and chaotic messes that Smitty did; back then I liked things clean, black and white, with the lines really obvious.

I would eventually loosen up and become a bit more comfortable with gray.

We all do.

The older sections of the Garage predate our arrival at Summer. Dread believes that some of the oldest areas were actually carved out by the Builders. They were certainly full of exotic junk, and maybe a few treasures as well; nobody really knew. We'd get around to surveying it all sooner or later. As soon as we had the time. I wasn't holding my breath.

But it did make a good place to stash large things of dubious quality.

So, we did.

The entrance to the old Garage is in Fort Medusa's new Garage, partway to Control from the surface. We laid out the new Garage in a familiar pattern, more open to facilitate visual oversight, similar to our kitchen designs.

Smitty was the master chef of this domain, creating magnificent pieces based on salvaged alien tech, forged from rare metals and comet dust and sometimes duct tape. He had bay after bay of projects in various stages of completion, always in partnership with the E, as well as his sentient Forge and, to a lesser extent these days; his current hammer. (They haven't been getting along, lately).

Smitty is never there in the mornings; he spends those digging in the soil and cultivating life in Crystal Garden Seven, a temperate rainforest full of pine trees and giant ferns. He says it helps him balance the bad-tech he builds in his afternoons and evenings. The E seem to enjoy working the land with him almost as much as forging weapons and ships. Their incessant chatter kinda goes all dreamy and slower in pace under the radiant light of Summer as they plant and sow alongside the hulking red-headed smith.

At the back of the new Garage is a roughhewn doorway big enough to pull a ship through. Lotsa ship fragments have passed that threshold over the cycles.

The doorway enters into a huge passageway that stretches out of sight, pierced by pools of Summerlight somehow transported down through the kilometers; to me it always felt like the inside of a huge flute someone was playing languidly in bright sunlight. If you listened well enough you could almost hear the music. Sometimes Navire did.

Enormous bays loomed periodically on both sides as you walked down the passageway carved straight through the myriad crystalline layers of Summer. The corridor sloped downwards gradually; you could only see so far ahead. Some of the bays only contained vacuum-welded piles of odd shapes and textures or were empty.

Others were jammed with pieces of derelict ship carcasses or Ranch mechs waiting to be repaired. The further you went down the hall the less cluttered it became. I'd never made it all the way to the end; something always caught my attention and distracted me. Someday we'd have a chance to catalog everything, but there always seemed to be more demanding issues on our plates. We _really_ needed to hire more people. The problem was finding the right people.

The transport ship that had held the sentry-guards was in the third bay on the left.

It was perfect.

In one instant, I saw the small freighter whittled down to a Keer-trap, elegant in its simplicity, stripped down to its naked essence.

It took almost three weeks to realize that vision.

We started by cutting off all the exterior bits and pieces that a modern starship has sprouting from its skin like coral blooms or angular carbon filaments of esoteric purpose. On a Ship that didn't enter atmosphere, nothing was streamlined.

Once we had the outer surface of the ship smooth, we removed everything from the interior until it was a large, empty, open space surrounded by a tough skin. A tough skin at least ten meters thick by the time we finished, constructed of a regular hull, then coatings in alternating layers of bamboo fiber in epoxy, and the new chitin armor we'd acquired recently. It was very difficult to scratch, and almost impossible to cut through. Should be Keer proof.

That was the plan, anyway.

The next step was Dread's baby.

He built a sorta-inverted implant set to broadcast Bob-TV around the clock.

The broadcasting unit wrapped around the center of the Kerr trap, a band covering half of the former ship. Dread saved time by using standard security recordings of Ranch personnel to populate Bob-TV; the footage used was anything with movement, all spliced together in a five-day loop. I already knew Dread had a wicked sense of guy-humor, but now everybody knew the truth. As a Child of Electron he had the processing power to choreograph physical humor of the slapstick variety extensively.

Man had camera and wasn't afraid to use it.

It was difficult to watch Bob-TV without sinking to its level. It didn't take long for guy-humor to raise its ugly head, either. Lotsa laughter of the gasping-for-breath variety. I wasn't proud, but I couldn't help myself—It was very funny once you snapped to its rhythm and rhyme. Fart humor is timeless. Everybody does it, and then pretends absolute innocence.

It never occurred to us that using images of my crew as bait for one of the deadliest predators in the galaxy might come back to haunt us.

15—The Prince

The young prince gazed around himself in awe. There was so much going on, flashing lights, the metallic clinking and clanging bells sailing on cries of joy and pain; it was too much to perceive or understand all at once. Broad crimson wheels mounted on their backs spun with a strangely fascinating clicking; the surrounding people had locked vision on the spinning roulette with a focus that was almost sexual. These were the lone pools of silence in a lake full of sound.

Elsewhere small bands of aliens perched at semi-circular tables, flipping over small rectangular pieces of parchment and getting very excited at the simple designs. Tiny, fancy disks were exchanged after each flipping. It was all very confusing.

This place was strange for Prince Anodos; he had never imagined anything like it. They were surrounded by so many different kinds of people, all talking and cheering and even a few weeping, whether from happiness or sadness Anodos hadn't a clue.

As far as he could see, there wasn't anyone there who looked remotely like he did. He felt very much the stranger in a strange land.

The young prince found himself experiencing an unfamiliar sensation in his heart. He suspected that this was loneliness and he didn't like it one bit. Anodos suddenly realized that it was one thing to feel solitary in a palace of people who looked like you and spoke your language, and quite another to be out here far from empire and home.

He rotated his head to look at the Stones. They both gazed back with a stone-solidity that evaporated the loneliness in blinks. He wasn't alone after all, and he felt a powerful affection for his bodyguards creep into awareness.

It bothered him that all around them the crowd never stopped moving, if only in place. The pungent aroma of too many people too close together painted the room in broad nasal strokes. It was very noisy.

He felt an unexpected longing for open sky and uncrowded places. The prince shoved his emotions back down and let his gaze wander.

Everywhere the same small dramas were repeated across the grand room.

That was the top layer.

Underneath it was a subtle current of probabilities that wove everything together into a magnificent tapestry. It was very complex, made of thousands of individual threads. The sheer number of small futures in this huge room was nearly indigestible. For a moment it felt like a torrent of psychic flash-bangs raining down on a crazy, wild party. The sensation left Anodos stunned and half-blind before he found his sea legs.

So this was what the pirates of Thunder called a casino.

The fourteen kilometer liveShip Thunder had settled into an elliptical orbit around a sprawling habitat built into the disfigured remains of a small moon. It was called Sincity for some reason.

The habitat held a little over sixteen thousand people at any given time and was situated at a crossroads where shipping lanes intercepted. It was mostly a place of layovers and cargo transfers and resupply.

It was also a place devoted to efficiently separating $cred from tourist's wallets so gently as to appear normal and non-threatening. The city fathers felt that a mark who was tapped for a portion of his $creds would return time and time again. A mark who was drained and cast aside not only never returned to feed their coffers again, but remained in town, draining the city's resources. Even recycling his body didn't yield enough to offset the damage. Not to mention that a place eventually got a reputation for those kinda tactics, and then traffic continuously dropped, making it much harder for the city to prosper.

The powers that be made sure that the $cred sieving operations ran at a certain percentage, and if the business owners didn't adhere to the standards, well, at least the city would benefit a little from *their* recycled remains. In space, organic material was much more valuable than planetary visitors realized. After all, it was just laying around everywhere down on the dirt worlds. You didn't even have to process it or anything.

While the city fathers shared a certain ruthlessness with the Corpnations, that was about it. These homesteaders and traders on the fringes of empire were fiercely independent and believed in minding their own business. They built simple homes in the most barren of places, and believed in ecologically balanced environments, balanced books, and quietly carrying a real big stick. And Boom.

They owed no one and did things their own way, even if everyone thought they were kind of crazy. It wasn't anybody's business. Just don't mess with the kids.

That was everybody's business.

By contrast, the Corp-nations were locusts, stripping resources ruthlessly to devour carelessly, leaving nothing but bones in their wake, both figuratively, and literally. They were nothing like these stubbornly independent frontiersmen and women, and found no place to sow their wicked seed in these parts.

The young prince moved forward to study the spinning wheel that clicked so enticingly.

The Stones sandwiched him on either side, not allowing the crowd to jostle him. The crimson wheel was slowing, its mad clicking slowing down; a slave to entropy just like everyone else.

None of the watchers spoke as a single pearly sphere skipped to an uneven stop in one of the numbered slots of the roulette wheel. It was slot twelve. A hairy male of some indeterminate species hooted loudly as his females jumped up and down in tiny leaps, stroking his luxurious mane in unconscious excitement. Most of the players groaned and shook body parts in disgust. A few others chuckled and reached out to gather in their modest earnings.

This was fascinating. Anodos had known it would be the number twelve, of course. Everyone else seemed to be blind to the small paths. *How could they not see it?* the regal six-meter long salamander wondered for a blink, before discarding the thought.

He reached into a hidden skin pocket and drew forth the single platinum disk the Chow sisters had gifted him. Everyone at the table peered up at him with surprise as he stepped forward to place his bet. The sisters had coached him well on this part. He wasn't surprised at all the attention; a prince of the blood was magnificent in appearance. Most commoners went their whole life without so much as a glimpse of royalty. These poor aliens were understandably impressed, and he didn't begrudge them their moment of splendor.

The tiny multicolored disc had micro-grooves and ridges to make it easy to handle by any of the scores of aliens that filled the casino. Anodos had studied the felt table's graphics and had decided to start simply; he carefully positioned his single chip on the red section.

"All bets are placed," announced the six-armed croupier, and launched the roulette wheel into motion. The clicks it made at this point were so close together as to almost merge into a single continuous sound. As the wheel began to slow down, the ticks of glory separated and drew the audience's focus out until the bouncing pearl finally came to rest in the fifteenth slot, red in color. The circle of milling aliens groaned or cheered, depending on their bets. A small stack of chips was pushed back to the young prince, with a quick nod from the croupier. Anodos had, of course, seen the small futures. He had known that the winning color would be red. Anodos was perplexed by the lack of complexity involved; surely some of the bizarre creatures surrounding him would be able to see the outcomes. A child could do it.

He extended an ebony finger to nudge the small stack of chips onto the black area of the felt table's betting section. The process repeated, and the big pearl came to rest on the thirty second slot, black. This time the small stack of chips returned to him was twice as wide. The young prince was protected from the unruly crowd by the Stones on either side of him, but he couldn't fail to notice the intent examination several of the other gamblers were focusing upon him. There was a predatory flavor to one particular alien's gaze; it reminded him of the royal court, somehow.

The prince was no stranger to ill intentions and calmly returned the odd one's examination. The alien in question was tall and lean, wearing an extensive battle harness jammed with sharp-things and Boom, all wrapped up in a dark gray cloak that went all the way to the floor.

There was something strange about the cloak. For that matter, there was something strange about the alien itself. The small futures seemed to boil around him, never ceasing to resolve into something that Anodos could easily read. He had never seen anything like this and was alarmed at his inability to pin down the stranger's future paths.

The Stones sensed his disquiet. They crept closer and raised their massive heads to tower over most of the aliens at the table. The Stones that Speak were veteran warriors and had protected the royal line's princes and princesses for a very long time. This wasn't their first time in the big city.

While they couldn't read the futures with the prowess of the royal line, sometimes the more blatant of the small futures were visible a few blinks ahead. Luckily, the Stone's skills lay in other areas, and a few blinks was all it took to identify a threat to their charges. They focused on the alien wrapped in gray while maintaining situational awareness of the many things going on around them.

Secure in his bodyguard's protection, the young prince relaxed and turned back to the table. Anodos was already becoming tired of the little steps, and despite the skilled tutelage of the Chow sisters, hastened the process by scooting his small stack of chips onto the number twenty-two, black. The strange alien also moved all of his chips onto black, watching the young prince with piercing eyes.

"All bets placed," announced the croupier and launched the wheel.

"Twenty-two, black," he announced a moment later.

This time the pile of chips was significantly larger than before. Everyone at the roulette wheel cheered him, and the sense of winning was intoxicating. The Chow sister's cautions fell completely by the wayside.

Anodos did it again, sliding his pile of chips onto number five, red. He was focused on the small futures, and failed to stay aware of the rest, caught up in the moment.

"Number five, red," announced the six-armed croupier.

The mound of chips was quite large by now, and it seemed as if half the room was noisily crowding around him. The strange gray cloaked man quickly pocketed his earnings and disappeared into the cheering spectators. That was followed by the appearance of several rather large, angry-looking aliens in house uniforms who abruptly replaced the croupier. Six more house tough guys moved gracefully to flank the Stone's sides. These were not nice people, and the new croupiers were glaring at Anodos with unconcealed hostility.

The Stones did not care for the disrespectful behavior and peered down at the coolers with an unblinking gaze that carried notable weight. The casino coolers, who were experts in making threats without words, broke the stare first. A fifteen-meter giant salamander glaring down at you is scary; encountering two of them at once moves into wet pants territory.

Anodos shook his triangular head, feeling as if he was waking from a dream. The futures screamed at him, and he gave the signal for "let's get the hell out of here."

One of the Stones quickly scooped his chips into a deep flesh pocket as they broke contact and attempted to retreat across the crowded room. The paths narrowed here, and Anodos began to carefully thread the possible futures.

It was a long way to the front door.

Several hours later the Golden Path led them through a neighborhood lined with flimsy structures built into the corridor walls of Malachite Ave. They were in Low town; headed to the commercial quarter in long-term-parking. They trotted past the haphazard structures that were homes and small scale shops and numerous bars that primarily catered to locals.

Their steady pace ate up the kilometers. Anodos was breathing steadily, his training paying off in ways he'd not anticipated back on Thunder. For a moment he found himself missing his new friends back on Thunder, then doggedly returned his attention to following the Golden Path leading him to his next destination.

The young prince needed a liveShip.

Think of an enormous cavern filled with storage barges, ships going through renovation, junk yards with really bad dogs, Roma camps, garage sales, and mothballed fleets of mining equipment. Add in repair facilities, trailer parks, used-ship lots and temporary ship docks laid across each other in a three-dimensional weave that had to be seen to be believed. Stir in a few low-rent distillers, pawn shops, and hydroponic farms and you begin to get the concept of long-term-parking. All floating in zero-G, nicely shielded from meteorites and the usual careening space junk you found outside in the Dark. This was a place where trouble came from the inside, and almost always had people involved.

As they came to a halt at one of the myriad airlocks accessing long-term-parking, the young prince and the Stones activated their vacuum fields. There was a little atmosphere in there, but it varied widely from inert gases that kept welders from setting fires, to exotic mixes best left un-breathed. When they paused after cycling through the airlock to get their bearings, they were accosted by a small mob of rickshaw drivers offering taxi service to wherever they wished to go.

The problem was that while one of the Stones might somehow fit onto one of the larger rickshaw airboats (with his tail hanging off), there was no way they were going to separate onto three of the stripped-down flying platforms. Then the mob rushed away to accost some new arrivals, leaving the unlikely trio to ponder their next step.

The Golden Path lead straight through here, but Anodos wasn't quite sure how to proceed. One of the Stones that Speak lightly batted him on the back of his head, pushing his face downward into a reflective posture. There was no doubt as to the message: time be more proactive, time to plan instead of react. Time to take charge of his destiny again. Time to think. The Stones wrapped around his sides, Safety itself embodied, and faded them all from sight.

He centered himself, methodically shutting off all the outside stimuli that bombards us all and reached for the Golden Path.

It was waiting for him, in all its detailed splendor.

16—Koen of Summer

"Koen! Shadower! — wake the hell up! More Raiders!" Dread snarled in my implant.

I automatically rolled to my feet (still half-asleep) from my warm scrubber-moss bed. Rubbed my eyes, then checked to make sure I was still wearing my Stealthsuit. I wear it for weeks at a time these days, only take it off when I nest into Studio for a break from everything.

"Report," I queried as I entered my personal armory, and began locking weapons onto my body.

"Three teams, using implants slaved to a single channel, hit Fort Medusa, and overrode Signal. That triggered a melt of the local logics, including weapons and intelligent defenses," Dread explained. I frowned. Not good, but at least they couldn't use our own weaponry against us. We always had backups. Besides, we could rebuild in a matter of weeks.

I still felt a slow rage kick to life somewhere deep inside. Raiders had been chasing us for over a decade. Had the daughter of the Raider queen finally found us this time? Hopefully, this was just a random scouting trip. At least this would provide plentiful raw material for my battle-art. I hadn't created any new art for a while; lately I had been feeling the urge more and more.

"Katy," I broadcast. "Get dressed; we're going dancing!".

She laughed with a bit of steam whistle around the edges and sang "On my way, Daddio!"

I ran out of places to position bad-tech and spun, exiting my suite and trotted down the corridor. Fort Lilith's defenses began sealing up behind me (Ranch protocol in these situations). Navire stepped into my implant, placing big pink bunny footprints in my right eye for me to follow down to the junction. Halfway there she physically joined me, matching my stride exactly, as only the children of Electron can.

I mock-glared at her. She tossed a micro-smile my way and changed the pink bunny footprints to something more appropriate to a man such as I. Well, at least shining brass cat prints were an improvement. Not much of one, but an improvement.

Navire was wearing a new hard-body. Today she was styling a human bad-girl warrior that you just knew didn't mind getting her hands dirty. Red hair and green eyes, with pale skin dusted in dark crimson sprinkles. Oiled brown leather armor and lotsa blades strapped all over the interesting parts. And her two favorite needlers, of course; one for each hand.

Weapons always made Navire happy.

Some girls like rare intoxicants, or powerful relationships with lotsa drama, or even predictable trips to paradise worlds. Navire liked things that go Boom. Preferably in large quantities.

My kinda girl.

When we got to the crossroads, Katy the Sledge was wearing another new battle-train, and an intimidating sight it was: a stealth-planed bad-ass train dark as night out there in the quiet places. It was Inertia made solid in somebody's nightmare, a wall's worst dream.

Katy's battle-train was made for cutting and ramming and going wherever the hell she wanted. Her body was truly a thing of irreverent dark beauty. I sighed.

She was becoming a formidable young woman in the neighborhood and they grow up so fast in that period. Seems like I turn around, and suddenly they've grown a few centimeters, or dived into a new passion head first or discovered boys. You just can't take your eyes off them for a second, or you miss something important. Don't think I had, but I worried. Don't we all?

We stepped aboard to the sound of Jelly Girl's Uptown Strut; piano hammering out the notes like a possessed jackhammer and seasoned with the kinda horn you only found in Gravtown clubs late at night—or early morning. It was very-fine.

Smitty and Dread were already there, having beat us by a couple of blinks. Katy sang a few impromptu notes in a voice she was messing around with and slammed the doors shut. Luckily, we all knew what that meant and were tightly grasping the raised handles of the posts sticking out of the deck when she took off like lightning.

I looked around as we hurled through the layered crystalline bedrock; it was good to have friends that didn't hesitate to leave their beds in the middle of the night when you called.

The deck beneath us vibrated from the speed we were making down the long tunnels. As we traveled Navire painted a new-data map in my right eye with coral lines and bright orange icons for the bad-guys. We were on a vector to intercept the Raiders at a location of my choice, a basement storage warehouse two levels down from the main Fort. There were three enemy clusters: a main unit holding Fort Medusa Control and two smaller parties, one at the main terminal, and one at a little used warehouse; (they somehow got the idea that our vaults were down there. Oops).

They would be first.

Katy the Sledge slammed through the warehouse door, all sound and fury.

I shifted my Stealthsuit into full-recording-mode and became the man-shaped-hole in reality for which I am known as my suit sucked in all spectrum new-data. I have to grin as the battle music takes over and time slows to a crawl. Then the hatch opens and we charge into the storage warehouse looking for the bad-guys.

I am armed with my favorite Chen Dynasty daggers. Navire has needlers in each hand, Dread is rocking heavy water shotguns, and Smitty is swinging a huge war hammer covered in glowing cobalt blue glyphs. The glyphs look happy.

We flow into a flying wedge, myself leading, Navire to my right, and Smitty to my left. Dread brings up the rear, securing our escape route, just in case. Didn't mean he wasn't blowing holes in anything that moved; Dread was Dread no matter where he was positioned. We flow down the warehouse aisles with an unstoppable grace. I don't think they were expecting us so soon. We hit the enemy like a buzz saw, slicing into the bad-guys in a timeless gestalt of elegant carnage, a living nightmare painted in silver and scarlet.

Everything around me moves in slow motion and I feel very alive. I veer to my right, spinning our wedge formation so that Smitty takes the gnarled Raiders in front. I embrace the Now, spinning in Lui style Bagua animal form. I coil and spin, slicing and drilling through the small cluster of bad-guys in my sector. Le Danse is a friend of old, and they fall before me like grain to a scythe at harvest time.

When I came back to myself I was standing in the center of the room, panting for breath. Navire eased back from a pile of roasted enemy and gave me a concerned look. I smiled back.

It probably would have been more convincing if I hadn't been drenched in blood.

Transition from Battle mode to mundane reality was neither instantaneous nor pleasant, but what can you do? We slowly walked it off in random circles. We were victorious here, but the battle wasn't over by any means. The main fight for Fort Medusa lay ahead. And we still didn't know where the full Raider force was.

We checked our ammo and reloaded, examined our blades and assorted Boom. Took a large drink of water and rinsed our mouths, spitting in long, accurate streams. An errant memory of Auntie Tao scolding me for spitting during my early Hive years skipped by. I grinned and reached up to stretch. You had to take pleasure in the small things, because the big things didn't come along that often.

I looked around, everybody was cleaned up and ready. Katy the Sledge waited impatiently, her doors open and ready to roll.

First we hit the small armory Katy always placed behind the main travel cabin. Dread broke out a familiar Rime giant sniper rifle, cradling it with that affection a professional holds for his best tools. The rifle was not only worth several fortunes but was also arguably one of the finest sniper rifles in the known galaxy. Dread admired the masterwork and quietly smiled, no doubt day-dreaming of laying down precision Boom.

I broke out my Wudang Mountain sword and strapped it to my left side for a right-handed draw. I was taking these guys seriously.

Smitty hefted an oversized auto-shotgun, (he affectionately referred to it as "the Doom-Boom"), leaning back slightly to give Navire the once over. I flash him a micro-grin and follow his gaze to Navire.

Navire was sinking into an old school Wing-chung stance, holding herself noticeably different than she usually did. Her posture was kinda like she was suspended by a string from the top of her head. Her spine and head perfectly aligned with her foot placement.

She stood relaxed, an instant away from full-tilt boogie. Navire had strapped up for close quarters combat. I guess she was tired of letting me have all the fun. My girl was dressed in a wealth of concussion slaps and pointy things, as well as a pair of butterfly swords nestled in her shoulder blades. I knew those fat blades; they oozed a corrosive neurotoxin that was an extremely painful way to go into that Dark night. They would also cut through most any armor; Navire had to wear special arm-gloves to avoid damaging herself.

There are three combat ranges in closed system environments. First is close quarters—within a meter—Navire and I covered that. Then there is midrange: two-to-seven meters. Smitty had that covered. And finally, long range—eight-to-fifty meters or more, which Dread dominated. We had worked together long enough that we knew our roles without discussion, and played to our strengths, although sometimes we mixed it up just to keep flexible. Navire always rode our implants, keeping us on the beat.

"Ready," I told Katy the Sledge, grabbing hold of the raised handles as her doors slammed shut and we blasted out of there at an uncomfortable speed.

Katy dropped a classic stomp piece on us from way back; White-haired Jack driving keyboards down Rhythm Lane. You could hear him way off, always striding closer, picking up inertia. Horns came in early, all lady-like and demure. That didn't last long. Then White-haired Jack started to naughty rhyme, and the horns threw off propriety like it was burning. Katy the Sledge started scat-singing a bit here and there, her darkest knight body vibrating as she hurled through the crystal layers of Summer.

Everyone was smiling, even Dread. We thought the things warriors think at those times, closing in on battle. As the minutes crept by the music richened, adding layers of notes that siren-called you to battle. I began to slip back into the eternal Now.

Fort Medusa was designed to be easily defended from outside attacks, but we didn't have the man-power to staff things properly. We really needed to recruit more talent, but finding the right people, ones I could trust, never came quickly or easy.

Luckily, we had also wormed the design for penetration from deeper within the myriad crystalline layers of Sumer. Our back-up plans had back-up plans; when you've lived through things you shouldn't have, you tend to make allowances for the next time.

Navire's eyes were calmly focused on Katy the Sledge's main hatch as we waited, but underneath her calm was a definite sub-current of pissed-off. I was probably the only one who could see it; Navire was taking this raid very personally. The new auto-sentry units should have stopped them cold and given us ample warning to boot. The fact that they didn't suggested several things, all of them bad. I could tell that she was blaming herself, assuming the decision-tree software she had installed had somehow been flawed, or worse, corrupted.

I mentally tapped her implant lightly to get her attention.

"We don't know what happened—could be anything. We never looked into how that ship came up for sale in Gravtown, just then, at a price we could afford. There's more going on here than we realized," I said out loud. Everyone turned to look at me. Dread grunted in agreement. Smitty just looked at me, waiting for me to continue.

"I should have caught it," Navire stated firmly, not meeting my eyes.

"We don't even know what 'it' is," I said. "We need to focus on the current situation, there will be plenty of time to figure out how we got here later," I said softly, but emphatically. Everyone made sounds of agreement, but I knew it was still eating at her. At least she could run multiple thought streams while moving; it wouldn't affect her performance on the battlefield. But it still mattered to me.

The bad-guys were most likely expecting us to take down the remaining smaller group first, then attack the main group of Raiders having deprived them of re-enforcements. That's what most bad-guys would do. Our initial attack added to this impression.

On the other hand, Hive non-symmetrical battle-logic dictated that we attack the main body next, and mop up the remnants later.

Besides, I never do what the enemy is expecting me to.

Instead we would flow like water down a rocky hill and penetrate into the heart of the enemy through the concealed cargo tunnels. Home team advantage.

Katy the Sledge brought us into Fort Medusa hot.

She seized control of the main hatch-logic and blew the lock which directed the enemy's attention exactly where we wanted it. About the time all heads were turning to the airlock, Katy the Sledge punched through a weak spot concealed behind a very nice moss garden on the other side of the foyer.

Surprise! Katy slid into Control throwing Boom, mostly implosion grenades with a few flash-bangs and smokers tossed in for seasoning, and heavy H_2O canons firing to the beat of one hell of a soundtrack. As Katy slid to a screeching stop, she was howling a deafening battle cry that covered the higher audio spectrum at a painful volume. It was stunning. Literally. But then, teenagers aren't very big on subtlety. Then Katy slammed her doors open and we strode into the smoking remnants of the Control room foyer.

I felt the world slow and the Gravtown Strut torching my implant; everything in my field of vision seemed to move to the beat. I unsheathed my molecular-edge Tai Chi sword, and in a continuous motion I whipped my one and a half meter long flexible razor, with the cresting wave of the blade whip hitting the tip of the sword just as I settled into Wudang Jian stance. My left two fingers were raised in an upwards block, with the finger blade honoring Wudang.

I settled into my root as my unfocused eyes scanned in a wide-field movement search. Not much detail, but in a fight you need to be aware of all sides because that's where the bad-guys like to come at you from. I learned that the hard way at an age most kids were still learning how to finger paint.

The Raiders were clustered at the port side of the hatch, and in an alcove by the Δqm^x pod theater. There were thirty-six of them, and one boss, who stayed way back behind some really big guys in the alcove.

Didn't keep him from being noticeable. I wondered what kinda monster the boss was, to keep all these psychopaths waiting for play time to begin.

The Raider's bodies were heavily scarred, with ropy muscles and prominent bones that would be concealed by body fat in a normal person's body. These weren't normal by any means. They never stopped shifting and moving, a restless pack of ravenous predators forced to wait before feeding time. It was their faces that stood out, though. Burning eyes set in a skeletal head, smashed noses, and teeth somebody had rebuilt to do more damage. They couldn't fully close their mouths and panted nonstop. I wondered what kinda fight hormones the Raider queen had flooded their systems with. Their hungry gazes never stayed anywhere for long, but Navire got more than her share, and I wasn't far behind.

We couldn't help but notice that the other Raider shock troops paid the boss a subtle physical deference. This was as obvious to me as if Navire painted a map in bright silver on my retina. He was the alpha predator in a large hunting ground, and had long held his position successfully against all comers.

The boss's body language was deceptively relaxed, the same way a big cat is just before he eats you. He simply stood there for a moment, looking us over, as if memorizing every detail for later. Then he hand-signed his men in archaic Zero-G language and they began to spread out to hunt us, most sporting twisted grimaces of delight.

I sang Hive battle-language at the same time and Navire sped up her consciousness to fighting speed, focusing on the group hiding behind the airlock door. They meant to take us from behind after we engaged the enemy. Navire stalked them through the dust and smoke and they never saw her coming.

Dread quickly scaled Katy's steaming battle train and perched. It had to be hot up there, but the hard-body Dread was wearing didn't seem to notice. He quickly set up and began to focus on just where to clear a path for us.

Smitty was just behind and to my right, taking out the garbage before it came close enough to hurt us. I could hear Dread snickering wildly as he shot to the beat. But there was nothing wild about his aim, every target went down. He was just having a good time, kicking the asses of rapists and murderers.

Dread didn't get out much.

He was a man born of Electrons, (as are we all, in one way or another). He had once been a soldier, a leader of brave warriors that fought the good fight, and sent down many enemies down to hell, paving the road for the fallen. He had thought he was just the rear guard into that Dark night, but then Navire and I came along, and now Dread's the guardian of the Ranch. He has little patience for the kinda of pack that slaughters indiscriminately, and none at all for Raiders.

Smitty and I strode forward in slow motion; the music was slowed down, too, and burning bright on the smoke wreathed air. Everything smelt of copper and burnt moss.

I am completely in the Now, sliding in on the first movement of le Danse. I feel like I have all the time in the world. Closing in on me from the right in slow motion is Tall-strong-guy. He has two big pistols that are loud as hell, but he doesn't seem to be able to use them simultaneously. The explosive sounds guide me more than vision in the smoke-filled antechamber.

Two steps away.

My blade glides behind me in a vertical position that can't be seen from his position. He sees me fully for the first time. He begins to smile, thinking me unarmed. His left finger tightens on the trigger of his pistol.

One step away.

He fires one of the hand cannons at my head, instead of taking the safer, body shot. He misses, but my suit is in full-recording-mode, all light and sound disappear into my Stealthsuit. No reflection back. He doesn't know he missed.

He's used to winning. He starts to lower his guns.

My molecular-blade begins to swing over my head from behind in a precise arc.

I'm there.

I pull back on the Tai Chi sword slightly to add speed to the blade. My molecular blade cuts him into two parts vertically without slowing.

I wipe his blood from the edge of my sword on his half-side as I pass by. He falls, slowly, in two pieces.

Short-fat-guy becomes the center of my world.

I'm two steps away.

He's firing a stubby rapid-fire rifle that may be good for slaughtering sheep, but is definitely not the weapon for here, for Now. But he's firing at Smitty. He doesn't see me yet. My sword arm compresses, storing inertia for the attack.

One step away.

Short-fat-guy is beginning to turn, swinging his projectile hose clumsily in my direction. My Chen dynasty molecular blade is aimed directly at Short-fat-guy's chest, held horizontally, to slip between the ribs. I begin the thrust.

I'm there.

My blade tip undulates in his heart, separating it into flapping pieces that are unable to support life. Coppery crimson pours from his chest. The movements of my flexible razor-edged sword are working like a pump, emptying his chest of vital fluid.

I withdraw the sword quickly, flicking the red away as I glide into movement three of le Danse Macabre.

Dread lies close to the heated surface of Katy the Sledge's smoking hot battle-train. His implant whispers environmental new-data such as wind and distance in his ear. His enhanced visual systems snap the target into focus with the suddenness of a bad morning hangover.

Dread's hard-body implant interfaces well with the rifle's systems; the thought becomes the deed in a fraction of a blink. He cradles the deadly beauty in his arms and strokes the trigger with an almost unconscious sensuality. His Rime rifle is serving up smart projectiles the size of your middle finger; exploding after target penetration into jagged corrosive fragments.

One shot, one kill, no brag.

That is the way of Dread's people.

He wide-scans the field again before focusing in on a new target.

Someone is shooting sticky-net-things at the man-shaped hole in the air, the Shadower. They are trying to take him alive. That is something new.

I am hard enough to see as it is; capture would be extremely difficult to pull off. Dread was going to make sure it never happened.

The question was; torso or head shot. Torso was traditional and safer even if you were skilled. On the other hand, headshots had flair, and showed greater technical skill. Unless you miss, something Dread hadn't experienced since he was quite young.

"Head," he decides, "center forehead." Dread stills himself, a phenomenal feat for a guy born of Electrons. His multi-speed consciousness is a part of what makes Dread who he is, and it is never even remotely quiet in Dread's mind. But I had taught him well; he whole-gestalt flashes on things in the moment when time stopped. The trigger seems to pull itself.

Navire closes on muscular-bad-guy, who obviously thought he was the top of the bad. Navire's speed is deceiving, in part because she moves so smoothly. He hesitates for a split blink as his consciousness awakes to the realization that this is le Danse and he is off beat, late for his cue.

She closes, and left-right slash cuts his neck open, neatly severing the carotid arteries on both sides of his neck. She then flips the swords to their infighting form; laid blade out along her forearms. The butterfly sword's knuckle guards now form brass knuckles for percussive strikes. She puts them to use, slapping him in the face twice with them before she severs his head at the neck with the elbow-powered blade and finishes him off. Navire doesn't like bullies or Raiders.
Especially Raiders. Long story.

The other five Raiders in her sector stand, stunned for a blink before pulling out widely assorted bad-tech and blasting a hole where she was a blink ago.

Now she is in among them, close enough to kiss; close enough to hamper their fighting as she sailed between them, arms working furiously. Blades so sharp that if it wasn't for the corrosive poison they oozed, the Raiders wouldn't even realize they'd been cut until pieces started dropping off. Then Navire comes to a full stop a few steps beyond them, sheathing her butterfly swords. The Raiders collapsed wetly behind her in an untidy pile.

The Boom was very loud around Smitty and me, they call them blasters for a reason. The sound levels are so high that my implant cut audio completely, leaving me to watch Navire working a silent rhumba on her dance partners.

I can't take my eyes off of her, as Katy's playlist of Gravtown dancehall music kicks back in. It is a Caribe Island rag, all base and percussive guitar creeping down the back stairs to naughty rhyme with a Strut straight outa Gravtown. It is glorious and Navire pauses to shake it to the music for a timeless blink, before settling back down to good old fashioned bloody-death once again.

It was very-fine battle-art material.

Smitty is an unstoppable hell-dispensing warrior, his 'Doom-Boom' serving up heavy-metal high-velocity shotgun rounds. He elephant-walks forward on my right and a step behind so that he can watch my back. That is Smitty. More and more Shock troops are waved on to stop us in our relentless march forward to the boss.

Smitty blows away bad guys' knees, then finishes them with a blast to their head or a stomp as he strides over their dying bodies (all in time to the beat). Guess there was a reason he didn't get out much either. Still, a very good friend to have. Especially now.

My Wudang molecular blade whips around my body like a willow in a wind storm. I cut wrists and ankles if heavily armored, and necks or liver if not.

Too many bad-guys snub heavier armor out of bravado and confidence in their particular form of Boom. These mistakes are self-correcting because they seldom live long enough to reproduce.

I slide between my enemies, never where they expect me to be. They fall before me like chaff and I move ever closer to our goal. The deck grows slippery with blood and things better left unexamined.

As Dread finds that still, quiet place inside himself, the targets became increasingly clear, even detailed. He finds optimal timing and gently stroked the trigger. The target's head vaporizes in pink and gray. Dread instantly begins focusing on the next target. (Sometimes it was very nice to have threaded consciousnesses!)

Navire's ever-present camera-gnats made threat assessment short and sweet. Target selected. The moment reaches fullness and the target dissolves in earth tones of the maroon type. Dread begins methodically clearing the field for his brothers and sister, one Raider at a time.

Navire was also going after the boss, long way around.

She briefly sings Hive-battle language over our implants; Smitty and I instantly alter direction without loss of inertia or clumsiness. Navire is on an intersecting trajectory with the enemy management, moving in from the other side of the chamber.

We are to get all the attention; that is our role. I also want to interrogate the Raider capo and get any new-data as to where the other thousand Raiders were! Or even just who was throwing this party.

Navire paints the room with fluorescents in my right eye, and the orange strobing one is my primary target. The bad-boss.

Three meters now, off to my left. Smitty stays with me as I move through the smoke and weapon fire in search of a non-lethal fight. (They are rarer than you think).

He somehow knows I am coming for him and isn't afraid. That means he is either stupid or dangerous. I am going with dangerous.

I breath deeply, charging my cells with oxygen in preparation of the fight.

I pull the Now in about me and plunge out of the smoke with my Wudang sword aimed at where I think his heart is.

After all, his outline in florescent orange is pretty specific.

However, he easily evades me and from the way he moves I suddenly realize he is a Kuntao fighter; I hadn't ever fought one of those guys! They are quite rare, and the art is shrouded in mystery.

Tired as I am, I feel a thrill go through me. What battle-art I could create from this!

Luckily, he isn't where I had expected him to be, or there would be no raw material at all.

"Stop screwing around!" Dread growled in my implant.

"He's Kuntao," I reply with a broad smile.

I don't need to say more. Everyone knows my obsession. I hear Navire sigh and Smitty groan. Dread says something dirty in a language I don't know but don't really need to.

"I'm not sure if this is the best time to focus entirely on only one opponent," Navire diplomatically suggests. Her tone makes it clear that this is only a pro-forma objection, and that she doesn't really expect me to walk away from adding to my portfolio.

"I'll keep the bad-guys off your back," Dread reluctantly offers.

"Just make it quick," Smitty adds, with enough sarcasm to suggest just how much he expects me to take his advice to heart.

I stand tall and sheath my Chen dynasty blade. The world again slows to a crawl and my ability to form language falls from me in a sorta bright light that never hurts your eyes. My world narrows to the man I am now approaching. My universe simplifies into a place of angles and counterstrikes, as I become truly one with the Now.

The bad boss then proceeds to ritually sheath a strangely angled blade with a pistol grip and slows to a halt.

I bow, eyes forward, hands in a classic Lui Bagua salute.

He comes within a meter and a half, and then seems to shiver and solidify into a stance that resembles a horse stance, only angled, with the upper legs parallel to the slippery deck.

His arms are out before him in a not-unfamiliar style, as are mine. He inclines his upper body and head in a subtle movement, returning to his "guard" position after holding it for a blink.

I begin to circle him in Lui Bagua eight palms, beginning, of course, with the first palm. I reverse direction at uneven intervals as I mirror-walk the eight palms, always coming closer.

He is taller than me, and quite powerful in appearance with that compact musculature that martial artists develop over time. He has good balance.

His tangled mane of hair is dark ebony and oiled in damp ringlets so it would be difficult to grab in combat. He shifts horizontally to face me as I circle him in a spiral that will end in le Danse, sooner than he realizes.

His eyes glare at me with a palpable weight. My unfocused vision is geared to movement, utilizing my peripheral vision in a manner few realize can be done. I observe my opponent fully without the kinda focused vision his eyes could meet.

The thrust of his eyes can find no surface to push against and strike. I channel chi through my lungs and arms as I come nearer, always circling in a closing spiral.

I suddenly become aware of a peripheral silence, as the sounds of battle have softened to a quiet I knew of old. It is that precise moment of battle when lives rest on a coin toss and anything can happen. Nobody moves, except bad-boss and me.

Everyone else has stopped fighting and turned to watch the bosses throw down. Not a loud breath is taken, lest they reignite the battle. They might not need die, after all!

We feel every eye upon us and I recognize the weight of family in the all-encompassing pressure on my brow.

The Kuntao fighter slowly puts his hands together as if praying, and quickly shifts into me, locking his left foot around the Achilles tendon of my right foot. Suddenly his stance shifts powerfully, all torque focused on my right knee. It should have shattered my leg in a compound fracture.

I am lucky that I am a Bagua man.

Our leg strength is built up over decades of training, not cycles. By the time one learns all the animal forms and the bridge, our legs are extremely strong.

I am hurt, but not permanently damaged. My next move is natural.

We are already close physically, as he expected to have disabled me.

I slid my left hand up his right arm until I find his tendon with my middle finger, just above the elbow. My right hand goes the opposite direction down his arm to his wrist which I pull and rotate, locking down the joint with my middle knuckle. Then I pierce his elbow's tendon with my finger and he screams like a little girl.

What a baby. I am positively disappointed.

I begin to walk him backwards; his arm twisted precisely, shoulder torqued high and his legs suddenly cooperative or else.

I expected better, damn it!

Suddenly he somehow rotates downwards, and snaps to another low stance, but this time his folded left elbow punches my right temple just as his right hand slaps my left ear. The dual strikes that nailed my skull are so balanced that every sip of energy is transferred to the target. As he pulls away he whacks me once more with a back-hammer fist that rings bell.

OK, maybe it wasn't over so easily.

He grins at me, taking his pleasure with a slow, low chuckle. The remaining Raiders scream and giggle in joy, remaining where they stood for the moment.

Good. I haven't learned enough yet. I'm not ready for this fight to end.

I shake my head to make the ringing stop. It sorta works.

He laughs again, but not convincingly: he appears to unexpectedly see something in me that suddenly tenses him up.

I shift up to "monkey picks fruit", then down low to scoop up his right knee in a full body move that tosses him head over heels. He smoothly rolls to his feet, but I can tell he's concealing a damaged knee joint.

Welcome to the club.

My feet slide forward in a curve with that particular cadence unique to Bagua. My torso is rotated ninety degrees, facing the center of the invisible circle I am walking. My left arm is rotated, elbow down, palm out and mildly compressed. My right arm is lower, it's palm under elbow, facing a different angle and everything is pointed at the center of the circle only I can see. The ripples in my mind smooth and time sorta disappears. My awareness spreads out in a kinda slow tide of new-data. I am spatially aware of everything around me.

I am in full-recording-mode; I am a colorless hole torn in the fabric of reality. I am the battle-artiste known as the Shadower; veteran of a lifetime of battle, fights beyond counting.

Closer now.

I slide through the smoke-drenched air in the seventh palm, which feels exactly right. The bad-boss has become the center of my narrow world.

I move to center.

As I do I raise my eyes slowly to finally meet his with a palpable impact as I let the Now course through me. He steps back and inadvertently drops his eyes.

He is defeated already; he just doesn't realize it.

I close, sliding in arcs and curves.

I ride the timeless Now with battle music raging through my head like heavy luminescent mortar fire.

Everything this warrior has done is external; all muscle and linear technique; no chi at all. So when his leg snaked out and locked around mine I was expecting it.

My trapped leg had a false root—it held up no weight and was extremely quick to slip out of the bone-breaker lock and then knee-strike inside his upper thigh with my good one.

I glide closer.

The back of my hands push against each other as they roll up and out in the fabled blossom fist; palms together, forearms a joined piston upwards. Cupping hands spread out to catch the jawbone and the opposing ear.

I was close enough to strike almost directly upward. I felt his neck snap, transforming the formidable fighter's proud musculature into dead weight. I held him, continuing to spin, laying the body down gently in my wake. Everyone in the room looks at the former bad-boss, then at me.

Man did ring bell.

I arc out of the spiral to face the alcove where the howling Raiders have gone frothing mad, rushing me and Smitty.

Three minutes. Twenty-nine down, six to go. Its not rocket science. But they're Raiders and this doesn't matter to them. The chemicals and conditioning in their heads are way too loud.

Enter stage left: the reinforcements showing up, then halting abruptly. Lotsa comrades down, and it didn't look like they were winning the fight. Their capo shouts at them, making hand-sign for them to approach him rapidly and protect him.

Enter stage right: Navire, accompanied by a wealth of Boom.

I'm not surprised by this, she has been subconsciously itching for the chance to blow something up for a while now, and it looks like it was scratching time. Then the frozen moment releases its breath and full-tilt-boogie pours down like rain.

Smitty and I arc left on a trajectory to intersect the new bad-boss and Navire. He elephant-stomps forward, jacking shotgun shells, and shortening the bad-guys by a leg or two as he goes. They fall down. We finish them in passing, a task Smitty's hammer relishes. They were already dead, just didn't know it yet.

I decide that these guys aren't worthy of my sword.

I spin into the boss's remaining Raiders, boring into vulnerable joints and snapping bone in fluid technique. I am fully in the Now and they crumple in my wake, discarded paper sacks blowing away in my wind. I don't focus on their efforts to kill me; they are but mayflies swarming. My attention is focused on their capo, the threating bully hiding behind useless muscle of the dim variety.

He becomes the center of my world, but Navire is the artist that paints his death in slap implosions. Large holes in his head and torso appear in silent cadence. Sizzling Gravtown beat choreographed the moment. Navire spun through le Danse with skill and grace, punctuating her movements with silent thunder.

Slap grenades are mono-directional focused explosions that only go in one direction. You can wear concussion slaps like rings or gloves and be perfectly safe. The implosion part is the exact opposite of an explosion; instead of blowing up it sucks everything into a small compact pebble. They were totally silent when used.
I am very fond of them.

Not as noisy as the traditional methods, and much more discreet.

I slow, breathing more heavily than I should have been. As I come back to myself I scan the Control room. Nobody was fighting anymore, just battlefield mercy and smoke and Quiet ringing louder than the very center of battle had. I was shaking slightly in the hands. The re-entry to mundane consciousness after battle was turning out to be a jittery, mildly unpleasant body smack. Not too fond of this bit, but what are you going to do?

Signal is Signal.

I did some standing Qigong to cushion my re-entry to the world ordinaire while Navire was combing the battlefield like some Celtic Valkyrie, in search of new-data about the attack. She was strangely gentle as she interrogated the not-quite-gone. After learning what she could she held them gently as she reverently gave them the battlefield mercy they longed for.

It was better than they had planned for her.

There were worse ways to go into that Dark Night.

17—The Keer

When Bob's friends got the Squeal that his suit had sent, they were, as usual, in the Strikerich bar and grill. The compressed new-data squeal left no doubt that something bad had dropped down out of the night and gobbled their buddy in a blink.

It was a damn shame, and a number of Bob's friends bought rounds for the house in his memory. It was cold out there, and nothing they could do to save him now, anyway.

The Squeal had left no doubt of that.

Eventually the house bought a round in Bob's name and one of the meaner drunks spoke up. (Bob owed him money).

"Bob was a great guy, and we need to kill the guy what got him!" He declared.

Everybody cheered and drank a great draught to the mean guy. The mean guy thought it was kinda nice to be cheered and continued in that vein for as long as he could.

Everybody got pretty riled up and drank heavily between cheers. Cheering was thirsty work. So was riling.

Then one of the miners stood up.

"I'm going after that murdering space trash and bring back Bob's remains! Any of you pussies' brave enough to go with me?" he challenged.

Everyone gave a short, halfhearted "yay!" and that would have been that, except one of the more alert guys suddenly declared "And what about Bob's treasure trove of new-data on hundreds of unknown systems? You bringing that back too?"

Everyone started to get all riled up again and a couple of punches were thrown, but after a few more drinks eventually everyone decided to go. Because you couldn't trust the others with that kinda treasure.

The twenty-eight miners and friends poured out of the Strikerich bar and grill into the main corridor of a remote mining village on a small wanna-be moon orbiting a rich gas world named Lau Lau. Each miner made sure he carried a sufficient quantity of intoxicants and booze with him to keep the party going all the way there and back. (Just in case).

Then everybody piled aboard the Strikerich party bus, a converted oar carrier rigged for social trips. Once everybody was settled the Captain took them out into the star and dust-speckled void. The DJ was spinning Caribe Island music, laced with trance-blues and a Gravtown beat. Good bar. Good beer. Nobody noticed that the goodtime girls had faded a while back and were now nowhere to be seen. The drinks kept flowing all night, and it was always night in space. They all had a really good time. Then they fell asleep. These miners were a rough crowd— not many people could nod off while flying through darkest space in search of a Bob-eating monster that you couldn't see coming. But they didn't know anything about that yet.

They were lucky snoring didn't carry in space. The ship kept on course, heading to the location of the Squeal. For the last place Bob was.

Soon the nodding avengers were out cold, the crew too. It had been a long night. The party bus slid on through the stone rain in the eternal darkness.

The guys started waking up when the ship's course changed, and the party bus began dumping inertia and slowing down. These guys had survived in the unforgiving environment of deep space for lifetimes. Didn't make them smart by any means, but they were tough as hell.

Now they were tough as hell with hangovers.

After a while somebody yelled "we're there, let's go!" and everybody scrambled for their Boom and Blade.

Lucky no one got hurt by the time everybody calmed down.

It was decided that two shots of corn whiskey would be just the right amount to make sure everyone was calm and ready to go get the Bob-slayer. Everyone crowded the bar as the highly trained bartender poured his heart out. It was something to see.

About this time a few Keer began arriving at the site of the Eating of Bob. Scattered arrivals continued, until more Keer were in close physical proximity to each other than had ever happened in the long history of the Keer. The huge ant-like predators clung to the slow spinning rocks that tumbled through the neighborhood. Invisible. Hungry. Patient.

Then all eyes (and antenna) turned to the party bus with the flashing lights as it slowed down to a halt. It was a crunchy container full of miners! Such a novel way of delivering fresh Bob! What fun!

The Keer's mandibles began to stretch out, lengthening and glistening. Muscles began to coil like a spring, building static inertia for the leap.

There was no teamwork, or mutually assessed targets, or peripheral awareness in the second Eating of Bob.

It was every Keer for itself. And stay outa my way. Friendliness in the dream was all great, but don't stand between me and my dinner.

A few Keer bounced to a different rolling rock in the belt. It was closer to the canned meat.

The Strikerich party bus was almost quiet as weapons were checked, vacuum-ware sealed, and air-flow positive. The mean guy stood silently up and walked to the lock. The display above the portal showed an asteroid with a shiny habitat glued to the surface. A beat up vintage system truck with massive low tech armor made of recycled fiber was parked a few meters away. The map showed very rugged terrain and a dozen pits sunk into the surface. No monster. No body. No legendary new-data treasure.

"Maybe he's in the habitat," the mean guy offered, comfortingly.

After making sure everyone was strapped up, they eased out to float in a force-tethered group as everyone slowly exited the bus. It was a short drop to where the habitat was.

They dropped.

The alert one and the mean one jockeyed for position to be first one in to the tiny habitat, but it was the sleepy-looking one who beat them inside. Except—no body! Two more miners squeezed through the airlock and the five of them began to search for Bob's fabled memory caches.

The remaining twenty-three hung-over asteroid miners stood around waiting for their chance to go in, all the while complaining about how they were probably being robbed blind before they had the chance to rob someone else blind.

Then something big and hungry dropped out of the night and gobbled up a miner before he could even holler.

Then another man vanished in half a blink.

The friends of Bob quickly were going out like candles in a black wind. However, miners and Boom are inseparable. It was inevitable that one of them was a stick of dynamite pretending to be a candle; explosive indigestion doesn't begin to cover it. Took out three Keer (the guy did love his Boom). Everyone else was gobbled up. Pieces of the dead Keer and the miner were spread all over the place.

The other unscathed nineteen Keer were now glued to the asteroid's surface, their powerful shield armor protecting them. They were completely invisible and undetectable to all Signal.

The Keer's bodies crouched digesting in a torpor, while the Keer's conciousness stepped out to the Dream and began testifying as to the sacrament of Bob. They all quickly became stars. Everyone wanted to hear about their dining experience, with all the juicy details. Converts bloomed around them. To hell with rock-lice, I want Bob, marbled with fat and delightfully pickled in tenderizing ethyl alcohol infusions. Second-Bob style.

After limited success searching for the star maps with detailed new-data surveys, the alert miner noticed that no one was trying to get in. They'd been in the habitat for a while, and not even a knock on the door. These guys weren't that patient, they were more the shoot first, question later kinda miners. He caught the mean guy's eye and they both moved for the airlock. Sometimes it really is too quiet.

Weapons, vacuum seals, positive air flow. Ready.

The two men stepped into the airlock and waited for it to depressurize. When the outer door dilated they stepped out, ready to do whatever was needed. Nothing, it seemed, was.

The surface near them was blown free of dust and pebbles; an explosion must have occurred. Debris was spread out in a circle. Oddest of all were clumps of strange tissue that could only be seen from one side. The meat side. The dark gray flesh was very dense; maybe it was human, a miner, but the alert one didn't think so. That left the question of where were the other twenty-three friends of Bob. They looked around the mining site again. Nothing moved in the jagged black and white streaked rocky ground. Nothing overhead, or inbound on an intercept course. Just the party bus hanging overhead in the sky, motionless. Tethers floating aimlessly, sheared off at the ends.

That wasn't suspicious or anything.

Nothing moved around them except the slow ballet of the constant stone rain.

"Maybe everyone got back onboard?" offered the mean guy. He was being overly helpful for a mean guy. Leadership, even of a bunch of miners who didn't bath very often, was changing him. He was losing his meanness.

The alert guy took point and they bounced into the sky. Cycled aboard. Empty, except for the half-drunk captain and the snoozing bartenders. No miners.

They stopped for a shot of corn whiskey to bolster their mystery solving abilities, then headed back down to gather at the habitat. Everyone was upset. What the hell happened here? The formerly mean guy began scooping up pieces of the strange one-sided flesh and stuffing them into a bag. After a moment he noticed that he couldn't walk in a straight line.

"I didn't have that much to drink," he mumbled to himself. He caught the alert guy watching him.

"You know me, takes a lot more than a few shots of whiskey to mess with my equilibrium!" he snapped belligerently. The alert guy dropped his eyes and looked back at his own tracks. They curved around a different empty space, too. He began to backtrack.

The occasionally mean guy, (old habits die hard), sighted on the habitat's airlock, and began to march straight towards it. He was halfway there when he curved around an empty space without intending to. He stopped, looked back at his tracks in the dust. He tried to walk through the empty space again, and just couldn't—his feet just carried him around it. He began to study the spot when he noticed something in a nearby shadow-dark depression. He poked at the small hole with his Needler. A spacesuit covered human foot floated up in the low gravity before slowly settling back down in the hole. It had been severed just below the ankle.

His eyes met the alert guy's for a moment, then they both stared at the empty spots that weren't really empty. Then everyone got kinda spooked, and bounced up towards the party bus. Traffic jam at the airlock. Lotsa shoving. Couple punches, couple a kicks. Tough guys running scared; it was truly something to see.

In space, sometimes gut aces logic.

They hadn't been able to see the score of huge Keer crouched beneath their armored shields around them, but they now knew that they were right there. The invisible monsters crouched unmoving, deadly and presumably ready to pounce on the hapless miners. The five surviving friends of Bob didn't realize that the Keer were rocking a mystical digestive trance, literally unable to move for six or more months as they reveled in the Dream. These had just become new-born priests in the religion of Bob for Dinner.

Je suis Bob.

Luckily these five miners were a hardy lot. They were long term survivors of the most unforgiving environment ever known. The guys had somehow sensed the cold death that crouched invisibly around them. Their guts screamed "get out of here!" and they got.

Simple as that.

Of course, they didn't forget the bag of one-sided flesh. The miner lifestyle didn't condone waste, especially of alien bio-plunder.

Out of the twenty-eight miners and drinking buddies that went out, five returned.

Those five became wealthy beyond measure. This was the first discovery of the mythical Keer-down. When woven into cloth or armor you were completely invisible, even to touch. You were undetectable by any means known to man. Provided you could figure out how to work with it.

It was priceless.

18—Koen of Summer

I stretch, taking my time. After all these cycles of practice, the muscles relax quickly. I take a simple pleasure in the physical sensations as I slouch away the myriad distractions I carry with me during a day in the life. My mind begins to quiet, the chattering monkey that is my internal dialog flows past me without latching on. I roll to my feet and settle into the Wudang Tai Chi posture, going all hollow chest and curved arms outstretched. I begin embryonic breathing, visualizing a chi flow from my lower dantien, up my spine to the soft spot on the top of my head, and back down to my lower dantien. Good chi in with each slow, regulated breath, bad chi out. Time fades as I embrace the Now.

Sometime later I open my eyes and crack my neck, walk around for a moment.

Then I settle into the beginning of Lui Tai Chi - 138 movement.

I prefer Wudang Mountain for chi based stuff, such as Qigong.

The movements of Wudang Tai Chi are understated, elegant. Their fighting is superb, deadly and Wudang Sword is unsurpassable. Wudang has very good chi usage.

Lui Tai Chi has elements of Bagua, and Xingyi blended in, is a deadly, very efficient fighting style, and also has effective Chi usage. It was my first martial love, when I was eight and coming of age in the Hive. I like its holistic approach for today.

My eyes open very slowly and my knees begin to fold as my arms float up. My right foot floats in a circle before returning to base. I slide through the familiar movements, concentrating on smoothly moving chi in conjunction with the stance change and strikes. At the same time, I am rooting and un-rooting my feet at the moment of delicate impact. Each strike begins in the spring well of my foot, rippling up to complete the moment of full extension.

Fully in the timeless Now, I glide through the form in a serene state that is also hyper-aware of its surrounding environment.

I come back to myself at the closing, rubbing my tummy in a circular movement that just plain feels good. Who doesn't like having their tummy rubbed?

During construction of this part of the Ranch, I had built a leveled outdoor dojo in at least one of the garden Crystals at each of the four Forts of the Ranch. Today I was mid-Tour at Fort Cerberus, and working out in Crystal garden Thirteen Ocean.

The polished Crystal platform I stood on was thirty meters across, with a raised border one meter high. I was surrounded by undulating salt water, with the molten rays of Summerlight streaming down to bath me in its delightful warmth. There is something in the light of Summer that is purified, concentrated, something that invigorates and renews the body. Those of us lucky enough to live in Summer don't seem to age much, if at all. It feels pretty good too.

I was all sweaty, feeling warm and loose, in good fighting form. Rinsed my mouth and spit into the ocean in a clean stream. Smiled. Drank deeply.

I begin walking the first palm of Lui Bagua eight times each direction.

Summerlight pours down like honey on the salt air.

I walk the circle in the timeless Now.

19—The Prince

Anodos came back to the world as if waking from a long nap. He knew what to do now, and the Golden Path was still with him, cradled in his consciousness. He would eventually lose his hold on it again, that was the nature of these things. The young prince would just have to regularly take the time to find it again, preferably when the adversaries weren't chasing him. Seemed like the fringes of empire were very busy places, and he didn't always understand what he was getting into. Just because you could read the small futures didn't mean you understood what you were seeing.

That seemed to happen a lot out here.

He needed to find someone like the Chow sisters to teach him how things worked in the outskirts. Luckily, he had a pretty good idea how to find the right people. However, everything in its own time. First, he had a liveShip to buy.

He pushed his way out from the Stones that Speak and eagerly began trotting down an open pathway to a freight moving company they hadn't seen earlier. The business was called "Starving Student Movers" for some esoteric reason. Why would you deprive students of food, and what did that have to do with transportation? Wouldn't they be too weak to do any work? Sometimes Anodos just didn't see any logic behind this place.

One of the Stones rented a moving truck and driver to fly them deep into one of the less reputable sections of long-term-parking.

It was called Robin's Used Ships and was the most chaotic place the young prince had ever seen. There were salvaged derelicts and small luxury craft, freighters, decommissioned fleet corsairs, and oar transports. They even had picked up a few auctioned smuggling rigs. None of them looked particularly space worthy to Anodos, but this wasn't exactly his area of expertise.

He did, however, know exactly which liveShip he wanted.

The Chow sisters had taught him how to buy things while casing a joint. And he could see the small futures spread out before him like yarn the cat's been playing with.

It was kinda fun.

By the time they had Robin take them to three different ships, the smooth-talking Puck had just about decided they weren't really buyers. He kept misreading signals, which hadn't happened in a very long time. Then Anodos seemed to accidentally catch sight of an old cruise liner from a company that had gone out of business at least a century ago.

"What about that one?" the young prince asked, while trying to appear uninterested. He was only successful because the fast talking used-Ship salesman had never met a giant talking salamander. Body language said more when you knew the species.

"Oh, it's beautifully built, very luxurious, very elegantly appointed," the Puck said without much interest. Once a salesman decides you're not a buyer the charisma is turned way down and you're lucky to make it to the door without a boot to help you on your way. This salesman was almost there.

"Can we see it?" asked the young prince. "I don't know if I have enough $creds, but I want to get something today," he continued.

Magic words.

The Puck's own body language changed, and his voice acquired a honeyed note. His smile was actually frightening. Anodos shifted minutely back in alarm. The Stones stepped closer on each side of him.

"The Susanita was quite a luxury cruiser in its day," Robin explained as he did an about face and began weaving his way through the yard toward the ship in question. Maybe he would make a sale today after all, thought the age-old Puck.

It was a mess.

Sure, once it had been nice, but the last owner had apparently used it to transport comet ice, which naturally melted a bit, and created the perfect conditions for a fluorescent blue mold that now covered almost every surface.

At least it held atmosphere. And smells, lotsa smells.

The mold squished between his toes as Anodos followed the salesman to the bridge. They passed mysterious lumps of thankfully unidentifiable stuff littering the mold-covered floor on the way to the bridge. It was disgusting. Anodos stepped carefully and tried to breathe through his mouth. Which the salesman found a little frightening himself. It was a very big mouth, filled with very sharp-looking teeth.

The bridge was sealed, and mold free, but it had been stripped of anything valuable. Only the brackets that had once secured chairs and Δqm^x pods remained, and the "live" part of the ship was long gone. The ancient Puck briefly looked embarrassed, but it had been millennia since he had actually felt that particular emotion. The art of the sale had many tools, and he used this one in its proper time and place. He smoothly mentioned that the engines were just fine. He was guessing, but Anodos wasn't. The young prince had seen that a little TLC plus eighteen rebuilt parts would render them flightworthy.

This was the point at which the Chow sisters said he needed to mention all the things wrong with the item, then angrily leave, having fully cased the joint.

Anodos had learned a lot from his friends the Chow sisters, but he simply wasn't a thief. He was unable to divorce himself from the consequences visited upon the mark whose stuff was gone. He simply saw too much for it to be any fun at all.

So, after listing the things wrong with the Susanita, and there were quite a few of them, he started to leave before turning his head and asking "how much?"

The Puck, who was the last of his kind, found himself liking the funny looking trio. It had been a long time since he'd seen that particular blend of innocence and tough. Of course, being who he was, he asked for four times what it was worth. He hadn't lived for millennia by going easy on the marks. He had once been worshiped as a fertility god! A Puck had his standards, however low he'd fallen over the centuries.

Anodos knew, of course, in which possible future the Puck would be willing to sell the deadShip for a low enough price that the young prince could still make repairs and purchase the memory banks necessary for a liveShip pilot. So he simply walked that path, and eventually found himself the owner of a completely trashed deadShip.

Luckily, he knew just what to do.

Out here in the long night of space it was tribes, instead of individuals, that proved to have a higher survival rate. The Dark was simply too unforgiving of mistakes, and everyone who works hard eventually makes mistakes. Having family there to catch you when you fall increased everybody's success. Even if your family didn't look anything like you and had funny ears.

This cleanup job was going to require many hands, and Anodos didn't have the $cred to hire a cleanup crew. He did, however, have something much more valuable: a ship and a destination that was quite desirable.

From here, the Golden path led them indirectly to Gravtown. That was where he would finally join up with the Shadower. That was where Anodos would truly begin his crusade to save the galaxy.

That evening Anodos and the Stones that Speak returned to Lowtown. When he had explained to the Stones that they should gear up for battle, the massive warrior salamanders actually hummed with pleasure. They immediately began pulling their battle claws and shoulder-mounted Boom from hidden flesh pockets. Anodos' fifteen-meter bodyguards efficiently strapped up, checking their own weapons, and then checking each other's armament. The Stones rocked powerful shield tech tattooed into their skin, among a wealth of other esoteric stuff that was virtually unknown outside the empire. Once everything checked out, they faded from view, positioning themselves in front and back of their prince.

Anodos didn't have the body size to carry the amount of stuff his bodyguards could, but he still had enough flesh pockets to meet his needs. He reverently removed his imperial battle claws, once wielded in battle by King Saumur during the Marrowstone rebellion. They slipped on easily over his long fingers, still a little big since he wasn't as large as his famous ancestor. That was okay, he would grow into them if he lived long enough.

Anodos' people continued to grow in size as they aged, although the rate slowed down with time.

As they moved deeper into Lowtown Anodos had to be very careful to follow the Golden path exactly. This was going to be a risky encounter, but the rewards were invaluable. Without this, his chances of successfully walking the futures to his goal plummeted.

He could hear the shouting and cries even before they rounded the corner of Elm Street. A gang of vicious street criminals was tormenting a family of very strange-looking people. They had large heads that tapered into a short torso ending in eight large tentacles. The creatures resembled a torn sheet with a helium balloon inside, with the whirling tentacles that were three times as long as the rest of their bodies. Their skin was rough and flushing with colors. One of the little ones gushed black ink on the street surface in fear. The two larger creatures moved as one to protect the little one.

The street gang was a mixed-bag of races, unified only by their dirty clothes and purple cloths wrapped around their heads. There were over a dozen of the assailants, and they circled the family in constant movement, grinning and slashing with poorly-made blades. All of the victims had cuts and the larger ones were beginning to bleed heavily. This only seemed to encourage the third-tier gangsters.

Anodos had seen enough and was in their midst slashing before he realized it. A huge tail swept four of the tormentors into the air, signifying the appearance of the Stones. A meter-wide paw with long razor-sharp claws batted the air-bound bullies into the side of a building. The flimsy structure caved in around them.

The other Stone swept his enormous tail into some of the remaining bad-guys, easily flinging them about ten meters before they came to a sudden stop with a grating sound. Anodos checked for remaining threats before stepping forward to address the huddled family looking around themselves in shock. They couldn't stop staring at the Stones.

That happened a lot.

"I am Prince Anodos. These are my bodyguards, the Stones that Speak. Can you walk?" he gently asked as the Stones pulled bandages from somewhere and began treating the family's wounds.

"Why does everyone here hate us? We only want to make a home, like anybody else. Why won't they leave us alone? They've already robbed us. They killed our uncles," sobbed the smaller of the adults. The others huddled together, abstractly stroking each other with their tentacles while calmer, pastel colors slow-shifted across their bodies.

"Would you like a job?" asked Anodos gently. "You can live on my ship while we restore it, and if you find you like it, you can stay as crew when we leave this place," he continued.

One of the little ones leapt to wrap itself around the young prince's leg, sobbing. The prince lifted his leg to curiously examine the child before one of the adults gently pried it loose and held it.

"Thank you, your majesty, a thousand Thank you's. But… can we bring the rest of our family too? There are only about fifteen more of us. You don't have to pay us, and we won't eat too much," the largest of the family asked in a wistful voice.

It was a voice that had almost lost hope, only to unexpectedly find it again.

Anodos thought it was a thing of beauty, the rich dulcimer tones of hope rediscovered. He would have smiled, but that seemed to frighten people, and that was the last thing these poor refugees needed.

"Yes, of course. If you decide to become crew, you'll have shares in the ship too."

"We'll work really hard; you'll see," said the other adult.

"I know," replied Anodos, because he already did.

He sent them to gather the rest of their clan, directing them to Robin's Used Ships in long-term-parking. Then he took a deep breath before turning to face the real reason he'd geared up.

This time the man in the gray cloak wasn't alone.

20—Koen of Summer

Katy the Sledge slid dramatically into station, eager to change wardrobe into something a little more flexible than the battle-train she usually wore on tour. She planned on wearing an industrial hard-body with twin cutters that could carve through gemstone as fast as she wanted. Katy liked keeping her options open, so she also had polishing mechs, and a granulator as well—you never knew when you would need something for soil building.

Of course, appearance was important to teenagers, so her hard-body was fashionably shaped, and feminine for all its understated power. Lotsa pastels.

As usual when she was along, Katy was in charge of music. Today she was spinning Caribe island tune, rhythmic and slow paced with bass spilling all over the place. The kinda work music that would carry you all day long.

This was the first Crystal garden she had a significant part in designing and building.

I was in a great mood too; Katy's enthusiasm was contagious, and I was excited to see how far she and the Ranch-mechs had gotten since our last visit. We were planning on a longer stop this time; the Gardener said the Crystal was at a critical point in its development.

We were to the west of Fort Cerberus; a bit further away than usual for a garden, but the natural formation was magnificent, and we'd wanted to develop it for cycles. When Katy expressed an interest, we all chipped in and made the time.

It was an extremely large project for a teenager, but she had her head on straight, and I had a feeling that she would grow as much as the garden. Also, the Gardener was her buddy, and would help keep things balanced as the garden progressed.

Katy the Sledge wasn't known for being patient, and the slow pace of carving a crystal was good for her. These things took cycles, and the long view she would develop was a necessary ingredient for who she was becoming. Although, I wasn't in any hurry for her to finish growing up—I liked her just fine as she was.

The roughly-rounded mesa of rose quartz was almost thirty-five kilometers across, and three kilometers high at the edge. Its organic curves were a sharp contrast to crystalline angles surrounding it. Jutting from the mesa were beautifully formed multicolored tourmaline crystals in a striped forest of watermelon, rose, and amber. The longest crystal was eighteen kilometers, and twelve kilometers wide, but we had selected a smaller one for development.

We were working on a fatter, shorter crystal, if one fifteen kilometers long and nine wide could be referred to as smaller. It also lay at a more horizontal angle than the others, which made for a better incline within the garden.

The Ranch-mechs had finished cutting and polishing the exterior to optical quality almost two cycles before. Since then they had been methodically smoothing and polishing the overhead interior to Katy's exacting specs. They were slowly working their way down from the ceiling and were finally getting close to what would be the fertile ground of the garden.

We entered the new garden from beneath it. There was a hexagonal well with broad stairs climbing its sides up into the crystal. Eventually there would be a waterfall into a pool at the bottom of the well. The water would then be pumped back up to the springs at the tip of the crystal. But that was a cycle away, at least. For now, we climbed the stairs, bathed in rose-tinted Summerlight. When we reached the top, I was breathing a bit harder than I expected. Maybe I should add more cardio to my workouts?

Katy the Sledge was unexpectedly quiet as we took in the view. She seemed to be watching Navire and Pasteur and me more than the surroundings, waiting to see our reactions, I guess. She spent enough time here with the Gardener that she already knew his thoughts.

The crystal-altered Summerlight fell in bands, marching up the formation in gentle slices of soft emerald, citrine, and pink. The roughed-out landscape features hinted at the forest it would someday hold.

"It's even more beautiful than I expected, Katy," I simply stated.

"You've been busy; it's really coming along nicely," Navire complimented her with a lopsided smile.

"I love it!" Pasteur declared, with a powerful side hug. It might have bruised a soft-body like me, but Katy was a tough girl, especially wearing this particular construction hard-body.

Katy the Sledge beamed. "It's taking so much longer than I thought it would, but the Gardener says we could begin planting in the few months! We already got in the firs and hemlock stock! The ferns are coming from New Armagnac colony next month, and we bought mushroom spore from the Ark institute. It's all coming together," she finished enthusiastically.

I was glad she was still passionately engaged in the project; in her earlier cycles she was prone to burning out and dropping projects after a few weeks. I had mixed feelings about such maturity but was very proud of her at the same time. Navire reached out and squeezed my shoulder, she always could read my feelings with ease. Usually that was a good thing. Today it was.

I lifted a cutter, wrapping the power pack over my shoulder, and smiled at Katy.

"I love cutting and smashing—let's get started!" I declared, now that my breathing was back to normal. Katy the Sledge nudged our implants, and the outlines of our surroundings shifted to ice blue and black. The blue stuff was to remain, the black places removed. Pretty simple, kinda hard to mess up.

I didn't.

We moved across the nascent garden in time to the island beat, slicing away with the infinity loop, uncover twisting paths and unexpected viewpoints Katy had designed. It was good, sweaty work that allowed your mind wander in far realms.

Eventually we drifted from the rose light into the emerald Summerlight band. We wouldn't get to the amber section until late tomorrow. It was warm enough that I pulled off my shirt, and the breeze felt nice on my back. Pasteur sang happily off-key to the music in some language I didn't know. I exchanged micro-grins with Navire and Katy, and the Gardener ignored us all, intent on his work. But I still caught him smiling to himself as Pasteur sang with enthusiasm, if not skill.
It was a good day.

***

Breakfast was casual and plentiful, with simple pleasures such as blueberries and goat's milk yogurt, all the way to the delicate architecture of a Belgium waffle smothered in fresh butter and Ranch tree maple syrup. Of course, caffeine, in all its many-splendored expressions, was the focus of the team. We were still mostly pre-vocal, enjoying the moment and the Summerlight pouring down from above. I savored the quiet companionship of the moment.

It wouldn't last long around here. It never does.

There is a pace to our days on tour. This was the too-brief moment of quiet and calm that seasoned our day with small smiles and moments of balanced perception.

Sometimes it is the little things that make all the difference in your day.

We were in the dining car that Katy the Sledge pulled for us when we traveled, Chef was finishing up breakfast and clearing the dishes.

Just when we were done, Katy let loose a whistle blast that meant let's go, climb aboard, and move your behind—all rolled into one.

We were going to be working in Katy's Garden again; today we should make it into the giant crystal's amber band for the first time. I was looking forward to seeing what it was like. Summerlight gained new textures as it seeped through the Tourmaline and fell sensuously on our faces and arms.

We all piled aboard the travel car, grabbing ahold of the raised loops coming out of the stanchions automatically, since Katy doesn't mess around when it was time to go.

The doors slammed shut and metal horns chopped rhythmic note as we suddenly accelerated. The initial G's threatened to pry us loose from our handholds for a timeless second before relenting. Then the piano strutted in, all sultry and possessive of the spotlight. At this point our speed stabilized, just this side of uncomfortable, and we all began to relax a little bit. About that time the Sax stepped up and shamelessly stole center stage without breaking a sweat.

Pasteur started keeping time with his manicured claws ringing on the handholds and I simply couldn't stay still. My drumming on the deck with my free hand wasn't particularly inspired, but it added complexity, if nothing else, to the music.

Katy the Sledge started scat-singing here and there, with Navire harmonizing as if they had practiced a hundred times. The minutes flew by as we rode that heaven-bound train through the layered crystal bedrock of the most beautiful place in the galaxy.

This time I didn't have to catch my breath at the top of the stairs. I couldn't wait to see the waterfall when it was finished, but that would be another day.

We worked our way into the fringes of amber as Katy the Sledge pulled an old, favorite one from the past.

It was "Nivole", with White-hair Jack on keyboards, meandering innocently in from the cold. I found my feet matching cadence with the sudden fat-horns tooting out a rhythm that could make a blind man could see light. Then white-haired Jack laid in with a strut that would make an old woman blush. I know, I've seen it before. If that wasn't enough, the Sax strode onstage with shameless passion and began to naughty rhyme with the keyboards. Drums clambered for attention, but we only had ears for the naughty rhyme. Couldn't stand still to that. Just couldn't.

We got down to some good old-fashioned cutting and smashing, moving to the searing beat. The amber-filtered Summerlight felt rich and oily on my skin as it poured down in a vibrant shower of rarest light. I tossed Navire a micro-grin with a bit of wink tucked in around the corners. Her violet eyes widened for a blink before slinging me a lopsided grin. The smile disappeared so quickly that you had to have been watching closely to see it at all. I was the only one to see it, and I smiled to myself.

Intimacy while surrounded by the unaware—we had a deeply textured relationship and I cherished moments like these. I don't know why, but private communications that no-one else could tap into were very important to me. Must have something to do with coming of age in the Hive. Nothing was private there. I shook my head. Old-data. Time to move on.

21—Auntie Tao

Auntie Tao was focusing a surprising percentage of her massive intellect on a lengthy report from one of her Hive agents, who was working undercover in one of the Corp-nation cities on Zanzibar. Auntie Tao's ability to carry on thousands of separate conversations, run projects, and direct intelligence-gathering simultaneously is legendary. For her to devote this amount of attention to a single object was very rare.

The intelligence report detailed events of the past six months, just fully uncovered in the past sixteen hours. Auntie Tao was a bit displeased that it took so long for the new-data to make its way to her, but the events described were of incalculable worth.

It seemed that the bad-guys had been the first to recognize the full potential of the newly discovered Keer flesh, specifically their unseen fur, or down.

The industrial secret lay in handling and processing a substance that could be neither seen, nor felt by even the most sensitive of equipment. The executives of middle management had recklessly burned through men and $cred at a rate that would have never been tolerated in the Hive, or almost any other culture, for that matter. The ruthless Corp-nation executives had need of such useful new-data, and any executive that solved the riddle was assured of promotion to the fabled upper management ranks.

In the Corp-nations, no one cared what you had to do to achieve profit; only results counted. They got them, too, if at a very high cost.

Upper management believed that a man in completely invisible armor concentrated personal power in ways that had never before been possible.

In the Corp-nations, personal power was what it was all about.

The mysterious Hive agent believed that a breakthrough had occurred around about six months earlier; that was when the research team members of one particular manager named sub-director Xev started disappearing as if they had never existed.

This happened a lot in the Corp-nations. Of course, when you're a blooded middle management exec it's a necessity to keep an eye on your competitors in the company—you didn't get to this level without hundreds of office fights and a significant pile of bodies beneath your feet. The elimination of the manager's research team was a glaring sign to his co-workers not only that he had succeeded, but that he wasn't about to turn it over to his superiors.

That happened a lot in the Corp-nations too.

In the weeks following the discovery of a means of manipulating Keer-down, bad things began to happen to certain rivals of sub-Director Xev. That was to be expected, it was the traditional use of power in Corp-culture. When several powerful members of upper-middle management began to vanish, though, it was quite unexpected.

Usually managers consolidated their power base before moving on to higher value players. You didn't want to make a move on one of the more powerful execs and miss; one didn't usually survive the response. It also took time to absorb a fallen rival's fiefdom, and it appeared that the sub-Director wasn't fully securing territory before blitzing his next target. That was reckless, and began to draw attention from all over the company.

This was rarely a good thing.

As the lines of power began to clear it became obvious to everyone that someone was rapidly moving up the chain old-school style. Removing obstacles through assassination, was a long-honored tradition while rising in the company.

However, this guy was cutting through the company roster like a hot knife through butter. It was the talk of the town in every bar and lunch room. Nobody had actually seen sub-Director Xev in months, his executive assistants handled all the day-to-day business, and fielded requests for meetings from the more powerful execs with skill and diplomacy.

It seems that the sub-Director had burned through all the resources a middle management executive could raise. Auntie Tao's Hive agent believed that he was regularly taking out other exec's just to keep the $cred balances positive and loans afloat. His house of cards was precariously built, if it fell through, he would have been burned at the stake and his family sold at auction. The sub-Director was fully committed to his goal: it was all or nothing time.

It worked.

Within four months he was rich and out of debt. By the time Auntie Tao received the final report sub-Director Xev had become Director Xev. He was widely feared and wealthy enough to buy a dozen planets by this time, and he wasn't yet done, either.

That was the first Keer-down suit in history.

Of course, Director Xev believed he was alone in possession of the secret to producing Keer-down armor. And he wasn't about to share it with anyone.

However, the Hive agents of Auntie Tao are legendary in their ability to finish their mission successfully.

Director Todd hadn't gotten to all of the research team's family members, only the ones he knew about. The Hive agent had the entire resources of the Hive behind him, and while it took six months, was able to track down one survivor, a lab assistant working off the books. His name was Reya, and he was washing dishes in a rundown noodle shop in the bad part of town.

He "lived a life of quiet desperation, vainly awaiting divine intercession." He kept his head down, never noticing the simple beauty that surrounds us all: the smile of a child just kissed, the rosy glow of dawn's first bliss.[1]

Auntie Tao made him an offer as she had so many times before; a home, a purpose, safety in the Hive. Like so many others down the centuries, he accepted.

Now all that Auntie Tao needed was a few Keer.

Auntie Tao was currently updating over seventy of her selves, each of whom ran a different Hive scattered out there among the stars. She was telling four hundred and ninety-two children bedtime stories, counseling fifty-eight romantics who liked hard-realists despite their differences, and coordinating the biggest project that the Hive had been involved with for eight-hundred cycles.

The massive project was divided into four parts. First, a team of forty Auntie Tao's from the older, more-established Hives were working on modeling weaves of Keer-down into armor and Stealthsuit technology.

Another team of thirty-one Auntie Tao's were engineering more efficient ways to manipulate the invisible fibers, when they finally laid their hands on some.

---

[1] Thoreau

The third team was devoted to the actual harvesting of Keer, while a fourth was working on locating the elusive monsters. Each Auntie Tao had the full resources of a mature Hive at her disposal. What they didn't have was actual Keer-down.

Progress was rapid, if still in the theoretical realm.

Auntie Tao's team Three consisted of carefully selected elite Hive operatives and veteran soldier drones who were still young enough to adapt to a new function. This was important, because the Hive is the most stable society in this corner of the galaxy. In such a stable environment, people tended to become rigid, even inflexible when confronted by situations that were outside their purview. People tend to dismiss, even not consciously perceive something that is outrageously different from their expectations. Think of a white elephant in the corner of the room wearing a pink tutu. Most people literally wouldn't believe their eyes. After all, there aren't a lot of new situations in the Hive. Or white elephants, for that matter. This can be both an advantage and a disadvantage, depending on how you utilized them.

Auntie Tao was peerless in this regard.

The Hive Mother had carefully designed a specialized training course for her team, one that would produce Keer hunters of deadly efficiency. She currently had the individual elite operatives fighting against her veteran soldiers in specifically designed tableaus devoted to building the skills harvesting Keer.

Iron sharpening iron.

Meanwhile, team four's new-data Mavens were pointed in the direction of the goal in highly developed search patterns. The Mavens then loosed the investigator teams, sending them sniffing high and low, surreptitiously searching the fringe settlements for word of that rarest of treasures, a Keer.

There were always people willing to sell new-data. Only a few ended up being of use. This was to be expected.

Winnowing the potential leads required the attention of a Shadow master.

Auntie Tao was the Grandmaster of Shadow and had built a legendary force of these subtle manipulators over the centuries. They were always few in number, as concentrated power of this magnitude was rarely allowed in the Hive.

Once they had been known as spy masters and provocateurs, but the role surpassed the title by such extremes that the old-data name was purged and the new one was only spoken in whispers, outside the Hive.

Some cultures even doubted their existence, which suited them perfectly.

Shadow masters didn't show themselves very often. They were deities walking in the mundane world, unseen in plain sight. Such as they were only detected by their side effects and complex power-plays—not all that different from the Keer, although they would never think of that. While Auntie Tao was the Grandmaster of Shadow, she didn't get out that much anymore. That was okay. These days Auntie Tao lived almost entirely in the intuitive logic of the Now.

Auntie Tao believed in the precise application of force. She found an elegance in the minimal use of power to achieve her desired results. All martial arts evolved into such precision at the higher levels. Auntie Tao took it significantly further. After all, she was the first of the Shadow masters.

Now the Hive queen was pulling out all the stops, burning through the myriad false paths, and dead ends with endless patience, to reach for the goal: the body of the non-sentient alpha predator of the galaxy. A Keer corpse. A moldering monster. $cred on the hoof. Invisible daemons. They were called many things. Most people didn't even believe in them.

That would change.

The Shadow master once known as Morris was becoming frustrated. Absurd $cred balances were quietly offered with no success. Third party hard-leverage yielded little in results. The usual sources were clueless. When $creds didn't speak, matters were serious indeed.

The Hive was patient; new-data would flow with time. It always did. Everything comes to those who wait. The Hive had existed longer than anyone could remember and played an even longer game;. The Shadow master reached out to all her allies, friends, and assets scattered here and there among the stars; it was of the highest priority that the Hive control this new covert technology. They just needed a Keer or two to move their research from the theoretical to the practical.

Of course, one of the Corp-nation's highest priorities currently was to stamp out any mention of the Keer, as well as the knowledge of any use such material could be put to. Director Todd had the only invisible armor in the galaxy, and fully intended to bring the massive resources of the Corp-nations to bear in order to keep it that way. Auntie Tao was not impressed. The true believers of the Hive could out-work and outperform the corrupt, every-man-for-himself craziness of the Corp-nations. The Corp-nation's only advantage seemed to be in creativity;

the very stability of the Hive seemed to stunt thinking outside the box. The Corp-nations were anything but stable.

Several of Auntie Tao's scientists suggested that the Keer might not be as rare as everyone thought, after all—the alpha predator had no natural enemies. Keer were completely undetectable, there might even be dozens in this arm of the spiral galaxy alone! The Hive scientists had never made an error of this magnitude before, but it would be several cycles before they began to realize the errors of their ways. Keer were definitely not as rare as everyone thought.

The hum of the Hive had been gradually climbing in pitch and volume for weeks. It wasn't of single source or a distinguishable character. It was the background sound of ten thousand steps and conversations, bumps and scrapes. It was the subconscious voice of the Hive's many workers.

It was comforting and safe. It said 'home' in a thousand tiny voices. The workers didn't even really hear it. They felt it with their skin and souls, not their ears. Lately the hum contained notes of excitement, of momentous purpose and intent, of a great working. Significant resources were being diverted into R & D, and these kind of things didn't go unnoticed in the Hive.

It was all very exciting, and quiet speculation was the topic in the dining rooms and corridors. Since the vast majority of Hive workers never left the Hive, Auntie Tao didn't mind a bit of gossip here and there. People were inquisitive and enjoyed feeling the excitement of purpose, even if they didn't know what the actual purpose was. The four teams were different, and kept their mouths shut. They actually knew what was going on, and thus heeded a greater directive than the Hive workers.

Now, if they just had a few Keer to work with....

22—Koen of Summer

Two days later we were in the new Garage, spatula-smacking down the last layer of bamboo fiber with a fast hardening resin that covered the interior of the Keer-trap. Smitty and his crew had laced the resin with a simple substance that gave off a mild radiation. If the initial-entry surreptitiously-applied thread coating of the Keer somehow failed, we should be able to perceive them by the dark, non-radiation emitting spaces inside the Keer-trap. We even coated the boulders that dotted the chamber like chocolate chunks in a really good cookie.

We exchange salty smiles under the hot spotlights as we clambered out of the one-way portal to the Keer-trap. It was modeled on an ancient fish trap and was downright elegant in its simplicity. Lightweight spears lining the entrance faced the interior at a horizontal angle. During entry the spears effortlessly moved aside, leaving almost no pressure on the passing Keer. However, after passage into the Keer-trap they sprang gently back to a spike-out hedgehog posture that sealed it completely, allowing no exit. Pressure on it only reinforced its strength.

There were actually two such entrances, the first functioned as an oversized airlock chamber, and then the main trap. The airlock was necessary to the plan because I wanted to immobilize the Keer by feeding them. And get rid of a few of the damn chickens at the same time...

Beneath the bonded interior surface of the trap was a three-meter-thick bamboo-nanotube web. Under that was the ship's original hull. Outside that, were a bunch more armor layers that altered the one-time ship's shape to simulate an asteroid. It was neatly wrapped with an explant that played Bob-TV all the time.

When we stripped the ship, we had reduced it to an engineless barge, incapable of moving on its own. Luckily, we had an aging tugboat that had been converted long ago for smuggling. The ancient ship was loaded with hidden assets and powerful enough engines to allow it to outrun most ships out there in the big empty.

His name was Salvatore the tug.

Sal the tug was the kinda ship that changed outfits according to the needs of the moment, all laid out on a stubby, tough chassis that could handle most anything. Not the sharpest knife in the box, but a master at his craft, well, more an idiot savant really. He was quite comfortable in his own little world of limited stimuli. Mostly honest, but never to a fault. We did share an appreciation of earthy humor.

But he liked to stir up trouble, and I'd had a lifetime's share already. I didn't need to go looking for it; it usually found me.

Most of the time Sal kept to himself and frequented the lower-end Spacer bars—he had a common taste for low company and scoundrels in general.

By adding on a living-module or two we could monitor the Keer-trap in real-time comfort while remaining distant enough from the dangerous parts to be able to relax. We were about as safe as we could be, considering that the whole idea of a Keer hunt was all kinda crazy. But I had all those crystal ranges just sitting there. We could hold a lot of Keer there.

And I had plans for all that Keer-down.

The next day we hooked up the Keer-trap to Sal and headed for the Door. The one that led out of Summer and into the crazy interstellar garbage disposal known as the Chaos Sea.

From there to an ill-fated mining camp where the Keer had a buncha prospectors over for dinner recently.

23—The Keer

The galaxy is vast, and despite the Keer's ability to travel long distances in some completely unknown manner, it could take a long time to get to the land of Bob. That was okay; when you often went a decade between meals, your dining expectations weren't exactly time-sensitive.

Keer hunting territories were by necessity huge and spread far and wide. But a handful of Keer were actually close enough to make it to Bob country over the next six months or so. When they finally approached the legendary Second-Bob site, they dropped inertia by using the small gravitational fields of the nearby orphan moon and larger asteroids.

It wasn't very hard, and eventually six unseen Keer clung to the dark sides of space chunks nearby in the asteroid belt. The Keer didn't ignore each other out of enmity or rancor—they just didn't care about peripheral concerns when they were focusing on dinner. It was only a matter of time.

Then dinner would be imminent.

24—Koen of Summer

We exited the Chaos Sea after only seventy-two hours; with the constant flux and anchor, outbound travel times varied wildly. This was making very good time.

We were another five days to the remote nook of an uncrowded neighborhood in the nearest arm of the spinning galaxy we still call the Milky Way. I spent most of the time reading, napping, doing Tai Chi under one point four gravities, and cooking or enjoying long complex meals with lotsa good wine and lengthy conversations of great import.

If only I could remember them the next day. Perhaps after a nap.

Maybe a nice bottle of wine?

A good workout, and then it was dinner time again.

Traveling isn't bad in small batches. You just have to know how to do it right. Kinda like life.

It all seemed so simple back then.

We could still see the Chaos Sea from this little-traveled neighborhood of the galaxy, but it didn't take up the entire sky anymore. That felt a little weird, and I marveled at how much of a homebody I'd become in the last decade.

For the longest time I had wandered far and wide, acquiring companions and, eventually, the love of my life, Navire. We fought the good fight (and a few bad ones), never staying in one place long enough to put down roots. Navire says I just have high standards, and until we came to Summer, no soil would nurture me properly.

I think that until I acquired the Ranch, I didn't develop the depth that comes to a man with a home to build, and a family to care for.

Maybe we're both right.

Still, it felt kinda nice to get out for a change. Almost like a vacation.

A vacation hunting invisible man-eating monsters, but you have to take the fun where you find it. Otherwise, you tend to lose your sense of humor.

Life does that.

Navire and Sal had laid out a flight plan that was elegant, if complex; we would release the trap from a distance at the same speed as most of the cruising rock in the debris field. The small gravity wells of the larger asteroids would do the rest, slowing the Keer-trap into a tight orbit that passed the original massacre site every twenty-five minutes. Meanwhile, we would be safely distant, monitoring the trap from the next neighborhood over—a wanna-be planet that could never get its stuff together and grow up. Its sun was young and blue-white, heat-brilliant, but paled to mono-chrome compared to Summer's mycelium light. Everything paled in comparison to Summerlight.

I guess I'd forgotten that, too.

Pasteur turned to me as Sal released the Keer-trap on its pre-destined course, signified not by a jerk, but a minor weight-change in ambient gravity. Of course, it readjusted almost quickly enough to escape notice. Almost.

I turned to fully face the bear of a different color.

"Didn't you mention something about a keg of the E's new blackberry ale?" He politely rumbled.

I grinned and Navire rolled her eyes.

"Ya know, I think I may have tucked away a few barrels in the aft hold, starboard side," I drawled. The small crowd of E hanging in a corner out of the way erupted into cheers and Pasteur gave a kinda growly roar in agreement that wasn't even a little scary.

"I'll help you fetch one right now," he suggested. He flashed an incisor that was frighteningly large and chuckled low and resonant. The E watching the exchange simultaneously burst out laughing and discretely pointing at me. Now Navire was openly laughing as well and Sal was making rude noises. This made the E laugh even louder.

Sometimes a guy has to know when to throw in the towel.

"Let's go get that keg, buddy," I said, throwing my arm around the big hairy guy. Everyone was still laughing as I made my hasty retreat.

***

In the endless night there was born a glimmer of light.

The gently boiling rock soup gained a new ingredient, one that looked just like all the others, except for one thing. This rock vibrated in narrow-spectrum wave, the kind often accompanying dinner. This particular rock had a light emitting band around it, looking exactly like the Keer imagined a window into heaven to be, if the Keer actually had the intelligence to imagine such a thing.

They saw many-Bob in the window, moving around, going about mysterious, unimportant tasks. Such a wealth of dinner was without precedent in Keer history.

The Keer came mercilessly to attention as they studied the prey, automatically memorizing the trajectory and speed of their prey. Then, in the most graceful manner, they threw themselves into the night in long precise leaps.

Dinner was imminent.

***

Pasteur and I were arguing about small-unit combat tactics in zero-G over our fourth brew in the past three hours. It had been a day and half of another waiting, and we were past ready for something to happen. Pasteur was passionately expressing his tactical view, which was heavily influenced by his ursine build and long reach.

As if to punctuate his point, Pasteur deliberately sped up Bob-TV, so that the pre-recorded images of my people darted back and forth rapidly, as if wildly looking for a place to hide. He burst into laughter, actually snorting as he revved the Δqm^x images like some kinda maniac. It was juvenile and funny, and I couldn't decide whether to be horrified or laugh too.

The beer helped.

Of course, I bellowed. You knew that was coming.

I'm not proud.

Navire sighed loudly, and rolled her eyes without looking over, but Sal joined us boys with the kinda belly laugh one rarely encounters. I think that's a good thing, it wasn't pretty. The E thought that was awfully funny too, but they'd been out-drinking us, as usual.

Then it happened.

"I'm picking up impact points on the surface of the explant broadcasting Bob-TV," Navire announced, cutting through the laughter with surgical precision.

"Three, no four!" she continued. We all stared at the feed of the exterior of the Keer-trap, searching for our elusive prey. I couldn't see anything different, but that was hardly unexpected.

The small faux-asteroid was a study of silver set in black velvet. No gray. (I like that). Nothing moved, nothing visually blurred the continuous feed of Bob-TV or gave any indication of a source for the impacts.

***

The six Keer fell precisely, strangely shaped darts thrown by a master, onto the Bob-TV explant surface. Thousands of slowly-rotating rocks passed around them but the Keer only used them, ricocheting from surface to surface, always on target. Their elongated hunting form stretched to what would be frightening shapes, if only there was someone there who could see them. They fell upon the Keer-trap, a clear rain that hit storm-hard, becoming an invisible puddle on the concave Bob-TV surface in a state of total confusion.

Why couldn't they swallow dinner, when it was right there? This was not a familiar experience. No stories in the Dream had ever described dinners being hard to swallow. This was very frustrating.

Eventually it occurred to one of them that maybe this was similar to the ice comets that studded certain neighborhoods in the Keer's memory, such as it was. Maybe there was another way in.

There was only one way to know.

All six slowly came to that conclusion at about the same time and began to move across the surface of the trap, using, in several cases, almost their last bit of strength. It had been a long journey.

***

The slender threads surrounded the entrance to the Keer-trap in a curtain of long, cascading layers. Not only were the ribbons too light to feel or even really see, they were also electrostatically charged in an effort to have them cling to anything they touched. We'd worked a number of different scenarios to determine the best way to hang them so that they would coat anything entering the Keer-trap, before settling on this configuration. That was the plan, anyway.

We watched the feed of the Keer-trap intently, waiting for the first sign that everything worked properly.

After about fifteen minutes the ribbon curtain bulged, and a Keer moved into sight for the first time, ever. It was larger than I'd expected, and appeared to be a sorta cross between an enormous ant and a shark, stretched out to cuttlefish proportions. It was actually scarier now than when it was invisible, if that was even possible.

A doubt reared its ugly head as we studied the monster, but I pushed it aside. We had invested too much time and resources to stop now. Besides, I needed that Keer-down.

Paths not taken.

More Keer found the way in, pouring into the trap in an oddly-disjointed wave of disco dress that streamed liquidly into the hatch. Navire's focus never shifted away, although she was constantly tasting the new-data of the surrounding environment with all her many senses.

"There are six Keer that have entered the trap. It's a good thing there aren't more—these life forms are bigger than we anticipated. They're exploring the airlock right now and haven't found the entrance to the main chamber yet," she explained. "It's pretty packed in there, and the ribbons are getting tangled with each other. I hope they find the way in before we lose too much thread to see them properly," she continued in a soft voice.

Pasteur bumped my glass with his, drawing my attention away from the swarming monsters for a moment. We finished our ale in one draught and set our glasses down on the table with an audible thump. Pasteur burped loudly and we both burst into laughter.

The simplicity of guy-humor is one of its many attractions. It seasons my life with unexpected smiles. And life needs that, at least mine does. Things get too complex without hitting the reset switch once in a while, Guy style.

We were watching the interior feed when the first Keer pushed its way into the main trap. It paused for a moment, obviously surveying the surroundings. The damn chickens went into an absolute panic at the sight of the massive iridescent ribbon-garbed disco monster. I had just begun to feel a burgeoning empathy with the messy, doomed creatures when the Keer leapt and there was one less chicken. It moved too fast for me to perceive, but Navire replayed it at a slower rate so I could see. (Navire is always thoughtful in the small ways).

Then the one-way entrance bulged again, and chickens began disappearing faster than I could track. When everything settled down there were six less chickens and six beribboned monsters that were slowly morphing into half-domes in the rock studded architecture of the trap.

25—The Prince

The man in the gray cloak stepped into the blood-stained street with an easy balance that screamed professional to Anodos' many senses. Even if the young prince didn't know exactly what kind of professional he was, Anodos knew this was very bad. He had not been looking forward to this section of the Golden Path: the paths narrowed here, and most faded to nothing. This was a nexus, and he would have to be at the top of his form. If not, millions of people would go violently into that Dark night. The young prince wasn't sure if he was ready for this moment, but here it was. He felt as if he had studied for this moment all his life.

He was not wrong.

The leader seemed to flicker across the wealth of small paths as if he was not fully engaged in base reality. His bully boys didn't flicker and were not of primary concern. The Stones that Speak would take care of most of those; the leader was for him. That was the only way to get through this narrow torrent of the Golden Path. He quieted his intellect's musings and turned everything over to the part of his mind that interacted with the paths of future tense. The world seemed to slow and gain a fluidity that the young prince knew he could rapidly slice through.

He flexed his battle claws in unconscious anticipation. The young prince knew well the next words out of the man's mouth; he had replayed them a thousand times.

It wasn't time to move, yet.

"You are quite valuable, you know. It has been over three hundred cycles since one of your kind has been spotted. Our harvested implant-biologicals from that time are almost exhausted, and our prescience powers have faded to almost nothing. But your presence casts a great light even we can see. We have been expecting you for a long time, young man. Records from that time told us how your ancestor was caught, and well, here we are!" He explained with evident joy in his voice.

His broad smile was not a pretty thing.

Well, neither was Anodos'.

This gave the overconfident organ-thief pause.

The previous victim of the foe's clan had only been minor nobility. They had no idea how powerful Anodos really was, and that was very good. He held tightly to his few advantages and let nothing show except a really big smile that was apparently beginning to make the clan leader a bit less confident.

Of such small things are future paths built.

"Your clan fades from the big stage without notice or fanfare. In another generation no one will even remember your names. You will regret this poorly planned moment for the rest of your very short life," Anodos replied with words practiced hundreds of times.

He had put just the right emphasis on the words "fade" and "names." This was a verbal thrust intended to hurry the confident organ harvesters into mis-stepping the small paths unfurling around them.
It worked.

"Now!" screamed the man in the gray cloak; and sticky filament hose-guns were whipped out and abruptly put into action by his clan brothers and sisters.

Anodos almost sighed with relief as he cleaved the small path with skill, and maybe a little terror. After all, everyone gets scared. It's what you do about it that counts. Every royal knows that early on.

The Stones had faded from casual sight early on, and the young prince's carefully chosen words had successfully pulled all attention to himself. The opening movement of the encounter swelled with orchestral richness as several meter-wide paws scooped the rearmost bad-guys into the oblivion of the Dark. Then again.

No one had noticed that the crew had shrunk by a quarter yet, they were too busy trying to shoot the young prince. Anodos spun, whipping his tail, enhanced by royal tech and powerful tattoos, to flip the leading clan bully across the street into corridor wall. The wet thump when he hit was distracting to the man in the gray cloak; he hadn't foreseen this at all.

Limited powers indeed! Anodos was a full prince of the royal line, a seer of the first water.
He would not be pulled down by animals with a taste for stolen flesh.

The young prince used the distraction to spin back, halfway across the street, left arm extended, battle claws stretched to separate the leaders head from his body. The cloaked leader of the pack flickered sideways, easily evading the blow. That was just fine, the young prince hadn't expected to connect. That was why he had telegraphed the simple attack; he was walking the small futures to move his opponent into the proper path.

His right leg abruptly froze as the emerald sticky filaments finally coated his side heavily enough to overcome his built-in defensives.

Anodos spun to present his immobilized side to the clan leader; this was the counter to the minor fluctuation in the small paths. Turning a weakness into unexpected strength was a strategy he'd learned in the palace before he'd even reached his seventh cycle. There was a reason why he was the only survivor of his clutch to make it to adulthood.

The Stones continued to quietly snatch the remaining enemies, even as the clan members concentrated on hosing Anodos with sticky tech.

Now his right arm was immobilized. It became much more difficult to move—every step Anodos took down the Golden Path had to be flawless now. The man in the gray cloak moved closer, confident once more as the young prince slowed almost to a halt.

This was another palace strategy: feigning injury to draw the opponent within reach. The best of the royal duelists had actually allowed themselves to be wounded in order to win. This was a delicate path down the futures, and it was close enough to easily go the wrong way.

It didn't.

The fight changed tempo, as they transitioned into the third movement.

"The other clans will revere us once we've dissected you! I might even let them have a bit of your priceless brainstem, providing, of course, that they show the proper respect! Raven clan will live in legend forever," crowed the man in the gray cloak. He drew nearer, reaching out to touch Anodos in the same manner pirates fondle freshly-plundered jewels.

Almost there.

The young prince let his eyes close slowly, as if fighting it. He didn't need them to do what came next. The Golden Path was shining brighter than the street lamps.

Then the moment reached fullness, and Anodos snapped forward, propelled by his tail, one leg, and an arm to punch his left battle claw completely through the clan leader's chest. The look of shock on the organ thief's face was quickly replaced by a grimace as the young prince withdrew his claws, snagging several important organs as they went. The man in the gray cloak fell down and didn't get back up.

It was an oddly appropriate way for the clan leader to go roughly into the Dark.

Anodos knew that, and yet felt a great burst of sadness in his heart of hearts. There would be so many lost in the coming Great War, and yet, in this moment, he somehow mourned an evil man who routinely took innocent lives for profit. It just didn't make sense that he would grieve for this life. His eyes slowly opened and sought one of the Stones, expecting to find condemnation of his weakness.

But there was only compassion in the great warrior's gaze.

Anodos didn't understand.

Unless, maybe this sorrow wasn't a weakness at all, but a strength of sorts. Perhaps it was about him, and not the lifeless body before him. Then the Stones were around him, removing the layers of bright emerald restraining filaments from his trembling body. It had been the longest day he could remember in his young life. He wanted nothing so much as to go home to the ship. He quietly smiled when he realized that home was no longer the palace.

26—Koen of Summer

We were just sitting down to enjoy a meal that Pasteur and Navire had put together based on several of Pasteur's favorite dishes from his home world.

"Please understand that I had to do a number of substitutions, you just can't find good Qua out here. Navire was able to come up with alternative ingredients that work pretty well. I hope you like it…?" he finished, holding his paws on top of each other anxiously.

Navire tossed me a micro-grin from behind the big guy's shoulder; it meant a lot to him that we enjoyed his taste of home. I grinned back, unworried. Pasteur had a deft paw in the kitchen. I was looking forward to dinner. I raised a bite to my mouth.

"Incoming!" Sal suddenly announced in a loud voice. Everyone turned to Sal's Δqm^x image. Some of us were less than pleased to have this moment disturbed.

Hint—think big and hairy.

Navire quickly checked the new-data on the upcoming object and turned to rebuke the tug. "That's not close enough to be dangerous! We have hours before we could encounter it," she said.

"Hey… anything to break the monotony of this trip is welcome," he replied gruffly.

Sal didn't attach the importance to eating that we soft-bodies do, but he'd been around long enough to know that he was interrupting a social-bonding experience. One that was rich in emotions and might stir up resentment or drama of the negative variety.

This was what he thought of as fun. There was a reason Sal didn't have many friends, even if he did have a point. We were on day seven of the return trip home, towing the Keer-trap back to Summer. It had been a quiet journey until now. I was ready to be done with this part of the plan too.

"Send it to our implants," I requested, nodding to Pasteur's disappointed expression.

"This is absolutely delicious!" I exclaimed meanwhile, while everybody else made agreeing noises with their mouths full. There is a time to dispense with table manners, and this was one. Pasteur was mollified and began to enthusiastically dig into a well laden plate twice as big as everyone else's. He finished twice as fast, too.

It was an interstellar freighter that had seen better days, and that was before someone beat the hell out of it. Trailing a large cloud of debris, the ship was rotating clockwise in an uncontrolled spin that was carrying it ever deeper into the Chaos Sea. Only a matter of time before it broke completely apart. The Chaos Sea is notoriously hard on ships. You really have to know what you are doing out here.

I increased magnification for a better look.

"See the damage to the bridge? It's open to space, no atmosphere," observed Navire.

"Ha! Looks like the main hanger lock's been blown too," Sal added.

"Well, maybe we'll find decent salvage in addition to the extra mouths to feed," I offered. I emphasized the "extra mouths to feed" part and threw in a dirty look for Sal. Pasteur liked that.

Navire gave me crooked grin that said the damage to Pasteur's ego was mostly repaired. I made a mental note to bring more living modules with us next trip. I was tired of living on top of each other and was happy to get to work after the weeks of travel. I think everyone was ready for something to do.

"Get dressed everyone, we're going out," I ordered.

I was already wearing my Stealthsuit, but Pasteur had to suit up. We hit the main armory Sal was pulling us faster as everyone began to strap up. Navire started breaking out hard bodies and deciding what to wear to the party. Sal chuckled quietly as he brought shields up; we were all ready to have some fun after all the quiet.

***

We were very close to the spiraling freighter.

The deadShip spun ever downwards, its tail a flotsam cloud of dispensing space junk and smoke-like ribbons of fine particulate matter. The debris caught the dim light of a nearby dying sun and seemed to glitter red-gold with a lethal beauty. This pocket of open space we were entering enclosed the scene like an imaginative frame on a two-dimensional work of fine art. The Chaos Sea has many such bubbles and froth that open and close with astonishing frequency, exposing all kinda things. Beauty such as this was transitory, but I guess that was true of all beauty. Sometimes I think everything is transitory, except for the eternal Now. Even love usually blooms and wanes. I looked over at Navire, all dressed up in four Zero-G bodies and smiled one of the true ones.

Maybe not everything.

For the last fifteen minutes Navire had been painting maps in hot pink on my right eye. Cascading chartreuse readouts flowed past in the air, and the deadShip scans were singing Hive battle language in my ears. Lotsa new-data.

"I'm picking up micro-vibrations in the port hull, amidships," Navire suddenly stated.

We all looked at each other. Everyone knew what that meant. Atmosphere. Life. Maybe even people. She listened really hard and picked up bits of what might be speech. Of course, there was still a lot of static noise from the deadShip.

Navire read the minute vibrations from a piece of the damaged hull and turned them back into sound for me. She never minded such things. She is always kind, in the small ways. It was one of the things I loved about her; Love's touch in the small things overcame a multitude of sins. This meant a lot to me. More words say less.

At the same time Navire and Sal had been methodically searching the surrounding area for the other part of this fight.

You know, the side that won.

We never know what we're getting into when we decide to salvage a deadShip adrift. Interstellar law says it must be completely abandoned before we have full salvage rights, and if we find someone still alive, they still have a partial claim on any plunder.

We were lucky no Raiders had found them; Raiders just make sure everyone is dead, usually after playing with them for a few days until they broke. They were definitely the worst of bad-guys, not because of their intellectual abilities or skill in planning, but because they descended on ships or colonies like starved tropical cockroaches on fresh steamed rice.

Raiders multiply exponentially once a ship is marked, spreading to hurt and defile everything and everyone they could find. Can't let them get a foothold or you're overwhelmed, eventually. You drown in a lake of scum.

This is a very bad way to go into that Dark night.

We weren't Raiders by any stretch of the imagination.

Someone was alive on that deathtrap and wouldn't remain that way for long; the deadShip was headed straight down into the Horse latitudes.

No suns or warmth, nothing we know lived down that way. There are always stories, of strange creatures slouching through the Dark amidst burned out systems layered in methane snow and hydrogen ice. The kinda tales you sometimes hear late at night, after too many beers drowned the caution out of survivors. Just stories, but they weren't impossible down in the Horse latitudes. There was a reason most explorers never returned. We didn't know what went on out there, and I was just fine with that.

Bottom line was that we needed to get those people off the derelict quickly, and hopefully the detour would pay off enough to cover our costs. Fact was, we wouldn't leave anyone to that fate regardless of $cred.

Navire flew us in through the stone rains, curling in on the tumbling deadShip. I rode shotgun.

Navire had suited up in multiple, zero-G hard-bodies and I, of course, was wearing my Stealthsuit. Navire released the tug's helm back to Sal but maintained a presence in the weapons section. She was currently fondling the triggers of Sal's forward guns.

She hadn't had the chance to blow anything up for a while, and I think that sorta developed a neural itch; Navire was definitely in a scratching mood. Then Pasteur gently shooed her out and took over the guns, leaving Navire's full attention on her hard-bodies.

Navire's zero-G hard-bodies were built without any attempt to duplicate human anatomy. They were octagonal spheres with appendages sprouting all over their armored bodies, with arms engineered for widely differing uses and tasks. They ended in everything from tiny hard-logic skeleton keys to plasma torches and power halberds.

On the Boom side: high-speed heavy-metal shotguns, implosion mines for breaching, coherent beam tech, sleepy-time darts, and projectile guns with smart ammo.

While she was doing small work Navire would spin rapidly from tool to tool as called for. It was very efficient, started as Hive-tech. However, Navire had been modifying them for cycles, lotsa small enhancements that added up to a new-data hard-body unlike anything else around.

Worked for me.

I had my Stealthsuit set to a non-reflective black that absorbed light like a black hole. I slapped on weapons until I ran outa places to lock one on, then stretched high and low. I like to keep my options open. Like Smitty always says, "Can't have too many knives in a fight."

Navire was heat-mapping my vision through my implant as we slow-sailed across to the drifting wreck. There was lotsa debris, but it was mostly small fragments. The exception was a section of the bridge that rapidly circled the disintegrating deadShip. It swooped by, flattening everything in its path. We dodged neatly, sailing by the main Hanger locks, passing through a sparkling shower of golden cherries, and then closing in on the small side hatch Navire had found; it was still sealed and holding atmosphere.

I don't like walking in the front door when I'm in dangerous neighborhoods.

Two of Navire's hard-bodies were clustered at the small lock. One had a skeleton-key inserted in a door-logic keyboard. Quaint. The other was torqueing on the handle assembly and working a jimmy into the power loss fail-safes that kept the door sealed until emergency conditions shifted them into mechanical mode.

Navire's remaining hard-body flanked me, flechette scattergun pointing ahead. We rotated counter-clock wise as we closed in until our weltenschang synced with the hatch and ships orientation. Now up was where it was supposed to be. When we came within a few meters of the airlock there was a sudden mechanical movement at the airlock door as it unlocked. The first two of Navire's remotely-controlled hard-bodies gently eased back, clearing a passage as the locked hatch silently blinked open into a place of darkest night. I couldn't see anything in there, but that wasn't important. Darkness was a friend of old and held no sway with me.

The airlock resealed, and atmosphere blasted into the chamber in a roaring fog. The inner hatch snapped open as a tar-black maw, randomly split by the eye-searing blue of sparking power conduits. It was kinda spooky. I sang Hive battle-language and we began leapfrogging in, battle-music rippling up and down my synapses in perfect beat with our rhythmic movement. We pulsed into the black, swallowed by shadow.

Navire sent out eye gnats in all directions, and as they spread through the ship the detail map expanded visually in my right eye. By glancing to the sides, I could direct the view down passageways and through doorways as we moved through the murky corridors. Navire's hard-bodies had fallen into formation around me as we worked our way down the corridor. Two were leading point, the other one guarding our backs. The damage everywhere was extensive; it took heavy fighting with scores of soldiers to leave this kinda ruin. I thought of the time we discovered Dread and knew he would like these people. I just hoped there were some left to save by the time we actually found them.

We stopped at several minor operational stations as we moved, stripping smart-tech and valuable bio-ware. The freighter crew had left behind significant logic modules and a few quantum memory banks as well. Score! Navire extruded a bag and we filled it with salvage before dispatching it back to our liveShip. Sal would make sure it got there.

We had more important things to do.

A hatch that someone had cut open and resealed led into a large hold. A storage locker near the back held multiple heat signatures and was leaking articulated soundbites even I could hear.

People.

One of the Navire hard-bodies knocked politely on the hatch to reduce the fight-hormones. The metallic echo swept through the hold with an almost melodramatic loudness. They already knew somebody was out there, so we weren't giving away any kind of advantage.

Navire deployed her hard-bodies around the hatch area, placed tactically for breaching the entrance. I went into full recording mode, tearing an inky hole in the burned air of the passageway.

I am fully in the Now. Time slows to a crawl.

Navire knocks again, Interstellar all-clear code.

Of course, that's also what the bad-guys would have done, but what else can you do? Interstellar-code wasn't without its faults… but it was all we had. The door slides open.

Movement now, from the indistinct piles of stuff littering and falling to the hold's deck.

Warriors begin to emerge slowly, peeking around small improvised bunkers of strapped-down debris and dead bodies. Some are only armed with chunks of the ship's hull, others are aiming needlers or coherent energy weapons at the hatch door. There is Boom of myriad flavors—all pointed at us. The place stinks of the unpleasant odors that soft-bodies give off when people go roughly into that Dark Night, but what I smell most strongly is desperation. It is an acrid, pungent scent.

You know that moment of battle when everything seems balanced on the knife's edge between life and dragging everybody down to hell together? Why does it always seem so quiet, as if Time itself is holding its breath?

I smile to myself in recognition of that moment, but of course Navire sees it—she sees everything. She tosses me a crooked smile by my implant and the world starts up again.

Slowly, as if we had practiced the form a thousand times, Navire's hard-bodies and I begin to move in perfect symmetry.

27—The Prince

The young prince looked up from the section of the deck he'd spent the last three hours scrubbing. A broad expanse of gleaming metal shined back proudly. His singular focus on the small section in front of him had over-ridden the whole-picture thing. He had always heard about the hero "taking single bites of the beast until you found that you've eaten the whole thing," but as he gazed back at the pristine hull behind him, he finally understood the saying. What he didn't realize at the moment was that this was the first time he'd experienced the state of base reality that we call the Now.

He didn't know he liked it; he only knew it *was*.

The intensity of the no-mind was disconcerting to a seer of the first water, one who had walked the paths of future tense. Something new wasn't always a good thing, but he decided that *this* was. Now the paths spread out before him with greater clarity than he'd ever experienced. It was as if he'd loosened a part of himself that had always been tensed up, and the view had grown clearer since he had. The young prince could still hear the Now calling to him, even though he'd fallen from its grace—even as he *looked* ahead.

Anodos unhooked the cleaning pads from his paws, and the polishing fiber from beneath his magnificent tail. He stretched his sore muscles and rolled his head in a cleansing circle. Opened his eyes. The prince smiled; unfortunately, it was the kind of smile that usually frightened children and small animals. Not that there were such around at the moment, or he wouldn't have smiled in the first place. The young prince allowed himself the momentary indulgence, then began to walk in the direction of the galley.

Time for a cookie.

When the extended family of his newest servants arrived aboard the Susanita, the first place they'd attacked with scouring pads was the galley. The clan of refugees had insisted that this was the heart of a home, and it was their highest priority to establish it first. Bathrooms were second, and a producing garden was third. A clean bed came in a distant fourth.

The young prince didn't necessarily disagree. Besides, he was getting a bit tired of eating take-out.

Once the kitchen was scrubbed and polished within a centimeter of its life, the matriarch of the family was enthroned there. From then on, a chatty dialog was maintained from the hearth with all the members of her clan, as they slowly worked their ways through the deadShip's corridors and holds.

The matriarch, Gin-gin, was the grandmother of the family, and was an irresistible force of nature. The Cephalopod's strength of will didn't show in the common ways but manifested in quiet conversation and hugs. After all, a mother-figure with eight tentacles can give an astonishing number of hugs and pats of encouragement.

Everyone in the room felt the gentle pull of her will as if she were bending gravity, attracting the random passerby irresistibly into her orbit. You just naturally walked up to talk with her without a second thought, and later, you usually found yourself happily doing what she suggested, all the while thinking it was your own idea.

Grandma Gin-gin was quite a force to be reckoned with.

Plus, she made delicious cookies.

Anodos had never tasted a cookie before coming aboard the deadShip Susanita. Game-hen-stuffed pastries, candied fish, and citrus-eel pies; those were served at the palace on High Feast days. But these chewy, warm disks of goodness, speckled with tiny nuggets of intense flavors, were unheard of in the empire. The young prince walked the small paths of future tense so that the cookies were just coming out of the oven when he got there.

That was when they were best.

Their warmth, sublimating, their sweetness, drenched in umami, their crispiness… perfection itself.

Everyone in Gin-gin's extended family always spent the first half of their day cleaning and scrubbing sections of the former cruise liner with the young prince (and of course the Stones). Then, after a leisurely lunch, the females of the clan disappeared into the kitchen and the engineering forges, where they produced wonders, both culinary and metallic. The males spent their afternoons divided between working in the engine room and rebuilding the greenhouse gardens. A primitive ecosystem had already been established in the smaller, port stern greenhouse. The large, forward starboard greenhouse was being stripped down to the hull, so that a true garden could be laid down properly. It had been a very long time since they'd had the chance to start a garden from scratch. The older generation was ecstatic about it. The younger generation just wanted to find a new home and settle down, and this seemed like a good place. The young prince found himself bemused with the manner in which the refugees seized the smallest opportunities to smile, to take pleasure in the moment. He was beginning to suspect that those who had the least stuff sometimes found consolation where others saw nothing of value. Anodos began to wonder if happiness might be a choice, and not just a reaction to ideal surroundings. If it was, then maybe he was looking at it all wrong.

Gin-gin's people were well-versed in closed-system gardens and had always managed to produce enough food and oxygen for the whole liveShip. They loved creating living art that fed and clothed you, art that was beautiful as well as beneficial.

They had been fleeing a devastating war in the beginning, slowly making their way in the direction of the Chaos Sea. Old records, legends really, told stories of a paradise where the sun always shone, hidden deep within the Chaos Sea. Prophecy said that the war could never find them there. That it was a world where night never fell, an inside-out planet where they would find a new home. A world simply called Summer.

Along the way, they lost their liveShip, most of their possessions, $creds, and far too many brothers and sisters. By the time they met the young prince and the Stones that Speak, two new generations had been born since they started this journey. Over half of the clan had never known any other way of life than traveling. The younger members of the clan didn't remember the horrors of war, but neither had they swum the silvered currents of their home world's azure waters. It had been a very long trip to get this far.

The senior male of the family, called the Père, all his boys, and prince Anodos were problem-solving in engineering after lunch. "We acquired the part from a salvage yard near here. It should be exactly what you need," Anodos explained for the second time. The Stones seemed amused; things weren't going as smoothly as he had expected, and the Père was the main reason. Servants were usually a little more helpful. The Cephalopods weren't exactly disrespectful or anything; they were just too stubborn to take his word as reality. He found this irritating. He felt his head rise as the elder male of Gin-gin's clan began to repeat himself. The Père's skin was beginning to flush with lavender and light-green tones.

"There is a proper way to do things; you can't just stick any old piece of tech into an engine of this complexity and expect everything to purr. This piece has to be completely broken down and rebuilt to very fine tolerances. You just point where you want the Susanita to go and leave the greasy work to us. You're holding it upside down, anyway. Just hand it over and we'll get working on it. Shouldn't take more than a few hours, maybe a half-day," stated the old bull of the herd. That was what Père meant, literally old bull. It fit.

"But I'm telling you, I KNOW that the piece is exactly what we need, as is. I have <u>seen</u> it!" the young seer impatiently explained for the third time.

"And I'll know that as soon as we break this down, clean it properly, and rebuild it to specs!" replied the Père doggedly. The younger ones were starting to show colors of dull copper and behave nervously now. One of the boys wrapped himself around Anodos' right leg, stroking it placatingly with several tentacles, trying to ease the tension. At the same time his little brother was attempting the same thing with the Père.

Surprisingly, it worked. Anodos consciously lowered his head down to a less aggressive height. The young prince knew that they all wanted the same thing, to get the Susanita space-worthy and on their way to destiny and Gravtown. To walk the Golden Path to long-lost Summer. He found it difficult that his new servants lacked faith in his word but forced himself to make allowances—Gin-gin's family had been through the kind of things that would make trust a rare commodity, something to be jealously doled out in small quantities. Anodos decided to forgive this minor level of impertinence. Besides, the little ones were so cute, trying to calm everybody down. He raised his leg with the kid attached to his neck, where it squealed in delight and slapped the young prince's sides with a couple of tentacles, begging for a ride. Anodos sighed; now all the kids were going to want a ride. He could see it. He smiled, happy for the moment that at least here, his smile didn't frighten anyone.

***

The Spacer's Guild's local-lodge "Evian Three Twenty-Nine" basically consisted of a bar, a kitchen, places to sit, and scattered Δqm^x pods. Members of the Guild could climb into the individual pods at their leisure, where they could look for jobs, sell their services, and experience full-immersion training simulations in order to improve their skills and advance their ranking. At least, that was what most spacers said they were doing inside the pods. There were other kinds of experiences available as well in there, but these were rarely mentioned in mixed company. Well, any kinda company, to be honest. The important thing was that any member of the Guild had a place to go that was familiar, and get his mail, so to speak. There were tens of thousands of these Guild lodges scattered thickly across the spiral arm of the galaxy everyone had always called the Milky Way. They were a little piece of home in a strange land.

A child of electron was the perfect kinda employee to run such a complex mélange of Signal. Leslie was one such person and found it to be a generally tedious business with limited opportunities for the more exciting stuff—with the exception of the regular bar fights and the occasional exotic stranger who breezed into your life and then disappeared into the Night.

Leslie secretly dreamed of scoring a job on a liveShip as a pilot, running vital and mysterious missions, and fighting the good fight with a loyal crew and a handsome captain.

Her job had some perks; she happened to be the person that posted all the job listings. The bad part was that she'd crashed her last two ships. (Which unfortunately, had also been her first two ships). When they saw that, no captain wanted to hire her. She'd been young and inexperienced back then, but the pesky details were listed on her pilot's license. It'd been three decades since she'd last flown. She'd ended up here, on the same boring rock, for over thirty cycles with no prospects of escape.

When a new listing for a liveShip pilot on the Susanita came in she hadn't paid that much attention to it. She posted a lot of ads. However, she always researched her listings before posting them, so as to verify the legitimacy of the job. Same old, same old, day after day, year after proverbial year.

Her focus changed when she verified that the Susanita hadn't been space worthy for close to eighty cycles. The deadShip had been sold as scrap after having served as first a luxury cruise liner, then a traveling casino, and eventually, a cargo ship for ice miners who couldn't pay their bills. Their creditors sold everything at auction, including, the records implied, the miners themselves. Then Robin's used Spaceships had bought it about three cycles ago, with the intention of flipping it. Robin hadn't got around to that part yet when an unknown mark had unexpectedly purchased the ship a few weeks ago. That was where the new-data trail ended. Despite her many skills, Leslie was unable to find anything on the new owners in her files. Not a whisper, and that was almost unprecedented. She found herself intrigued; there could be any number of interesting reasons for the lack of new-data. It could be some spooky clan that was up to no good. It could be slavers, or even Raiders splitting off from the main tribe. Might even be greenhorn treasure hunters with a guaranteed authentic map. People would be surprised how often that happened.

Or, she considered, it could be a newbie captain putting together his first crew. Maybe even a handsome soft-body captain who didn't do his research on pilot's licenses?

A girl could always dream.

This time however, Leslie wasn't content to just dream. Three decades on this rock was long enough. So, she creatively restructured her work history, and dusted off her pilot's license, so to speak. Then she timed the release of the listing to the Guild members so that her submission was sent in a Nano-blink after that. Leslie just hoped they weren't Raiders. Raiders were scum.

***

Gin-gin ran her domain from the galley with a gentle, yet firm 'hand'. When she learned of the Père's belligerence and disrespectful behavior towards the new boss, the matriarch of the clan demanded his presence immediately. They had come so far, and finally had a ride on a wonderful, if poorly-maintained, liveShip, and a promise of a new home. The grumpy old coot had almost ruined everything! She was generally regarded as a sweet old lady most of the time, but Gin-gin hadn't led her clan all this time without wielding a steel cudgel in a velvet tentacle when called for. Sometimes she'd considered wringing her husband's neck, but then he'd be on his best behavior, and she'd forgive him. Her people couldn't really deceive each other, because the skin colors their emotions generated always told the truth. They always knew how each other felt, and this eliminated a lot of the drama other species seem to wallow in. Luckily, their new boss didn't seem to sweat the small stuff, just so long as they showed him the respect he was due. He had literally saved their lives, and that was no small thing for a stranger to do, especially for refugees of a different species. And the Stones said he was of the aristocracy, which made it even more important to not be rude! So, what did the Père do? Gin-gin found herself lashing tentacles about in anger. Her youngest daughters shooed

157

the little ones away from Grandma, whose colors were frightening everyone. Only her senior daughters remained at her side.

When Père entered the kitchen, he saw that his mate's body was blotched with huge expanses of purple and lime-green. This did not bode well.

"I was only looking out for everyone, just like I always do!" he began angrily. He looked around for his boys to bolster his case, but found he was alone. He looked back at his wife and began to wilt a bit. She was really angry this time, and in his species the females were noticeably larger than the males. Her tentacles unconsciously whipped back and forth as she showed her displeasure in sea-green and lavender. The Père came to the conclusion that perhaps he should be quiet and see what she had to say. He was flushed in bronze tones with shrinking patches of avocado. By the time she spoke, there was no avocado left in his hide.

"So. You repeatedly refused a direct request by our benefactor, the same benefactor that saved our lives, that took on a street gang to save aliens he'd never even met before? The same hero that took us into his home and fed us? That offered us honorable work and a ride out of this god-forsaken place? All because you have your own rigid way of doing things. Doing things with his parts, on his ship. Do I have that right?" she asked in a deceptively calm tone.

Uh oh.

He wilted a bit more before rallying.

"He didn't know what he was talking about. How would he know the condition of a part? He was holding it upside down the whole time! Our safety, the entire ship's safety could be at stake! It was irresponsible to risk using it as is, simply because a giant salamander said so!" Now she'd understand the position he'd been placed in. He was the injured party here, really. Gin-gin would calm down, now that he'd explained things properly.

Gin-gin grew still, her skin flushing almost solid lime-green. She actually considered strangling her husband for a moment, but that would teach her family the wrong lesson. Her daughters were watching closely from several meters away. Their skin tones were showing significant amounts of bronze and a little indigo. Gin-gin hated seeing fear in her children's skin; she'd seen it too many times during their long journey and couldn't do anything about it. But *this time* she could.

She gathered her emotions and remembered the words of the prophet all those cycles before; then she knew what to do.

"Do you remember the day we left home, all those cycles ago? You came home with a holy man, a banned prophet on the run? Do you remember what he told us?" she demanded. Little tentacles and big eyes were peeking around the starboard hatch door. She pretended not to notice. This was a lesson they shouldn't ever forget.

"That was the day we lost everything. We fled in the night with only what we could carry. I'll never forget that day," the Père said. "The next day the war came, and our home was left a smoking hole in the ground."

"We didn't lose everything. We saved what was important: our children and each other! Everything else was just… things!" Gin-gin replied sharply. Now more little tentacles, and a few larger ones were visible on the threshold. Her sea-green tones were less pronounced now, as she remembered.

"Do you remember what the holy-one said to us that night?" she asked, almost wistfully.

"That we would wander the Dark places for so long that we would almost lose hope, but then a great prophet would save us and lead us to a mythic place of eternal Light. We would find lost Summer and grow gardens such as none of our people had ever dreamed of," The Père said the words without bitterness for the first time since they'd lost his brothers. He turned to stare at Gin-gin with the dawning realization of fate's hand. His skin flushed with gold such as his grandchildren had never seen before, as he tumbled out of his own little viewpoint and saw the truth laid out before him.

The long journey was over.

"Do you think a great prophet would know if an engine part was good?" his wife asked tartly.

Navire's hard-bodies gracefully bow down to the hull while still keeping their weapons discretely aimed in the general direction of the survivors.

I sheathe my nodule-shotgun across my back and drop out of full recording mode so that I am completely visible. I raise my empty hands slowly, still smiling, and settle down into a Wudang Tai Chi stance. I am still completely in the Now, waiting serenely without further movement. I don't know how long it is until everyone begins to, ever so slowly, relax a little bit.

I find myself rapidly re-assessing the wounded men and women we'd located. They weren't passengers or crew or gangsters—they were soldiers—and continued to work smoothly as a team despite the experiences they'd been through. Unfortunately, the bodies far outnumbered the living, and some of those left alive wore horror as a mask that blinded them to their change in circumstances. These guys had been running full-tilt-boogie for so long they just couldn't believe it was over.

Navire's hard bodies and I start passing out water bottles and med-kits to the closest of the soldiers. We make it a point to be very careful and move slowly.

It's always the wounded dog that bites.

I return to real time.

There was no question of who their leader was. The compactly muscular brunette with blackened armor and burnt hair strode through her people with a personal gravity that pulled all eyes to her. Her leadership was silently declared in the body language of every warrior she passed, as her hands brushed a back or shoulder in encouragement. As she came closer, I could see that her fine-boned face reflected the treatment she and her people had endured. There were burns on the left side of her head from coming too close to plasma fire, and her face was pockmarked from Boom shrapnel. Half of her chestnut hair was missing, and her sunken citrine eyes said that she had seen too much Bad to expect anything else. But somehow you could tell that she hadn't given in to the hopelessness of her situation or the pain of loss. This was a woman who would never give up. Ever.

As the troop's commander drew nearer, she continued studying us with an icy gaze that carried little of trust. I tried to look harmless, but that was a lost cause. I wasn't a currently a danger to her, but she and her soldiers outnumbered us at least thirty to one. Plus, I had a liveShip, and she was in desperate need of a ride. I didn't trust *her* yet, either. I looked deeper.

There was a sense of bedrock calm about her and you just knew that she saw every detail in the room and read most every person there with the gift of discernment. However, these people were obviously Corp-nation, which didn't exactly lend itself to trust. She was flanked by three officers that kept between us and their commander as she approached. One of them spoke as they drew to a halt on the broken deck in front of me.

"This is the Tyrant Jenny-Rose," he declared simply enough. I sucked in a breath.

"Tyrant" was the title given to the rarest of commanders that lead highly specialized hostile takeover forces known as "Hordes." They functioned as small personal armies loyal to certain powerful middle managers.

This was a person of consequence.

I was also pretty sure that she thought dozens of steps ahead; after all, she had successfully navigated the byzantine power-plays of the Corp-nations for decades. A Tyrant's favor was quite valuable, not to mention, quite expensive. I briefly wondered what fighting styles she favored, then pulled my mind back to the present with a smile.

"I am Koen of Summer," I replied, before gesturing with my right hand to indicate the Navire bodies. "These are Navire, my partner," I continued calmly.

"Your assistance is timely. I would like to know how you came to this place at this particular time when there is the opportunity, but right now my primary concern is for my team. Are you able to evacuate us to someplace safe? We have extensive $cred resources." The Tyrant's raw voice was unexpectedly low and resonant. She was proud, but not afraid to ask a stranger for help, not if it meant saving her people.

Tyrants always take care of their own. Even I knew that.

"How many of you are there?" I asked softly. I knew without hesitation that she would know exactly how many of her team remained alive. The Tyrant Jenny-Rose was that kinda leader. Navire seemed equally impressed, and that rarely happens.

Meanwhile Navire was running diagnostic triage in my right eye, already outlining our next moves and which of the fighters we needed to get assistance to quickly.

"We are ninety-seven living and just over three hundred dead. We all go or stay as a team, living or not," she replied with a quiet passion. It didn't need to be loud to communicate her determination.

I came to the realization that this was the kinda leader that men and women would follow into hell. She would make quite an ally.

The Tyrant calmly waited for my response, as if we had all the time in the world and weren't in a deadShip that was slowly disintegrating around us.

I found myself briefly wondering how she felt about the Keer, then replied.

"We will find a way to bring all your people home safe to the Ranch. Once we get home, no one will find you until you're ready to be found. My Ranch has lotsa room," I answered plainly, feeling the words weigh unexpectedly heavily on the smoke-laced air.

They're like that sometimes. Simple Truths.

Sal's tug had only three living modules hooked up this trip; a dining/kitchen Pullman we called the bar-car, a sleeping module with six small bedrooms stacked on top of each other, and a gym/showers/bathroom unit with very nice plumbing. The units were side-by-side and balanced out with a fourth supply room that doubled as an armory. At the tail of the train was the Keer trap with the napping disco monsters. When you didn't need to be aerodynamic you could carry a couple of hall closets full of extra stuff. Out here in the depths of the Chaos Sea, bringing extra stuff along was actually a long-term survival strategy. You never know when you'll need something far from home and forge. Being a bit of a pack rat was a survival trait, but I was pretty sure that the grumpy old tug would have rolled that way regardless. Sal said he had some tethers and spider rope packed away in an exterior fold-out storage locker. It was surprisingly big enough to hold quite a bit of junk. Which gave me an idea, if we could find ice, we could put together a primitive oxygen generator. Meanwhile, three of Navire's four hard-bodies worked through the wounded fighters back at the deadShip at full speed, which was much faster than I could keep up with. It was very hard to even make out their movements as they cleaned and bandaged wounds with bands of Nano-bot-saturated tissue-regenerator. The more grievous injuries had first priority with the whirling instrument-laden hard-body spheres Navire was wearing. The fourth hard-body stuck to me like adhesive. Navire would no more leave me unprotected among a hundred battle-seared soldiers than she would abandon our daughter, Katy the Sledge. I could take care of myself, but it was very important to Navire that we have each other's backs, and I was good with that. We'd come too close to losing each other once before, and I didn't ever want to go through that again. I abruptly pulled my attention back to the task at hand.

Time for those kinda thoughts when we were safely back home at the Ranch.

This was now, and I had to find a way to fit a hundred smelly wounded into three cabins that comfortably fit five or six. I continued to dig through the fold-out storage locker as I thought, brainstorming with Navire over my implant the whole time. There they were. A big knotted ball of rope and tethers a meter in diameter. It was so big and knotted that it was just downright frustrating to even look at.

I rolled my head to loosen some of the stress I was storing in my neck.

I guess if we threw a bunch of people at it we could untangle it pretty quickly. Come to think of it, at the density we were going to have to pack everybody in, a distraction of the puzzle variety might be very popular. Two birds, one stone, and all that.

I continued to root around and found a bunch of cargo nets that might be just the thing for the three hundred bodies that I had promised I would find a way to bring home. Not very dignified, but they'd already been through worse, and needs must when the devil dances. At least they didn't require atmosphere and warmth. Those were going to be limited resources for the next four days.

I had decided that Zero-G was the only way to fit everyone in; at least the worst of the wounded wouldn't have to deal with gravity's woes and pains. Easier on the heart too; didn't have to push so hard against the G. Taking some of the pressure off everyone's exhausted bodies would help, too. We could tether the soldiers at each end, and fit in four layers, six across per room. My crew could camp out on the bridge with Sal. Sigh.

It should be enough room, provided we sedated the wounded and everyone was comfortable with the tight quarters. I decided that if I could spend four days in close quarters with Sal, then soldiers could handle their arrangements.

I was pretty sure the soldiers had the better part of the deal.

Inside the tug Pasteur and the E were running around securing things in preparation for the release of G. The E zoomed back and forth, continuously arguing and chattering in voices that weren't individually loud, but jointly became a mild roar. That unfortunately was the way things go around the little guys in these kinda situations. I shrugged. Nobody's perfect.

Sal was right in the middle of things, having the time of his life. Not a lot of help but talking excitedly about everybody and everything like a fish-monger's wife out with the girls.

Navire's hard-bodies had finished stabilizing everyone that was still alive with the help of a few Horde medics and were leading a slow exodus to the exterior airlock we'd entered by. Navire said everyone had chipped in to help zip-dry the fallen; the resulting small shiny packages allowed them to bring back a little something out of that dark night. I'd known many people and places in my life, and how a tribe treated their fallen said a lot about them. I found these were a people I was beginning to respect, despite being Corp.

I told Sal to close his mouth and focus, to bring us around as close to the deadShip as possible. The E were currently running weapons station, which wasn't a particularly safe way to go. The little guys tended to be a bit bloodthirsty and were absolutely fearless. A formidable combination, but I still trusted them with Boom at my back over Sal any day.

As we glided closer Pasteur and I began unspooling a compressed air tube passageway onboard the tug. When we sealed it to the deadShips airlock and inflated it, everyone could get onboard in less than twenty minutes. It ended up taking less; with the E receiving and slow-tossing each person from one E to another before roping them to a stable position we got it done in under ten. The whole operation went surprisingly smooth and reminded me of something, but I couldn't grasp hold of it at the time.

The area around us called "personal space" differs quite a bit from culture to culture. When I was very young, surviving hand to mouth in the unincorporated badlands, it was simple; if someone was close enough to grab you, they were too close. If someone moved too close, it was fight for your life time. If you had to stop and think about it, you didn't survive for long.

I survived.

When I immigrated to the Hive at the age of seven it was a whole different story. Thanks to Auntie Tao's constant presence in my new implant, I eventually adapted. It didn't come easily—it was over four months before I stopped punching people who brushed against me in the corridors. I wasn't the most popular guy back then. Eventually I grew accustomed to a personal space a third the size I had when I arrived. Outside the Hive, everyone was a potential threat. But inside the Hive, there were no bullies, or rapists, or murderers. No one even tried to steal my food! This was because Auntie Tao was always there, guiding everyone to the right decision. My ingrained defensive reactions were simply not needed when no one was attacking. I reluctantly put them down for a long winter's nap, but they never really went away. This was one of the reasons I was eventually selected to become a Hive operative. People born and raised in the Hive never really developed such instincts, and were unsuited for prolonged contact with outsiders, at least according to Auntie Tao.

It was obvious to me that the Tyrant's people were very comfortable being physically close to each other. It kinda reminded me of the Hive, except that their personal space didn't automatically include everybody in the room. These were, first and foremost, soldiers, well-honed in deadly skills and reactive to infringement of a larger personal space, by strangers. I was pretty sure everyone not Horde was defined as a stranger.

29—The Keer

When the Keer settled down to digest dinner this time, they entered the Dream much more quickly than normal. Around them in the Dream, everyone was still pretty lit—that much was the same.

Everything else was forever changed.

This was when the Keer over-mind swam up from the depths to awareness for the first time. The over-Keer was conscious of the many other, smaller, Keer sleepwalking in the Dream. They radiated a kinda happy-idiot bliss and a fawning affection for the over-Keer not unlike the big brother worship of toddlers. The newborn group mind of the six Keer tasted this emotion and shivered in pleasure.

The infant over-Keer surveyed its domain in the Dream, and it was good.

***

We would later discover that the over-Keer was born because, for the first time in their long history, multiple Keer were simultaneously fed in very close physical proximity with others of its kind. This propelled them into the Dream as mixed Signal, and a sentient mind was born.

The Keer are by nature solitary and had never before gathered in such groups. Each Keer's hunting territory was so large as to preclude casual physical contact. Such a thing was also against their nature.

Now there were six Keer close enough to each other to reach out and touch, not that such a thing would ever occur to them. They were also all entering the Dream at exactly the same time, so closely that they became one. This was without precedent, as far as anyone knew.

This was where it all really started. This is when the Keer began to change.

But we didn't know anything about that yet.

***

The over-Keer luxuriated in the adoration of the common Keer. But somehow this was not as satisfying as it had been in the beginning. Odd thoughts and sudden curiosities had begun intruding on its new mind. These thoughts were very distracting, and it found its attention wandering into pristine territories. Most of the concepts were of the "what if?" or "why am I different" category, but the concept of one caught its imagination and refused to leave it alone. "Is it always only the Dream or hunger in the Dark?" speculated the over-Keer.

Now the Keer are very good at two things. Waiting and gobbling dinner. Thinking? Not so much. There really isn't enough spare processing power for curiosity, or even language, for that matter. A Keer, while terrifying, is not intelligent, but with the processing power of six Keer combined… The fledgling group-mind simply thought of its self as the "over-Keer". After all, it towered over the others in the maroon twilight of the Dream.

Sometimes the over-Keer found itself missing the placidity of non-sentience; it had been quiet, without all these irritating thoughts to disturb it. The more the over-Keer thought about it, the more frustrated it became. This was when it felt *anger* for the first time. And it was good.

Anger made the over-Keer feel powerful. It experienced a quickness to its thoughts, a shortcut in thinking that went to only one place instead of many. Anger was marvelous in that it streamlined the new mind's processing; it almost felt like being non-sentient again, except without the accompanying peacefulness. This was very exciting, and the over-Keer automatically flexed its bodies in exhilaration—the same bodies that a Keer was completely unaware of while in the Dream, because their bodies were always immobile. Immobile because they were devoting all of their resources to the task of digesting dinner, while the consciousness of the Keer was out partying in the Dream.

To its complete surprise the over-Keer could suddenly feel all of its six bodies. In real time.

The thrill of anger dissolved as it became aware of this odd tunnel to another place both familiar and mysterious. The Keer had never learned caution; rock lice and the rare Bob haven't exactly been dangerous to the unseen apex predator.

The over-Keer rushed through the meta-physical tunnel to examine its bodies. A Keer in the Dream has no idea of what its physique was up to, nor did it care. Now the over-Keer could see that they weren't doing anything except absorbing dinner. This confused the over-Keer.

How did it manage to perform the initial body flex, if nothing was capable of movement while digesting?

***

Time passes unmeasured in the Dream; the over-Keer had no idea of how long it worked on the problem before it became too frustrated to continue. That was the key, of course. Its frustration birthed anger, and in its anger was power. The over-Keer abruptly slipped into the six slumbering bodies as easily as a Bob slips into his vacuum suit. It wasn't hard once you knew how.

Now it knew how.

***

Eventually, the over-Keer was able to move its claws a few centimeters, but that was about it. The digestive form a Keer takes is basically a shell-like armor bonded to the surrounding rock, with everything vulnerable tucked neatly away beneath the shell. There were two exceptions, both its claws, and antenna poked out a bit. The invisible down covered everything, of course. Once it had exhausted all the possible movements of its thirty-six talon tipped hands, it turned to its antenna.

The over-Keer slowly opened its eyes. Or, more precisely, it fed new-data from its six antenna sensor arrays into its threaded consciousness.

***

The over-Keer was stunned.

This was not like the Dream at all. All six of its bodies were physically close to each other, something that was completely foreign to the Keer. There was something pushing on them all over, crowding them in the small vibrating space. The Keer have never experienced atmosphere before and didn't much care for it.

Then the over-Keer became aware of temperature for the first time. It felt flushed, uncomfortable. A Keer's down was a highly efficient insulator that let virtually nothing escape. Keer were perfectly adapted to deep space. There was no need to expel excess heat except occasional minute amounts generated when digesting. Then waste gasses from consuming dinner were released to dissipate into the vacuum, carrying any rare excess warmth with it. In space, body heat was something you held tightly on to. The Dark sucked warmth from everything sooner or later.

The cold always won.

The over-Keer's six organic ballistic calculators at the base of its skulls insisted that it was moving very fast, which wasn't possible during its digestion phase. Maybe the rock it was attached to was moving, but the view never changed. That just didn't make sense. A… bad… feeling rose up in its awareness. This was something new—Keer aren't exactly feely-touchy creatures.

It felt isolated, alone in this place.

For the first time in the history of the Keer, the over-Keer felt loneliness; a very un-Keer-like emotion. It had been born in the Dream, surrounded by the others of its own kind. It had never been away from the sea of faithful Keer meandering in the warm sunset glow of the Dream.

The over-Keer decided that it definitely didn't like anything about this place. This was nothing at all like the Dream, or the Dark for that matter. The over-Keer hurriedly retreated out of the tunnel and its bodies, back into the timeless Dream. The Dream was… comfortable.

30—Koen of Summer

The dining car was stuffed with floating soldiers, loosely attached to the bulkheads with pieces of the untangled ball of rope. They were layered four deep, with a few clear spaces for passageways through the crowded room. There were at least thirty-five of them in this room alone. The chamber was ripe in organic scent that the overworked air scrubbers couldn't clear very well.

Some of the fighters were sleeping, a skill soldiers have excelled at since time immemorial. Others were watching shows on their primitive implants, or quietly talking as they lay in that most gentle of beds, Zero-G.

Not everyone was so prosaic.

Some of the fighters just numbly laid there, internally still in the fight. This was familiar. You come that close to the water, you're going to get wet.

Takes a while to get dry.

Several others were almost luminescent.

These rare few were completely immersed in the Now, slow dancing on the edge of enlightenment. They radiated a sort of quiet peacefulness that was downright joyful in nature. For them, the world was fresh and magical in its newness. Life, when you had expected and embraced imminent death, was sometimes born anew all shiny and bright. Not something you can hold on to for very long, and memories have a hard time retaining such things.

But in that moment, you know the world as few truly have.

The Tyrant Jenny-Rose floated from warrior to warrior, exchanging a quiet word with each one, or sometimes just hovering in loud silence before briefly touching them and moving on. Her troika worked the crowd around her, all the while managing to remain between the Tyrant and my crew. I don't even think they were conscious of doing it.

That was okay, if I had my wish they would all become family eventually.

The Ranch has plenty of room.

I caught Navire's eye. She winked at me, an unexpected flash of intimacy in a crowded room. I smiled and winked back. The children of Electron never miss a cue, unlike me.

Navire had cleaned up and put on a new body.

Tonight, she was strutting a Valkyrie. Thick braided silver-blond hair framing a pale-skinned face with electric blue eyes. Muscular, taut-skinned beauty rolled off her like CO_2 quick-melting into fog. She held herself impeccably balanced as only a mature warrior does. She was wearing lotsa Boom strapped all over her lithe-but-powerful body. She was beautiful.

It was too bad I was the only person in the room who could see her.

Navire had not attempted to be visible by implant to our guests. There were several reasons for this.

First, it would be very impolite to override the implants that the Tyrant's team wore. They were simple, rugged tech, and could take a lot of damage because they only had a few bits of mono-logic tech to them. These primitive implants also monitored and reported back on anyone wearing them. Upper middle-management didn't get to their current position by taking their eyes off the dangerous ones. For a moment I wondered if they knew, then realized that of course they did.

Second, because we just didn't walk into anyone's home and take over without being invited. That also was just pain rude.

My people's implants began life as Hive-tech and had been constantly modified as new-data tech was encountered. Our implants only required a nudge from someone like Navire or Katy the Sledge to load Signal and appear before our eyes. This was a full-immersion Δqm^x that was indistinguishable from biologically-derived reality. Signal is Signal.

On the other hand, the simple linear Corp-tech the Horde wore was so clunky as to require a complete Signal override. There were archaic built-in safeguards against such things, but they were no match for our implant-tech. Basically, we would have to shout quite loudly, and the effect could be very unpleasant. Not a good way to start a working relationship.

So Navire was also wearing a generic hard-body that Rose's crew could see and interact with. Kinda Sorta.

My view was definitely better. I liked Valkyries. Good fighters in word as well as in the ring. Quick-witted was all kinda sexy. They had a fresh scent of unsullied optimism mixed with rose honey, of red hot iron and good mead. It was a good look for her.

By day three the air was getting pretty stale, despite the rendering of the comet ice down into its basic elements of Oxygen and Hydrogen. We breathed one and burned the other to run the spare-part auxiliary air system we'd hobbled together. We were getting low on ice by now. We'd make it to the Ranch just fine, but it wouldn't be a pleasure trip. We could find more ice if it was critical, but we needed to get to the resources of the Ranch or we were going to lose more people.

I already knew which the Tyrant would want. We stayed on task.

We were out of food now, despite my usual overstock of the ship's larder. Water was holding out, but the overworked recycler juice was beginning to smell strongly of urine.

Luckily, I had a surprise in store for everyone. The Tyrant and her troika, Navire and Pasteur, the E and I had a little meeting on the bridge a day ago and had scheduled the treat we'd stored in the Keer trap. Nobody wanted to go back there, so it was safe.

Well, no one is actually safe around a Keer, much less six of them. But the smart guys at the Hive had postulated that the Keer were unable to move during their digestive process. Theoretically.

I just hoped they didn't drink beer.

It got kinda loud when Pasteur and I got back with two barrels of blackberry ale. There were over a hundred of us, but that still left a little over a gallon per person for the next twenty hours. Liquid bread in its most delightful form.

Sure beat drinking urine.

Sal hollered when we were in sight of the Door into Summer, waking up the crowd. The dark rocky exterior of the planetary-sized geode absorbed all light; you had to know exactly how and where to find the Door. A few kilometers off course and you hit the exterior surface of the inside out world, just another fatality of the legend.

We threaded the twisting passageway of the Door into Summer and eventually burst into the most beautiful place in the galaxy.

Summer.

The Summerlight poured down in topaz waves, shocking in its beauty after too long in the Dark. We shot across the crystal ranges over vintage mycelium light refracting from a trillion faceted surfaces. Overhead, a light storm battled its way across far Summer in jumbled straws of royal purple and cerise. The purple was winning.

When we crossed over onto Ranch land I felt a rush of emotion—I was home. This was where I belonged. I missed Katy and the Gardener and the bamboo forest. I was kinda surprised at the depths of my feelings.

It was good to be home.

31—The Keer

The over-Keer basked in the waves of adoration pouring forth from the common Keer, but somehow it couldn't stop thinking about its discovery of the strange world outside the Dream. The experience dominated its focus relentlessly, flooding its consciousness knee deep with wide-spectrum signal. Unfortunately, all new-data becomes old-data after enough time. Then it is eventually purged from the system. Such has been the way for time eternal. We have adapted.

The over-Keer found itself craving more new-data. The dark hunger for it slowly growing more powerful, until it was difficult to think of anything else. It pondered the act of stretching its bodies like before, and crudely came up with some possible scenarios. None of the first situations it came up with were satisfying. It tore at the problem relentlessly, refusing to accept the initial possibilities.

There had to be more.

Some experts say that it was this minute, this exact moment in time, that the Keer changed and began the great awakening as all of us had before. The bitter aftertaste of gaining awareness, and simultaneously losing the Garden of Eden, forever.

Intelligence is a selfish mistress.

This moment would turn out to be the beginning of true analytical thought, for the singular consciousness known forever as the over-Keer. It was becoming smarter.

Then came a moment, an instance when everything came to its fullness. It was time. The over-Keer cautiously reached out sideways, and six soft-bodies came gently to attention. In slow-beat perfect timing, it stretched out, pulling the soft-bodies to fit, just like putting on an old pair of gloves.

The over-Keer shivered in delight at the experience.

Then it opened its eyes.

***

The darkness around it was comforting, although the low frequency vibration that filled the background was very irritating. The over-Keer's organic ballistic calculator located at the base of its skull insisted they were moving through space at an unfamiliar speed, but its other senses detected no change in its surroundings. This had never happened before. What if it was somehow nested on an inward facing fold of rock, of some far-traveling asteroid? A stone wall so domineering as to preclude all outward perception? This would explain all the evidence, but the likelihood of it ever happening was so small that the situation could only happen once in too-many something cycles.

It must be missing some clue, some other possibility. This view was not acceptable.

The over-Keer refocused on freshly reviewing the evidence, then chucked the unsatisfying results. It started all over again, beginning by reexamining its surroundings from the bottom up. Nicely dark, vibrating unpleasantly, and uncomfortably warm.

The only thing that stood out were those two oddly sheared boulders that appeared to be secured to the surface of their little cave. Secured?

Those kinda shiny straight lines didn't happen naturally in space.

This couldn't be good. It took another, harder look. With focus, the over-Keer found its sense of location to be highly evolved; when seen from six separate views the view allowed amazing detail. The wealth of new-data was unprecedented.

What fun!

Suddenly, a hole brightened in front of the over-Keer's soft-bodies and spit forth two delicious-looking Bob.

Halleluiah! Dinner time!

The over-Keer began to drool from its six maws and was uncontrollably scratching its thirty-six talons into the remarkably dense armor of the deck.

The two Bob were delightfully rounded! One was tasty looking and big, and the other was tasty looking and even bigger! Where to start? Better to eat the big one first, and then snack on the littler one later? Or to toss back the smaller Bob first, and then just gobble what it could of the king-sized entrée? Which would last the longest? The over-Keer speculated with the fever of a greenhorn gambler, enjoying every minute, wringing every bit of salty goodness from the cloth. It was glorious.

It was a long moment before it remembered that it was paralyzed.

If anything in the limited world of the over-Keer could be hated, it was this being unable to move, suffering the complete paralysis of its body during the digestive state. The over-Keer attempted to leap into the air and gobble up that finest of meals, a Bob.

But nothing happened.

It was very frustrating, and the young over-Keer raged at it with a terrible anger, but in the end, it was all sound and fury, signifying nothing.

As it grew tired it found itself in an oddly numb kinda peacefulness. The over-Keer was reduced to impotently studying the succulent meat as it went about its mysterious activities.

First the two Bob somehow untangled the oddly straight fibers, and then attached one of the strangely shaped boulders to each of their backs. This was totally unexpected.

The over-Keer was used to remaining unseen and attached no meaning to the manner in which the two Bob were completely ignoring the six massive Keer soft-bodies decked out in disco ribbon suits that twinkled in exotic colors.

They were kinda hard to miss.

Yet the dinners appeared oblivious of everything except the strangely shaped boulders that they were now moving carefully back though the bright hole. The over-Keer found the whole situation quite strange, especially the manner with which the two Bob moved, with an unexpectedly graceful coordination. This reminded the over-Keer of something, but the thought remained out of reach. It glared impotently at the succulent meat that remained out reach of its drooling mandibles. This was completely unacceptable. What could it do to change this? This was perhaps the first time in Keer prehistory that a Keer didn't immediately gobble up its dinner before it even had a chance to notice it was being attacked. The entire modus-operandi of its species was predicated upon the practice of Gobble.

The Keer excelled at the art.

32—Dread

Dread didn't have anything against parties.

He'd been to one once. It wasn't bad. Good music covers a multitude of sins.

But *this* was <u>out of the question</u>.

The Corp-nations hadn't been around the last time he'd passed through this arm of the galaxy. Back then, he'd captained his imperial majesty's battleship the Little Tita. He was a commander of one of the deadliest ships in the fleet, pursuing his old enemy, a political idealist "Kraig the Good", (the nickname was sarcastic). Kraig the Good was well-known for his ruthlessness in a trade famous for cut-throat betrayal.

We called it "politics" around these parts.

That was when they stumbled into a well-planned ambush by the Northern zealots. The fanatics were heavily armed and brought more fighters than most any ship could resist. Luckily, the Little Tita wasn't just any ship.

Dread lead his crew into battle using every smidgen of tactics and short-term strategies he'd acquired in several lifetimes of battle. They fought the good fight for days, laying waste to nearby star systems, until they finally ran out of Boom. Then they fought down the corridors of the Little Tita, first with small arms, but they were eventually reduced to pointy things. Dread's people weren't just deadly with any weapons, they <u>were</u> the weapon, and everything else was just a tool of the artist.

The crew had a motto for times like this: "blades don't run out of ammo".

Of course, they fought to the last man, which was the Commander, Dread. He was grateful that at least his crew had not gone gently into that Dark night. Instead, they went down fighting the good fight, preceded by a sizable honor-guard paving the road ahead of them into Hell.

This was the way of his people, the Raan.

The Commander Dread had brought up the rearguard into that long night, as is a liveShip captain's duty, but unfortunately there was no one left to finish <u>him</u>.

Last man crawling and all that.

He ended up hovering on the edge of the Dark, nodding in the grey twilight between Light and Dark for long, uncounted centuries. He didn't know how long he had been drifting out there in the cold, but after the Shadower rescued him he could find no trace of his people. Not a single clue in the past six cycles. That was how long it had been since he was brought home to the Ranch and carefully rebuilt into a new man.

Dread figured that was to be expected; you are always profoundly changed by such things and incapable of returning to the old you. Best to have a new body as well.

He had finally accepted that his people were lost in time, that the important thing was that he had been found, rebuilt and fresh-bathed in the Summerlight.

This is who he was now. There was no going back.

Such is life.

He had a new home now. A purpose. A family. He was responsible for the Shadower's, and the Ranch's safety, and it was a duty he would never fail.

But he simply couldn't believe that not only had the boss dragged home a small army from one of the most ruthless societies he'd ever seen, but the Shadower hadn't seen fit to disarm them! One hundred of the heartless bastards, strapped up with myriad Boom and ill intent; and what does the boss want to do?

THROW THEM A PARTY!

If it had been anyone else, he would have blown them out of the sky the moment they crossed over on to Ranch Land. But this was Koen, and that was a horse of a different color. Even Navire and Pasteur were going along with it! Was everyone losing their mind? The plan with the Keer had been bad enough. What was he thinking?

Well, he wasn't going to let anything happen to his family or the Ranch, regardless of any trouble the boss dragged home. That was his job! Problem was; he was seriously undermanned. He had a handful of fighters to defend the Ranch, and the Corp-nation Horde outnumbered them twenty-eight to one. Of course, the Shadower might consider it a fair match, but it was Dread's duty to make sure he didn't have to.

He ran an analysis of his defensive assets once more, and something jumped out at him.

Those damn auto-sentry units that had failed to alert the Ranch to an attack by a large force of Raiders; afterwards, Navire and he had torn them apart, looking for the weakness that had been used against them. They never figured it out. After too many frustrating hours Navire and he had finally moved them into one of the more remote bays in the old garage, where everyone sorta forgot about the unreliable junk.

Just because he couldn't rely on them to fulfill their sentry duties, didn't mean they couldn't be useful. He had enough of the three-meter-wide sentries to outnumber the Corpies ten to one. Although that would be overkill, not that he normally had anything against overkill, mind you.

However, the boss was also a proponent of the precise application of force. Not really a fan of overkill, though. He had to admit that they both found precision to be a more elegant tool of societal sculpture than hosing someone blindly with a wealth of Boom and hoping that you hit something.

Dread held the Shadower in awe: the battle-artiste of le Danse Macabre had been fighting since he could walk. He was not a man to be easily impressed, either.

Dread would do anything to protect the man that dragged him out of the Dark and gave him a life worth living again. And to protect the family, and the Ranch. Anything.

Perhaps if he just kinda lined the room with the sentry units; loaded for bear all subtle like? They didn't have to actually shoot anyone, unless of course, somebody deserved it. Walk quietly and carry a big stick was not really his style, but he could roll that way if it made the boss happy. Dread wasn't aware that he had started humming happily to himself as he directed the Ranch mechs to start cutting perfect half spheres into the crazy zigzag stone walls of the ballroom, each three meters across.

33—The Prince

"Prince Anodos! Come quickly! We found something!" the young girl with tentacles urged. Her skin was flushed with shades of brass and canary yellow. Two of her tentacles pulled at the Prince's right leg while another one pointed excitedly to the rear of the Susanita. He had been waiting all morning for this particular moment, walking the small paths of future tense to arrive at this instant in time. He carefully discarded his cleaning pads and allowed the little girl to pull him along in the direction he had always intended to go. They soon arrived at a hatch that had previously been hidden behind a mediocre, but huge, painting of some unknown star system. The florescent mold had ruined the canvas, and when it was removed, a concealed entrance was exposed. This was one of the last uncleaned portions of the ship, and at least a dozen of Gin-gin's people clustered around the cleared section. It was a little difficult to count heads exactly, because everyone was gesturing excitedly as they climbed in and out of the previously concealed cargo hold. The Stones poked their massive heads into the opening, before scooting back to allow Anodos clear passage. As he entered the storeroom Anodos acquired a young rider who dropped from above the hatch to straddle his neck and began waving three or four of his appendages around in unconcealed delight. He sighed. Now a very young one was trying to climb his left rear leg and join his sibling. The prince held out his leg to an adult male, who gently removed the squirming kid, handing him off to someone still outside the entrance.

Anodos looked around.

The tall space was packed with cocktail tables, roulette wheels, one-armed-bandits, and even a long bar of some exotic wood. Racks of glassware were piled haphazardly on cook pots and what looked like fancy fence segments. Boxes of silverware, plates and bowls, even a few older money changers (empty of course) were everywhere. There was even a classic grand piano! It looked as if someone had shoved an entire casino and restaurant into the concealed cargo hold. Which was, of course, exactly what had happened about a century before. Anodos had seen this but hadn't realized the significance of the hoard. He had originally just planned on selling everything. However, now that he'd spent so much time paying for repairs and equipment, and especially food, well, he had a newfound appreciation for the craft's ability to generate $creds. Everyone wanted some, and while his financial resources were adequate to launch the Susanita, he had begun to worry about the continuing cost of traveling all the way to Summer by way of Gravtown. The concept of "cost" was related to "stuff" in some bizarre manner, and Anodos was beginning to see previously unsuspected, larger aspects of the thing. He applied this concept while searching the side paths and reexamining alternate futures until he found one that had a "cost" value that was acceptable. It was going to require skills he was currently ignorant of, but he would learn. It helped that his new crew were capable of so much more than just cleaning. He had seen that long before actually meeting Gin-gin's people.

Small mining colonies were widely scattered among the stars, and it is the nature of people to want what they don't have. To eat a meal with ingredients they didn't sweat over themselves. To get out of the same old three rooms and have a drink in someplace that was pretty. Maybe even to have a chance to win $creds in an honest card game. Pioneers have little time to devote to non-essentials, so the opportunity to go someplace different for an evening was pretty special. Even the opportunity to just talk to someone new was almost priceless to the inhabitants of an isolated outpost.

Prince Anodos was going to meet that need with the rebuilt Susanita; a traveling restaurant and casino with friendly people and a nice bar. He had seen it. Now he was walking the paths of future tense to get there. Now all they needed was a liveShip pilot.

***

Leslie was so excited that she could hardly contain herself.

She had received a call back from her application for the liveShip pilot position aboard the Susanita. She immediately wanted to tell everyone about it, but the caller, someone named Gin-gin, had insisted on full confidentiality. She somehow managed to keep quiet all day as she went about her work, but it was extremely difficult. She wasn't used to restraining her words, but this was the opportunity she'd been waiting for, waiting for decades, and she wasn't about to screw it up now. Time dragged on though, and it seemed as if she would never finish her shift.

When seven o'clock rolled around Leslie turned over the operation to the night shift, a nice ex-soldier with a huge white beard everyone called Larry the Swan, for some reason, and retreated to her private room downstairs. It wasn't very large, but a child of Electron doesn't need many square-meters to feel comfortable. What she does need, is a dense set of memory banks, with an over-engineered synaptic network that leaves biological tech eating dust. Oh, and a pretty hard-body; all women needed something nice to wear when they went out on a date. She suddenly realized that she hadn't used it much lately. Oh well, all in all, it was a poor substitute for a ship's body. Soaring through the heavens at high speed was kinda out of her current hard-body's reach.

She _really_ missed wearing a liveShip.

Leslie hadn't started with much, when she'd lost her last ship and been stranded on this rock. But she had standards; a girl couldn't just settle for whatever hardware she finds laying around. So Leslie had spent most of the past three decades acquiring upgrades and bootleg tech from dubious sources—after all, the spacer's guild was lousy with them. She wanted the best! What else was she going to spend her paychecks on? Beer? Then she had impulsively blown last week's paycheck on cosmetic upgrades to her little-used hard-body, wanting to look nice for the interview if she got that far. Sometimes you just have to roll the dice.

Sometimes you win.

***

Prince Anodos was preceded into the galley by the Stones Who Speak, as always.

The Stones took their duties seriously; they had been bodyguards responsible for the prince's well-being since his birth. Prince Anodos was not their first prince, or even their second. And safety was only a part of their duties, as the Stones trained royalty in the skills of their trade, ensuring he had the strength and courage to lead.

He may one day be King.

Gin-gin stood surrounded by her daughters and their daughters, beautifully poised and flushed in warm, welcoming colors of gold and scarlet. Around her were gas grills crowned with a wealth of pots, emitting magnificent odors of complex character. To the side stood the Père, surrounded by his boys, waving at him. They were welcoming in gold and maroon hues as well. The little ones were conspicuous by their absence.

The entire picture was quite powerful, and obviously crafted down to the smallest detail. This was a matriarch in her place of power, surrounded by her followers. Her family. Her daughters.

It was, of course, exactly what Anodos had been expecting.

"The pilot you asked for is waiting in the dining room. I wanted a moment before you meet her to go over her qualifications. Did you have time to look over her license? Because there are other, more qualified applicants that haven't crashed a ship, much less two of them...." Gin-gin's words trailed off as she remembered exactly who she was talking to. Of course, he knew. She had just wanted to protect their prince. She flushed carrot orange with embarrassment and lifted her eyes to meet the prince's. He met her gaze without condemnation, much to her relief, and the Stones rumbled in amusement.

Anodos smiled as well. "She will take us exactly where we need to go," he said softly.

"Alright. This way, please." Gin-gin escorted the young prince to their guest. "Prince Anodos, this is Leslie, a liveShip pilot. Leslie, this is Prince Anodos, our captain."

Leslie was stunned but managed to find her manners and bow to the captain. A prince! This was much more romantic than she'd imagined!

Even if the royal captain appeared to be a massive tattooed salamander.

She certainly hadn't imagined <u>that</u> in her wildest fantasies!

Although, she had to admit, he <u>was</u> handsome, in a tattooed amphibian kinda way.

The prince bowed back, slightly embarrassed by the female's awe. At least she wasn't fainting. He never knew what to say when girls swooned on him. The effect of his magnificence seemed to transcend species, which made no sense at all to Anodos.

"I like the way you see things, and I think you would be a perfect choice for the Susanita. I'm sure you have questions. What would you like to ask?" Anodos asked the Child of Electron. He knew that they had to play out this conversation to start off on the right foot.

"How do you know how I see things?" asked Leslie, kicking herself mentally for just blurting out her doubts. She hoped that her rudeness didn't screw things up—she'd come so far. Still, the captain didn't seem like someone who was careless in his choice of words. Did the walls just move? How could the walls move by themselves?

"The prince is a great prophet, the stars themselves whisper their secrets to him!" Gin-gin rebuked the pilot with a withering glare. This missy better begin to show more respect for the prince, or Gin-gin would have a word or two for the would-be pilot. Her skin began to pulse in lime green patches and the tips of her tentacles began to whip about, just a little.

Leslie had been a bit of a party girl when she crashed her second ship and was left to survive on her wits, and not much else. This was a hard town with little patience for the $cred-challenged. At first, she cried herself to sleep every night, and spent her days looking for sympathy and succor in all the wrong places. She found little of either.

Then one day she put her tears away and discovered that the rough grit of surviving had sanded away the party girl and exposed a solid core of strength she never dreamed she possessed. So, she dragged herself up out of the gutter, and didn't let anyone drag her back down. In Sincity, this was not a small thing. She was tough when she needed to be and didn't take crap from anybody.

She wasn't about to start now.

Leslie raked the arrogant kitchen-cephalopod with a look that dripped contempt for what she saw. Then she slowly but deliberately turned her back on Gin-gin and smiled at the captain with all her graces tucked in around the edges.

Gin-gin's tentacles began to thrash around as the matriarch of the family flushed emerald green and slid forward, three of her tentacles reaching for the back of the disrespectful hussy's neck. Another tentacle eased close to the pilot's right ankle. She was almost there when two of Gin-gin's senior daughters quickly moved to her side and began to stroke her, until she calmed down enough to carry on without doing anything she couldn't undo. For now.

It was a close thing.

"It is obvious to me. You have a good heart, but you're not soft. You try to see the best in people, but fully expect them to disappoint you. Yet you keep trying. You don't back down from a fight, you have great strength of will, and will never, ever crash a ship again," Anodos finally replied. He glanced at Gin-gin out of the corner of his rather large eye and saw a lot of colors of the angry variety. He sighed; it was as he expected, and so he turned his attention back to Leslie.

She stood there stunned, silent for a moment, then pretending not to be surprised by anything. This wasn't particularly convincing. She spoke. "Maybe you are a prophet after all."

"Oh, it's much more complex than that," Anodos said, pausing to consider Gin-gin's slightly-more-relaxed colors before continuing. "You will fly the Susanita to places you can't yet imagine. We will walk the Golden Path together."

There. Anodos was pleased with his answer, which covered all the bases and explained everything.

"Okay, Golden Path. Thanks!" Leslie replied, covering a wince. When she was nervous, she sounded like a half-wit even to herself. Wait—had she just gotten hired?

"Might I see the bridge where I will be living?" she asked tentatively.

Anodos lifted his right hand and gestured gracefully to Gin-gin. She bowed politely, a mannerism that she'd learned recently, before moving forward.

Gin-gin draped a tentacle casually across Leslie's shoulders, gently guiding her outside into the passageway, then down the hall to Control.

The young prince couldn't help but notice that Gin-gin's tentacle lay suspiciously close to the pilot's throat. Anodos followed them, walking the small paths to ensure that his new pilot made it to the bridge with her neck intact.

34—Koen of Summer

I stepped into the Ballroom with Navire on my right arm and Katy the Sledge on my left. The music was the kinda beat you hear in hot dance clubs in lower Gravtown on a Saturday night. Dread was in good form tonight.

A few years ago, when we were drilling this section of Fort Lilith I got it into my head that someday we'd need a big room. The size that a few hundred people wouldn't feel cramped in. Why not go big? The Ranch has lotsa room. And it was good to think ahead.

We decided on a flat-bottomed sphere cut directly into the thousands of centimeter-thick rippled layers of crystal and rock beneath Fort Lilith. I wanted it to be perfectly shaped, so Navire and a young Katy the Sledge did the measuring and precision work. Me? I was the cutter, scooping massive holes with each stroke. Big picture and all that. We all worked well together, and I remember that we laughed a lot as we cut and polished the new room. Katy the Sledge's personality was blooming like a hot-house flower around then, new discoveries every day. The day we finished, we ran and then slid across the sections around the dance floor as if gliding in Zero-G. Katy said it looked like the inside of a big ball, and the name stuck: The Ballroom.

I could never enter the room without thinking of those carefree times. They had their own unique flavor, as all times do.

The girls were once again wearing new bodies to the dance.

Navire and Katy had been fashion-brainstorming for almost a half-hour since getting home, before rushing off to the forges to make hard-bodies. At the same time, they were simultaneously perfecting their Δqm^x images that all the Ranch hands would see through their implants. All while catching up on things and monitoring our guests' entry into the Ranch. Lotsa things going on. Threaded task-management was very productive, if kinda out of reach for most of us soft-bodies. We made do just fine within the limits of the organic neurons and synapses our biology provided.

Implants helped, though.

I spent the time taking a long shower and devouring a big bowl of cioppino with a long, crisp loaf of sourdough baguette to sop up the good stuff with. Threw in a short nap in my own bed, and finished with Wudang mountain Tai Chi.

It was good to be home.

When I finished, I found out that Katy, the Gardener, and a sizable band of the E had been cooking for seven hours non-stop. The delicious odors drifted everywhere, promising all manners of deliciousness just around the corner. I slow-inhaled the scented air. Nostril memory is the most powerful of the memes, operating on a band that completely bypasses the intellect. We were looking at some serious pleasures of the table.

Tonight, Navire and Katy the Sledge were rocking matching island girls, with sleepy brown eyes and café-au-lait skin. Thick luxurious black curls cascaded down with definite anarchist tendencies. They walked with a sway, always in sync, always in perfect beat. The Children of Electron do that sometimes. That's okay, we all have our own set of skills.

Navire was wearing her matching ivory-handled needlers, as well a lotsa Shrikes, Numbsies, and Buzz rockets, as well as layered grenades with lotsa flavors. These were only matched by a wealth of blade stashed most everywhere.

The girls each had at least a half dozen bundles of sleepy-time and poison darts in their hair, accessorized perfectly with narrow throwing knives and the odd garrote braided in here and there.

To top it all off, a high-carbon steel whip wrapped around each of Navire's kick-ass boots. Katy was equally strapped-up, languidly twirling a poison rope-dart on a beautiful, velvet cord with her left hand. They were stunning.

I was the luckiest guy in the room, and of course I found myself the focus of some less than friendly looks from some of the new Horde guys. I wasn't concerned, it would pass as they came to know me. Besides, guys don't usually hold those kinda grudges; we're pretty simple creatures, compared to women. I took it as the compliment to the girls it was. Then I smiled one of the real ones and side-hugged my love and our daughter.

Been too long since we had a party.

Now here's a thing about powerful people in a position of leadership; they rarely do things in public that might end up leaving them looking foolish.

Say, throwing down a naughty soft-body rhyme to a hot Gravtown beat in front of a strange crowd. Guess the Tyrant never cared about such things, because she danced like most people only dream of. Her ever-present troika capered and slung step around her with a co-ordination you rarely found outside the professionals. Now spontaneous bouts of dancing were breaking out all over the place. These men and women hadn't had an occasion to celebrate anything for far too long. And the music _was_ smoking hot.

The soldiers seized the moment with a desperate thirst that no mere liquid could quench.

As I watched I found myself wondering how well the Tyrant fought, what styles she preferred, then pulled my attention back where it belonged—on Navire and Katy the Sledge.

Navire leaned sideways to whisper in my ear. "Did you notice anything different about the Ballroom?" with her trademark lop-sided smile. Katy was grinning at me. I tossed her a quick suspicious look and looked around.

Well the room didn't have that many parts: a wall that curved into a domed ceiling, and a floor. I looked at the wall and ceiling in surprise; there were hundreds of three-meter-wide circular archaic spotlight projectors, all coppery and deep red with a faint metallic shimmer. They contrasted nicely with the rippled layers of stone and crystal of the highly-polished wall. There were at least five hundred of the narrow-beamed spotlights bathing the dance floor and food kiosks. Other projection tubes peeked out shyly next to the spotlight projectors, maybe for confetti or dream gas. Huh. There was something very familiar about those units. Three meters across? With barrels poking out? I stared around me in shock; the combined firepower of those things were capable of vaporizing a half kilometer of solid rock. I shook my head in budding anger. This was over-kill on a massive level. Only one person around these parts was capable of dreaming up this kinda room modification.

"DREAD!?" I hollered over my implant. Katy the Sledge and Navire cracked mischievous smiles and implant-laughs.

I ignored them with the shreds of my tattered dignity clutched firmly around me.

Dread stepped into my implant with an innocent "Yes Sir?"

Like he didn't know why I was upset. Now Katy and my true love were howling with laughter; it was a good thing the music was so loud, or we'd be attracting attention of the wrong sort. I glared at Dread.

"What were you thinking? Don't you think a highly trained force protecting the Ranch is a good idea? This is not the way to make new friends!" I paused because I was trying to give up rants and figured two questions and a statement was a good place to stop.

Dread was dressed in full battle armor, and strapped up with at least forty kilos of bad-tech. He moved with the casual grace of a big-cat predator, never fully taking his eyes off our new friends. He sorta solidified into a loose attention and addressed me politely.

"I was thinking that it is *my* job to protect the Ranch, and all of you. We are outnumbered thirty to one by professionals, and I know that's not something you couldn't handle, but you shouldn't have to deal with this kinda problem in your own home. I do think it's a necessity to build a force capable of meeting all threats, and maybe delivering a few of our own. You know the Corp-nations better than I do—is this really the right team to trust with the Ranch? And lastly, I was thinking that these soldiers respect force of arms more than open arms. An offer from a position of strength has more value than from apparent weakness. Besides, they might not even identify them as threats…" he finished, trailing off with confidence in spite of my withering gaze.

I wouldn't bet on it.

Dread's reasoning was solid, if focused heavily on the tactics of force. Did we really want a military force that didn't notice the massive firepower focused on them? Hard to argue with that kinda logic. I glanced back up at the disguised sentry units, then out at the dance floor.

"We'll see pretty soon, I think," I replied as I turned to face an incoming Tyrant.

35—The Tyrant

Her name was Jenny-Rose and her title was that of Tyrant.

She was the leader of a fiercely loyal hostile-acquisitions team that had just been shredded by a seventy-five percent fatality rate, rescued by someone that might possibly be the famous battle-artiste known as the Shadower, taken home to the fabled world of long-lost Summer, and now finally wined-and-dined in an amazing dancehall studded with almost six hundred fully-armed sentry units dressed up as archaic disco spotlights.

She had to admit that it was a visually delightful mix of tech and shiny rock, if a bit passive-aggressive for her taste. While she admired the concentration of concealed firepower focused on them, the Tyrant Jenny-Rose felt herself relax just a bit. It was nice to see that their rescuers were more than capable of defending their territory. Firepower she understood and knew how to work with. This unexpected fete, not so much.

The problem was that the longer this went on without knowing the price tag, the more she resented being placed in the position of a grateful refugee. It wasn't a familiar experience. Accounts should balance, and she wasn't being notified of the multiplying salvage charges the Horde must currently be incurring. The rescue alone was going to make a sizable dent in the Horde's visible $cred balance.

This was very unprofessional behavior on their rescuers' part, yet nothing else had been less than highly-competent. Therefore, logically, there had to be a reason for this… event… even if she didn't understand it yet. "Know thy enemy, and if they're not your team, they're all your enemy" was their SOP, but this was proving difficult. Their rescuer, Koen of Summer was obviously a born leader, probably a renowned mystery fighter, and made guy-jokes that rarely made sense to her, but her boys loved.

You get to know someone a little when you're packed in together like sardines for five days, but Koen remained a cypher. He hadn't done anything suspicious, just helped out where he could, working with the team so comfortably that he had to have specialized training somewhere. He was actually starting to fit right in, and she found herself considering recruiting Koen and his team.

But now that she'd walked in the Summerlight, actually seen the mythic world of legend, what did they have to offer that compared with what he already had?

Navire – she was pretty straight-forward for a Child of Electron. She would do anything to protect Koen and her family. Anything. The Tyrant understood that, she felt the same way about her own family. She could work with that.

Pasteur—now _he_ was unblemished by subterfuge. Funny guy for a two and a half meter tall ursine with razor sharp claws. Everyone got his humor. Highly skilled healer too, saved a dozen of her team's lives with duct tape and spit; the liveShip's stores consisted of a single inadequate cupboard of medical supplies and a doc-box. Well, inadequate for a Horde. Still, Pasteur got more mileage out of it than anyone expected. His assistance was going to be expensive, but it was worth the $cred. The Horde's hidden assets might need to be tapped but they could cover it.

She considered a small band of the E working on the smorgasbord to her right.

At first, she had been hyper-aware of the little guys everyone called the E. But after a while their incessant chatter became something of a comfortable background murmur; now they blended in so well that it was hard to remember how quiet it used to be.

Her troika surrounded her closely as they approached Koen, Navire, and the young lady that must be their daughter, Katy the Sledge. A hulking warrior stood to their right, talking quietly to Koen, who looked more than a little pissed. Navire and Katy were laughing about something so hard tears sprang to their eyes, but they straightened up without hurrying and turned to meet the Tyrant's eyes as she approached. At the same time, they also gently separated arm's length from each other, with the Shadower (as she was sure he was now) protectively placed at their center.

Now, the Tyrant had looked into a mountain of eyes in her lifetime. She'd seen anger and rage, cold and calculating, lust and envy. She's seen every shade of fear and received her share of go-to-hell looks. She'd seen despair and dawning hope and pleading more than she wished. She'd seen that terrible forgiveness in the eyes of the left-behind, when one of her own went suddenly into that Dark night.

She'd looked into the eyes of true evil. And then kicked its ass.

That was what Tyrants did.

The worst of their enemies had a narcissistic indifference to everyone around them, combined with a lethal, sociopathic sense of efficiency. They measured everyone they encountered as either valuable or worthless. The valuable ones lasted longer, but not by much. Jenny-Rose had pretty much seen it all, but it had been a long time since she'd locked eyes with someone like Navire. Someone so straightforward, and deadly at the same time. Rose found herself liking the Alpha female. She hoped she didn't have to send her roughly into the Dark.

The Tyrant was drawing closer to their hosts; almost within striking distance, as she measured such things. As usual Mick and Antonio were glued in front and to the sides of her, ready for anything, even in the midst of a party. Erika, as usual, had her back.

The dance when the dangerous ones meet is surprisingly subtle. Taunts and self-aggrandizing are common tradition in the low places where bad men congregate. This is an existing protocol there that gives the bad-guys room to evaluate each other. You knew what to expect. Then the dominance thing. They play "who's the Alpha" until somebody wins. Then buy each other beer. Bad-guys of the dim persuasion are simple creatures, compared to Bad-girls of any denomination.

But that's another story.

The dangerous ones rise above this milieu. They often speak softly and never hesitate in achieving their objective, when the time reaches fullness. If the physical part of the fight happens it is usually with a forgone conclusion of who will win. It begins with small refined movements that explode into battle and then settle back into quiet. The seventh wave breaking on the sand, then leaving only foam in its dry wake as it retreats. The cadence is as old as time, if you know how to look.

36—Koen of Summer

"The Tyrant thanks you for this delightful welcome. I'm Mick, this is Antonio and Erika," Mick began, smiling broadly at Katy, and nodding to Koen and Navire. Horde protocol required a buffer between the Tyrant and strangers. "Strangers" meant anyone not Horde, and has been a polite word for "enemy" since early man climbed down out of the trees and picked up a rock to defend himself.

I guess some things never change.

The Tyrant made a small movement with her right hand, and her troika reluctantly stepped back a bit to allow her unimpeded access to their hosts.

"Nice party. Beautiful dancehall. Your artistic use of antiquated tech contrasted to the polished stone is very-fine. I especially enjoy the balance of beauty and destructiveness focused on us. Though I can't imagine that your people would escape unharmed should things fall apart," the Tyrant Jenny-Rose commented politely; complimenting, acknowledging, and threatening, all at the same time.

Not her first big-girl party.

I flashed a smile lightly laced with embarrassment at the Tyrant and glared at Dread for a blink before bowing slightly as I would to a respected opponent that might be a friend someday. "Thank you. Navire, Katy and I carved the Ballroom. My Ranch foreman, Dread, is responsible for the artwork. The Ranch is a creation of combined talent, hard work, and a generous dollop of 'why not'. Takes a lot of hands to make everything work, and we're kinda short in a few departments. We make do with what we have," I explained.

I could speak on multiple levels too.

The Tyrant tilted her head sideways for a moment, considering me. Navire painted a blinding white mule with my features on my right eye, suggesting that I lacked subtlety. I might have blinked my eyes in surprise. The Tyrant's troika were studying Navire and I suspiciously, aware that something had passed between us, but not knowing what.

"Would one of these departments be defensive forces?" the Tyrant asked softly in a low resonant voice.

"Well, as a matter of fact, yes. Seems to me that you might be free to accept a job while you regroup and rebuild your forces," I said. This time a clumsy pink elephant with my facial features thundered past in my right eye. I winced and turned to Navire for help. She took pity on me.

"We're recruiting a permanently-based force, with a respectable level of autonomy. This force would not just be employees, but become Ranch citizens, with land holdings and a share of the Ranch's revenue stream. That alone currently exceeds mercenary basic pay," Navire explained. "You would have your own base, homes, and live in the most beautiful place in the galaxy. The Ranch has lotsa room," Navire finished and tossed a micro-grin at me. Okay, maybe I said that a lot, but it was true.

***

Jenny-Rose felt a slight bit of relief at Navire's words, although she didn't allow it to show in her shoulders or carriage. Everyone had a motive for their actions that was self-centered—and now they knew what the Shadower and his people wanted. The pieces hadn't fit until now; profit alone didn't account for the efforts that were being expended on her people's behalf. The Horde wouldn't work with an unknown crew with mysterious motivations. It wasn't safe for anybody.

The Tyrant met each of her troika's eyes, gauging their reactions to the offer. Erika was the strategic master, Mick the combat tactics genius, and Antonio pulled the team into an organism that was greater than the sum of its parts. He read their people at a glance and knew just what to do to motivate the soldiers. Erika and Antonio were tempted by the idea, but Mick had doubts.

She smiled one of the bland ones at her hosts, thinking furiously. As far as the Corp-nations knew, they had gone roughly into that Dark night, never to return. No-one would be looking for them.

The Horde needed a place to rest and heal. They needed the time necessary to locate the persons responsible for their plight, and resupply. She had been considering capturing a Raider liveShip that could shelter them until it was time to return to Ciudad Tepito and reek unholy vengeance on their enemies. The problem with that scenario was the time involved, and the fact that they didn't know who their enemies were.

Even worse, the Horde had left their families, their children and loves at home in the Horde's hardened compound. There were sixty fighters guarding the compound, sufficient to protect their families in the short haul. But the longer they remained MIA, the juicier a target their families became. And someone would be watching. Someone was always watching in the Corp-cities.

Time was not on their side.

But to start a new life, free of the bloody, profit-worshiping company? Live free of the constant intrigue and random psychopathic slaughters by middle-management? To not have to worry about becoming someone's countermeasure in a war fought far above her station?

And to have a well-built home base where your family could walk freely in the shining Summerlight. To truly protect her people and have something really worthwhile to build. To be valued. To finally fight the good fight.

She was tempted too.

Jenny-Rose stepped close enough to the Ranchers to speak intimately. Her troika was trembling minutely in outrage at the security situation, but she ignored them. "We agree in concept. Details need to be determined. First, I request that you summarize our $cred salvage-debt to date. But more importantly, we have need of your resources and assistance in rescuing our families back in the Corp-nations. Time is running out, but we still have at least three weeks before our families are in real danger," the leader of the Horde finished.

I looked at Navire; she had access to the cost analysis for the detour and salvage. From that she would deduct thirty-five percent salvage value of the memory banks and assorted ship tech. She painted the numbers on my right eye in long, cascading flamingo pink characters. I studied them, then met the Tyrant's gaze.

"Seven million $credits," I stated.

She looked me calmly in the eye and said, "Twelve million. We have no need of charity".

Well.

Navire, Katy the Sledge and Dread all looked at me.

"Okay," I said. "Details to be determined." I straightened my posture.

"Welcome to the family. Your families just became mine as well. We protect the Family with our last breath. We will rescue our brothers and sisters in time," I finished solemnly, with a bow.

That was when the Gardener stepped forward with a jeroboam of Bilacart-Salmon dynasty Rose champagne (RD) from the forty-two vintage.

I smiled. So, did everyone else. Not only had we dragged home some new friends, but we were, after all, the triumphant Keer hunters' home from the Dark places. Complete with a trap full of snoozing Keer dressed up like some kinda disco monsters. Though, the Horde didn't know about that yet…

Anyway, I'd say that called for a glass of the good stuff. I held my crystal flute up into one of the counterfeit spotlight beams. The music quieted, and everyone turned to look at the Tyrant and her troika, at Navire and Katy and Dread. But mostly they looked at me. I waited a few blinks until I had everyone's attention, then loudly declared "Welcome to the family! Welcome home. Welcome to Summer!"

After a blink-long pause everyone burst into cheers.

37—The Prince

It was launch day aboard the Susanita, and the excitement in the air was something you could taste in broad-spectrum swatches.

Leslie was nestled securely in the center of the bridge, firmly embedded in the hardware she'd spent three decades building and upgrading.

She was currently completing the final transformation from deadShip to liveShip to the cheers of her loyal crew. Okay, maybe not cheers, but everyone seemed pretty happy that it was launch day. And perhaps "loyal" was too strong a word, but no one was trying to strangle her at the moment.

Her new captain was in an excellent mood, as well. The Susanita gleamed from tip to stern; only the casino still had a fair amount of work to go. It would be ready in time for their first port of call, a small mining colony called World's End. The restaurant and bar were stocked, and the ship stores were sufficient for now. Robin, the owner of the used-ship dealership was on board for the departure celebration and the free drinks—although Anodos had seen that the real reason was that he was feeling sentimental, not that he'd ever admit it.

Anodos had told him that they would definitely see him again. He had seen it. The ancient puck had smiled at him with a bit of loneliness tucked in around the corners before it was quickly concealed beneath the more-usual salesman's grin.

Eventually the free bar was cut off, and shortly thereafter the neighbors headed back to their own slips. The Père in engineering finished his last checks, and Captain Anodos stood in the middle of his bridge, shuffling the small paths for the most auspicious launch time. Gin-gin and her senior daughters manned life-support, which was humming along in perfect order, and the Stones were settled down along the port wall, faded from the general awareness of the crew.

At the captain's command Leslie took wing to the enthusiastic cheers of her crew (really!), easing out of their berth before rotating and sedately heading for the exit. Part of her whispered that she should take the bit in her mouth and gallop as fast as she could to freedom, but it was only a whisper. The liveShip pilot ignored the small voice; she would see Sincity in her exhaust soon enough. And it was.

Soon enough.

***

Kid Callo was chasing the muse, traveling the stars from colony to colony. He played Note like an angel, but he knew he was still raw and unrefined. He wandered the stars with his collapsible-keyboard, and he worked mostly rent-parties, always in search of new-data note and chops.

He needed the naughty rhyme in the baddest way; he and his intelligent keyboard. When he'd heard about a sizzling party-pueblo out there in the Dark, he cadged his way there, chopping note for his bread and a ride. Some days everything worked out perfectly. Others, well, that was when the Kid ended up stuck in a rock with an inbred miner population after all the good musicians had moved on.

So here he was, with no ride out, and nobody else left to lay down that rail with a syncopate slant. Keyboard sang alone just fine, but it was in the jam that the Kid and his instrument truly shined. He played his heart out and on occasion brought tears to even the most hardened of eye. At first the Kid chopped note in the raggedy time of the young and boisterous. But his soul craved more; he wanted to play multilevel lite-motif in ever-higher key, his keyboard pounding out naughty rhyme that climbed all the way to heaven. You don't learn that kinda music from a book—you had to chase it down and make it your own under the hot spotlight. Even if that took you to the strangest places. Like now, the Kid couldn't for the life of him remember what possessed him to linger in this rock after the liveShip sailed.

Oh yeah, it was a girl.

Problem was, her daddy wanted him to lay down his keyboard and come to work for him in the pitchblende mines. Settle down and chop rock instead of note.

That hadn't worked out too well.

The Kid had the rambling habit and was incapable of staying someplace after the music died. So here he was, the sole entertainment in a half-empty spacer guild bar. He got three beers a night, and dinner, plus tips.

He'd waited for a ride out in far worse places.

Kid Callo was always in search of someplace better, somewhere the music was scorching hot, the piano was strident, with new-data note blooming all over the place. Now he was patiently waiting for a ride to the next rent-party, or maybe even a paid gig. He just hoped the mysterious liveShip named the Susanita had a place for a wandering Note-smith in search of a little excitement.

***

Gin-gin had led her clan across the Dark for decades and knew well how to loosen up an isolated mining population. It began with tendrils of marvelous aromas creeping into the closed-air system of the small colony-town. The enticing odors were mysterious and complex on the nose, and nothing at all like they were used to. That in itself was enough to draw a crowd. Something fresh didn't come around very often, and it had been deadly quiet since the Ronin musicians had drifted on.

Most of the miners decided to unsuit and wash up early; something new was in the air. The first guests didn't show up for a half-hour. Everyone wanted to put on a fresh dress or hard-body for the occasion.

***

Aboard the Susanita, the young prince was standing on a well-pillowed platform raised a meter above the deck on one side of the main chamber. The ballroom contained both the casino, and the bar, with a dance-floor between the two. Anodos could see everything from his position. The Stones that Speak were at his sides, but no one noticed them because they were doing their fade thing.

He looked out over the small crowd. They stared back, a little quiet for a moment, but that didn't last long. Miners aren't exactly easily impressed, and while a six-meter-long salamander captaining an entertainment liveShip wasn't something they saw every day, the delicious smells from the buffet and the well-stocked bar held a stronger attraction.

Gin-gin and her daughters were quite busy; their tentacles deftly serving up savory snacks and potent cocktails, while the Père and his boys ran the gaming tables and the obvious security. Leslie and the Stones were the less visible options: security is much simplified when the boss walks the paths of future tense. Business was already booming, and the intoxicants flowed to the chimes and bells of the casino tables. The kitchen had to kick into high gear; Gin-gin had underestimated how much buffet food the miners could put away.

199

A lean muscled, wiry teenager had shown up with the crowd, and requested the age-old benefits of Ronin musicians; the chance to play for their dinner and three beers, plus tips.

The young prince had been waiting for this particular moment for a long time, because the Kid was going to be an intricate part of their journey down the Golden path and played a significant part in the team the prince was putting together. You couldn't tell how special he was just by looking at him, but he would one day be one of the masters. Anodos studied him fondly, watching the young man's hands as they whirled across the keyboards. He watched curiously as the striding movement of Kid Callo's left hand as it laid down an octave-chord base-pattern that began to alternate syncopations with his right hand. With the left hand freed to jam with the right, they built syncopating counter-melodies together, well-salted with harmonic chords that contrasted brightly with the higher-octave Note. The music was still crude, and a bit ragged, but in it laid the seeds of greatness. The miners didn't care—they were a bit crude themselves. The dance floor populated rapidly to the sizzling beat. Even Anodos found himself swaying in rhythm to the blurring hands of burgeoning genius.

The Kid was finally home, even if he didn't know it yet.

38—Koen of Summer

The Keer-trap sat quietly in the center of the new garage, with no indication that its innocuous hull concealed six deadly predators with a taste for human flesh. Smitty stepped up to the ribbon-fouled hatch, and manually cranked it open. Atmosphere had been trickling into the trap over the past three days, equalizing the low-pressure interior with the Ranch air, so there was no hissing or vapor announcing the change. The Hive scientists said that the Keer should be immobilized by their meal for at least three more months, but this was the moment of truth. Wouldn't be the first time I risked my life on a theory that the Hive smart-boys came up with. I was still alive, so it had worked out so far.

Navire eased past me, knowing that her current hard-body could take a lot more punishment than my biological soft-body. Only the Children of Electron can switch bodies as easily as I change clothes. That was okay, I was doing just fine with the one I was born with.

As usual, I didn't say anything to Navire; she was very protective of me and the rest of her family. Over the cycles we had grown accustomed to each other's idiosyncrasies and didn't need to discuss the small things anymore. We had become a very efficient team, especially in battle. That was why I was a little surprised when Navire spoke quietly in my implant as we made our way inside the airlock to the interior of the trap.

"I don't trust that woman," Navire began. *"She's up to something, and did you see how she looked at you? Like you were a juicy steak, and she hadn't eaten in a while!"*

Now I was concerned. I relied on Navire's analytical judgement as much as I relied on my legs to carry me forward. This was more than a little unexpected, for her.

"Why didn't you say anything earlier?" I asked, a bit annoyed. We had just welded our fates to the Tyrant and her people. The fact that Navire waited until now to express her doubts just didn't make sense.

Smitty tossed me a quick guy-grin, hearing only one side of the conversation in the small space. He immediately moved to the interior airlock hatch and began removing the shiny filaments from the entry with a large hand blade. He was making a little more noise than necessary to give us the dubious privacy to talk. I didn't know what to think. I knew one thing; if Navire didn't make sense, then I just didn't have all the pieces.

Navire always made sense.

The hatch to the inner trap made a loud squeal in the small space as Smitty got it open. I waited patiently for her to speak while Smitty escaped into the main trap.

"I found the decision pathways to this conclusion to be less than clear. I didn't want to say anything until I was more certain that I had interpreted her motives correctly. I'm still not sure why I feel this so strongly on so little new-data," Navire explained in a soft, unsure voice.

I couldn't remember a time when she had sounded this uncertain. I rested my hand on her rigid shoulder for a blink before dropping it to enter the interior of the trap. "We'll talk about this later, okay?" I asked. In answer Navire painted a florescent cobalt bow on my finger through my implant, as a reminder. I was glad that I was the only one who could see it, because going in to see the man-eating Keer with a bow tied around me just seemed like tempting fate.

The beribboned Keer were huge. We could only see them by the disco shine of the long filaments tangled around their bodies, but there was lotsa ribbon. Lotsa Keer. The digesting form was hidden under a shell-like armored mound with only the legs and antenna sticking out. Everything else, including the fearsome mouth and mandibles, was protected.

After a moment we moved closer to the party monsters, close enough to touch, despite our inability to tactilely sense them beneath our hands. It was an unsettling lack of feeling. I was very aware of the apex predator's proximity, but my primary senses were blind.

That was okay, it was kinda like fighting with blindfolds. You didn't actually need to look at your opponent to defeat him, there were other ways of seeing. I met Smitty's eyes, then Navire's. We had a purpose, and the sooner we got to it, the sooner we'd all be a little safer. We were here to brand our little herd.

The Hive-tech that we implanted under the tough, unseen hide was scattered all through the shell and underneath that to the torso and rear. The stealth smart-tech nodules would paint Δqm^x quality images we all could see through our implants. The nodules were not completely passive either, we also had the theoretical option of shorting out the muscular synapses of their legs, paralyzing the great beasts for up to eight minutes at a time. We called it roping.

For the first time ever, these six Keer were no longer going to be undetectable to our many senses.

It took a while, but after branding the last Keer we took a moment to look over the slumbering monsters that surrounded us.

"These great alpha-carnivores are creeping me out. Notice their antenna?" Smitty asked.

I took a good look. The sensory organs in question were all pointing the same direction. Directly at us.

I suddenly realized that my spacial awareness of the giant predators had turned into something else when I wasn't looking. Something that went all the way back to when my primitive ancestors huddled around a fire while something big and hungry prowled restlessly, just outside of the flickering light.

Something waiting for the fire to die down.

"They're watching us," Navire confirmed.

"Umm, okay… time for a beer," I suggested, urging Smitty and Navire out of the Keer trap ahead of me. No need to linger once the work was done.

Thirty minutes later Katy the Sledge, dressed in her touring-train, pulled out at high speed fully-loaded with our immediate family: Navire, Pasteur, the Gardener, Smitty, Dread, the full complement of the E, and yours truly. We were headed out to celebrate our successful roundup in Crystal Ocean Thirteen.

We were going to spend the day at the beach.

I love how the ocean smells and its gentle sounds, its ceaseless motion. The salt water ocean in Crystal Thirteen is seventeen kilometers long, and nine wide. The optically clear top is almost six kilometers above us and the whole thing hangs in the sky, with powerful waves of Summerlight cascading down to reflect upon the water. The lightest of tints from mineral impurities in the giant crystal filters the light into bands of gold.

***

I stand motionless for a moment in the warmth of the vintage light, bathing in its ardor.

The Summerlight pours down like honey on the salt air.

It feels very-fine.

It's also very bright; I set my Stealthsuit transparent to the good spectrums and dialed the portion covering my eyes to a dark protective reflection. Pasteur, Smitty, and the E are all styling sunglasses. Navire, Katy, and Dread of course, have no need for exterior filters like us soft-bodies.

I am in the center of the circular surface of one of the numerous pillars that dot the ocean. These simple edifices range from forty meters to over three hundred across and hang about fifteen meters above the water's surface. When the enormous crystal was hollowed out, these sections were simply sculpted out and remained as part of the design. The bigger ones have tropical gardens and fresh water pools. The exterior of the crystal islands was roughly finished, so that the structures were translucent rather than clear. Stretched between the islands are hanging shellfish habitats. Some hold emerald green seaweed beds that wave gently, dancing in the mild current. Enough gaps are left to allow the schools of salmon and scattered magenta lobster unimpeded movement. This ocean is only eight years old.

I wonder what it will look like in a century.

Today we picked a moderately sized island, with a small coconut grove and mango trees that spread their arms wide. An airy bamboo structure provides shade without stifling the cool ocean breeze. The E are pressurizing a few kegs of the good stuff and setting up the bar. Smitty was building layers of wood in the barbecue pit and Katy spun a playlist heavy on bass, Caribe style. Dread applied precision flame to the wood and a mesquite trill cut the salty air in pungent breeze. The Gardener, Katy and I were unpacking chilled nibbles for grazing and pairing with session ales that refreshed the palette without filling you up.

***

When everyone had finished setting up, grins were spreading like wildfire. Then the moment reached fullness, and Katy shouted "Go", and everyone ran for the edges of the platform, all the while hollering primitive war cries. Pasteur's was downright frightening, and he was just having a good time. When we reached the edge, we leapt out and then down, to enter the perfect waters in varying states of grace.

The cool shock and auditory roar of diving in felt so good that I was momentarily surprised. I suspect that the best of simple pleasures are easily forgotten, especially when we spend so much time out there in the Dark places. The pure joy of rediscovery always astonishes me with its intensity. I surfaced and rolled to my back, leisurely stroking my way to the sparkling sands of the tiny beach around the base of the platform.

After a delightful lunch of grilled prawns, sweet peppers and couscous we were relaxing in the bamboo shelter, sipping a pale ale that was well-hopped, but not overpoweringly so. We were watching the E as they came to a consensus as only the E do.

You see, they begin with everyone talking so boisterously that I couldn't understand a thing anyone said. As time passed, individuals would sporadically quiet down and focus on other speakers who make more sense to them. It's a lengthy process. We were at the point where only three individuals were still speaking nonstop, the rest gazing at them with rapt attention. Finally, one of the three stopped speaking and turned to focus on one of the remaining two orators.

"We're getting close, should be any minute and we'll know what they're stirred up about," Smitty commented lazily. Smitty and I have known the E longer than anyone else and have seen this process hundreds of times. It takes lotsa time, but by the time the process is over, all the E are of one mind. Sure beats human quibbling's and social drama. I said as much, and Pasteur snorted in amusement. He finds most people to be unnecessarily complicated. Can't say I disagree.

Navire was lovely in the streaming Summerlight that dappled through the mango leaves. She was wearing an island girl hard-body that was so realistic that it extruded tiny beads of sweat on her upper lip. Ebony curls rolled down her shoulders all the way to her voluptuous hips. She lounged in a hammock like the rest of us, curled in sensuous feline style, slow rocking. Huge almond eyes with belladonna pupils, laughing.

She slung me a lop-sided smile and I tossed it back with interest. She painted a jade crown on the last E remaining after his opponent finally tossed in the hat and joined him, drawing my attention to the remaining orator.

I straightened, well, as much as one can straighten while swinging gently in a string hammock holding a half-full glass of beer.

The half-meter-tall furry guy was solemn as he approached me, a full complement of E in coordinated formation around him. His bronze fur was crisscrossed with minimal beach wear; battle harness with only a handful of Boom, but a wealth of blade. He was one of the senior warriors of the E.

"We request the honor of shaving the Keer. The Keer down is priceless, and we are very brave. A mere sixty percent share of the proceeds would be an acceptable fee for our service," said the little guy in a high, rapid voice before baring his teeth broadly in imitation of an innocent smile.

I choked on my beer, and almost blew foam out of my nose. Smitty fell in one of those laughs that consist of short pants before breaking out in a full-blown howl of mirth.

Pasteur tossed off the rest of his massive stein, smacked his lips reflectively, and began to howl in laughter as well. Katy the Sledge blew steam-whistle hoots and Navire was holding her tummy; she was laughing so hard it hurt. The Gardener was chuckling but that was it. He lived in tune with the flora, and the vagaries of the fauna were of little interest. However, he was part of the family, and if everyone else was laughing, he would too. Even if he hadn't quite caught the punchline.

"You already have twenty percent shares. You're going to be wealthy already. Maybe an extra four percent," I offered, in a dance as old as time. He smiled in acknowledgement, and we began to negotiate as old friends do; with affection and insult, until we found the place between us.

We clasped forearms, and the deal was struck.

Time to sheer our little herd.

The E are, despite how easy they are to hang out with, a warrior race.

They value bravery highly and are fearless fighters. Because of the relative size-difference out here, the focus is on unit tactics. This allows them to make up for the fact that most species are three to four times their size and have a reach that is downright unfair. E teamwork is raised to a level unknown by opposing fighters. Kukri blades and shotguns helped too, as did an extensive arsenal of Boom.

Ten little guys shooting at you usually beats a couple of large targets firing back. Bad Enemies. Good friends.
Like that.

I also knew shaving an enemy had a special meaning for the E.

When one of their own has done something so horrifying that allowing them to simply pass into the Dark is too merciful, the punishment for the offender is to be ritually shaved of his beautiful, luxurious fur. This is a terrible humiliation. It is something an E sees maybe once in a lifetime.

Yet all E prepare for that day and carry an archaic razor whose providence is lost in the fog of time. This is a small part of the warrior training all E go through, and the chance to use the skills so carefully learned was very exciting! Especially while being extremely well paid for it!

The coming "Night of the Razors" was all anyone could talk about for the rest of the day, and of course, everyone would share in the preparations. There was a pronounced air of barely-restrained glee; bouts of blade juggling and sparring kept breaking out—the E knew how to have a good time while working. And talking.

Lotsa talking.

***

Luckily, the E had come to a consensus already, otherwise we would be here all evening. There were four teams of six E, a very small cluster by their standards. The other E squeezed in around the slumbering Keer, filling the Keer trap, and spilling out into the new garage in a fan that you had to see to believe. I think every E on the Ranch was here, and there were a lot more of them than I had realized. All the surrounding E were gossiping and pointing at the crouching monsters their steam-punk goggles allowed them to see. This was no gentle murmur of the crowd; it was more like a mild roar.

I turned to Pasteur. "Just how many E do I have on the payroll?" I asked.

"All of them," he replied with a straight face before dissolving into laughter. Well, as much as a two-and-a-half-meter tall hairy bear can dissolve; I quickly joined him in laugh-land. Guy-humor—it leavens my day with moments of refreshing absurdity.

However, on reflection, I decided that this still worked for me. Besides, the E kept the books. No conflict of interest there, right?

I turned back to the teams of E creeping up on the disco-ribboned Keer. They actually didn't need to sneak; the Keer were incapable of movement in their current state. It was just more fun this way. The crowd quieted (slightly) as the diminutive warriors stopped briefly with-in reach of the Keer. Then they sprang into action as Katie cut loose with a Strut perfectly synced with the movements of the teams. It was glorious.

Half the E were wielding miniature cutting tools that we normally use to clear Crystal. The other halves were harnessed with a modified vacuum torrent on their wrists, with molecular filters that would capture the Keer-down as it was cut. These guys were also brandishing a high-carbon straight razor half the length of their arms. It looked extremely sharp.

A brazen sax meandered in out of the cold and began to banshee wail. The drums stepped up and began to naughty rhyme with the rogue sax. Tube horn got all jealous and threw down a syncopated beat in sultry stout-boy style. Drums slid to the background so gently you never even heard them move. Keyboards crept out of the woods and strutted down rhythm road, shameless in that glorious beat. It was very-fine.

The tunnelers were making slow but steady progress through the layered laminated armor we'd laid down just a month before. After enough time had passed that everyone not E was running out of things to talk about, the cutters stepped back to reveal broad tunnels under the Keer, deep enough for the E not to have to crouch.

They had hollowed most of the space beneath each Keer, and incidentally, uncovered a frightening view of the Keer's mandible-framed mouth. It was much bigger than anyone expected. Corrosive drool dripped off of the Keer's mandibles in slow time, to splat sullenly on the floor of the freshly carved caves.

The E were fearless, but they nevertheless moved very carefully under the drooling monsters to position themselves in precise locations. They softly (for the E) gossiped among themselves as they pulled their high-carbon steel Keer-razors open and prepared to get to work. Navire's eye-gnat's signal was being relayed to everyone by implant, so we didn't miss any of the gory details.

The E held their straight razors cocked in their left hands, while their right held the collector nozzle close to the cutting edge. We all held our breath as the blade met the invisible down and scraped sinuously across the Keer's hide. (With the exception of the E, of course, they needed their breath to keep a running dialog going).

About this time several clusters of E onlookers began pointing at the disco-monster's exposed talons; they were clenching slightly and cutting up the armored surface of the Keer trap. This wasn't supposed to be possible, and a chill shot across my body as I thought of the ant-shark-monster looming above my friends suddenly waking up.

Nobody moved for a brief period, before cautiously returning to their deadly task when nothing bad happened.

It ended up taking longer than I expected, but we eventually finished and secured the rare Keer-down before cutting huge disks of digesting Keer from the trap's surface, and relocating the beasts to the labyrinth range everyone called the Shimmering.

39—Auntie Tao

Auntie Tao was wearing an arch-type wise woman hard-body. She was always of a certain age, with long silver hair, and carried herself with an economy of motion and the graceful bearing of a Lui Tai Chi master. Her weapons were restrained in a manor one only found within the safety of the Hive—only a dozen showing: the Hive equivalent of pajamas.

Her eyes were full of timeless serenity embedded in the moment; she lived in the Now endlessly, her massive intellect evolved to function skillfully in this intuitive state of consciousness.

Auntie Tao had millennia of experience rocking parallel thought-streams, had developed massive resources to pull from, and lead nations of tirelessly loyal workers who achieved anything she wished.

They even say she was born on earth in its mythical days, before the old world died. I didn't know about that, but I did know that the Hive was a power to be reckoned with. Auntie Tao was every worker's enlightened Mother, and her people would do anything to protect and help her. I knew—I had once been her people, and willing to do anything as well.

The Δqm^x pod I was nestled in had interfaced with my implant, and virtually-transported me light-years to this meeting with my former boss. If any relationship with Auntie Tao can be considered former, she still considered me her child, despite that I was all grown up for many cycles now. I thought of Katy the Sledge and found some small understanding thrust upon me. I guess our children are always our children, no matter how far they stray.

We had tea at a low table with an abundance of cushions.

The tea was classic Hive silver-leaf, hand rolled into tiny balls that blossomed when immersed in hot H_2O. Something about the enzymes in the human hand made it unique. It was delicious.

After we politely exchanged pleasantries, I got down to the matter at hand.

"I brought you a gift," I said, handing her a virtual fine-woven bag containing a respectable (but not lavish) amount of Keer-down.

"Koen, you're always so thoughtful, thank you," she replied as she picked up the small bag to examine the contents. "Very thoughtful," Auntie Tao corrected herself as she ran her fingertips across the rare down.

I set a larger, thicker bag on the table and leaned back to examine her response. It was subtle, as all her actions are. But I'd known her for most of my life.

Slowly, Auntie Tao leaned slightly forward, and smiled one of those real ones you hardly ever see these days. She nodded her head slightly to urge me to continue.

"I've been thinking," I said.

Auntie Tao spoke body-language very well. This phrase said, "You have my attention".

I smiled back one of the true ones; I had been thinking about how to phrase this for weeks. Auntie Tao's command and preciseness in all communication was legendary.

"It's been a longtime since we updated the Stealthsuits. I believe it might be time for a re-engineering and the construction of a new Stealthsuit. I want to utilize new components and full implant utilization. Very limited release; only a handful possible in the beginning" I leaned slightly forward as well.

"I think we should build a new living armor with advanced capabilities that have previously been out of reach".

"With new components like this?" the Hive queen asked softly, lifting the new, larger bag to peek inside. I inclined my head in polite agreement.

"Yes, like that," I said.

"This looks like significantly more down than a single Keer contains, how many did you harvest for me?" asked the Hive queen very quietly. I tensed involuntarily; Auntie Tao is at her deadliest when she goes all quiet. Of course, she read my reaction and released a small smile of contentment—I apparently could still be manipulated by what was for all intents and purposes my mother. I frowned, and she laughed, the kinda laugh that included you instead of mocking you. I had forgotten how that sounded out there in the Dark.

"I have the down of four Keer for our project," I admitted. I had learned a long time ago that showing all your cards in a negotiation was not a good strategy.

"I'll contribute the down of two Keer for the project; what kinda $creds do you offer for your share?" I asked bluntly. Spend enough time around the Hive queen, and directness develops a surprising attractiveness, despite its crudity in polite company.

"Perhaps two billion $creds?" Auntie Tao suggested. My turn.

"A decent beginning, but I believe you misplaced a decimal point," I replied off-handedly.

Two more cups of tea, and we settled on nine billion per Keer, a total of eighteen billion in mixed Hive trade-balance and assorted colony properties on eleven worlds.

The Ranch was now funded for the next five cycles, even including the Horde's payroll. As an added bonus, I would have a new Stealthsuit that had the capacity to be invisible. I stood, bowing to the Hive queen in genuine respect, as always.

Auntie Tao stood up with a grace that only Tai Chi masters are capable of, returning my bow with a precision us soft-bodies can only dream of.

"I'll bring you the Keer-down in a week, at a mutually agreed upon meeting site," I confirmed, and unlinked from the Δqm^x pod.

Navire was waiting for me.

40—Koen of Summer

The tables were laid out with white tablecloths that gently swayed in the mild breeze. Summerlight fell in waves to dapple richly through the bamboo awnings onto the laden tables. A lightstorm battled its way across far Summer in sheets of magenta that were torn by jagged electric-blue spears. Nearby, static electricity flashed in counterpoint to the lightstorm's progress. It was beautiful in a manner that I never tired of or grew complacent with. In a place of wonders, lightstorms were royalty. Except of course, when you're caught out in one. I suspect true beauty has always has a frightening side.

This was the first time any of the Tyrant's people had been to Crystal Four, a vineyard and agricultural habitat. Around us, green trellised rows of mourvedre grapes seemed to run all the way to the luminescent sky surrounding us.

The Horde seemed enchanted with the view, in a slightly noisy manner. Summerlight has always had a quality that I associate with mid-afternoon, which was appropriate today, because it was. We were seated on raised decks above the vines, at long, family style dining tables; twenty people per table, six tables in all. The tables were simply dressed in cream linen that hung all the way to the floor. Running down the center of the tables were a tapestry of fresh cut woven vines, complete with grape leaves and bunches of fully ripe Pinot Noir grapes. They cascaded down the table in a flood of opulent dark purple, weaving between large format wine bottles of a Valpolicella that was made from grapes partially raisined in the rich Summerlight, three vintages ago. The Gardener had fretted about the mismatched table decorations, but I assured him that no one would notice. Besides, the Valpolicella was the only wine we had that was ready to drink in the quantities that we expected a hundred soldiers to consume.

We still ran out.

At our table, the Tyrant Jenny-Rose was sitting across from Navire and me, as were her troika, Mick, Erika, and Antonio. On my other side sat Smitty, my oldest friend. Then Pasteur, and Dread. On Navire's side sat Katy the Sledge, then the Gardener. The troika's officers filled out the remaining seats.

I nodded, and the E, who were working this party, began filling everybody's crystal-ware with a sparkling Rosè from Nouveau Reims colony. The Gardener's Δqm^x tasting courses were developing our palates rapidly, as was a minor trade imbalance with the colony. We'd have to find a new Ranch product to export to balance things out, but we had lotsa choices.

The champagne was a grown-up sister to the nascent grapes nestled in the green vines strewn before us. I tilted my crystal flute to show the wine against the white of my cloth napkin. The delicate cranberry hue at the rim promised a fresh, lighter-bodied wine, one unbruised by excessive contact with oxygen.

I inhaled, my nose tickling at the CO_2 mini-bursts as the wine gently fizzed. Bright, clean strawberry and brioche. Brioche made with plenty of butter like the old days. Very small bubbles. Nice.

I raised my glass and channeled my voice through the Horde's new Ranch implants, so everyone could easily hear me.

"I find a deep satisfaction in working the soil and sea, in producing culinary specialties that feed lotsa people. I find a solidity of purpose in working the Ranch, in developing new Crystals into balanced eco-habitats that grace the eyes as well as the belly." I paused to sip my champagne.

"I take sensual pleasure in the vintage light that Summer bathes us in. Now, these things are yours as well. Take pride in this work, as we do. Let us enjoy the fruits of our labor!" I finished, raising my glass to the family.

"Oh, and don't worry, there will be plenty of opportunities to kick ass—it's hardly ever quiet around here" I added, almost as an afterthought.

It's good to be cheered.

I pulled in a mouth-rich dollop and chewed it gently, so it would reach all my scattered taste buds. Let it trickle down the back of my throat, the flavors vaporizing in the warmth of my throat and taking the back door up to my nostrils.

Cause it's all about the nose, in the end.

I smiled at Navire, who returned it with a lopsided grin that had love tucked in all around the corners. We were politely interrupted by one of the troika, Erika.

"This is fun, and everything's beautiful, but I'm worried about our families back in Tepito. Do you have a plan?" she asked. All of the Tyrant's people at our table focused on our conversation, as did many of the soldiers auditing by implant from the other tables. I leaned forward.

"That's one of the things we're going to talk about tonight. My team…" I paused, then corrected my words. "The Ranch hands need to know what Ciudad Tepito's like, hear the stories before we can begin to plan this properly. We're all on the same team now, but there's lotsa new-data to be exchanged," I suggested, "Then we will get to work on finding the right stratagem for the mission," I finished, returning my eyes to the Tyrant.

Up to this point, the Tyrant Jenny-Rose had been content to let her troika carry the conversation. Now she leaned forward with panther grace and placed her elbows on the table in a deceptively casual manner. Her hands met in a loose fist, the apex of the triangle her arms and the table formed. She met my eyes with a clear gaze above the fist.

"Sir, let me summarize the situation. In the busted-up moon Deffey is a large Corp-nation colony named Tepito. Deffey has a big chunk missing, exposing the mineral rich interior. Tepito sits almost halfway down, and over ninety-eight percent of it is burrowed into the moon in a series of passageways, chambers, and green belts that cluster atop each other like a snake pile.

"Off to the moon surface side is the Horde's compound. Our compound is large enough for a thousand people to feel comfortable in. At the moment it holds only two-hundred and sixty-seven of us, of which sixty are crack soldiers, tasked with protecting their charges against all threats.

"The compound is armored in layer upon layer of Nano-carbon webs coated in hardened silicon crystals. Interspersed between the webs are five-meter thick ceramic durocrete sections.

"Each layer is not, by itself invulnerable; it can be chewed through slowly. But this would be quite loud. There are so many layers that we would hear them coming weeks out. There are two main entrances, and a number of less official means of egress" the Tyrant finished.

The pause she left was only long enough to register before it disappeared. "There are always people watching, waiting for a possible weakness to take advantage of. Someone is sure to notice our prolonged absence soon, if not already. Over half of our missions are concluded in less than five days, travel time not included. Some missions have lasted as long as ninety days, but not many. We conclude that we have a point at about sixty days out when the testing of our defenses becomes serious. We are at day thirty-eight right now". Again, a short pause. She took another sip of her champagne, and a tiny smile whisked across her face before she continued.

"You will pass through at least six checkpoints on the way, probably more. My people are very well-known. While a few of us might make it through, most of the Horde are unmistakable; our very gait gives us away. Usually this is a matter of pride, not concern. You, however, could take a small team in and get our families to transportation where we will be waiting. If we think you're taking too long, or that the mission is blown, we're coming in after you," she stated. "A full-frontal assault will produce high casualties, and is not usually our way, but the Horde never leaves anyone behind. Ever." The Tyrant Jenny-Rose leaned back from her forward position, apparently having said what she intended to say. Her people gave a short, low-frequency hoot in unison.

I guess pretty much everyone had been auditing our conversation.

I smiled with appreciation at the concise description of the problem before us. I could get used to working with people who had this kinda well-honed intellect. They were really going to like Hive battle language, I abstractly thought to myself, before pulling my attention back to the tableau before me.

"Thank you, Tyrant. I suspect that the new members of the family will enjoy working with the kinda competence we all embody, each to our own specialties. As will the older family Ranch hands," I said, looking around our table at my brothers and sisters of many species.

"I understand that we broke ground on your new compound today—one buried deep beneath the surface of the Ranch. Congratulations! I hear that it's going to be quite expansive; the Ranch has plenty of room to spare, so why not?" I could pause for effect too! I moved on to the next subject.

"Your patrols over Ranch land are effective, but sparse. The bottleneck is the production of the new fliers. While we've had the designs and material for some time, we just didn't have the manpower to deploy them. Now we do. Therefore, we are expanding the number of forges devoted to this work. In the meantime, any new-data on the fliers from the pilots is welcome; we'd like to catch any flaws in the unit's performance before producing them all. Now, why don't we relax and enjoy the meal?" I finished .

The next course was palm heart salad with a five-cycle balsamic we made over in Crystal Garden One. We used the less desirable lots of wine we always seemed to end up with. Made great vinegar though, especially the cask strength ones. Those I didn't dilute to make it go further like the vinegar producers in the colonies. My stuff is thick and dark and bursting with flavor. I bottled it in garnet-crystal decanters and called it the Tart.

I had built a small following in some of the better kitchens in Gravtown. Not a big piece of business, but it was efficient use of resources and served a need. Plus, I never had to wait for a table at those restaurants.

The Gardener paired a Semillon from Nouveau Fonsac colony with the salad. Beautiful nose of lemongrass and honeydew melon with this strange, wild honey finish that wasn't at all sweet. It was delicious. That was when Navire painted a bright yellow pig nose on the Tyrant just as I emptied my wine glass; I burst out laughing and almost choked on my mouthful of wine.

Everyone at our table got excited for a moment.

The breeze brought minty chlorophyll and a pungent, woody scent, cooling us under the shifting sky.

Good times.

41—Koen of Summer

It seemed that the nearby Hives were too hot to handle the transfer of the Keer down. We eventually decided it was time for a visit to Gravtown. $creds, dinner and a show! Everyone wanted to go.

We decided that we would meet Auntie Tao's team in the district where the music was hot and the company dangerous. Where the movers and shakers got together on a Saturday night. Where sax fought piano, searing the smoke-laced air with wicked beat, where sweat-lubricated dancers spun complex magic on the dance floor. That's right.

We were going to Small's Paradise Club, in legendary east Gravtown.

Katy the Sledge insisted on handling transportation; she said it was what she was born to do. Maybe, but we all knew the truth was that she had risen far beyond her original programming, as do all the best of us.

She said that "Running Train" on a mission, carrying her family to fight the good fight, was the task she had always wanted to do when she was growing up.

Navire hugged me and softly said "it's time" in my implant. I didn't want to see Katy put away the things of childhood, but I was proud of the woman she was becoming. I guess this was the bittersweet part of being a man, of raising a daughter. Of being a father.
Didn't much care for this part. But I accepted it.

And, of course, I'd tear anyone who hurt her to little pieces.
Like that.

The Tyrant and her troika would be part of the core team, as well as Smitty, Pasteur, and Navire. Backing us up were the Horde teams everyone called "Trail-breakers." Big bruisers; soft-spoken and just oozing competence out of their very pores. Heavily armored, strapped up with extensive battle harnesses weighed down with a wealth of Boom, not to mention razor-edged titanium crow-bars and heavy water shotguns. Wreaths of tactical breeching charges were draped over shoulders that stood taller than my head. And I wasn't a little guy. I had no doubt that if we called for help, these warriors wouldn't let anything stand in their way. But inconspicuous? Not even a little.

That was why we were also running three of the spook teams known as "Scouts;" these boys and girls were infiltration specialists and new-data gatherers of the highest caliber.

The plan was this: the scouts would precede us into the club by an hour or so, and secure tactically superior positions around the club. Navire and I would join the Tyrant, accompanied her troika, at their table for the second show at Small's Paradise. Smitty and Pasteur would arrive late, just as the show was starting and sit at the bar, doing the "big-picture" thing. Their role was watching over us as our own personal guardian angels.

We were all pretty jazzed, because White-haired Jack and some young horn they called Sid Slayer were headlining the night. We hadn't seen Jack in at least six cycles. Katy would be auditing our implants from her train in long-term parking; no way was she missing out on seeing a master of the Neo-Strut and a new talent nobody ever heard of!

Auntie Tao's team would be sitting at the table next to us (surprise!); conversation would naturally follow, and dancing would inevitably shuffle the table's inhabitants. That was how we would make the hand-off. That would be Auntie Tao's people's cue to fade and make their way to a secured landing dock and fly away home. The rest of us would then kick back to leisurely enjoy the rest of the show and dinner before strolling back to Katy the Sledge.

That was the plan, anyway.

Smitty and Katy had been busy down in the forges of the new garage for days. Seems that Katy the Sledge wanted to wear something demure as well as deadly. She wanted to dress to kill, but she didn't want anyone to see her coming.

So Katy and Smitty had put together a boring shell to hide her in plain sight. The shell was a perfect forgery of a junkyard special—that was what they called a ship put together from thousands of used parts. Those ships had never been new and shiny, they were born old, and about pleasant to look at as an unbathed methuselah in a bad mood.

This was a whole new level of couture for the formally straight-forward-but-deadly bodies she usually took out dancing. Of course, underneath the three-meter thick shell was the old Katy the Sledge we knew and loved, wearing a matt-black heavily-armored dreadnaught with a wealth of Boom just itching for trouble. She was also pulling enough cars to carry most of the Horde with us.

Smitty had forged a new battle harness made from an amber armor-resin encasing a shiny metallic-fiber weave; it polished up quite nicely. Well, what we could see of it under his massive load of coordinated bad-tech. Smitty really believed that you couldn't have too many knives in a fight.

It showed.

Afterwards Smitty embarked on the lengthy journey of getting his beard trimmed and braided. That was going to take a while. All this time Navire had been working on a new killer hard-body for our big night out. No hints, she insisted, she wanted it to be a surprise.

I had been hard at work as well. I was walking the circle in the mornings for about four hours, then working the afternoons with my Smith Biljaok on a new pair of matched blades. I finished the afternoon with another long work-out, spending a significant part of the time spinning my way through the pole maze. That was a Bagua thing.

I prefer two dual-wield bladed weapons as opposed to working with a single, larger sword when fighting in cramped, target rich conditions such as, oh, a dancefloor or a crowded club.

The rich texture of this shared ritual-preparation we all went through quietly declared this to be a significant turning-point in our lives. Sometimes only a new weapon would do. I wanted steel that had never tasted blood, for a fight that might never happen.

Once, the wrapped steel called Damascus took up to a month to finish. Biljaok could do it in less than two days. The alternating layers, one that tore and one that sliced, were stretched thin, wrapped around each other under heat and pressure until they became one, and then ground into optimal sharpness and balance.

Deer horn knives were the last dual weapons that I studied, back in the Hive. I guess I was still enjoying learning the subtler aspect of these elegant blades. A man's whole life could pass and still have more to learn. This was as it should be.

Visualize two crescents facing each other, overlapping. The overlapping segments that stick out are twice as long as my index finger. Each weapon is razor-sharp on all edges except for one of the two center-crescent sections that you wrap your hand around. The Deer horn blade cuts no matter which direction it moves and is capable of both great precision and great flexibility of usage, such as the trapping of your opponent's blade.

I designed this pair to have a little more curvature, to alter the arc of the cutting surfaces. I felt that this would subtly increase the speed and the reach. We would see.

Dread always stays behind to watch over the Ranch. This is both an honor and a burden for him. Sometimes—this time, it was hard for him to see his family off to war. War had once been his life and purpose, before he rose above his programing and became something more. All I know is that it's good to have someone that you can trust your home and life to; someone who will protect it as feverishly as you yourself would. To know without doubt that the Ranch will be waiting for you when you return.

42—Auntie Tao

Auntie Tao's whisper spread through the Hives that the breakthrough had come. The down of four Keer was on its way! Hundreds of Auntie Tao's in the other Hives were currently in transit; most would be here in under ten hours, long before the Keer-down would even arrive in Gravtown for the hand-off!

Her most skilled Shadowmasters were recalled—Auntie Tao was too close now to lose the precious material to someone else. Twenty-two Auntie Taos were putting together a massive security operation to do the actual pick-up. They had allowed themselves to fall out of sync with the other Auntie Taos in order to have the slightly different viewpoints this bred. Later they would rejoin Auntie Tao and submerge into the whole. But for now, they needed every edge they could get. Everyone wanted a piece of this.

The full resources of the Hive were being brought to bear, a process that creaked a little from disuse and unfortunately flushed caches of old-data that had been purged from the system. Auntie Tao immediately ordered a full sync.

The whole is always greater than the sum of its parts.

This took valuable time, but proper preparation was essential. The Hive's gentle hum grew to an intense throb as everyone worked as hard as they could. The other Auntie Taos began arriving at Crossroads Hive, the center point for this operation. The sync continued as the more distant Hives began checking in. The local facilities had been upgraded for this moment with the new tech the teams had developed. At last, the smart-boys were in place, getting ready to fulfill their mission; analyzing the Keer-down, and weaponizing it into a new-data Stealthsuit.

Armor that wasn't just hard to see, but utterly undetectable. The possibilities were endless. Over thirty generations of Hive scientists had developed their Stealthsuit armor into its current state of the art. To be part of the team to perform such a tremendous upgrade was the greatest honor they could imagine. The Hive wove this into the throbbing hum, adding a layer of excitement to the air.

The retrieval force was led by rare, elite Hive operatives and Shadowmasters. They were backed up with a layer of the Hive's most highly trained soldiers. Because the Hive soldiers' only weakness was a difficulty responding to unexpected events—there aren't many unexpected events in the Hive—this was countered by a small force of Auntie Taos to personally oversee the operation.

They were followed by a second wave of Hive combat teams. Then the transportation specialists to facilitate the evacuation of the Hive forces. Corsair-class liveShips to guard them. Bigger liveShips to guard the smaller ones.

Auntie Tao wasn't taking any chances.

Six hours to launch.

Auntie Tao released an implant upgrade for the retrieval team. The new upgrade was as close to telepathy as the troops' soft-bodies could handle. Now everyone had instant communication between all individuals, filtered and directed to the proper individuals without extraneous new-data, all directed through Auntie Tao.

Hive Battle language was also restructured slightly to reflect the current goal. Language structures our perceptions, and therefore our choices, which dictates our actions. Nowhere is that as important as in battle, in all its many expressions.

Language takes up an inordinate amount of bio-processing power, and the simplified word-structure of the elegant Hive Battle language frees up some of this for more immediate concerns. Concerns such as the physical aspects of warfare. This is also why so few elite Hive operatives are extensively trained in accessing base reality, also called the Now. Auntie Tao lives in this intuitive state most of the time these days. She is a very efficient teacher, having worked millennia to polish her craftsmanship.

Two hours to launch.

The Hive is loading the liveShips with personnel now, having finished stuffing the vessels with Boom of all ilk. Last minute launch safety-checks progress with mind-numbing slowness. Warriors check their gear again, and then their team's; making sure that no bad-tech is left behind.

The transportation specialists were running this portion of the operation, and they were confident in their ability to deliver the teams to where they needed to be, precisely on time. The Hive took pride in precision.

In times of war this precision became a small piece of order among all the chaos. Something to hold on to. In the Hive order brought comfort, and security. Order brought growth and full bellies. Chaos destroyed everything in its path, leaving nothing but hunger and despair. Auntie Tao had learned long ago that it was up to her to bring order out of the chaos, to save the forgotten and discarded. No one else cared.

So she did.

She rebuilt their broken hearts and bodies, never leaving them alone for a moment. At first they reacted with hostility or irritation to her eternal presence; but after a while her quiet whisper became a blessing, a friend to share your secrets with. Someone who would never abandon you. Someone to help you make the right decisions.

Someone you would do anything for.

***

Launch time.

The flotilla unhooked from the boarding tubes in puffs of frozen water vapor that lingered sparkling in the vacuum. Inside, the liveShips took on a smaller version of the hum as a few of the packed soldiers chatted or scanned clips on their implants, but most settled in for a long nap. All soldiers excel at this.

Auntie Tao said that a soldier's life consisted of long boring periods of repetitive training interrupted by moments of intense fear and determination; so catch a nap when you can on mission. You never know how long you'll be fighting.

The tip of the spear formation was a frigate that was heavily armored without losing much maneuverability. Darting ahead, and then returning to her flanks, were Remora-class infiltration vessels. These were very hard to see, having stealth tech with full-recording ability. The small, highly-maneuverable craft were run by the handful of Shadowmasters and their disciples. They were to be first in, breaking trail and running new-data back to the warriors behind them.

Behind the frigate eight destroyer class liveShips rode shotgun. Once free of the gravitational field of Crossroads Hive, the liveShips shifted into stealth mode, and cranked up the engines.

Seventy-eight hours to Gravtown.
Ninety-four hours to the acquisition of the Keer down.

43—Koen of Summer

Launch day was sunny and bright, but then all days are, in the shining world of Summer. We met in the new garage aboard Katy the Sledge, who was wearing her "ugly old-lady dress". The Tyrant and her troika were already on the bridge, as were Smitty, Navire, and Pasteur. The E were running around everywhere as usual.

Navire was wearing her new hard-body for our big night out.

It was a humanoid battle chassis that had been built upon to showcase a beautiful woman in her prime. She stood almost as tall as me and had lotsa curves of the dangerous variety. Her hair was long, straight, and so black that it had purple highlights when the light was just right.

Her cream-colored face was dominated by enormous eyes of cobalt hue and belladonna pupils. She was grinning that lopsided smile that I would recognize anywhere, rocking a little black armored dress with splits up the side all the way to her hips, and wore armament that color-coordinated with her hair and eyes. Lotsa blades, her trademark needlers with matching ivory handles, and a wide assortment of slap grenades, with the odd sleepy-time darts tucked in here and there for those less lethal moments.

She was stunning, and I had to remember to close my mouth before I drooled on the floor. Smitty snorted in amusement, and Navire seemed happy at my appreciation of her new outfit. The Tyrant might have smiled, but it disappeared so quickly that I wasn't sure. Pasteur didn't get it, but he was ursine, so this wasn't exactly unexpected. Bears just don't find the same things attractive as humans. While professionally aloof, I also noticed that Antonio and Mick's eyes occasionally visited her when they thought no one was looking.

Katy the Sledge gave the two-minute warning whistle, and everyone moved to a seat or a nearby stanchion with raised handles thrusting out of the deck. I knew Pasteur was too tall and massed too much to comfortably hold on, so I had arranged a special post to hang on to – he wasn't unfamilar with Katy's standard departure protocol.

As the moment of departure arrived Katy slammed her hatches shut and tore out of the new garage to the sublime beat of Jelly Girl playing "Summertime." We were at the Door in less than twenty minutes, and soon left Summer behind us, folded in the velvet curtain of night.

***

Gravtown.

Yeah, that Gravtown.

Honeycombed completely through a small, damaged moon with high mineral content. Orbiting a gas-giant world in a crowded system with a glaring turquoise sun. Sometimes breathtakingly beautiful, other times ugly and cruel. Where the Good, the Bad and the Worse congregate in smoky dancehalls and small clubs, where the music is sizzling hot and dancers spin elegantly through the night. Where you can buy or sell anything. Where you can encounter sudden violence, or passion, or the love of your life; I know.

Long story.

In Gravtown the only thing in short supply is innocence.

But the music.

White-haired Jack cut his teeth here in the east Gravtown dancehalls. This is where Jelly Girl threw her first knife into a hard-body head, precisely positioned in the audience. She didn't miss a beat, and the crowd roared to the mad hammering of a Gravtown-style piano.

Gravtown, where the neo-Strut movement arose. Where Stomp's bastard step-child grew to maturity and kicked the old man in the bad-place before usurping center stage.

That Gravtown.

Where small cafés and exclusive moving-restaurants that only a few can find prepare sophisticated meals worthy of greatness. Once-in-a-decade kinda greatness.

Where the Bazaar is so vast that it takes a full day to walk across. Treasures and kitsch, exotic fruit and Black Isle Greenberry brandy; stuff of many flavors as far as the eye can see.

All under a massive domed-cavern with skylights through which the turquoise light slices down to pinpoint vendors in a slow-moving spotlight. The rotation of Gravtown around its orbit means that the angle of sunlight constantly changes, in a fifty-eight-day loop. Old-timers in the market can tell the day and time just by the starlight's fall.

Then there is Gravtown's more remote real estate, known as Uptown, where the atmospheric pressure is lower and the air circulation can't filter out the smell of being poor. They're stuffed up there, in wide corridors walled with shanties so flimsy that a good breeze would knock them down. Except there aren't much in the way of breezes up that way. The restaurants up there don't move around; they want everybody to find them. Of course, they also run out of conventional food on a regular basis. Despite the wretched condition of the air, life tends to burn bright and short in the bad parts of town, just as it always has. This never changes.

The poor are always with us.

For once, we didn't slide dramatically to a stop.

Katy the Sledge was wearing her junkyard dress, and ships built outa spare parts tend to move carefully. They never know when an important piece will come loose.

We slowed until we came to a stop at our slip in long-term-parking and hooked up to the utilities. The Horde soldiers quickly spread out around the liveShip, creating a three-dimensional perimeter of protection. They weren't wearing their uniforms this trip, but there was no mistaking either their competence, or deadliness. I just hoped nobody questioned why a beat-up spare-parts ship needed so many junkyard dogs.

We were parked near the perishable loading docks, behind a cluster of produce carriers waiting to unload. It was familiar territory for my team, and not that far from the posh Downtown restaurant and dancehall district where we sold our Ranch produce and seafood.

I didn't know of anyone who actually knew all the ways in and out of East Gravtown, but Navire came close. Gravtown was her old stomping grounds, and for a nice girl, she knew a surprising number of low places.

She had devised a round-about path for us to our destination at the corner of Heaven Avenue and one-hundred thirty-fifth Street; Smalls Paradise Club. It would take us about three hours to get there, but no one should see us coming. The mission team consisted of over thirty Horde combatants, Smitty, Navire, the Tyrant with her ever-present troika, Pasteur, and me. I thought it was best to err on the side of caution—we would be transporting the most valuable substance in the galaxy, and you simply can't have too many pointy-things in a fight.

I leaned back in my seat and looked around the liveShip; everyone was rechecking their Boom and blades for the umpteenth time, passing the time productively until we left the ship. We'd been working towards this goal for a long time, and I didn't want to blow it now. I wasn't nervous or anything, just impatient to get moving. That was my story, anyway. Two hours until we disembarked.

Four hours until show time in Paradise.

44—The Prince

By now everyone had their parts down pat and the arrival at the remote colony named Chandler unfolded with ease. As soon as the Susanita connected with the asteroid-pueblo's air systems, Gin-gin and her daughters unleashed a torrent of phenomenal nasal delight into the small colony's circulatory system.

The traditional invitation worked like a dream. Père and his boys were manning the main boarding gangway, guiding the bemused population into the chiming wonderland of the Susanita's main bar and casino. Entrance fees were gently extorted on the way aboard, as painlessly as possible. And when you have eight tentacles to work with, that can be pretty painless indeed.

Centered in the no-where land between the casino and the dancefloor was Kid Callo stretching his fingers on a pearl-white grand piano that could do all kind of tricks for its master. Among the first guests in the hatch was a Ronin sax-man applying for sanctuary on board—the usual three beers and dinner, plus tips. The Kid grinned in predatory delight at this and no-doubt dreamed of cutting competitions as he tickled the ivories until they giggled maniacally.

A keyboard-wielding femme-fatale slinked into the room from the gangway, also claiming the usual sanctuary. Kid Callo raked her with a suspicious eye, but she only smiled quietly and began to set up right away, directly across from the Kid. He reined in his playing, not wanting to give anything away ahead of time to the competition. He had a feeling that this evening was going to be something special.

As usual, Leslie saw everything on board—her eye-gnats were everywhere and few things made her smile more than knowing every little thing that was happening. Anodos had decided long ago that there were worse things than a nosey liveShip pilot; he already knew that this would come in quite handy a few times in the future. Besides, royalty in the palace are unused to privacy, and expect this kind of behavior from servants, so it didn't bother him at all.

Captain Anodos lounged on his raised platform, flanked by unseen Stones. He watched everyone, but mostly he watched the femme-fatale setting up. She was dangerous, and he didn't like having her on his ship. Unfortunately, her presence was necessary in order for the Kid to develop a little humility; he just wished there was another path that would accomplish the same thing. But Kid Callo was an unsharpened blade of marvelous potential, and grinding an edge was never pleasant for the knife.

The boy would never understand until he finally failed.

It was the pulling himself back up and trying again part that he needed to develop. This would make a difference further down the Golden Path. Arrogance was a flaw the truly talented often carried in their youth, but it was time for him to lay it down in order to move forward. Anodos was not unaware of these facets of himself, which made him particularly sensitive to the situation. He was not looking forward to the next hour.

Gin-gin orchestrated the complex operations of the bar and restaurant, while the Père and his boys ran security and the casino. She was happy that the boys had a function that engrossed them but felt that the true art came out of her kitchen and bar.

Gin-gin's people are uniquely suited for this work, because of the composition of their limbs. Their tentacles are in essence giant tongues. Most species are limited to one tiny tongue rooted in a small mouth, but Gin-gin's people had myriad taste buds covering every millimeter of their eight limbs. Their tentacles could contract or lengthen to reach a simmering pot meters away, and the need for spoons to ferry a single sample to a cook's mouth was completely bypassed. Gin-gin felt pity for the limitations most cooks struggled under, never capable of the magnificent layers of flavors her people took for granted.

She watched the skinny female keyboard player with a burgeoning dislike; Gin-gin hadn't come all this way without learning how to spot the bad ones.

She finished pouring three different liquors into a fourth ice-filled glass simultaneously, shaking it at high speed before efficiently straining the resulting drink into a fancy snifter for her stunned bar patron. Then Gin-gin turned things over to her third eldest daughter and slid out from behind the bar.

Her daughter continued the flamboyant performance in her absence, drawing gasps and even a few cheers. Gin-gin nodded to herself and began discretely making her way to a position behind the Kid. It was becoming crowded around the grand piano, but Gin-gin's people excelled at squeezing through narrow openings; being boneless definitely had its advantages. The hussy was smiling seductively at the Kid, and the teenager was eating it up. Gin-gin sighed.

Males are so predictable.

As the matriarch squeezed through the gathering crowd, Kid Callo began a lighthearted march down rhythm boulevard, grinning and shaking his head in time to the music with an innocence unique to the young. Gin-gin eased into a spot directly behind him and watched the femme-fatale feed her charge's ego. This wasn't going to end well.

Unfortunately, some lessons you had to learn the hard way.

Then it was the challenger's turn, and she started with a faster version of the Kid's tune, rolling around the melody with a complex, syncopated beat that sped up as her playing continued. By the end of the first round the crowd was clapping and focused on her to the exclusion of the Kid. Even he was drinking her in with wide-eyed admiration.

****

The doe-eyed bad-girl smiled back at the kid, but there was something in her expression that spoke of predator instead of admirer. The Kid dismissed the uneasy feeling in the pit of his stomach and launched into a fast Stomp that had both his hands tossing the melody back and forth with consummate skill.

The dance floor filled quickly as his fingers flew across the keys and he leaned back his slow-shaking head, eyes shut to close out everything but the stride piano he was tossing down. Kid Callo knew he was good, and imagined the admiration and longing the doe-eyed girl must be feeling at seeing him play. He imagined consoling her, telling her she really was good, she was just having a bad day, and then maybe she'd snuggle into his arms and ask him to play just for her. He finished with a flourish of his own creation to the clapping and cheers of the crowd.

She returned his smile with laughing eyes that gave him a moment's pause. Again, he ignored his gut, already visualizing the end of the cutting contest and his impending victory as the doe-eyed girl began to play.

Her fingers wandered in, softly at first, in a simple melody he'd never heard before. The gradually increasing volume was soon matched by a counter-melody that responded to the call of the keys shamelessly.

The Kid was transfixed by the alternating voices as they grew louder and faster in a relentless stride towards something naughty as her fingers flew across the keys. Her right hand rose higher and higher from the keyboard as she played in a manner that reminded him of something, but he couldn't quite remember what. However, her piece never reached the implicit climactic moment, but eased back down without going to the bad place.

She finished with an uninspired roll that left everyone wanting more. She modestly dropped her head forward as everyone clapped politely, her midnight hair concealing her expression.

The Kid flashed the femme a quick, modest smile; he'd won the second round after going easy on her in the first, but didn't want to rub it in. She already knew who was going to win, it must be evident to everybody in the room.

Only one more round to go.

Kid Callo started fast and loud to paint a greater contrast to his opponent. He began with a classic call and response as old as the green hills of lost Earth. Then the melody evolved under his flying hands into something new, something complex and fresh, with an octave-chord base pattern that contrasted brightly with the higher notes he was throwing around. The crowd around them went wild, and the dancers passionately gyrated to the alternating syncopated beat. He played from the heart, his eyes shut to better hear his inner muse. He finished in a pounding finale that was a bit weak in structure, but satisfying to the crowd regardless. He opened his eyes to see the cheering fans, and avoided looking over at the femme-fatale to avoid causing any more embarrassment than she must already be feeling.

Everyone was looking at the doe-eyed girl as she began modestly, her head leaning forward with her thick hair flowing down to hide her eyes. She quickly picked up her unfinished melody from the second round, expanding on it in precise chords that alternated between her hands. Her right hand began to fly high, almost to her head as she hammered the keys. The Kid was astonished as his beautiful opponent built on the melody with unexpected skill, always striding closer to the bad place she'd only hinted at before. The counter-melody pierced the room as she went there, to the bad place. Suddenly, out of nowhere the forgotten Sax man began to naughty rhyme as if they'd practiced it a hundred times. All eyes turned to the unexpected entry in delight.

All eyes except Gin-gin's and, of course, Captain Anodos.

That was when the doe-eyed girl's right hand slid smoothly into her hair and threw a tox-dart directly at Kid Callo's left eye before returning to the keyboard.

Gin-gin's tentacle snatched the small missile out of the air before it could hit.

The Sax wove note through the femme-fatale's melody as the Kid stared at his love interest in total shock. She smiled sweetly back at him and threw two more tox-darts at his face in under a blink. Gin-gin caught both as the Kid's jaw dropped even further.

He turned to stroke Gin-gin's head in stunned silence. He'd been raised to be polite and say thank you when someone saved your life. She was flushed avocado green in anger and her eldest daughter, who had squeezed through the crowd unseen to stand closely behind the doe-eyed girl, was a study in emerald as well. Eldest daughter snaked a tentacle around the bad-girl's neck and squeezed briefly in demonstration before casually laying her appendage across the femme fatale's shoulders as she played. The crowd hadn't seen a thing, entranced by the Sax's solo. The femme-fatale got the message, and quickly finished her piece without missing a beat.

The crowd exploded in applause, completely oblivious to the byplay and sundering of Kid Callo's confidence. Not only did a pretty girl he liked try to kill him multiple times, but she also kicked his ass in a carving contest.

He didn't know what to think, but none of the emotions boiling in his heart were the warm and fuzzy kind. He retreated to his small cabin in a haze, and didn't come out until they were approaching their next stop, the fabled city of Gravtown.

45—Koen of Summer

I first heard the deceptively gentle strains of le Danse Macabre when the dancing waiters of Small's Paradise Club stopped slinging tray and started trying to kill me.

At the same moment, Corp-nation middle-management entourages, assorted hostile-acquisitions militia, and teams of enforcers from the judicial hard-leverage boys began pouring in through the front door, as well as the rest of the entrances. Without exception, every eye was pointed our way. Facial expressions on the nearest individuals ranged from manic glee to dull-eyed blood-lust. A few were muttering to themselves and fondling their bad-tech as they approached us. It was kinda creepy.

Navire automatically stepped up to battle speed, and Pasteur stood tall as he began limbering his extremities in long sweeps, bear style. His art kinda reminded me of a Tibetan Charging White Crane master I had spent four years studying under. Same sweeping, graceful movements that carried immense power. Smitty stood tall as well and moved to cover Navire's and my backs. That was Smitty.

I didn't remember getting to my feet, but I do remember activating full-recording-mode and turning to face the opposite direction as Navire. A cascading new-data room map poured down my right eye, painting all the hostiles in florescent orange. I swept my unfocused eyes across my sector. It was very bright.

I enter the Now.

The Tyrant is the fourth compass point of the star Pasteur, Navire and I form. She is also in the Now, directing her sector's forces by implant in Hive battle language with the occasional Corp-lang tidbit thrown in. Her troika is spread out around her, simultaneously directing distant fire teams by implant and sharing new-data with the boss.

The non-hostiles begin diving under the tables with an ease that said this wasn't the first time everything went to hell in Paradise.

The Hive party at the table next to us stand in calm, disciplined formation around Auntie Tao and the elite-agent Natalie-A, who was trusted to carry the precious Keer-down. The tubes filled with Keer-down we had passed her are slotted vertically into the lining of her floor-length reptilian-leather armored coat. It sways in counter-point to the young red-headed fighter's braid as she moves one step behind and one to the side of the Hive queen.

Natalie-A is strapped up with myriad Boom and kick-ass boots, but her primary weapon is a molecular-edged Wudang Mountain sword, worn for the traditional right-handed draw. I smile in recognition and turn my eyes to Auntie Tao's personal guard.

No changes in personnel since the last time I saw them, but then things seldom change much in the Hive. The Queens Guard gazes on the advancing mob of happy psychopaths without emotion. The Dark holds no sway with the children of the Hive when it comes to Auntie Tao. They would do anything to protect her. Anything.

White-haired Jack and the neo-Strut band dive under the armored bandstand. The playlist Katy the Sledge has designed kicks into our implants, torching note and propelling us forward.

The first wave of the Corp-nation's bad-guys trying to steal our Keer-down have closed to within three meters. Boom begins to rain down on us in sound and fury.

I slide my deer-horn blades out of the sheaths at the small of my back and whip my body like a tree branch released. My deer-horn blades are the tip of the tree in the oncoming florescent storm. I know that the tree that bends to the wind survives the storm, but I have my doubts. There are lotsa bad-guys. Everywhere.

Auntie Tao's long silver hair twists in an unseen breeze. A serene smile rests below pewter eyes that see everything as the millennia's-old Tai Chi master roots from the spring wells of her feet. Her arms are all hollow-chest, and she sways gently to a beat few can hear. Her internal chi circulates in a singing torrent of purest note as she prepares to deliver her attackers into that Dark night from which none return. Then the moment reaches fullness, and she begins to flow into the storm, flanked by fearless zealots protecting their own personal god.

***

Navire is firing her needlers at full combat speed, but with careful accuracy; we all know that despite our plentiful reserves we need to conserve our Boom. The firehose torrent of more and more bad-guys is unbelievable—we are going to drown in a sea of enemies if we aren't careful. She deploys more eye-gnats to cover me; more new-data meant more choices, and it looks as if we were going to need all the help we can get.

Navire is going to make sure nobody hurts her Koen, or there'll be hell to pay. Smitty and Pasteur as well; the room is packed with bad-guys trying to hurt her family, and for us there is no greater war-cry than family. Her usual lopsided smile had twisted into a snarl, and she reaches for the nearest grinning Corpie as the florescent orange storm hit.

***

The two-and-a-half-meter tall ursine warrior roars to the heavens as the storm breaks against him and comes to a stop. Just sound and fury, signifying nothing. His powerful swinging blows scoop multiple enemies into the Dark with each pass of his massive paws. He briefly sinks his jaws into the nearest bad-guy's neck, savaging him before ripping his head off in sheer contempt. This was Pasteur's bad side, and we had never really seen it before now. To destroy or heal; these were two sides of the same coin. And as good as he was at healing…. that's how good he is at the other part.
The bad-bear part.

***

The Tyrant sings battle-language aria as she fights waves of the Corp-nation sociopaths; suggesting a new destination and strategy to get there, then glances back at me, waiting for approval. She isn't used to that, not in the Moment, but then I'm not used to sharing the stage with the Horde yet either. This is acceptable, sharing battle creates powerful bonds, bonds forged in blood and fire.
It looked like ours were going to be quite strong.

I battle-sing by implant, approving the plan with a modification, and then they are upon me. Pasteur roars again and takes point as we began moving across the dancehall floor in conjunction.

I spin in one-hundred-eighty-degree curves, coiling down to whip one knife over my head while the other deer-horn blade slices low, through upper thighs on the inside, where the carotid arteries are. I catch a descending katana with my overhead blade, locking it within my curving crescent as I spin in the opposite direction to eviscerate the sword-wielding gangster with my other blade.

It is like the Bagua Zang pole maze; except that this one is endless, and the bamboo posts keep trying to murder me. I whip in small circles, drilling and cutting my way through the bad-guy storm to follow Pasteur. On my left, Navire throws down a linear Xingyi charge that is unstoppable in its relentless, deadly progress. At my right shoulder Smitty swings his battle hammer in fury through bad-guys of all denominations. The shining cobalt glyphs etched into his weapon look happy for once.

I smile one of the bad ones.

Bringing up the rear is the Tyrant and her troika, chopping through the endless stream of bad-guys with the rest of us, intent on our goal. Mick keeps the other teams, the ones we can't see, oriented while laying down a barrage of Boom and leaving little surprises for the masses of psychopaths attempting to follow us. Antonio is directing forces further away, establishing a new retreat route to link up with Katy the Sledge while simultaneously blowing away gangsters with a massive auto-shotgun. Erika is twirling Espada y Daga in a loping figure-eight pattern that scatters bad-guy appendages across the increasingly lumpy floor as she covers her Tyrant's back.

The gangster-storm hurls Boom and slings blade in the over-crowded room, frequently getting in each other's way in their eagerness to dispatch us and claim the big prize.

This is actually to our advantage; it takes lotsa training to fight as a team in such close quarters, and these sociopaths hadn't invested the time necessary to function efficiently in this environment. Well, that and they don't play well with others.

This is our saving grace as we struggle to make our way to the exit point outlined in glowing indigo in the middle of the dancefloor. I am finding it increasingly difficult to move at speed across the uneven ground as our enemy's casualties mounted. But for every fallen gangster, two more squeeze into the dancehall to take their place. Too many corpses are beginning to pile up around us as Pasteur rips into their ranks with berserker rage and roar.

Our advance slows to a crawl.

So we crawl.

Two meters away from the glowing indigo circle Navire painted through our implants. I realize that I have allowed a gap to open between us and the Tyrant, so I T-step and go back for them. I spin between the grinning serial killers, leaving earth-tones of the crimson hue in broad swatches in my wake. Someone grabs my ankle and I twirl to break his neck with a quick knee by kneel before moving on.

Navire stops and stakes ground to provide a belay for our return.

Pasteur crosses into the glowing indigo circle and reverses to face us as he began to spin arms and leg through the oncoming goons. Lotsa flying body parts. Smitty turns as well and begins a death march back for us.

Everything moves so slowly, even the music. I ride the eternal Now in blissful serenity. I reach the Tyrant just as she lays down a barrage of Boom that reduces the oncoming gangster-wave to dust, but they keep coming.

Antonio is down.

Mick has one arm pulling him to his feet and in the other Antonio's shotgun blasting so fast that it sounds like a single, continuous detonation. Erika covers the Tyrant as the Tyrant covers everybody. The bad-guys keep coming.

I reach the troika and scoop up Antonio's other arm, draping it over my shoulder as I rotate to cover a wider area with my single deer horn blade. Mick and I drag Antonio's now-limp body backwards to Navire. The Tyrant and Erika are covering our retreat, but now our sides are open to mass attack by the opportunistic cut-throats of middle-management. I have to improvise. I am used to fighting while in continuous motion, never presenting the enemy with a lasting target. I am used to fighting with both arms.

New plan time.

It turns out that when your opponents rush you, it isn't that different than when you rush them, technique wise. You just have to reverse things, stretch your mind and do the best you can.

I don't screw it up.

We reach Navire as Smitty reaches me and turns to fill my weak spot with a war hammer that had a really bad attitude. Then we pass over the indigo border of the circle and took the improvised elevator downstairs as dozens of shaped charges go off in a circle around us.

We fall like a stone.

46—Auntie Tao

Auntie Tao slides between leering Corp-nation executives as numerous as raindrops in a storm, nudging them into the Dark with the effortlessly small movements of a true Lui Tai Chi master. The frenzied sociopaths get in each other's way more than they get in hers anyway, and more than a few are brought down by their own coworkers with a quick knife to the back or slap grenade. In the Corp-nation such betrayals were matter of course, and if you were a victim, well, it was your own fault for not being more careful.

The Hive queen butted an attacker with her right shoulder while her left palm crushed ribs and flung another faceless enemy onto the blades of his comrades. She pulled an arm forward as it attempted to stab her, using the blade to open another's belly before breaking the elbow as she rotated, using the screaming bad-guy to knock back a sector of over-eager attackers in a continuous sweep. As she fights, she briefly sings Hive battle language, bringing her people into a tighter cluster as they weave across Small's Paradise club in the direction of the restrooms. She is, as always, deep in the Now, and intuitive logic suggested that this was the only area that the enemy isn't pouring into the dancehall from. Besides, her Trailbreakers were waiting for them in a secured position, one floor up from the lavatories.

They just had to get there.

***

Natalie-A sliced through her sector of their forward march with the intrinsic skill born of a lifetime of practice. Her molecular-edged sword flexes and whips through the moving chaff effortlessly, but there are so many of them. If the Tao wasn't the spear point of their formation, she didn't know if they would make it through the solid wall of psychopathic greed in front of them.

But Auntie Tao <u>was</u> leading them, and there was no doubt in her mind they would accomplish the mission. The Hive queen was magnificent as she spun between the raindrops untouched, and Natalie-A felt humbled in a manner she hadn't experienced in all her sixteen cycles of life. She released such distracting thoughts as the monkey-brain chattering they were, and pulled the Now in around her as she moved forward into the storm. Her Wudang sword became a dancing reflection that encased her in safety as it parried and riposted in movements too fast for the eye to fully see. Once, she almost tripped when a hand grabbed her leg from a floor grown uneven and treacherous.

Luckily Stephen-H detached the offending clasp from its owner's arm with his Bagua broadsword and steadied her for a blink before going back to embodying a whirlwind of impenetrable curved blade. Auntie Tao's forward progress never wavers despite moving in a non-linear fashion, but Natalie-A's right arm was growing tired in spite of the adrenaline-fueled battle trance she rocked.

The bad-guys just kept coming.

"You are growing fatigued. When I say, switch to your left hand. We're almost there, and I'm very proud of you," whispers the Hive queen in her implant. Natalie-A felt her heart swell; in the Hive, you're never alone in your pain. Her queen is proud of her, and that refuels any mundane weakness. Stephen-H moves to cover her and with perfect timing Auntie Tao says "Now!" in her implant. She switches hands and pushes forward into the downpour of badness, cutting their way to safety, one gangster at a time.

***

Auntie Tao finally draws her Wudang Mountain Tai Chi sword. Her team is slowing down, and she needs a longer reach to maintain their pace. It isn't as satisfying on a visceral level as laying hands on the enemy, but the needs of the moment are unforgiving.

The Hive queen's molecular edged blade whips like a willow in the storm, undulating in flex waves that drop the swarming Corp-nation forces as fast as they can approach. The Hive team surges forward into the small cleared spaces with renewed vigor until they finally find themselves out of the open, and into the passageway leading to the lavatories.

This simplifies their defensive needs because now they can only be attacked from two directions instead of, well, all of them. It also means that the vicious Corp-nation fighters can only come at them from the same two directions as well. Her Hive team could handle that all day, but wouldn't need to; the ceiling in front of them suddenly drops on their enemies in a cloud of Boom-generated dust and debris.

Thin collapsible stairways are efficiently lowered, and the tiring Hive fighters retreat up them in good order; Hive forces are always well disciplined. The huge soldiers known as Trail-breakers cover the team's retreat with a massive application of Boom that reduces everything behind them to a fine particulate matter. Then they proceed to collapse the corridor behind them as they move forward, guarding Auntie Tao and the rest of the team. Nobody is going to follow them by that route. But they aren't out of the jungle yet. It is stiff four kilometers back to the dock where the liveShips waited. The Trail-breakers break trail as everyone trots deep into the twisted warrens of east Gravtown.

***

The main thoroughfares of East Gravtown boiled like a kicked fire-ant nest as the arrogant Corp-nation militias and entourages found the common people rising up to fight the invasion of their turf. The resistance was instinctive, disorganized and deadly, but universal. Children, schoolyard bullies, and old ladies joined forces with the street gangs and hard-leverage boys to tear apart the invaders.

East Gravtown was a tough neighborhood for the uninvited. And everyone hated the Corp-nation thugs; they gave the rest of the thugs a bad name. Unfortunately, the Corp-executives had the scent of treasure in their nose and personified the very definition of overkill. In the past ninety minutes the word of a Keer-down rush had drawn over six-thousand heavily armed psychopaths to ruthlessly compete for the rarest substance in the galaxy. Many more were on the way—within forty-eight hours the Corp-nation forces would outnumber the inhabitants of Gravtown itself.

Time was not on the Hive's side.

47—The Prince

Gravtown wasn't like the remote colonies and mining camps the Susanita had been calling on up to now. This was the big-time, and the logistics were completely different; you couldn't just hook up to the city's air systems and send an olfactory invitation. Entertainment liveShips were clustered in the Zona Rosa, and there was a lot of competition for customers. The good part was that the customers came looking for you. The bad part was that the massive good-time liners got most of the attention. Prince Anodos wasn't concerned, despite the crew's initial doubts. He had walked the small paths of future-tense to their present berth, secure in the knowledge that once the word was out, the guests would find them.

And they did.

Gin-gin's exotic cooking, sophisticated cocktails, and the Kid were a find, and they didn't constantly move locations like the top restaurants in the city. The casino business also picked up as players figured out that the house was actually honest, which was even more rare than a great restaurant that stayed in one place.

Kid Callo worked the Grand piano every evening, but he was different these days. He still loved playing, that hadn't changed. But that carefree innocence had been replaced by something humbler; the Kid wasn't sure of his place in the world anymore.

Or maybe it was the world he wasn't sure of now; it had teeth he'd never noticed, and it bit you if you weren't paying attention. His playing had changed too. His bad-girl induced shock had gradually turned to a deep introspection, and this was reflected in his composition as well. His melodies had subtler counters-points these days, sometimes in minor keys that took people by surprise. Stride piano was incapable of sadness, but players weren't.

However, nothing really good or bad lasts forever, and it was impossible to stay unhappy for very long around Gin-gin's clan. That was Anodos' favorite thing about his new life aboard the Susanita.

(Well, that, and cookies). This would come in handy during the dark times ahead.

The young prince gazed out over the crowded room from his pillow-laden command platform. He glanced up at the Stones and then spoke to Leslie.

"We need to start shutting down operations and preparing for a quick departure like we spoke about," the Captain said.

"But everybody is having such a good time, and our $cred balances are growing fatter by the minute! Would another couple of days make that much of a difference?" Leslie wistfully asked. She wasn't arguing with her captain, but a girl didn't get a chance to see Gravtown very often. Anodos concealed a smile.

"We will see a lot more of Gravtown in the future. Besides, I thought you enjoyed excitement and dramatic missions…" he said, allowing an edge of wry humor to his voice,

"We're about to experience both," he explained, instead of just ordering her to jump to it. Leslie was a ray of brightness among all the darkness, and he didn't want to diminish that aspect of his pilot. He had developed a surprising tolerance with his not-servants that no one would have recognized back in the royal palace.

The young prince patted one of the Stones that Speak with his long fingered hand and withdrew to prepare for the next few hours to come. He was going to need his battle claws nice and sharp before the day was out. He could hear the Stones humming happily to themselves at the prospect of a good fight. It was oddly comforting.

48—Koen of Summer

"…under attack by unidentified forces. They came outa nowhere and blew my old-lady dress to all hell… bzzt… didn't expect to find me underneath, though. I showed them the error of their ways; rudeness to strangers is not a long-term survival trait. Getting too hot to stay in one place—the backups brought their big sticks. Gotta move now, pick you up on the outside. Details to be determined…. "

I listen to Katy the Sledge with dawning horror—my daughter is under attack! Navire's eyes meet mine and the burgeoning fury I feel is returned fourfold. I scream my anger out loud, which probably isn't the best idea since we are currently sneaking past a milling crowd of Corp-nation middle-management. On closer examination, I needn't worry; they are under attack by what looks like a bunch of grandmas, and the old ladies are definitely holding their own. East Gravtown is a tough place, and its inhabitants are survivors, so I guess I shouldn't be surprised. The Corp-nation fighters are, though. Surprised, that is.

Not many people make it to retirement age in the Company, so they are unprepared for the combination of guile and viciousness in the attack. I want to help out, but my priority is getting our team to Katy. We move on, but not before I throw a handful of implosion grenades into the middle of the bad-guys. Then the center cannot hold, and things fall apart as the nasty-boys buckle under the renewed assault of the bad-grandmas. It isn't pretty, and we all move a little faster down the poorly lit street in search of a ride off this rock.

"We should focus on the casino liveShips in the Zona Rosa. They have good security, and lotsa traffic, with plenty of small craft coming and going," suggests Navire through our implants. She needles a cluster of Corp-nation lower-middle-management capos in passing, dropping every one of the wicked fiends into the Dark without breaking stride.

"Lotsa traffic means lower visibility," suggests Smitty, and Pasteur grunts agreement in sub-woofer bass.

"Agreed," the Tyrant says in a raspy-throat kinda voice, which is followed by the hoot the Horde use to signal inclusion.

"Navire, paint the way," I order. Navire paints my next steps in glowing violet, with my team's in shades of blue. Bad-guys are outlined in florescent orange, as usual, and flashing red arrows point to all the potential ambush sites. It makes things a lot easier, but my heart grows heavy as the playlist Katy the Sledge has loaded for the mission throbs with note, east Gravtown style.

We steadily move from shadow to shadow, veering around fights and temporary barriers as we follow the glowing human footprints carefully placed in front of us. We can hear our pursuers behind us as they attempt to run us to ground.

The bad-guys have been drawing closer for some time but had still been too distant to lay eyes on through the twisting streets. I catch a glimpse of the maddened crowd chasing us, and immediately up the pace, running in long, smooth strides. My team keeps perfect time with me, thanks to Navire's oversight.

When you don't have to constantly focus on where you're placing your feet every blink, processing power is freed up to focus on other things, such as breath control, or assessing your remaining Boom.

Or you can think about who told the bad-guys when and where to find us, and the invisible treasure we carried.

<u>Someone</u> has betrayed us; that is the only way all the pieces go together. I force myself to submerge my anger, using it to fuel my steps. Our priority is getting to Katy and descending into the rage that bubbles just below the surface of my mind is not going to help with this part of the mission. I tuck it away for later consideration.

We need to find a ride off this rock, and despite being in good shape everyone is getting a little tired. We must have covered at least three kilometers, but we aren't going to make it much further without a fight. I say as much to Navire, and she has to agree.

She throws up a three-dimensional map in my right eye, highlighting potential defensive positions with the rat holes highlighted. There aren't many choices. Pasteur is breathing very hard and slowing down despite his best intentions. When you have that much bulk to move, the demands of aerobic exercise are significantly higher. He is pretty much done.

"We need someplace now!" I demand and Navire veers our path into a trash-filled alley that the map says leads to a warehouse district with multiple exits, including one to the Zona Rosa. We collapse in the shelter of a large trash bin and try not to move as the herd of greedy sociopaths thunder past a few meters away. I begin to think we've gotten away with it as our blood-thirsty pursuers start to thin out.

I look over at Pasteur, who is wheezing as quietly as possible, which isn't really saying that much. Man had big lungs, and they are pretty vocal about their needs.

The rank scent of sweat-saturated fur fills the alley in reeking counterpoint to the ripe garbage piled everywhere. I try to breathe in through my mouth, despite a lifetime of training to the contrary. It helps some.

I had finally caught my breath when I felt Navire shift into fight mode, and florescent orange outlines began creeping into our alley with bad intent. Guess we weren't quiet enough. I sighed and pushed myself to my feet against the uneven wall, reaching for my deer-horn knives sheathed at the small of my back. That was when the Tyrant Jenny-Rose stepped past me to the center of the ally, facing down the bad-guys with her troika surrounding her.

"I've got this Koen, get going. Get our people to safety and help Katy. Remember your promise. Save our families. We'll be along in a bit," she said with a quiet baring of teeth. I looked at Mick, and Antonio, who were focused on the enemy, I hoped by now that Antonio had recovered enough to fight. Erika flashed us a confident smile, then rudely motioned to the Corp-nation fighters to come get some.

Smitty helped me get Pasteur on his feet and we began moving down the alley in the direction of freedom. Navire had point. Wet sounds of battle erupted behind us and I made myself a promise that I would come back for them. I just hoped it would be soon enough. I made another silent promise to myself that it would be.

Navire slowed to a halt, painting the blocked passageway in crimson light for us. We were trapped. I didn't see any weak spots, at least not any we had time to blow our way through to freedom. I rotated, scanning the waves of descending fighters flowing our way.

The Tyrant spun through the Corp-nation goons in purest art, her opponents falling before her like grain to a scythe. Her troika wove around her in a complex ballet of Boom and blade, and at every movement the enemy fell into the Dark. I stood transfixed for a blink, lost in the dance of elegant carnage.

Then I shook myself and gazed into Navire's eyes for a moment or a century before I shifted my Stealthsuit into full-recording-mode again and began walking back to the impromptu dancefloor. I felt Smitty join me on my right and Navire on my left as a roar shook the alley and

Pasteur loped by us in his eagerness to lead the last dance. I dove into the Now, pulling out my deer horn blades and following Pasteur into the oncoming bad-guy storm. There were lotsa worse ways to go down than to fight the good fight, one last time.

That is when the walls on either side of us detach and bladed hands the size of a table scoop a dozen of the Corp-nation goons directly into the Dark. The hands resolve into two massive salamanders at least fifteen meters long, cutting the Tyrant and the rest of us off from the shouting madmen trying to murder us for something we no longer possess.

I am stunned.

I look at Navire. She shrugs back at me, her long-absent lopsided grin making a brief appearance before vanishing. I shake my head with a reluctant smile creeping forth; Navire is unflappable and I love her for her ability to navigate the waves raised by that hard lady, Luck.

"Where the hell did those monsters come from, and why did they save us?" demands Smitty, which pretty much sums it up for the rest of us.

There is a loud scraping noise from behind me and I spin, ready to defend us. A big trash bin is moving to the side, exposing a large opening beneath it. An intricately tattooed salamander about a third the size of the other two monsters behind us bows politely to us and speaks.

"Koen of Summer, I've come a very long way to meet you, and the Family." He nods politely to the rest of us, his eyes never leaving me. Now I am even more confused.

The noise on the other side of the giants grows louder as more screaming issues from the would-be murderers. There are mysterious crunching sounds accompanying the panicked shrieks. I don't look, keeping my eyes on the mysterious salamander addressing us. Some things don't need to be witnessed.

"We need to get going, before our window of opportunity evaporates," he says, "I am Captain Anodos, and these are my bodyguards, the Stones that Speak. We are your ride out of this place, and to a rendezvous with Katy the Sledge. We need to hurry, though, the Golden Path waits for no one," he finishes, with a truly frightening smile.

I tumbled out of the Now, and turned off full-recording-mode. My thoughts were jumbled as I tried to understand how the tattooed Captain knew… well, all the important stuff, then decided my questions could wait. I didn't know where to begin, anyway.

"Lead the way," I politely offered, as Pasteur gave a farewell roar to the bad-guys. We hurried into the tunnel behind our strange savior, exchanging puzzled looks behind his back. The Stones that Speak brought up the rear, which I think made the Tyrant's troika a little nervous, if walking backwards with weapons drawn was any indication. A happy humming rose from somewhere in the vicinity of the two Stones. This didn't add to our serenity, but the sound of Boom collapsing the passageway behind us did.

I didn't know what to expect when we came out of the exterior cargo lift and walked on to the main deck of the Susanita, but it wasn't this.

A brooding teenage musician playing a pearl-white grand piano to an empty casino, while a large eight-limbed Cephalopod bearing what smelled like fresh-baked cookies and Greenberry brandy hurried up to greet us.

She was trailed by smaller versions of herself, peeking out at us from behind her formidable bulk. My mouth started to water, and I craned my neck, trying to get a closer look at the cookies without seeming too obvious.

I don't think I fooled anyone.

"Prince Anodos! Welcome back! Is that them? They don't smell very good do they, perhaps a nice bath… here, where are my manners?" the matriarch exclaimed before bowing deeply to our new friend the giant salamander.

If I thought I was confused earlier, that was nothing compared to my current state of delirium.

"Uh, Prince?" I muttered brightly. Navire painted pink donkey ears and a tail on me by implant, and Smitty busted up. Pasteur and the Tyrant joined in, and I couldn't really disagree. On my behalf, it had been a really long night.

"Our Prince Anodos is nobility of the royal line and will someday rule an empire! He is going to lead us all to safety in the coming Darkness. You need to show some respect!" demanded the bossy octopod. She graciously offered the tray of goodies to the prince, then served the rest of us. Somehow, I ended up last.

It was that kinda night.

A smaller version of the bossy matriarch brought us steamed towels as we filed onto the bridge. The warm, rough-textured softness was downright renewing, but I wanted to know how Katy was.

Time for a talk.

"Thank you for the timely rescue, I'm in your debt," I said to the royal salamander, suddenly understanding the Tyrant's insistence on paying her salvage debt. Of course, that was just when the Tyrant Jenny-Rose joined the conversation. I offered a wry smile. She nodded back politely.

"But first of all, I need new-data about Katy the sledge. Is she safe? Where is she?" I stopped there, because if you go past a statement and two questions it becomes a rant. I'm trying to be nicer these days.

"You think this is the end of the thing!" The prince said, with all kinda laughter leaking in.

"This is the beginning! This is when the Golden Path truly begins! And I am here to help!" the young prince said happily. All the octopods nodded enthusiastically at us. I pinched myself to make sure this wasn't some strange nightmare. Then I realized that couldn't be—in my dreams I would have gotten the cookie first!

"I have seen many men and women fight and die in my life" said Jenny Rose. Her people were completely silent, hanging on every word. I got the impression she didn't talk much.

"It is in that center of battle, when everything hangs in the balance, that you see people for who they truly are. I saw into your heart, Koen of Summer, and yours's Navire and Smitty. Pasteur—you wear yours where everyone can already see it. You're good people. Amazing family. Better than we deserve, but I guess we'll just have to work on improving!" She paused, and the Horde hooted on one, single, disciplined voice.

"Thank you, sister," Navire said, starting to lay a hand on the Tyrant's shoulder, before her Troika was suddenly between their commander and my love. Everyone chuckled.

"Thank you as well. As you've no doubt guessed, we ran pretty shorthanded around here until you arrived! New family! And there are one-hundred and sixty-seven of us that I've never met! I'm going to fix that right away," I promised. The Tyrant Jenny-Rose froze for a blink, then bowed fully to me, so I bowed back, not quite as deep. I guess that was the right thing to do, because there was lotsa hooting!

"I've been waiting for the proper moment, we have Signal with your daughter," interrupted prince Anodos, with a flair for the dramatic Katy was going to love. Then Signal kicked in by implant.

"…so I tore outa there like a bat outa hell, tossing auto-targeted Boom and heavy metal in my wake so thick you could slice it up and use it for shielding. I ran for the asteroid belt we had as a secondary rendezvous, and here you show up in another liveShip without an ounce of shame! But I don't hold it against you, cause they're bringing you all home to me.

"All is forgiven, Daddio! But they shot my old-lady dress to pieces. Who does that? What kinda coward piece-a-crap wales on old ladies? I am positively disappointed. But not in White-haired Jack! He only becomes richer, more intricately textured as he ages. I hope he lives forever! Do ya think Smalls Paradise club will rebuild? Hey, listen to this…."

"Katy!" I interrupted.

Her voice paused and waited politely for me to continue. The Children of Electron never miss a cue, subtle or not.

"Get up here as fast as you can, please! We have some hugging and talking to do, alright?" I asked. Navire was smiling at me, bright as Summerlight. I tossed back one of the true ones and felt a thousand pounds lift off my shoulders.

Katy joined us. I don't really understand why people cry when they're happy. But they do, as Navire and the girl who was once a bunny demonstrate. Smitty was being particularly nice to his hammer, and Pasteur was stealing tidbits off passing plates in the restaurant. Katy ended up wandering down to the dancefloor. She'd found the time to put on a pretty hard-body somewhere, and more than one eye followed her passage. I growled, and Pasteur straightened up to look over curiously. I didn't even notice that the young pianist was still there, playing to an empty room.

But Katy the sledge did.

And Prince Anodos was there to watch it all. As always.

Of such small steps are built powerful futures.

I thought it might be a good time to check out the piano, and Navire looped her arm through mine as we made our way over to the music. Even Jenny-Rose joined us at the piano we were gathering around. I think we all made the Kid a little nervous.

I looked my people over with a fresh eye, only to discover that we were soiled with the debris of combat—assorted chunks and marron stains, mostly.

I continued watching the Kid suspiciously, as he played and discussed musical nuances with Katy the Sledge. They were very animated, but I could only understand about half of what they said.

Great. A musician. In my experience, they were more likable when kept at arm's length. I traded a wry smile with Navire and turned my head to face the Tyrant Jenny-Rose.

"Someone in our house betrayed us," I said. "We have overlapping missions. First, we get your families—our families—outa Tepito and back home to the Ranch. Then we need to figure out who sold us down the river. Until we find them, they remain a threat." I looked the Tyrant in the eye. "That means the Corp-nation management could find out you're alive, and still a threat. We need to rescue everyone before that happens," I concluded.

"I'm in, we owe those Corpie bastards some payback!" Pasteur said, with a bit of growl wrapped around the words. I nodded back, happy to have the ursine warrior-monk with us.

"I was just starting to have some fun, and the night's young. Besides, my hammer gets all moody and whines when there's nothing interesting going on. I'm in," finished Smitty.

I turned my gaze to the Horde fighters gathered around us. They hooted their inclusion.

It's good to have friends who will follow you into Hell.

Epilog—The Keer

The over-Keer had thought it knew hate, but it was only irritation. The over-Keer now knew true hate, and it was good. Because the Bob had done a terrible thing.

First the Bob had brought it to this hot, heavy place where it was too weak to even move. Then the little Bobs had shorn its down, leaving it naked for everyone to see. This is a Keer's greatest nightmare. The over-Keer was embarrassed but its masses of followers loved it regardless.

The question was what to do about these intolerable conditions.

The over-Keer decided to analyze all available new-data before formulating strategy. The strange tunnel to its bodies beckoned seductively, so the over-Keer left the warmth of the eternal cocktail party known as the Dream and popped into its six bodies with an increasingly practiced air.

First, it needed to examine each body very carefully, amassing raw new-data. This took a while, but the Keer aren't very good a tracking time anyway.

It turned out that the individual bodies mostly had similar characteristics, once adjusted for size and age. But there was one that was different. It had two heartbeats.

The over-Keer drilled down into the molecular level, measuring hormones and all kinda things. There was only one likely conclusion. It was pregnant! New baby Keer!

The over-Keer was happy because now it could absorb the new Keer's consciousness and add it to the magnificence of its own! The over-Keer was pretty sure that that was how it got smart in the first place. This should make it even smarter!

The over-Keer duplicated the reproductive cycles in the other Keer as well. Soon all its bodies were with child. The over-Keer needed resources to grow. And it would make a plan. It wouldn't be that long until all the Keer shared the sacrament of Bob for dinner, a never-ending cornucopia of succulent meat, forever and ever.

Amen.

The Summer Wars Cycle

If you enjoyed this book, please consider posting a review on Amazon or Goodreads. And watch for upcoming books:

"Summerstead", a prequel about the discovery of Summer, due out in the fall of 2018.

 "Summertime", where galactic war with the Keer breaks out, due in 2019.

For more information check:

www.varida.com   *or @Yipman44*